THE

END

OF

MUSIC

THE
END
OF
MUSIC

JAMIE FITZPATRICK

A NOVEL

Breakwater Books

P.O. Box 2188, St. John's, NL, Canada, A1C 6E6

www.breakwaterbooks.com

Copyright © 2017 Jamie Fitzpatrick

ISBN 13: 978-1-55081-685-3

A CIP catalogue record for this book is available from Library and
Archives Canada.

We acknowledge the support of the Canada Council for the Arts, which
last year invested $157 million to bring the arts to Canadians throughout
the country. We acknowledge the financial support of the Government
of Canada through the Canada Book Fund (CBF) and the Government
of Newfoundland and Labrador through the Department of Tourism,
Culture and Recreation for our publishing activities.

Printed and bound in Canada.

 Canada Council   Conseil des Arts   Canadä
for the Arts   du Canada

Breakwater Books is committed to choosing papers and materials for
our books that help to protect our environment. To this end, this book
is printed on a recycled paper that is certified by the Forest Stewardship
Council®.

Interior Layout: JVDW Designs

1

The woman across the aisle is watching. They've landed in Gander and lurched to a halt. Herb Carter is on his feet, pawing at the overhead bin, raised arms shielding his face. He pretends not to notice the woman, her pupils full. Biting her bottom lip. He sneaks a look as she draws dark lipstick across her mouth. She catches his eye.

"It *is* you!" The woman reaches as if to touch him, but they aren't close enough. "That band!" she says, still reaching with long glossy nails. "I loved that band!" A smile crinkles her eyes, the lids folding to obscure her gaze.

"Thank you." Carter sucks in his stomach and tugs his carry-on free from the bin. The little tube of a commuter plane has him hunched like a Neanderthal.

"We saw you play at Grossman's, like, a million times. My girlfriend and me." Her voice carries through the cabin, too loud now that the shuddering grind of the propellers has let up.

She's short and square. Built like a hotel-room fridge. Must have been a fine-looking girl back in the nineties, red mouth singing along and face deathly pale under the gelled lights that spilled into the crowd. Most of the kids pushed towards the middle, drawn to

Leah at the lip of the stage, catching the sweat that dripped from her as she leaned into the microphone. A few might stand apart, watching Carter make his simple chords, riding the reverb. They were usually boys, taut and serious. Sometimes they closed their eyes and bucked their knees in time with the song. One summer there was a kid who followed the band to several festivals, where he would respond to the unrelenting drone by draping over the stage and pounding it with his fists.

Everyone's in the aisle now, and sunlight streams through the windows like there's a breach in the aircraft. A grey-haired man in a tank top comes between them, wrestling an oversized bag. Carter's head still aches from the propeller din and the recycled greasy-coffee air. He imagines himself as a boy on the wide-open tarmac, unfolding and stretching under blue sky.

The woman shimmies into the aisle, where her bulging shoulder bag nudges the tank-top man aside. "Are you here for the gerontology conference?"

"No." Ten years he spent with Leah, pulling and coaxing the music from her. He had nothing left when they were done.

"But of course you're from here. We were so proud of you back then, you know. Two bay girls from Newfoundland, and you were one of ours! We were so lonely in our smelly little apartment off Borden. We went to every show at Grossman's."

"There weren't many of you," says Carter. The band slogged through countless dreary nights at Grossman's. In his recollection it's always a drizzly Tuesday. The room smelling of dishwater. The crowd sparse, but hanging on every phrase. Every note. Even on a poor night there'd be a ring of kids who came to them with a kind of yearning, and the band could feed off it, forging ahead with showy confidence. Music raged in Carter back then, as innocent and dumb as a tornado.

"Do you still play?" the woman asks. The plane wobbles as the doors release and open.

"No, not anymore."

2

"I know what you mean. I hear music now and it's like, oh, that's a nice song. But it's not the same. Nothing feels like it did back then." She looks away when she says this, embarrassed by their shared disappointment. People are moving, and a teenaged girl coughs loudly because they're holding up the line. The tank-top guy is on his phone, in agitated conversation. "Well, what time did you leave Burin?" he asks, and sighs.

"Oh!" The woman gasps, and grabs Carter's arm to stop his turn. "Remember that CD you did? The one with the sparkly cover?" A strand of salt-and-pepper hair has escaped her ponytail, trailing into the open collar of a white blouse. She's blushing from the neck down. "Remember?"

"Of course," says Carter. His bent posture directs his eyes to the open collar and the grip on his bare arm.

"Oh my God." She looks to the ceiling, offering the perfect pink of her throat. "I think that album saved my life. The kid I was back then."

/////

The bungalow is dark and featureless, the front lawn ankle-high and overrun with dandelions. Water pools in the empty driveway and plump spiders dangle under the eaves.

Carter's arm still tingles with the damp grip of the woman on the plane. The bay girl. He's never been picked out of a crowd like that. Well, maybe once or twice when the band was active. He might have been sleeping with girls like her back then, waking up in their smelly little apartments, had he not been so devoted to Leah and so zealous about her music.

He knocks on the front door and opens it, making deliberate noise.

"Hello, Mom! It's Herb!" The living room walls are bare and the bookshelf empty, the furniture gone save for the couch and coffee table, the area rug rolled up and yellowed curtains heaped in one corner. The dining room is empty, patches of polished floor indicating where the table and buffet used to be.

3

"Mom? You there?" He follows the hum of the refrigerator through to the kitchen. A cup of tea, its attending cigarette burned down to a tube of grey ash in the saucer. An overturned chair. A white curl of smoke shifts as he steps into the hasty, furious silence of the room.

There's been another episode. She's in the ambulance now with a mask clamped to her mouth, eyes searching. Carter fumbles for his phone. Did he have the ringer off? The sharper smell cutting through the smoke—could it be a trail of cologne left by a paramedic? Who found her this time? Mrs. Primm again? In the driveway, oblivious? In the middle of the road, staring blankly at the cars that pull up before her?

Nothing on his phone. A rapid pulse throbs in the arch of his right foot. He only gets it in moments of terror, and occasionally at the brink of orgasm.

"Yes? Hello?" The basement stairs creak, and his mother appears at the opposite side of the kitchen. "Hello!"

"It's Herb!"

"Yes!" They're both shouting.

Joyce Carter crosses the kitchen and holds his arm, almost in the same spot where the bay girl gripped him. His mother and the smitten girl, both reaching for him. His younger self would have found it a profound coincidence, would have pondered it and picked up his guitar. Is that where music used to come from?

"Are these capelin any good?"

"What?"

Joyce raises a plastic grocery bag in her hand. The lump inside is mostly frost, with ribbons of black showing through, and an occasional fish eye.

"How old is this?"

"Oh, since before your father died. Someone gave it to him. But he never bothered with capelin." The hand on his arm trembles slightly, but she's clear-eyed.

"Throw it out, Mom. You can smell the freezer burn."

Joyce walks to the garbage and steps on the pedal. She's slowed a good deal, though her stride retains a tight, military precision. Her navy stretch pants are cinched around her tiny waist, with hipbones poking through. She must be losing weight.

"There's hot dogs," she says, nodding at a second bag on the kitchen counter.

"You've already cleared out a fair bit, Mom. A lot of furniture and junk."

"Some fellows are coming with their truck. They've come three or four times now."

"I'll just get my bag." Carter returns to the vestibule and carries his suitcase to his old bedroom, his pulse easing. He's been skittish since the bay girl. The things she said made his teeth chatter and legs twitch. Music used to rush through his body like this. The excitement of it often brought on headaches, nausea, vertigo, itching. More than once he had to interrupt a great show and dash backstage to sit on the toilet, his insides churning with adrenalin.

He won't be sleeping in his old bed. It's gone, as is the dresser. The closet is empty. He had left old records and CDs in there, and a few colourful shirts and scarves from his brief attempt to dress like a high-school rock star. He didn't mind that the boys snickered and the teachers grinned. Bunch of rubes. But when sweet-faced Simone from Quebec told him he needed a cucumber in his pants to complete the look, and her friends covered their mouths in scandalous laughter, the humiliation left a deep scar.

The bathroom is unadorned, with only a few toiletries and a small set of towels, like at an inn. Joyce has emptied the house of its history. He peeks into her room, where two open suitcases and two tote bags sit at the foot of her bed.

Hot dogs boil on the stove, a yellow scum rising to the surface. Joyce uses a bread knife to separate frozen buns. The wieners are cheese-injected, according to the package. The overgrown backyard waves in the window, weedy and brown in the late afternoon sun. A mower might not get through it.

"I talked to Howley Park yesterday, Mom. Your room'll be ready anytime tomorrow."

But his mother has slipped away, opening the front door with a loud greeting. "Ha-ha!" replies a deep male voice. "Ha-ha-ha!"

Carter catches up in time to see two thick men pull the rolled-up area rug out the door. The rug sags, leaving a trail in the grass as they carry it to a pickup in the driveway. Joyce tosses the bundled curtains after them and watches from the front step as Carter joins her. She turns to him and blinks, as if surprised to find him there.

"Where's Leah?"

"I'm not married to Leah anymore, Mom. I'm married to Isabelle."

"Yes, that's right." She grips the wrought-iron rail.

"Remember I told you? When we split up?"

"But what about the baby? He can't grow up like that."

"No, Mom. That's Sam. With Isabelle. Leah and I never had kids."

"Ah, yes, yes. Okay, yes." Joyce tosses her head.

One of the men returns to grab the curtains. "Ah, Jesus," he grunts, sweating through a skin-tight black T-shirt. His belly is huge but solid, and his fleshy face doesn't jiggle, not even the big pink wedge under his chin.

"He's hardly a baby anymore," says Carter. He takes the phone from his pocket and holds it to Joyce's face, flipping through several photos of Sam.

"Now then, missus," says the sweaty man, approaching them after throwing the curtains in the truck. His partner follows, a younger man with tangly seaweed hair and matching T-shirt and sweatpants. He squints to keep his glasses pushed up his nose. The T-shirt says, *Not in this lifetime, Mthrfckr!*

"Come in," says Joyce. "Have a hot dog."

/////

6

"Is she okay?" asks Isabelle.

"She's fine. You know... She drifts." That's not quite it. She takes hard turns he can't track. "But it's okay. She's pretty much there."

"That's a relief."

Relief. It's the only thing they ask for now. The relief of avoiding another day like last February, when Mrs. Primm looked out her window next door and saw Joyce at the end of the driveway, half-dressed and in a panic. Talking gibberish.

"It'll be a hard for her tomorrow. Is she anxious?"

"She's already cleared out most of the house, like she can't wait to get out." Carter is in the basement rec room, where nothing remains but a box of empty mason jars and dead moths silhouetted in the bowl of the light fixture. The electrical outlet is still scorched black from the day his amp blew out.

"How's Sam?"

"Fine," says Isabelle. "He had it out with Raccoon this morning."

"Raccoon? Really?"

Sam is a mild boy who has lately discovered malice. Toys have been pitched over the basement stairs, stuffed animals scolded and locked in his closet. Raccoon is a long-time companion and sleeping partner, so some kind of rupture was inevitable.

He tells her about the bickering flight attendants at Pearson, the bladder-bursting line-up for the single onboard toilet, the hasty transfer at Halifax. Finally he mentions the bay girl who loved the band, how she blocked the aisle to talk to him. He leaves out the flushed throat, the open neck of her blouse.

"You flirt," says Isabelle. "Was she another of your ugly ducklings?"

"No, not really." But she's imagining the right type. At its peak, in the mid-nineties, the band found its audience with a gloomy crowd. Young men in army surplus gear, playing at nihilism. Young women in plaid shirts, rejecting the feminine straightjacket. Kids who had given up on ever being part of anything. Proud to have given up.

7

They moved furtively, heads down and shoulders turned inward, and danced fitfully, as if shaking off a chill. They recognized one of their own in Leah, a wiry redhead delivering gnomic scraps of lyric, her shaky alto coming in and out of range. Carter had heard the power in that voice, and worked relentlessly to bring it out.

"Leah called."

"Hmm?"

"Leah. She called."

The name deflates him. Leah in the here and now.

"When?" Carter crosses the basement to the laundry room.

"Just a few minutes ago. I told her you were flying."

"How did she sound?"

"Urgent, kind of." A hollow *whoosh* pulls at Isabelle's voice, rising and falling, echoing to a high pitch.

"Her cancer's probably back."

"Oh no. Really?"

"I don't know. It's just…" He can't imagine any other reason.

Carter flips the lid of the deep freeze, next to the washer and dryer. Steam rises, with its pungent freezer smell. Bricks of grocery-store bread line the bottom. There's meat as well, black, frosted chunks of something. He'll have to scrub the smell out. There's bumping and shifting overhead. Joyce's muffled voice. "Ha-ha-ha!" from the sweaty man. They must be finished their hot dogs and heading on their way.

"You still there?" asks Isabelle.

"Sorry."

/////

The couch is gone, and the men are in his mother's room, using mallets to knock her bedframe into pieces.

"Wait," says Carter. "We're sleeping here."

The men pause. "Wha?" says the young one with the seaweed hair, speaking for the first time.

8

"We still have to sleep here." Carter looks around for Joyce, but she's still outside. "Tonight."

"Missus!" shouts the sweaty one. "Hey, missus!" The screen door creaks and slams, and Joyce's slippers swish-swish to the bedroom door. "Fella here says we can't take your bed."

"Or the couch," says Carter.

"We're after driving all the way in from Carmanville," says the young one. The two of them are on the floor, legs splayed like toddlers. "I mean, come on," he adds.

"Tonight?" says Joyce, gripping the doorframe.

"Your room at Howley Park," says Carter. "We can't move in till tomorrow."

"What room?" Her tremor starts up again.

"We got to haul that couch back in out of the truck?" grumbles the young one.

"At Howley Park. Where you're going."

"Wait now." Joyce begins massaging her hands, rolling one over the other.

"Tell you what, missus," says the sweaty one.

She waves frantically, as if to quiet them all, and backs away from the door.

"Mom…"

"Tell you what, now."

"Give us a minute, will you?" Carter also waves at the sweaty one, and follows his mother. She stares into the empty living room.

"I don't know about all this, Marty."

"No, Mom. It's me, Herb." His Uncle Martin has been dead for years.

She extends a hand, as if to grasp the absence in the room, a dusty summer-hot odour of disturbance and abandonment.

"Tell you what, missus." The sweaty one comes up behind them. "We'll bring the sofa cushions back in so buddy has something to sleep on."

"Please." Carter has had enough. "We need—"

"Yes," cries Joyce. A clap of her hands echoes in the open space. "There you go." She smiles and presses the hands together, as if offering a prayer of thanks.

/////

She'll call, they all said. Perfectly normal, Mr. Carter. She'll call and say, please come and take me home. It's all part of the adjustment. They all do it, a kind of mourning for their former life. But she'll be grand. Do you want her kept from the phone for a couple of days, till she settles in? That helps sometimes, they said.

No, Carter said. Let her call.

She's left the microwave, so he goes to Shopper's for a stack of frozen dinners, only to find that the microwave doesn't work. Why didn't the guys with the truck take it? He stops at the Co-op for bananas, milk, a rotisserie chicken and a twelve-pack of sausages. Sees people his age, knows none of them. The temperature tops twenty-five degrees, with a blurry, liquid sun. Carter eats the chicken from its tray and moves his couch cushions to the cool of the basement rec room, laying out garbage bags underneath to ward off carpenter beetles and earwigs. He wakes in the middle of the night with his T-shirt soaked in sweat and his butt slipping between the cushions, and hears music in the dark. In a high-school essay he dared not show anyone else, Carter wrote that he craved music for its beauty and strangeness and confused striving. He wrote it in this room, records blaring.

The cleaners, Pamela and Jocelyn from Traytown, arrive at eight that morning and follow him from room to room, grinning at his instructions. Don't worry, sir. We've scoured many an empty house. They're amused by him, somehow. He leaves them to their work and explores the exterior, where vinyl siding is cracked and coming undone. Takes a broom to the spidery eaves.

Joyce calls while Carter is dragging her mattress to the curb. "I'd like a drink at lunch, and before bed, and they should give it to me."

"But they can only let you have one drink, Mom. It's all you're allowed."

Howley Park agreed that there was no point in cutting her off altogether. "That won't make anyone happy," said the doctor. So it's been written in her chart: An ounce-and-a-half of Scotch, with water, every day before dinner.

"Have you got anything at all? A job or something?"

"I'm still at the bakery, Mom. I've got a good arrangement there."

In fact, he left the bakery last year to focus on grad school. Joyce would be appalled if she knew the truth. Isabelle supporting the family while Carter still dabbles in archaeology. Still trying to get started, she would say. Sitting in a classroom with youngsters half your age.

He pulls the mattress up the driveway, letting it buckle and flop to the ground when the phone rings again. Isabelle reports that Sam isn't sleeping, and she might have a migraine coming, and Leah called again. "Left a message last night," says Isabelle. "Said she had to talk about the band. She mentioned a guy named Will?"

"He was our bass player." Will was the sensible one. Band manager, booking agent, accountant, archivist, driver. The one who wheedled a better deal out of night-shift motel clerks and threatened to beat the shit out of scummy club owners. Later he went to northern Alberta for work and was nearly killed in some sort of industrial accident.

"Maybe she wants to get your band back together."

"No, Iz. That'll never happen."

"That new friend of yours, who you met on the plane. She'd buy a ticket."

Carter laughs nervously.

He gets the mattress the rest of the way to the curb, fighting for a good grip. Then the microwave, frozen dinners stacked inside it. Gathers the couch cushions, bags the last bits of kitchenware and contents of the deep freeze, and retreats to the front step. The street is quiet. Mrs. Primm's house dark. She must be out of town. He'd like to thank her for keeping an eye out all these years.

Leah would never propose a reunion. Unless, if the cancer was back? Maybe one last go?

He won't play music again. It would be like relapsing into a nervous disorder.

"I'm not a musician anymore," he had told Isabelle when they met. It felt good to say it.

The town truck pulls up, and Carter waves to the garbage men as they dispense with the last of Alcock Street. Then he sets out on the short walk to Sinbad's Motel, pulling his suitcase.

The route takes him through the town square and past Dee-Jays Music. It's a bottle depot now. Carter cups his hands to peer through the plate-glass door. Empties are stacked against the back wall, where a bin was always reserved for vinyl, even as CDs slowly took over the rest. It's still got the checkout counter, where Jane the Punk propped her big boots on either side of the cash register while she rolled a cigarette against her belly. Carter spent so many after-school hours here that Jane gave him free access to the 99-cent bargain bin. He could pick through it and take home as many records as he liked, as long they were back for end-of-month inventory.

Carter loved those records, how every song purred with aspiration and nerve, like a fresh-faced schoolboy angling to get by on charm and good looks. It was exactly what Carter needed. Music became his consoling belief system.

It was this belief that would carry him to Toronto a few years later, to the damp little music shop on Queen Street, where he found Leah and stood in front of her until she took him home. He was in her bed before he knew how to ride the TTC or where to order a pizza. He was still living out of a suitcase when they started making demos in her living room. She had a boyfriend and went to North Bay to be with him to teach high school. Came back at

Christmas and said she was engaged. Came back in June and agreed to start a band, just for the summer. They called their band Infinite Yes. "We will make art as realists," Carter told her, quoting from a book he found somewhere. "The true realist does not present the world as we see it. He reveals the world as it would appear if only we could see it fully."

Had there really been a time when he could talk such nonsense and be taken seriously?

Weeks later, Carter had picked up a fungus that festered in the quicks of his fingernails, with tiny blisters popping into sores. Unable to put any pressure on his fingertips, reduced to playing gentle bar chords, he began messing with the effects units. Little black boxes with pedals and coloured buttons that he talked Leah into "borrowing" from the music shop. That's how he discovered the droning, heavily processed sound that would come to characterize the band. When he finally went to a clinic to have the fungus looked at, the woman at the desk asked how long he had been in Ontario, and told him he should have applied for an OHIP card by now. But I've been making music, he wanted to say. I'm playing guitar and I've got a band and I'm fucking the lead singer. Can't you tell? Don't I look like the new guy who blew into town and formed a band? Don't I walk like the guy who fucks the lead singer?

/////

Her cuffs are stained and crusty with food. Her hair hangs loose. There's no excuse for that. The photos on the wall show her in a bun.

"You must be doing alright," says Carter, his voice bouncing off the lavender walls. "It's nice here."

Joyce pushes herself up from the rocking chair with quivering arms. "Let's go for a walk."

They start down the long hallway, the gleam from the linoleum rippling ahead of them like moonlight on water. Doors are open on a Saturday afternoon. Visitors perch nervously on beds while residents doze in rocking chairs or lean against stacked pillows, half-following the trail of small talk: the food, the aches and pains, the grandkids. And the weather, always the weather.

"I'm leaving this afternoon, Mom."

"Okay then."

"I'll try to get back soon for a visit."

"Okay."

A chalkboard at the end of the hall promises games of chance in the activity room at two and *Coronation Street* in the sitting room at three-thirty.

"Games of chance this afternoon, Mom. Do you think you'll go to that?"

"Go to what?"

"Games of chance. In the activity room, it says."

"Will they have a cup of tea? A bun or something?"

"I don't know. I would imagine."

"They were singing those bloody old songs this morning. Her eyes they shone like the diamonds, da, da, da. Beating the piano to pieces." She lifts her arms and flaps them in front of her. "I said to the girl, get me out of this. Did you know Mr. Bussey's wife got sent away?"

"Who?"

"Sent her down to that place by the lake. I'm not going there. I already told them. So if that's what you're here for you can forget about it."

"No, Mom. I'm just here to see you before I go." He reaches as if to touch her elbow or take her hand, but shrinks back again.

They complete the circuit. Joyce returns to her chair and Carter examines the room, finding a photo album on his mother's bedside table. The usual scenes: birthday suppers, young women cradling babies, Christmas mornings, and what looks like a retirement or anniversary party. Back into the hallway, he catches up with the familiar-looking nurse. He doesn't know her, but she strongly recalls the girls he knew in school. Thin and unadorned, with quick eyes behind small glasses. He finds her outside the kitchen, with dishwashers grinding.

"I don't know these people," he tells her, showing the album. "This isn't our family."

"Stuff gets mixed up all the time," says the nurse. "They scatters it everywhere."

"What's the place down by the lake?"

"That's New Horizons, our facility for the Level Three and Four residents."

"Marty! Marty!" Joyce is outside her door, her voice urgent.

"She's worried about being sent there."

"Right now Joyce is classified as Level Two," says the nurse, trailing the nub of a pencil along the clipboard. "Feeds herself and manages alright in the bathroom."

"Marty!"

He sprints back down the hall and touches her elbow.

"It's Herb. I'm Herb. Uncle Marty isn't here."

"I'm through with the house." She flicks a hand, like brushing crumbs from a table. "I can't go back to it now."

"We're selling the house, Mom. It's on the market."

"Yes, but I don't want to be in a racket over the money."

"There'll be no racket. There's an agent, he'll get the best price."

"Yes but… People like that will tell you anything."

"I'll watch him. Every move. You don't have to worry."

The two of them stand silent, until Joyce seeks out the rocking chair, gripping it with shaky hands. Carter follows and reaches to help. "No," she says. Sets her jaw and settles into the seat.

On the high shelf of the open closet, the black gloss of the jewelry chest peeks through a woolly tangle of gloves and hats. The chest has a satisfying heft, but it feels small in his hands, no bigger than a meatloaf. As a boy, Carter called it the Night Box. When its hinged lid was open, it meant his parents were going out for the night. Carter liked to sit on his mother's lap while she dug through her treasures, choosing pearl earrings or a chunky necklace. His father claimed the Night Box had been a gift from "a real Arab." His version of the story cast Joyce as a headstrong young woman working a night shift at the airport. The Arab ("Rich as Croesus!") touches down for a few hours en route to New York. He is smitten; falls at her feet. But Joyce turns him away.

"Imagine that, Herbie!" says his father. "You might have been half-Bedouin! The next Prince of Persia!"

"Go on with your old foolishness," says Joyce.

The lacquer finish is spoiled by what looks to be dried glue left by strips of tape. But the lid is as Carter remembers. Painted with a crosshatch of gold trim and the portrait of a brown princess in white turban and crimson robe. The toes of her slippers curl back to make full circles and her dark eyes are as big as the palm of her open hand. She's a daring princess, with substantial cleavage on display. This was Carter's first cleavage.

The blue carpet inside darkens when his finger sweeps against the grain. But there is no jewelry, only a dog-eared postcard and a photo in a Ziploc bag. The postcard shows an egg-shaped map of the world. Newfoundland is at the centre, and has the map's only identified location, a black star labelled *Gander International Airport*. From the star, red streaks shoot in all directions, curving across oceans and continents. *Crossroads of the World* is the inscription across the top. The reverse side is blank.

By the time he was in high school, Carter chafed against this glorified history. What was the so-called "Crossroads of the World" except an accident of geography? A suitably flat stretch of land at the edge of the continent. A service station, where international flights could top up the tank while everyone had a pee and a sandwich. Even that trivial role was fleeting, over by the time Carter was born, as more powerful jets crossed the ocean straight to cities like Montreal and New York and Toronto. Places that mattered. He had made this argument excitedly, nurturing a fierce urge to take his father down a peg or two. But Arthur Carter only smiled and shook his head.

The photo is a black-and-white of his mother, with her head tipped back and lips parted, blurry points of white where her gown shimmers. Three fingers hold the microphone stand. The other hand makes a fist at her side. She's alone in the spotlight, darkness all around.

"You'll take the money, then. Is that it?"

"From the house? No, no. You'll get every penny, Mom. In your bank account."

Joyce is on her feet again. She makes for the window and yanks at the handle.

"Here," says Carter, rising from the bed and easing her fingers away, then turning the window open a crack. "Bit of fresh air."

She returns to the chair, lowers herself slowly, pulling the blanket around her knees.

"Where's Leah?"

"Isabelle, Mom."

2

Joyce saw it first. A dot against the pale blue, coming for them.

"Look!" she said.

One of the men shaded his eyes. "Now then." He glanced at his watch. "Three-oh-six from Idlewild, late again."

Joyce watched its descent, which seemed too fast. It tilted and seemed to break apart, and her heart was in her throat. But it was just the wing flap opening. A moment later, three-oh-six was on the tarmac with a screech of rubber, slowing to a crawl against the wide horizon. The side lettering identified it as Air France.

"Ha!" snorted a tall man, smoothing the hairs that blew across his head. "Late again. Skinner'll be having fits."

"When will it get to France?" asked Joyce.

"Depends on whether Skinner murders the crew."

They were walking on a road that skirted one of the runways, bending left. Looking across the runway Joyce saw what she took to be their destination. A few low buildings cut from the woods.

She didn't cover her ears for the next one. It passed over the road ahead, close enough that she could trace the rivets in its grey, burnished belly and see the landing wheels spin as they emerged.

The women clapped their ears and the men shouted to continue whatever they were arguing about. It bounced lightly before settling on the runway like a giant toy. She didn't recognize the foreign name, and the men took no notice of it. She liked the French one better. Long and lean, with a huge wing at the back.

Darker clouds crowded the sky by the time they reached the Legion. Tall, billowing clouds like she never saw at home. Within an hour rain was beating hard on the low, wooden rooftop, throwing the dancers off their rhythm.

"That system blew in quick," said Frank, who worked at the weather office.

"And how do you plan to get me home in this?" asked Gloria.

Joyce sat with Frank and Gloria and three couples she had just met. The only one she could name was the fellow who made a lot of jokes, because the women would laugh and shriek, "Oh, Kenny!" in response to his frequent wisecracks. Joyce didn't get Kenny's jokes, but perhaps she would in time.

She had arrived the day before, dragging her father's old duffel off the train as the stinging dust blew down the platform. Her father had begged her not to leave, feigning illness. Her brother Marty had come at her with his fists. By the Jesus, your place is in this house and you'll stay in this house. But they were seven hours away now by train. She had a bed and a roommate named Rachel. She had yet to work a shift, and had slept poorly, waking with a fright when the first of the early-morning arrivals passed over and the whole building trembled. In the morning she had walked through the wrong door returning from the bathroom, frightening a pair of girls in slips as they stood shoulder to shoulder at the mirror. Gasping and backing out, Joyce glimpsed the grey skirt and jacket of Trans Canada Airlines laid out on each bed. She would soon meet these two as co-workers, and hoped they wouldn't remember her.

Gloria was seven months pregnant, so Joyce and the other women took turns dancing with Frank.

"I warned you," said Gloria, as he pushed back his chair and extended a hand to Joyce again. "You can't get him off the floor, the fool."

Joyce had seen bands in movies, and knew some of the songs from the radio. But the attack of the music jarred her. Drums pounded in the bridge of her nose. A recurring low note found her legs. In the lull of a slow dance, the horns blared so loud they gave her a terrible start. For a moment she thought it was an alarm to signal some sort of attack.

"Lovely," murmured Frank, guiding her between couples. "Where did you learn to dance like that?" Before Joyce could answer, the wind shifted and rain pelted the high windows behind the bandstand. A window flew open and sent a spray of water down on the musicians, staining their light blue tuxedos. The hush of the song was spoiled.

A horn player stepped up to a microphone and bowed with mock formality. "Another lovely night on the Gander," he said. The crowd responded with derisive laughter. "Hold on to your hat!" cried one man. "Now you're in a pickle!" yelled another.

Joyce was glad for the interruption, and took the opportunity to shift away from Frank and the pressure of his hand against her back. It was 1952 and she had a new home. A place so new that almost everyone lived at the airport's edge, in military barracks refashioned as apartments and hotels. A few modest bungalows housed the families. It would all be abandoned when the permanent town site was ready.

All of this Joyce had known when she arrived, thanks to letters from Gloria and a film Father Coles had shown on one of the days when he brought his projector to school. What she discovered on her first night out was the spirit of lawlessness that must have been left over from the war years. The dance floor lights were kept low. People drank as much as they liked. Women wore perfume and men leaned into their necks to sniff it. She liked Frank, but after two verses and a chorus of "Blue Moon," she had decided there was no good reason to leave his hand on the small of her back.

A barman was mounting a chair to close the window, to shouts of encouragement. The horn player with the microphone kept talking, sweat shining on his rosy face. Other fellows in the band were sipping the drinks they kept at their sides and calling to friends in the crowd.

"They're not smart," Joyce whispered to Gloria.

"Smart how?"

Joyce shook her head. She had expected something more in line with Father Coles' film. In the dark of the small classroom in Cape St. Rose, with the damp smell of mitts and boots drying over the wood stove, the film had trumpeted "a prosperous Newfoundland in a prosperous Canada" and "a people ready to embrace the future." It showed nets bulging with fish, rivers jammed with logs, a mighty waterfall, and grinning, black-faced miners heading underground in cages. Music swelled and stirred, putting the island in motion, fish squirming and water rushing and lights shining from the miners' hats. Gander had been identified as "a thriving hub in this new era of trans-Atlantic travel." A huge airplane climbed into open sky. There were paved roads with cars, and women browsing racks full of clothes, and men in an airport tower talking into microphones while they gazed at the far horizon. Most intriguing was a glimpse inside a spacious home, where a man carved a great roast of beef while his wife ushered children to the table, all of it in the glare of electric lights.

At the end of the night, people lingered in the lobby. Rain slapped at the door and trickled under it, making a stream down the middle of the floor. Frank went to find a ride. Gloria wiped her brow and pulled at the V-neck of her wool dress, flapping it for air. For all her adventures, she didn't seem much different. She had been just a few days finished school when she left Cape St. Rose, her letters to Joyce filled with thrilling reports from St. John's. Gloria doing her commercial certificate at Prince of Wales College. Gloria

21

getting steno work at the American base, full of young men, then at Job Brothers, where it was all local fellows, and married, then at the phone company, where her supervisor made "shocking advances." Gloria finding a husband and moving to Gander, because the new airport needed young people with skills and smarts.

All the while Joyce had been working at her father's store, stocking the shelves with fat pork and slab cheese and kerosene, or in the cellar, salting a barrel of livers to make cod-liver oil.

Now that she was here, she suspected she could catch up in no time.

In the glare of the lobby, whiskey racing in her head and under her skin, Joyce felt different about the band, more open to the music. The words of the songs had lodged inside her. They made her want to fall in love and have her heart broken. She wanted to risk everything for a man, or toy with him and refuse him, or walk out on him and slam the door.

Frank came through the door, his black curls holding rain drops. "They've only room for two," he said, gesturing to the car behind him. "I'll be back to see you home."

"No, I'll be fine," said Joyce.

"Don't be ridiculous," said Frank.

"Really."

"Are you sure?"

"Stay with your wife." Joyce squeezed Gloria's hand and kissed her damp temple. She looked like she might be sick. "Night, love. Thanks so much."

The car pulled away, headlights flashing in the window. Behind the swinging doors to the bar, there was loud, sputtering male laughter, and a voice shouting, "Get out of it with your friggin' and foolin'!" A woman next to Joyce tut-tutted and her escort hid an embarrassed smile.

A soaked head poked in from outside. "Room for one more out here," the man said, and looked at Joyce. "Miss?"

Joyce dashed for the pickup. The street was all muck and she'd ruin her shoes. But what odds. Ugly old pumps. She'd get paid soon enough.

A hand reached from the cab of the truck. "Up we go, missy." Someone slammed the door behind her. Joyce sat next to a man who said, "Come on, Eric. Let's get the fuck out of this."

It was the trumpet man from the band, the one who appeared to be leader, beginning each number with the rhythmic snap of his fingers. Where Joyce grew up—a town hardly known for its delicacy—men tried not to swear in the company of strange women.

"Not a bad time tonight, eh?" he said. "Not like that Pan-Am party, though. My God, they went wild that night. I told the fellah on the bar, you just keep the drinks coming."

"Huh," said the driver, guiding the truck onto the paved road and swerving around a monstrous pothole.

"And what was that smell in the cloak room? Someone and their lady friend must have got lost in there, eh, Eric?"

"Hah," said the driver, and muttered something Joyce didn't hear.

She was meant to be shocked. So she said, "Perhaps it was those suits you wear. Ever get them cleaned?"

Trumpet Man erupted in a wheezing laugh, his belly expanding. He was bigger than he looked on stage. "Yes. Old tux gets quite the going over. Good deal of sweat and blood."

He turned and looked at Joyce for the first time. "You're that girl danced with Frank Tucker half the night."

Joyce already sensed the imminent departure of Frank and Gloria from her life. The effort required to maintain the connection would be wearying. She nodded to the black hard-shell case in Trumpet Man's lap.

"How did you learn to play that thing?" She was thinking of the long, aching note he held at the end of one of the last songs. The song was about falling asleep alone and dreaming of a lover who went away.

"Here and there. A Salvation Army fellow showed me a good deal. The Sally Anns are where you go for brass. I believe he thought he might convert me to the cause. But there was never much chance of that."

"You're at the hotel, then?" asked the driver. "The Airlines?"

"Yes, thanks," said Joyce. They were on the main road, reversing the route she had walked earlier. Wind and rain blew hard across the runway, shaking the truck.

"Do the airplanes fly in this?" she asked.

"They fly in anything," said Trumpet Man.

"That song you did, the one about drinking coffee all night."

"'Black Coffee.'"

"You forgot the words."

"Christ, didn't I though?" The wheezing again, and his cigarette ash dropped on her coat. "That's a woman's song really. We need a proper girl singer. You ever sing?"

"Church choir."

"Never seen you in choir."

"Back home." She had been good enough that Sister Marie gave her "O Holy Night" for midnight mass one year. But Joyce had been so nervous that she cracked on the high note.

"Well, now. Perhaps you'd like a turn with us. Give them something to look at, eh, Eric? "

"Huh," said the driver.

"This is the fellah what holds it all together," said Trumpet Man, elbowing the driver. "Without Eric at the piano she goes off the rails entirely."

The driver didn't acknowledge the compliment. Joyce looked out her window into the black rain. She said nothing more until they pulled up to the hotel, where she stepped into the mud.

"Thank you." She tried to direct her voice to the driver. All she could see was a dark profile topped with little swirls of hair.

Trumpet Man leaned out the door, the porch light shining off his red cheeks and crooked red nose. Everyone here was red, it seemed. The whole town overheated with late summer and drink and dancing.

"See you to the door?"

"I'm fine, thank you." The rain had eased, leaving her rumpled and damp.

"Where are you working?"

"Trans Canada Airlines."

"TCA? Wait till Dennis Shea gets a look at you. Tight little operation over there."

The door slammed. The pickup sprayed mud and drove on. A gust of wind cut across the denuded landscape, rattling shutters on the boxy hotel. Pinpoints of light—she now knew they marked the runways—brought a little crawl of sadness to Joyce's stomach. Was it homesickness? She was never going back there.

/////

She lifted her foot, but it barely moved. She yanked at it, then tried to kick it free. Her leg bounced off something hard and sharp. Joyce gasped and opened her eyes.

"Dad?" The word dry in her mouth.

Wait. Was she with someone? The warm pressure of a boy next to her.

There was no boy.

"Marty?" Her throat closed around the word.

Joyce wouldn't panic. Surely Marty would be coming to help.

She pushed the sheets away. The leg wasn't trapped at all. Up on her elbows, she wiggled it and drew her knee in, freeing the foot from the metal bars of the bed frame.

In the blue shadow of the room she recognized the door, the open closet, the mound in the other bed. She sat up and placed a palm where her back had been. Soaked through. Mopped her face and neck with a hand, spotted the glass on the bedside table and drained the tepid water. Stood and pulled the window blind.

The aircraft couldn't have been more than a hundred yards away, wet and silvery white, blinking and humming. It was flanked on either side by a truck and what appeared to be a long, snaking jeep. Puddles shimmered in the dark of the runway.

A rustle and squeak from the other bed. Rachel sat up and yawned, gathered curls and dropped them behind her shoulders.

"What were you dreaming of just now?"

"I don't know," said Joyce.

"You were talking a good bit."

"A man, maybe. A fellow lying next to me."

"Mmmm," said Rachel. "Wrapped all around you."

"I was wrapped around him, I think."

Rachel stood and turned on her lamp. They stared out the window, side by side, half expecting the airplane to move any second.

"They can see us," said Rachel, breath stale with tea and smoke and sleep.

Most of the tiny windows were dark or hidden in shadow. But Joyce saw a few faces turned in their direction. One wore glasses. Another—a woman, probably—drank from a cup. Another looked out, then disappeared.

"Marty would be appalled," said Joyce. "Showing my bedclothes to the world. He'd lock me in my room. Then he'd die."

"Boyfriend?"

"Brother."

The airplane rocked in the wind, clinging to its little wheels. Propellers whirred to a blur and slowed to a halt, as if preening and settling in for the morning.

"Think you'll ever get on one of those?"

"I hope so," said Joyce.

Rachel shook her head. "Imagine being in that thing, above the clouds when the motor gives out." She picked up an alarm clock and tilted it to the light. "Won't get back to sleep now." She groped for cigarettes at her bedside and offered the open package to Joyce.

They were silent for a minute or so. Joyce wanted more faces in the airplane windows. A man rubbing his bristles because he hadn't shaved since London. A French woman in an exotic hat. Maybe a darkie from the States.

"You have brothers?"

"Four," said Rachel. "And three sisters."

"They keep tabs?"

"Hardly. I don't say Joe would know me if he passed me in the street."

Rachel puffed and exhaled. She had a good three or four inches on Joyce, and could have been pretty. But she wasn't built for a tall frame. Her skin pulled tight around her eyes and mouth, giving her a severe look.

"Is your brother so awful?" she asked.

"Marty? Always suspects the worst."

"Do you give him cause?"

"Not much. Not until last summer. Stayed out all night with a fellow."

"Oh, yes? Did you lose your virtue?"

"Misplaced it for a bit. Went swimming naked. That was the best part."

"Your poor brother." Rachel giggled. "Must have been beside himself."

"I did it to spite him as much as anything. Do you know the fellows in that dance band?"

Rachel shrugged. "I work so many nights. They gave you a run home last night, didn't they?"

"Not before I took them to the edge of town."

"You didn't."

"Behind the American side. Isn't that the place? For a bit of fun?"

"You're joking."

"I'm not."

"Seriously?"

Joyce smiled. Took a moment to stub her cigarette in an ashtray on the windowsill. "No," she said. "Just fooling."

Rachel gave her a shove. "Holy mother," she said.

"So I needn't worry about everyone knowing my business around here," said Joyce.

"Right down to your dirty drawers and how they got that way."

/////

Joyce found the employee entrance and waited, as instructed in the letter. The letter was on Trans Canada Airlines letterhead. She carried it in her purse.

The eight o'clock shift change scattered people every which way. They wore coveralls or airline uniforms or shirtsleeves, and headed across to the hotels or out to the main road and towards the little houses that showed their peaked roofs behind stands of birch and spruce. A few hung about smoking, or walked the border of the tarmac, rubbing night-shift eyes in the morning sun. Joyce watched the women. Some strode with purpose, shoes snapping. Others looked exhausted. Her legs itched under her wool skirt.

The skies were quiet for the moment. Three hulking aircraft sat silent, far from the terminal. Nothing beyond them except the low-cut woods skirting the runway. A dark scribble on the horizon.

A short, baby-faced blonde hurried past.

"Hat! Hat!" she said to Joyce, reaching up to tap her own.

"Sorry?"

"Cripes, you're the new girl, aren't you?" She stood with her feet splayed and flipped a page on the clipboard in her hand. "Phyllis? No, Joyce. What are you doing in winter kit?"

"Sorry?"

"You don't have a summer uniform? And your hat. Come here." She took Joyce by the sleeve and pulled her into the shade.

"See here," she said, and pulled a compact from her bag. Joyce flipped it open and watched in the mirror while the blonde circled behind. Hands appeared and changed the angle of her hat, realigning the pins with thick fingers. The nails chewed ragged. "If the men catch you with the wrong tilt, they'll make you recite some awful limerick. It's one of their filthy games."

"I was told to see Mrs. Power?"

"Gert. That's me, I'm afraid. Look, the shift schedule is gone to pieces, so I haven't much time. But you're a bright girl, eh? You'll catch on."

The blue sky put Joyce in mind of a song, the one about telegraph cables on bending highways and skiing on mountainsides. Whatever it was. The music from the dance nagged at her. What odds about Frank Tucker or a couple of fellows in a truck—men of that ilk were as common as rain, and about as mindful. But the songs had shaken her, making the world sound more beautiful than it was.

Inside and blinking away sunspots, Joyce found her new workplace hardly appropriate to the dashing business of air travel. Mrs. Power showed her the ladies' with its cupboard of sanitary products. The coatroom. Supplies. Assigned her a rusted locker with a stale, powdery smell and a dead housefly on the shelf. Into the crowded, windowless warren of desks and offices for a rundown on how to write up a ticket, read a flight strip, and check a passenger manifest. ("Don't worry. It'll come to you.") Unsmiling women squeezed past, dressed like Joyce but in lighter skirts and short-sleeved blouses. Too much rouge or foundation. Men pecked two-fingered at typewriters, squinting through fluorescent gloom. They made phone calls, barked technical gibberish—"...backed up at blue jay...That's all we've got on four-check"—yanked at their ties, and noted Joyce without looking up from their work.

"New girl, Gert?"

"Send her over here, Gert."

The women were all on their feet. The men all sitting.

After tracking down her badge and nametag, Gert gave her a final once-over—"By God, you're a lovely girl"—and led her out to the ticket counter. Joyce paused before the sudden space, the concourse with its echoing voices and electric hum. Gert gave her a half-second before touching her elbow. She was all St. John's. Probably the eldest of a big Catholic brood, keeping the rest in line.

Joyce was left with a frowning woman named Mary.

"I hope you're better than the dumb tit they gave me last week," said Mary.

"We'll see," said Joyce. Told herself not to flinch when aircraft roared overhead. She touched her hair, which had been brushed until it gleamed, and tugged her jacket.

A man appeared before her, looking through smudged glasses and a straggly grey beard that reached all the way up to his eyes.

"Can you tell me, please, how long we'll be stopping?"

He hugged a fat leather satchel to his chest with both arms, holding it just like Marty had held the pig that got into the potatoes. The pig screaming and spitting and shitting on him, and Marty saying he'd kill it, and Mother saying, "No, dear God, Marty, that's Mrs. Kennedy's pig, we'll never hear the end of it."

"Miss?"

"Yes, sorry. I'll check. Just a ... one moment."

Mary had disappeared. Joyce couldn't remember a word of her morning tutorial. She turned and lifted her chin. Crack-crack went her shoes, around the door and into the sweaty room. There was a man at a desk that had previously been empty, a head of perfectly parted black hair bent over a lengthy sheet of paper.

"Excuse me."

The head looked up, mouth open and fishy eyes squinting, his face yellow-green in the lamplight.

"A gentleman, a passenger wants to know..." Joyce raised a hand in the direction of the counter.

"Yes?"

"How long it will be. His stopover." That was the word: stopover.

"What flight?"

"Oh!" said Joyce. "I'll just go—"

"Never mind. Tell him 45 minutes. He's not military, is he?"

"No. Englishman. Well dressed."

"Tell him 45 minutes."

"Yes, Mr. Shea," said Joyce, catching a look at the nametag. She resumed her post and delivered the news.

"Well," said the Englishman, releasing one arm from the satchel to remove his hat and scratch his bald head. "That's not the arrangement as I understood it. Not the thing at all."

Joyce remembered to smile. "They'll stand you a coffee at the sandwich bar," she said, having picked up the strange expression while dancing with Frank. I'll stand you a drink, he had said as they finished a box step.

The Englishman brightened. "That's alright, eh?" Joyce knew it was the smile that shifted his tone rather than the prospect of free coffee. "Is there a telegram kiosk, then?"

"Certainly, sir." She straightened her shoulders and leaned across the counter, her starched white sleeves crackling. He leaned as well, and touched her forearm, as if she was confiding in him. "Ah-ha," he said, as Joyce pointed to Posts and Telegraphs. The satchel had fallen to his side.

Joyce was smoking when Mr. Shea came in from the tarmac. The engine noise rattled teacups on desks. Men in overalls followed him, smelling of exhaust.

"Your first day, then?"

"Yes. Joyce Pelley." She stood and smoothed her skirt.

"And where do your people hail from?"

"Cape St. Rose."

"Eh?"

"It's down around—"

"How'd they vote down your way?"

"What? Oh! Mostly confederation, I think?" Her father had not revealed his vote to anyone. "I mean, I wasn't old enough, so—"

Mr. Shea waved a hand. "Never mind, girl. Just having you on. You'll want your summer kit on a day like this. Gert!" He was shouting all of a sudden, head turned over his shoulder. "Gert! Do we have summer kit for the new girl?"

"What?" The voice booming from around a corner.

"The new girl." He looked at Joyce. "Sorry?"

"Joyce Pel—"

"Joyce!" He was shouting again. "She'll want a summer kit."

"I'm waiting on Supply. They're hopeless."

"What about the dress? The frock? You've a closet full of them."

"She's too busty, Den."

Joyce felt herself blush. But the men weren't watching. Everyone was busy, the day's pace picking up.

Mr. Shea leaned back in his wooden chair, which creaked on its pedestal. His waist was tiny as a schoolgirl's. Maybe he had been a sickly boy. Probably from some big-house merchant family that voted responsible government.

"We've got you on the counter, then?"

"Yes," said Joyce. Her thighs itched fiercely.

"Good. Look, when someone gets all in a huff about being delayed, tell them forty-five minutes. You'll be right as often as not and most of them just want to know if they've time for a drink. Got that?"

"Yes, sir."

"Call me Den. Where's your nametag?"

"I was told to leave it on my jacket."

"You've only got the one? Gert will have to see to it."

Joyce feared he would start bellowing again. But instead he stood, took his clipboard and disappeared down the hall, skinny hips rolling in an exaggerated manner that might have been a limp.

3

Carter stands in the doorway, watching Sam run to the car, trying to guess whether he might pee at the mall. He's getting bolder with outside bathrooms, even peed at the airport with hardly any help.

Sam shouts, "Bye, Daddy!" and disappears behind Isabelle, who leans over him, hips shuddering as she yanks at the straps of his car seat. Confined by belts and pads, he looks strangely fragile. In a few weeks they have another checkup at SickKids, where the doctor will listen again to the slosh and flow in his chest. Sam has a heart gallop, which is probably nothing. He might have a murmur, which is likely innocuous. It could indicate a tiny hole in the upper heart wall, though such defects are often harmless. Probably, likely, often.

Isabelle's skirt balloons up around a tanned thigh as she stands straight, and dry leaves race at her feet. The trees in this young neighbourhood are thin and reedy, easy pickings for the autumn breeze.

"I'll text you if I get the early bus," calls Carter from the doorway.

"We'll come get you regardless. Right, Sam?"

"Right!" cries Sam, who loves the bus station.

"Don't be afraid of the magic toilets," calls Carter, as the car door closes on Sam.

The washrooms at the mall will surely be a fright, full of women, stall doors banging and industrial pipes roaring with water. But nothing scares Sam like the automatic flush toilets, the sudden and seemingly random flooding and sucking of the bowl. They've shown him the blinking red sensor, and waved hands in front of it to set it off. But he can't bear it, clapping hands over his ears and whining a painful, "Noooooo!"

/////

Grossman's is unchanging, with its green floor tile and church-basement furniture. Its daylight pong of dishwater and disinfectant and fermentation is the smell of afternoon sound checks. Thirty people would make a decent crowd. But stepping through the door reminds Carter that there were good nights as well, when so many people came to see Infinite Yes that squeezing up to the bar was impossible and the cops should have shut the place down.

The club is empty at one-thirty on a Sunday afternoon, save for Leah behind the bar, her mop of faded red hair hanging over the dishwasher. She greets him without looking up. Asks after his mother. The two women have never met.

Carter takes Suzy Q's old stool at the corner of the bar. Suzy was a hobbled woman who drank brandy and scratched her arms raw. Supposedly one of the boat people from the Vietnam War, with bulging blue ankles and a red vinyl raincoat full of cracks. Red flakes fell around her, and sometimes she fell too.

Leah approaches and lays a slim black box on the bar between them. A hard drive, much like the one Isabelle uses to back up their computer at home. "The new cancer is a lump in the corner of the lung."

"I'm sorry, Lee."

"Everyone's sorry. You wouldn't believe how sorry the doctors are. You should have seen them delivering the news last week. Like they just found out there's no Santa Claus." Her hands, long troubled by arthritis, rest on the table like rubber Halloween props. She's forty-nine, two years older than Carter. The hollows of her eyes have deepened, much like his. The crooked red lines spreading from each side of her nose are new. Is she a drinker now?

Leah's first cancer diagnosis had brought her back into his orbit, four years after their divorce. Carter had just met Isabelle. Euphoric in the early days of new romance, he'd responded generously when Leah called. He visited her several times following her lumpectomy, pleased that she had found no replacement for him.

She lifts the hard drive from the bar and turns it in her hand. "Will brought this along when he came to see me. He's got everything on drives like this. All of it."

"Right."

"But there's some kind of glitch. A software problem."

"A glitch?"

"I'm not sure about the details. He sat here, where you are, and he's showing me this thing and rambling on." Leah shakes her head. "Have you talked to him at all?"

"No." Carter had sent a card after Will's accident, but never followed up on a promise to call or visit.

"It did something to him, whatever happened in Alberta. He's really hard to talk to."

Carter takes the black box and turns it in his hand. It's heavier than the one on Isabelle's computer. The shell tapers to a row of silver teeth at one end, where it plugs in to some larger machine.

"Anyway, it's crapped out, one way or the other," says Leah.

"But he's still got the three-inch reels." Will had kept and catalogued the tapes from every studio session. Infinite Yes completed just one fifty-minute album in ten years. But they were constantly recording and rejecting material. Nearly a hundred hours of music, by Will's reckoning.

Leah reaches below the bar, this time producing a cardboard case. "Part two of our show-and-tell," she says.

The lid hinges open, and Carter breathes the magnetic residue of a long forgotten studio. He wraps both hands around the fat reel and lifts it. The lead end of the tape begins to fall away, and he shifts a hand to stop it unravelling further.

"Look," says Leah. She nods at the open box. There's a fine layer of dust at the bottom. "They're flaking away."

"That's from the tape?"

"Whatever we played that day." She dips a finger in and draws a line through the dust. "It's just about gone. Apparently they're all like this. Unplayable."

Carter tilts his head to read the faded pencil notes on the spine of the box. *IY 10/5/98 best takes: 5 mid/end 6 mid 12.* He returns the tape to the box, and his fingers come away black. "We have to save those hard drives, then."

"He says he can transfer it to a new format, whatever everyone's using these days. But it'll cost around five thousand dollars. And there's no guarantees the software will hold up."

"He fucked up here." Carter's anger rises. "He's got to pay for it."

"Will doesn't even have a job."

"This is ..." Carter grasps for a dramatic statement about legacy. "My boy's nearly four years old, just like that. I mean, when you're young it feels infinite. You don't understand the way things ..." He swoops a flat hand through the air. "You don't understand the velocity ..."

"I've got maybe two years, if that." Leah pushes the tape box aside and reaches to lay a dry hand over his. "I have to settle things. And with this, I think we just let it go."

"Did he say how long we have to do this? Before the software stops working, and it's all gone?"

"You're not listening, Carter. Look at me." Her voice falters and a dim memory stirs. His head resting between her small breasts, rising and falling as she breathed. "We don't do anything. The tape falls apart and the digital stuff fails. The band dies a natural death."

36

"What?"

"Remember how it used to drive you crazy?" she says. "All that old music on the radio? You'd be screaming at it. You said the past was weak and lazy."

"I said all kinds of stuff back then." Carter must have been an exhausting partner in those days, going on with his grand, over-heated ideas.

"And at the end, when we broke up, you said we should erase it all."

"I didn't say erase."

"Of course you did."

"But letting it go on purpose, Lee? It's a crime. Against our legacy."

"Or a crime against our vanity. Let's not confuse the two."

"How about we don't get personal."

"How do we not get personal? I put ten years into this, Carter." She lifts the drive and slaps it on the bar. "I left everything else because you told me to."

"Could I get a glass of water?"

Having her serve him, briefly forcing her into the barmaid's routine, might restore the balance between them. He feels ambushed, and shamefully suspects that she's coordinated all this, her own demise and that of the music, for full effect. It's true that he marched into one of the final band meetings and said they should destroy the archive. But that was just a stunt, a way to show Leah he could dismiss everything they had together.

She comes around the bar with his water, and sits next to him. He drinks, and she reaches for the glass to take a sip. "We made a mistake," she says quietly. "Lots of people pick the wrong career, the wrong partner. They figure it out and move on."

"You're talking about us," says Carter. "Maybe that was the mistake. But these recordings..."

"It's all the same." Their marriage failed, and that failure is written into the music.

Isabelle knows it was all just blind, headstrong youth. Carter has told her how he and Leah set themselves to music with the tenacity of a child sitting a difficult exam, head bowed to the task, vexed and jittery, the answers coming in spurts. How they lived as distracted ascetics. Minimal eaters. Occasional teetotallers. Night owls. Income-tax truants. They were kids, so devoted to the vitality of experience that they overdressed for shows, so they might more readily drip with sweat.

The marriage was fatally humourless and often sexless, even in the early days. It was only in the final months that he and Leah started screwing all the time. They did it quickly, with a kind of grim vigour that felt adulterous. He suspects now that Leah was not a fully willing partner in this final flurry. He recalls her body twisting and shifting as if trying to evade his. She worked hard to overcome this resistance, as if determined to swallow a pill that caught in her throat. Taking extra water to force it down.

Carter prepares for every meeting with Leah by girding himself against regret. But regret always finds him.

Straightening and leaning back in her seat, she pulls up her pant leg to scratch a reddened shin. The pants are blue and limp and shapeless, probably with an elastic waist. She's dressing like a hospital patient, concerned only with comfort and easy access to a leaking body. "What did we move on the album? Was it a thousand?"

"Closer to two," says Carter. "Eighteen hundred, at least." For years Carter kept his share of unwanted CDs, several hundred of them, shrink-wrapped and boxed. They went into a dumpster when he and Isabelle bought the house.

"So there you go. Anyone who really wants the music has it anyway." She sneezes, and Carter imagines a cloud of poisoned air shooting from her lungs. "Can we at least think about an agreement that we won't release it, or let anyone sell it?"

Carter excuses himself to the bathroom, hunching low to get down the cramped stairwell. Like the rest of Grossman's, it's plastered with yellowing photos and flyers for bands like Danny and the Devils and the Swamp Juice All Stars. A club dedicated to middle-aged white-guy blues was a poor fit for Infinite Yes, and the regulars despised the band.

The Mens is freshly disinfected, and his eyes water with the sting. He leaves the door propped open, and is standing at the urinal as Leah descends the steps and turns for the Ladies.

"Jesus Christ, the roll's empty in here," she calls. "Can you grab me one?"

"Hang on." Carter zips and takes a roll of paper from a cardboard crate in the middle of the floor. One step out the door and another to his left brings him to the Ladies.

"Whoever closed last night…" says Leah, from her stall. "Un-fucking-believable."

Carter takes a step into the washroom, side on to the stall, and offers the roll. When she stands to take it, he catches a glimpse of thin calves and the panties stretched at her ankles. Still she can't reach, so Carter leans, and sees the pouch of flesh hanging over a thin and ragged patch where he once knew a red expanse of pubic hair.

In the sanctuary of his fifty-minute bus ride home, Carter will come to hate this moment. Leah orchestrated it, obliging him to look. She knows that he can't separate their music and their bodies, and wants to remind him that one is in the other. By the time Isabelle and Sam collect him—"I peed, Daddy! I stayed and it went all the way down and I wasn't afraid!"—he will decide that the body Leah showed him can't last much longer.

In the moment, he can only apologize. "Sorry," he says, and averts his eyes. He's truly sorry about the marriage and the band and the music, about the part of him that's been waiting for her cancer to return. Every day he's waited, and every day he's been sorry.

/////

First he hears a low, droning noise. Then whispered sounds like half-formed words. She's closing in on the bit where her legs flex and her breath shoots little hisses through gritted teeth. Carter lifts his eyes to look at her face. She doesn't like him to, but he knows her eyes are closed.

His neck is tired, so he climbs down to the floor and shifts her to the edge of the bed. Careful with the ankles. They've been achy of late, and swollen. His phone starts up like a bee in a jar on the bedside table. Probably Howley Park again. He already signed off on his mother's new prescription. Another brain pill. Ratcheting up the medication.

Isabelle's fingers knead his head, easing him back a bit. She arches and gasps. There's a gurgling sound—the kind of throaty noise Carter recognizes from movies, when someone is eviscerated—then the hissing breaths.

The phone stops. Carter doesn't trust the doctors at that place, the way they wrangled him into it. We'll just give it a try, Mr. Carter. Just five milligrams per day. It slows the progress a bit.

He releases Isabelle's legs. Waits until the muscles release.

"Okay?"

Her chest jumps with little convulsions that turn into laughter. Not her real laugh. More of a mad, slippery giggle. Finally she opens her mouth and takes a long breath. Wipes her chin with the heel of a hand.

He crawls up and lays his head next to hers.

"Good joke?"

"Very."

"Care to share?"

"You wouldn't get it." She gives him a sleepy, not-quite-there look, and turns her back to him.

It took Carter a long time to understand that this is simply her way, that she dims and flares like a faulty porch light. It's better than it was with Leah. Making love with her had always been a pursuit, like he was trying to close a gulf between them.

"Back to school for you on Monday," she says, still looking away.

"I hate that phrase," says Carter. He runs his teeth over his tongue, moving the bitter-salt taste around his mouth.

Isabelle snorts a laugh.

In fact, he doesn't mind being the forty-something student. It was Isabelle who pushed him to finish the undergrad degree. Filled out the application, examined his ancient transcripts from Memorial University, brought home the calendar, and flagged courses with sticky tabs." Don't think about money or career," she said. "Just engage yourself. You'll die working at that bakery. The drudgery of it."

Carter flipped through the catalogue and settled on archaeology. He recalled being interested—or half-interested, anyway—in the archaeology course he had taken at Memorial.

She turns and takes his arm to pull him near. Carter reaches a hand between his legs to tease himself back to life.

"Relax, Carter. It's not a race." She shifts her legs to either side and takes the full weight of him. A rangy woman with broad shoulders and thick legs. She carries it well. Walks like a ballerina, toes out. Long, lovely nose. Long eyebrows and heavy white lids that seem to descend over her eyes in slow motion.

It's taken them a couple of years to get it back. Ordinary sex. The watchful grind of baby making had imposed a peculiar, abrasive kind of intimacy, even hateful at times. Isabelle hunched on the bed, taking her temperature. Reclining with knees splayed to check the quality of her mucus, stretching it like raw egg between her fingers. The practiced fumbling before Carter emptied himself into her. Waiting and not talking about it until the used pads appeared in the bathroom wastebasket, neatly rolled in their pink wrappers. Start again. Then the miscarriages, with their knee-buckling, crimson-faced cramps. Peeling away her soaked pyjama shirt, pressing a cold cloth to her blotchy face and neck and chest. Isabelle squeezing his hand so hard it ached for days after.

Later, as he dips in and out of sleep, the phone starts again. "Go away," says Isabelle, with a drowsy wave.

A nursing home wouldn't be calling at night. Unless…Carter rises on one elbow to check the phone, but the caller ID is blocked.

He's heard stories about old folks homes measuring quality of life as whatever keeps them catatonic, whatever makes it easier on the staff. Joyce is getting the new pill to ward off depression and anxiety, is how it was put to him. But maybe they just want her manageable.

Isabelle rolls into his back with a sigh, irritated to be awake. "So with your band, isn't the music out there anyway? It's probably online somewhere, isn't it?"

"Probably. She just wants us…she wants the band to have a final end."

"How do you feel about that?"

"The music's not great, I know that. But the older you get, you've got to own up to the things you did and move on."

"Unless you're Leah."

"What do you mean?"

"Her moving on days are over."

Carter sees Leah wasting away in time-lapse photography. Hips and elbows and vertebrae poking against wounded skin. Cracks and open sores running with weak blood. But he doesn't really know what cancer looks like.

"Does she have anyone? Family, or a partner?"

That question, and the hitch in her voice. It's nearly a decade since Isabelle left her brother to die alone. It was the only thing she could do, after all the days and nights spent at his apartment, the groceries delivered and meals cooked, the futile efforts to hide his dope, drain his booze, and push him into rehab, the drives to Emergency as he slumped beside her, barely conscious or doubled in pain. Ronnie was out of his mind, and dangerous. That's what Isabelle said on the day he died. She called Carter to come get her. He found her at the street corner. They drove away and went to a movie. A ridiculous old French film about a boy and girl falling in and out of love. The actors sang their parts, and it was almost too much for Carter, this relentless singing about hopeless passion. When the love expired and the boy drove away, the lights came up and everyone in the theatre looked around blinking.

Their combined body heat is too much, and Carter rolls out of the embrace.

"No boyfriend, I don't think. Leah's family is pretty small. Brother still in Kenora. A little sister who died. That was a sad tale."

"What happened?"

"I'm not sure. But she was never quite right. She always thought she was pregnant. Her period would stop and she'd be gaining weight, throwing up in the morning. The whole thing. But there was never any baby."

"Pseudocyesis," says Isabelle. "Hysterical pregnancy, they used to call it."

"Have you ever seen it?" Isabelle almost never talks about the kids she sees at the student counselling centre.

"No. Was she married?"

"The sister? I don't know. I never knew her, never really knew any of them. We did a song about her, though."

"A song?"

"About the fake pregnancies."

"My God, the poor woman's privacy!"

"But the way we did it, no one would ever know. Leah changed names. The woman in the song dies, and within a year or so the sister died too."

"That's awful!"

"Yeah."

In fact, he and Leah had been proud of the coincidence. Here was proof of their artistic intuition, a sign that they had hit a rich vein and songs were now bursting from them as thunderbolts of pure truth.

Isabelle rises. Her feet pad across the carpet and make sticky sounds in the wooden hallway.

There was a time when the old French film wedged between them. But they worked through it until Sam appeared and made everything that came before seem insignificant. Ronnie was hopeless, doomed no matter what, and hardly worthy of his sister's loyalty. One night he even tried to offer Isabelle to one of his drug buddies, in exchange for a hit of whatever they were on.

"Remember how sweet it was when we were trying?" says Isabelle, returning to the bed, tossing and settling. "Before Sam? Trying, trying, trying."

"What made you think of that?"

"I'm getting my period."

"It wasn't sweet. It was really hard."

"I know. But sometimes it was, I don't know. Nice."

"I hated it."

"You didn't. You loved it."

/////

The telephone rings, and Sam responds, singing nonsense words from his perch at the kitchen nook. He's ignoring his toast, though it's been cut into shapes, the way he likes it. Another ring.

"I have to pee," says Sam. He scrambles to the floor and strips off his pyjamas. Sprints up the stairs using hands and feet. At the top of the stairs he shouts, "Daddy! Answer the phone!"

It's Howley Park. What if they want to shift Joyce to the place down by the lake? He can't blame his mother for fearing the prospect of diapers and spoon-fed tapioca and bodies slumped like dead infantry in the TV room.

The third and final ring. Carter watches through the window as a car hits the dip in the street and creaks like an enormous mattress. He can imagine the stream of invective from the driver. Locals know to slow down when they approach 19 Vickers Street, with its

44

nasty hollow. The subdivision is barely a decade old, but its roads are sinking in spots where they weren't properly graded.

Upstairs, he finds Sam in his favourite underwear. Nautical blue, patterned with whitecaps and orange fish.

"Sam, where did you get those?"

"Where's Mom?"

"She had to go to work early. Tell me where you found those underwear, please."

"In my room."

"In your laundry basket. What have we told you about taking clothes from your laundry?"

Sam turtles, face down and rear end raised, the curve of his white back shielding the unsteady heart. The fish on the underpants swim front to back, around the side and across the cheeks.

"Sammy, you wore those underwear yesterday. They have to be washed."

Squirming and sliding, the boy dangles his head over the side of the bed. "My other underwear are fake."

"Fake how?"

"Fake on my bum."

"Come on, Sammy. You know better."

"I don't!"

They're calling it his defiant phase. Though Isabelle suggests it might not be a phase at all. Maybe it's the real Sam. "It's gone on so long now," she said. "It could be part of his personality coming to life. A contrarian streak." How might they explain this in the child development books? *When your boy acts like an asshole, the parent might assume it's a passing phase. But we should consider the possibility that maybe he's just an asshole.*

"Time to go see Miss Kristen."

"I have to pee!"

"You just went."

Any mention of Kristen sends him dashing to the toilet. He has

45

loved her unconditionally since his first day in the three-year-old room. It was never this way with Miss Tricia, though he adored her as well. When he switched rooms, the shift in his affection was quick and absolute, and went straight to his bladder.

Carter leaves him to the bathroom and returns to the kitchen.

A message on the phone.

"Herbert? Could I speak to Herbert please?" His mother's voice begins loud, then softens. The swish and rustle of a hand against the mouthpiece. "This is Joyce Carter and Herbert Carter is my son. He was raised on Alcock Street. My husband, Arthur, is passed away. There are no other children."

Someone interrupts her. A man nearby. "What?" says Joyce, her voice drifting. "Talk right into the phone, my love," says the man.

A delay. Then she speaks slowly, measuring her words. "Can I speak to Herbert, please."

"Daddy!" shouts Sam. "Daddy!"

Muffled voices. A tumbling hang-up, his mother struggling to match receiver to cradle.

Carter saves the message. Sam crashes into him, face to crotch. Tugs at the zipper of his jacket. "I can't. I can't."

Carter fixes the snag. The zipper runs smooth, prompting Sam's first smile of the day.

"Who you talking to, Dad?"

"Nobody."

"Was it Mommy?"

"No. Where's your knapsack? You still need pants, Sam."

When Carter leans in to buckle the car seat, Sam exudes a mild stale-water scent. Not only has he escaped the house in his orange-fish underpants, he's pulled his entire wardrobe from the laundry basket.

"You're dirty," says Carter.

"You're dirty," says Sam. "We didn't brush teeth."

//////

His mother won't remember calling. Or she'll get indignant about the booze again. "It's not right that they keep it from me." He lifts the phone and finds the call display. *Howley Pk 3 Fl.*

"Third floor nursing station."

"Hi. My name is Herbert Carter. My mother is a resident there."

"Mrs. Carter? Yes?"

"She called a little while ago. From this number."

"I'm sorry? You're calling for her? Did you go through our switchboard?"

"No. She called me. Just an hour ago. Or…"

"Resident calls don't normally go through here, sir. I could transfer you to the switchboard."

"But she called from this number. This is the number that showed up. She left a message."

"One moment, sir. Nora? Nora? NORA! Who covered off when I went downstairs?"

The voice breaks into shards of syllables. A second voice answers. Distant agitation. Carter sits at the front window. Counts eight black ants belly up on the sill. A live one flexing its legs in the corner.

"…and tell them they better. That crowd. They got to figure it out. That bloody crowd." A moment of throat-clearing as the voice returns to the phone. "Is this about the fee increase, sir?"

"No. I'm returning her call."

A flapping of pages. "Only we had a few calls about the fee increase. But it's no good calling us. Oh, here we go. Someone had a complaint about Mrs. Carter."

"A complaint?" The word feels like a terrible defeat.

"From another resident. I wouldn't worry about it, sir. Some people complains about anything. Mr. Foley complained the other day because a fellow at his table had two pieces of pie. A formal complaint, mind you."

"But she was the one calling me. I don't know what it was about."

"A couple of them were riled up about the fee increase."

47

"But that's got nothing to do with her. Anyway, can I talk to her?"

"I wouldn't worry about it, sir. I'll have the office get back to you, all the same. Anyway, we got to get everything sorted out here now."

Carter takes the hint and says goodbye.

A letter about the fee increase arrived last week. An extra $176 per month is far from insignificant. But Joyce is financially independent, thanks to a frugal life and a surviving-spouse pension from the feds. Art Carter did well for himself. Got out of Bonavista Bay at a young age and hooked into a good government job, just in time for all those big post-war salary leaps. One child. Nice split-level with a two-car driveway, a maple in the yard and a wood stove in the den because it's nice to have a wood stove. Trips to Montreal and Nova Scotia—Florida one year, though none of them could take the heat. An annual reminder of their good fortune was the summer trip to see Dad's crowd in Bonavista Bay. The chilly, damp little cove and its weed-choked pond. The grubby cousin with the scar on his lip. The local boys and their nasty street hockey games. The creaking gloom of the general store, like something from a horror movie.

Carter suspects that he was never meant to enjoy Bonavista Bay. The trip was meant to be instructive, an illustration of his father's progress in the world. A reminder to the boy that he had narrowly escaped a grim and backwards existence.

Prosperity nagged at Art Carter like a nervous condition. Bonavista Bay nipped at his heels, prompting repeated wisecracks about boiled cabbage, horrible outhouses, frozen well water, and nothing but an orange for Christmas. He voted for Joey Smallwood, attended Sunday mass out of obligation more than devotion, and scoffed at those who waxed on about simpler times and the good old days. "Poverty," he would say with a snort. "Misery." He was careful of his dignity, keeping his tie snug and jacket buttoned. Didn't dare haggle with tradesmen or bankers, for fear of appearing cheap. Leaned too close and agreed too readily when addressed by a hotel clerk or car salesman, eager to show that he was equal to the exchange. An evening at Sinbad's Steakhouse made him giddy, though he always placed his order with gravity, hands folded across his belly. The bill left him anxiously fingering his patent leather wallet. Ten percent? Twenty? Inevitably he over-tipped. Overcompensated. An apology for his inexplicable good fortune.

4

Joyce unzipped and pushed the dress down to her ankles. The pale blue taffeta billowed up around her legs and she punched at it with her feet to get clear of it. A shiver went through her, back to front. The radiator ticking and banging behind her, hopeless. She danced on the balls of her feet until she was into her robe. Pulled the blanket from Rachel's bed to wrap around the robe. Wool socks and into bed with the covers to her neck. She wanted a cigarette but didn't want her hands out in the open.

What a night. If it was going to be like this all the time, Joyce wanted no part of it.

Rickety old cabin down by Deadman's Pond. Wouldn't last five minutes if you put a match to it. Those men with their pocket flasks out. Sitting right up front, shouting and carrying on, and their women laughing. Not laughing so much as screaming. You'd have thought they were being murdered.

Den had warned her that afternoon, as she was leaving work. Better watch your step, he said, when she told him she was off to do a show with the band. Especially down at that cabin, he said.

The savages will be out. Den was no innocent. Joyce took him to be around her father's age, but he carried himself with the vitality of a much younger man. She'd seen how he leaned across the lunch counter, chattering like a magpie, coaxing a smile from that little one who was always rinsing the dishes. If Dennis tells a girl to watch her step, it might be advice worth heeding.

The night had started well enough. A few nice dance numbers before Joyce stepped up to sing "Carolina Moon."

Then the crowd arrived from steak night at the Base, drinking from their pocket flasks. "Steak night's a bugger if you're trying to keep up with the Scando boys," said Reg Pritchett, who had been with the band longer than anyone.

"Who?" asked Joyce.

"The boys from Scandinavian Airlines. Try to match drinks with them and you're asking for trouble."

The microphone still gave her a fright, the way it sent her voice booming off the walls. She kept backing away from it, and the more she backed away the louder she sang. Then she'd catch herself and lean in for a low note, and the microphone would set it howling like wind in the eaves.

She'd like to slap Gord Delaney, the way he kept after her all night, chasing her across the room during the break, slopping his drink on her. "Don't be shouting, Joyce. You're singing like a tavern girl." What in God's name did that mean? Tavern girl. Joyce didn't argue with him, wouldn't give him the satisfaction. She was near tears by the end of it, but wouldn't give him that satisfaction either.

Delaney with that tarnished old trumpet, standing there singing "Don't Fence Me In" like he was showing her how. Big red face on him.

She'd caught a ride home with Eric and that new fellow, the Frenchman with the saxophone. They hardly talked. That's when the shivers started, in the cold car with the sweat drying on the back of her neck.

51

Joyce exposed one hand to pull a cigarette from the bedside table. A second hand to strike the match. Rubbed one foot over the other, then switched. The taffeta was still crumpled on the floor, a ring of blue fabric with a hole in the middle where Joyce used to be. "I can't carry it at all, even before this," Gloria had said, draping the dress across her very pregnant belly. "But on you? My dear, you'll be a proper Peggy Lee." She was almost right. They had to let out a couple of stitches so Joyce could breathe, and that was fine for a while. But as the night went on, it was like the dress gave up on her. It went floppy at the shoulders, and when she was singing "I Got It Bad" she felt it sag around her chest and back. She must have looked like a marionette, hanging limp until the puppet master returned. Not that anyone noticed. Not that she gave a tinker's cuss if anyone had.

She didn't mind the crowd in the back, playing cards and hardly looking up from their tables. But the pocket flask fellows up front, drinking and shouting. Then heading out on the dance floor, not dancing so much as just making fools of themselves. Their girls laughing like it was the funniest thing. Then somebody was throwing up. Inevitable.

Joyce checked the clock. Could she sleep at all between now and seven? She'd be dropping by lunchtime, head aching when the mid-afternoon flights touched down. The shift schedule was relentless. Good thing they never eased up with it. Otherwise people might expect a decent night's sleep. The days held no shape, marked only by tides of darkness and light. She was always due at work in five hours or three hours or before she was through dinner or before the laundry was dry. Which is how she had ended up going in yesterday with wet bra cups stuck to her and the blouse damp on her shoulders.

Burnt toast somewhere. The hotel tossed and turned at all hours. Doors squeaking and slamming. Cold air rushing up the hallway. Whistling kettles, muffled squeals, the crash of a stumbling drunk, the operatic rise and fall of a card game. A shift change every eight hours, with its hurried steps, curses and sighs, barks of laughter. At any given hour there was a crowd at work, a crowd trying to sleep, and a crowd at liberty. Itching with liberty. The women were no better than the men. But the men were louder about it. Acting drunker than they were, egging each other on. They knew when they were being watched, but that just made it worse. They wanted to be watched. The boys here wanted everyone to know that they could do whatever they damn well pleased.

Still, she wouldn't mind having one here now, just to take the chill off. Like last fall when her father sent her around the point to look after Aunt Nance for a few days. Jack O'Mara said, I know that house. And Joyce said, you wouldn't wake Nance with a shotgun. So she left her window ajar. Jack slipped in and warmed the bed until daylight. But of course it's never that simple with a man. Never enough to wrap up together, get cozy, maybe fool around a bit. Because then his piece of business is sticking up like a broken bedspring, and you can either do something with it or forget about getting any sleep at all.

Joyce shrugged off the blanket, twisted out of the robe and stockings and left them on the floor. She pulled the flattened pillow from behind her head and tried to punch some life into it. Gloria would hear about tonight, because she heard about everything. Then she'd say, Oh Joyce, I don't know about that crowd. I don't know if that's the crowd for you, hanging around those parties at all hours.

She closed her eyes and a heaviness settled in her legs. Sleep when you can, was the rule. The relentless traffic set windows shaking and lights blinking. Nobody complained, not after the first week or so.

Gordon Delaney was the last man she wanted to see in the morning. But he managed the commissariat, doing up food trays for refuelling flights. He never looked busy. Often she would see him in the company of other men in suits, striding with purpose in the direction of the Big Dipper. He never looked her way, though he knew she was there. On a cigarette break a few days ago she had met a rather dim girl who worked at the commissariat. She said they were all treated poorly.

Summer had come to an abrupt end, but the sudden frost didn't stop people going out all the time. There wasn't much point staying home at night, not in this freezing room with the radiator hammering away. If she gave up now she could just imagine the boys in the band going on about her. Guess she couldn't take it. What do you expect? Only a young one from around the bay. Never seen a damn thing in her life. She wouldn't have it. She didn't mind any of them, not Gord Delaney or the band or the drunk fools with their pocket flasks.

Mary said next pay packet, a crowd of the girls were flying into St. John's for a day's shopping. Step on the plane and they'd be on Water Street within the hour. Joyce resolved to go and come home with a couple of decent dresses of her own, properly fitted. She'd be ready for the next dance, the next crowd. Wouldn't back away from the microphone anymore, either. Step right up to it. It won't bite.

/////

They were the first to board, and sat in the front, where they could hear the goings-on in the cockpit. Joyce wasn't sure she wanted to hear any of it. But at least she wasn't sitting next to Maeve Vardy from the post office. Woman could talk. She had introduced herself to Joyce in the terminal, and declared that she knew St. John's like the back of her hand, from working the entire war at the Caribou Hut.

"What's the Caribou Hut?" Joyce had whispered to Mary.

"The hostel where they put up servicemen during the war. She got a husband out of it, but he was lost in the merchant marine."

Now Maeve was going on about an owl. "It was Gisbourne shot the owl himself, I guarantee you. Boom! Just like Davy Crocket."

54

Between the nattering, Joyce could hear the pilots talking. Shouldn't there be more than a curtain separating the cockpit, because what if they had to talk about engine trouble or bad weather? People shouldn't hear that. Both pilots were former RAF, and looked the part, with their practiced calm and brilliant hair going grey at the temples. Joyce had seen them at the Airport Club, one showing a diary he kept during the war. Every bombing mission recorded, noting the target cities, payloads dropped, and the number of crews lost.

"Gisbourne's on the river, fishing the big pools just past the turn," said Maeve Vardy. "Henley's Turn, you see? Every year he's out to the same pools. He looks up and wouldn't you know there's a big old lopper staring him right in the face. Plugged it with one shot. Well over a foot long, it was."

"Nonsense," whispered Mary, settling into her seat next to Joyce. "Gisbourne wouldn't know a twenty-two if it took his own head off. Still lives with his mother."

The pilots talked the sort of gibberish Joyce overheard every day. "Thirty-six can … ceiling ragged … generator three." But it sounded different, like everything was urgent and it all might go wrong at any moment. "Come on, darlin'," one of them said as the third engine coughed. Then all engines were going, and they were moving. The shaking went up the back and into her throat.

"I know," said Mary. "It settles after."

"It's alright," said Joyce, and closed her eyes to the shudder that turned everything blurry.

When plans were hatched for a day in St. John's, Joyce had said she might have to work. "Someone will change shifts," said Mary. Then she said she already had two new outfits from Scheffman's, including a green dress with a sheer overlay that looked like something from a magazine. All the girls laughed and said Scheffman's smells like mothballs, just wait till you see the racks at Bowring's. But ten dollars to get to St. John's, and as much again to get home?

Nearly a week's pay gone, just like that. Think of it though, the girls said. Barely an hour to get from your room to the shops down on Water Street.

"You know Briscoe? In that band?" asked Mary.

"What?" Joyce turned, and for a moment saw ground rushing in the window, like fabric being ripped apart.

"Roy Briscoe is in the band with you. Works at British Overseas."

"Yes?" The blur was nauseating. Her hands, Mary's knees, the seat back in front of her.

"He's in for it now. Laid out some Englishman last night."

"Englishman?" A tilt, and lift, followed by a little dip that turned Joyce's legs to water, before they settled into a steady climb. Someone let out a gasp behind her. But Joyce liked it better. Not so much noise and shaking.

"Last night he's having words with his wife outside the bar," said Mary. "And it gets worse from there." She leaned across Joyce's lap and called to Maeve Vardy, "Tell Joyce about the racket last night. Briscoe and the British fellow."

"Oh my word!" cried Maeve, turning to Joyce. "But hadn't you heard? Right outside the Big Dipper, Briscoe and the wife are having words. He gives her the back of his hand, just a little tap. And this little Englishman comes over and gets between them. Well, buddy, Roy doesn't even blink. Lays into the stranger like this." She mimed a punch with her small red fist. "And one of these." A high jab with the other hand. The plane gave a surge, drowning out her voice. Joyce gripped her armrest, but no one else seemed alarmed. Maeve kept talking, pushing her nose to one side with a finger.

"Not just any Englishman. No, sir," she said, coming back into range. "None other than the Vice Chair of British Overseas, about to board for LaGuardia."

"Poor luck for Briscoe," tittered Mary. "He's in for it now."

"He's in for it for sure," cried Maeve. "B'ys, oh b'ys."

Joyce's eye caught the window over Mary's shoulder. The plane bobbed lightly against the horizon, level with small white clouds under an overcast canopy.

"Do you want me to close it?" asked Mary. "Some people, the window makes them sick."

"Yes, maybe," said Joyce, her insides lifting and falling with the horizon.

Mary leaned into the aisle. "Someone said this morning that's just a lot of old talk. There was no British fellow."

"Well, I got the rights of it, I'll tell you right now! Never mind what someone said."

"But you egged her on," whispered Joyce.

Mary smiled and opened a magazine.

///////

Joyce made it to St. John's without need of a sick bag, though she nearly lost her stomach in the lurching taxi that delivered them to the waterfront. She had ideas of a sequined dress with three-quarter sleeves. But in her excitement at the Royal Stores—more clothes than she could wear in a lifetime—she bought two wool skirts she might just as easily have found anywhere. A girl she didn't know beckoned her to the appliance section and pulled at a creamy white door, which opened with a sucking sound. "Sensational new advanced design Philco," said Joyce, reading the tag. "All the conveniences and refinements of modern refrigeration for the modern housewife." Unspoiled by food, the interior was clean and inviting, especially the smooth dark of the ice box.

They spanned the sidewalks and crowded the shops, lifting the lids on console radio sets at City Radio and Music and stroking the furs at Ewing's. Joyce wrapped a fox stole around her shoulders. It was the full length of the fox, head and all, a polished clasp in place of its nose and jaw. They admired the men smoking outside the sailworks, and turned from the direct looks of the fellows outside Marshall Motors.

After a nice lunch at Bowring's, Joyce gave up on dresses and found a simple striped pullover that was just right. "Flattering!" said one of the girls. "Whoever you're buying that one for, he'll be drove mad." She liked the racy figurines—nymphs with pubic mounds and pointed breasts—in the china cabinet at Thompson's Jewelers. Maeve headed east to visit the Caribou Hut—"To say a prayer and shed a tear"—and the group scattered, agreeing to regroup at McMurdo's and replenish their Beecham's Pills before heading back to the airport.

Joyce picked her way through a lane filled with dog droppings when a cold rain came on, driving her into a cramped shop where a gloomy-looking man offered her a free sample of Campana's Italian Balm. Joyce extended a palm for a drop, and he watched her hands roll over each other. "Rub it right in," he said.

He asked where she was from, and invited her to freshen up in the little room out back. There was a girl who worked for him sometimes who kept her things there. It had a mirror, and free makeup samples.

Joyce hesitated, and rounded the counter to step into the room, just to straighten her hair. A small table was crowded with cosmetics, the familiar smell mixing with a heavy, salty odour that made her anxious.

"I'll close up for a few minutes, so you won't be embarrassed by anyone coming through," the man called from the front. He bolted the door and flipped the sign in the window. Joyce found a hairbrush as he appeared in the doorway of the little room. "Where did you say you grew up?"

"Cape St. Rose."

"Do all the girls from there look like Jane Russell?"

"Who?"

"We've a fine selection of stockings, like nothing you'll see in Gander," he said, filling the doorway so he nearly touched her knees. "If you want to change out of those old damp ones, eh? You're all wet from that rain." He lifted the hem of her jacket.

"But I've got my flight," said Joyce, near tears all of a sudden.

"Hold on a moment. I've got the perfect shoe for you."

When he turned to his shelves she could see the shop door, its deadbolt like the one that locked her room. With a few steps and a quick turn of a hand, she was out.

The flight home was sparsely seated, the plane buffeted by wind. Joyce, who had been nauseous since the strange encounter at the little shop, made use of the sick bag. Rinsed with stale water brought by the stewardess. The wind surged, and the aircraft strained against a leftward tilt. Joyce gripped the armrest and stared between her buckled shoes, head pounding. The sour taste in her mouth felt like her awful insides bubbling to the surface. She had abandoned her father, her brother. Shamed her mother's memory with her willful behaviour. She swallowed, forcing back her disgust and humiliation.

The turbulence ended, and a weak wash of sunlight filtered through the grey twilight.

"Who's Jane Russell?" she asked Mary.

"You've seen her in movies."

"Have I?"

"Maybe not out where you're from. Did a man say you looked like her?"

"How did you know?" Had Mary been to the same shop?

"Your figure, it's all they see."

One of the pilots came back to chat. "Eight years ago today we bombed Mainz," he said. "Six crews lost in our squadron."

"My brother Lester flew over two hundred missions," said Maeve. "Over two hundred. Easiest thing he ever did, he says."

/////

Joyce thought she might show her purchases to Rachel. But Rachel was on her the moment she came through the door.

"Come out with us."

"No, Rach. I'm on at eight."

"We're going to the Officers' Mess. George is taking us."

"George who?"

"I don't remember. Come. Please?"

George was a green-eyed British man who came in a car and brought them to his apartment in a building overlooking an old rubbish pit from the war. "RAF," he announced. "Pathfinders Squadron 614. Navigator." He poured drinks of gin, warm as bath water, no mix. Joyce was still reeling from the flight home. But George said they couldn't go to the club until the gin was gone. He sat close to Rachel, an arm disappearing behind her back.

Joyce had imagined the Officers' Mess as exclusive and richly appointed. But the tightly packed tables and chairs had people colliding and stumbling, and a band playing Irish tunes brought Joyce's headache back. They found a table, and George spent the next ten minutes talking to a man over his shoulder. Some story about leaking fuel. He was a bore, with his eager camaraderie and tattered sports coat.

The large woman singing Irish waltzes had big fleshy arms that swayed in time to the music. There was no room to dance and nobody listening anyway, and bottles were going around with little glasses, and you had to drain a glass if someone put it in front of you. Rachel fixed her gaze on the table, mouth half open. George muttering into her ear.

Joyce fell into a woman's lap en route to the washroom, spilling her drink. She didn't understand the toilet, yanking its long chain to no effect. There was a fire exit at the end of a hall, propped open with a brick. The stoop looked out on an empty lot where three soot-faced boys piled grass on a small, choking fire. They paid her no mind. She must have stood there shivering for a long time.

At eight o'clock the next morning an elderly couple pushed a ticket at her, saying, Toronto, Toronto. Joyce tried to explain that their ticket was with KLM Royal Dutch, not TCA. She called the KLM desk, but the couple wouldn't let up. Toronto, Toronto.

"Jesus in the garden," said Joyce, tapping the logo on her jacket. "You're with KLM." The old man tugged at his white silk scarf and clutched his silvery head, and the old woman snarled something that sounded a lot like swearing. A KLM agent arrived, and determined that while the couple had crossed the ocean on KLM, they were booked through to Toronto on TCA. The silver-haired man had simply pulled the wrong ticket from his raglan pocket.

Joyce used her break to make herself throw up, but her thick papery tongue wouldn't let anything past. She was sweating cold when Den called her in and said there was a complaint about her language from a couple transferring from KLM.

"They didn't even know English," said Joyce.

"They knew enough, apparently."

"The men swear all the time."

"Not in front of passengers," said Den. "By the book I ought to suspend you a day. But never mind. Just a little more patience next time, yes? KLM doesn't service Toronto. That might have been your first hint. Anyway, let's get on with it. There's weather in the Maritimes."

Joyce felt her insides turn, and rushed for the toilet.

Anything routed through Halifax or Moncton was grounded, so she spent the afternoon dealing with that crowd. Mike Devine next to her, in his usual panic, sweating through his shirt and barking at her. Den raging into the phone because the rooms weren't nearly ready, and Gert cursing Heathrow for the illegible baggage tags.

She finished the shift in tears, wishing Den had suspended her so she wouldn't have to show her face again in eight hours. The rain let up and the cool air felt good, so she opened her coat to it, walked for a bit, and stopped at the Goodyear's Canteen. It was empty, save for a boy and girl occupying the first booth, hands linked across the table. When Joyce took a booth at the back, the girl stood and shooed the boy out the door. Joyce asked for tea, and said, "Sorry to interrupt you and your fellow."

"I'm trying to break up with him," the girl said, laying out a cup and saucer. "But I have to see him at school every day. Anyway, the train'll be along any minute."

Joyce couldn't imagine what it must be like to grow up here. The girl was only a few years behind her, but she could make a bit of money at the canteen, have a boy visit, and break it off with him. Rejecting a half-sensible boy might stain a girl for life in a place like Cape St. Rose.

The booths filled as people gathered for the five-forty train, which boarded just up the road. Most of them looked to be heading home after seeing a doctor. Many of the adults moved slowly, gasping with the effort or leaning on arms. It was impossible to tell which children might be sick, as they could barely contain their vitality.

A woman with a plate of chips asked to share Joyce's booth. "Are you just off shift?" she asked.

"Back at midnight," said Joyce. "Are you a stewardess?"

"How did you know?"

Joyce indicated the TCA blue of the woman's uniform collar, peeking out where she unbuttoned her raincoat. But it was everything about her, really. The hair bun; the eyebrows, black as oil slicks; her slender form, as pale and long-limbed as a newborn goat. She introduced herself as Katie, stranded overnight by the system in the Maritimes. The rest of her crew was already into a bottle back at whichever hotel it was. But she wasn't in the mood. She sized up Joyce and said, "Hard shift?"

Joyce described the last two days.

"When did you eat last?" asked Katie.

Joyce shook her head. She was too tired to eat. Rarely hungry at meal times, ravenous at odd hours.

"Eat," Katie said, pushing her plate to the centre of the table. "Go on. Put ketchup on. Anything helps. You don't want a big meal when you're on a quick turnaround," she continued, as Joyce picked at the chips. "It'll leave you logy. Just a little something to set you up for a nap. Then a little something after the nap to send you back to work. You have a kettle? You want a kettle in your room, and tea, and biscuits."

There's a few other tricks, she explained. Simple things to ease the day. You're better off sleeping in snatches. Save your big sleeps for the end of the shift cycle. Keep your hair in a tight bun, like so. Same bun every day, don't even think about it. Sprinkle baking soda in your hose to keep them fresh for an extra shift. Keep an extra deodorant at work, and apply a new layer when you're on break.

"What does your husband make of it?" asked Joyce. "Wouldn't he rather you were home?"

"Husband? Oh!" Katie laughed and turned the golden band on her finger. "This is only for keeping the dogs at bay. It works on some of them, anyway."

/////

Two days later a man stopped her outside the chapel. "Well, Joyce, I wonder if we'll have that drink soon."

"We'll have that drink directly," said Joyce, trying to place him.

"No time to lose, I'd say. But you got home alright after?"

There was a touch of gallantry in how he rushed the conversation along and dashed as soon as they set a date. He knew her humiliation from the night at the Officers' Mess and was at pains to relieve it.

"Well done," said Rachel, after watching the encounter from respectable distance. "He was with that band. Remember?"

"No. God only knows what I said."

They met the next day after work. The Big Dipper was crowded, but there weren't many she knew. They found a table next to a Chinaman, who turned away when they sat down, and started taking hasty bites of his sandwich, as if fearing they had come to take it from him.

Jules—he worked his name into the conversation early—worked at American Overseas, and had been assigned to Gander four weeks ago. He was back and forth to Argentia a good deal, coordinating fuel and other supplies. He kept a room at Mrs. Pinsent's.

"No drinking, no women, no singing, that's her motto," he said. "She manages to keep a damper on the singing, at least."

Joyce laughed. She could see he expected laughter.

His last name was Walser and he came from somewhere in the States, somewhere she had never heard of, and planned to settle there in time. A shadow of black stubble went down into his collar and nearly up to his eyes. His round, rolling accent was new to her.

She sipped her whiskey, her first since the Officers' Mess, and listened for hints of what she might have said that night.

"You said I should talk to the man running that band," he said.

"Gordon. Gord Delaney."

"To see if they need a clarinet."

Joyce unbuttoned her TCA jacket and pushed the flaps aside.

"You don't travel overnight with them, do you?"

"Who?"

"That band."

"I've only done a couple of dances around here."

Jules nodded and sipped his drink. "I'm sure you're careful with your reputation."

They played crib and he won two games handily, so there was no need of a rubber. Jules asked if there was a good poker game to be had around town. Not penny ante. A real game. "You don't know what kind of town you got until you know how the men play poker," he said.

/////

The man who took the beating from Roy Briscoe wasn't the Vice Chair of British Overseas. But he was the Vice Chair's son-in-law, close enough to cost Briscoe his job. Mike Devine said a toffee-nosed limey should know better than to get between a man and his wife. Gert said it was bad news for the wife, as losing the job wouldn't do much to improve Roy's mood. By this time, Joyce recalled Roy Briscoe as one of the horn players in the band. A big, shoe-leather face surrounded by curls of black hair. A rumour got about that he was part Jack-a-tar, but Mary said it was nonsense.

"Sure the Briscoes don't even have children," she whispered. "The Jack-a-tars are always at it, you know. Back in school I had a friend was sneaking around with a Jack-a-tar. She was off with the nuns in no time."

With Briscoe out of the band, they might need Jules. Joyce didn't welcome the prospect. She wanted to see him on her own terms.

/////

She was singing the second verse, an abject lover begging for pity, when Gordon cut her off.

"Don't be going after it so hard, Joyce." He paced the floor in front of the stage. "You want to string it along a bit. Hold back a little. A girl needn't spread her legs as soon as she gets a nod and a wink."

He could have said, "A girl needn't drop her skirt" or "needn't bed down." But he chose to be vulgar. Still, Joyce took his point about the singing. She retreated from the microphone, placed her hands in the small of her back and arched.

"Are you thinking about anything when you sing?" Gordon sat at a table and reached into a bowl of last night's peanuts.

"What do you mean?"

"When you sing the words? Do you think about an old boy-friend, something like that?"

"No." Joyce thought the suggestion odd. Her life was no match for the brilliant visions brought on by the songs, with their romantic picnics on the beach, heartsick nights on lonely city streets, and new love always turning up in Paris, or on the Isle of Capri. "Sometimes I picture the things in the song."

"As long as you don't try to make them about real things."

It hadn't occurred to her to think about real things. She didn't even know whether Capri was a real island. What did it matter?

Gordon tossed peanuts in his mouth and chewed, his entire fleshy face in motion. "People don't want that, to be reminded of anything real. This is a show we're putting on. A lark. A fancy dress-up ball, in its own little way."

Eric hunched at the piano bench. Despite the chill of an empty nightclub at eleven o'clock in the morning, he was down to a yellowed undershirt, his faded leather bomber jacket crumpled on the floor behind him. "So what happened with the hospital party?" he asked.

"I told them we can't do it," said Gordon. "Not with Mike Healey gone to Fox Harbour."

"Again?"

"Says the wife makes him go. She misses the ocean."

"What about Ivany?"

"Working."

"Buddy in Grand Falls? He could use Mike's drums."

"Never again. Plays like a bricklayer."

"Bloody Healey."

The scrape of a door, and the janitor emerged from the kitchen with his mop and pail. Wheels of the bucket squeaking as he crossed the dance floor, through another swinging door and behind the bar.

"Church Lads are in here at noon," he said, gathering empty bottles and lining them up on the bar.

"Somebody likes their gin," said Gordon.

"Crowd of Frenchies come through last night." The janitor tipped an empty gin bottle bottom up. "Drank every drop. I don't imagine they were fit to fly this morning."

"Another go?" Eric asked.

"Let's try the up-tempo number," said Gordon, snapping his fingers. "Get the party going."

"Sure thing, boss." Eric rolled his hands up the keyboard in an exaggerated flourish, fingernails rimmed black with grease.

Joyce cleared her throat and sipped from her glass. Gordon had convinced the janitor to unlock the bar and pour them drinks. But the whiskey scalded her throat without warming it. She waited for Eric to start and tucked her hair behind her ears. Breathed in and out.

I'll take you on, you might regret it.
I'll take you on, you won't forget it.
You never know what you're in for with a girl like me.

Gordon was right. Songs turned the world into a dream place. What could a song say about Roy Briscoe and his wife, or the strange man cornering girls in his shop? Or about Joyce being courted by a man who had already seen her at her worst?

The janitor's stringy mop slapped the floor. His tattered railway shirt suggested a son or daughter working with CN. They were the only old folks in town, the ones who came to be with family, to watch their grandkids and pick up a bit of work. Gert Power's mother had come for the electric lights and flush toilets. Though the toilets gave her a fright.

Joyce had thought it might be easier, rehearsing with just the piano. Without the whole band looking at her and waiting for the next mistake. She listened for Eric's timing and watched his fingers hit the keys, but every line seemed to snag on the wrong end of his chords.

She pushed on to the safe harbour of the chorus, and was ready to try another verse. But Eric stopped and reached for his cigarettes. Gordon was sitting again, hands folded over his belly and chin lowered like he might be sleeping.

"Anything big this afternoon?" Eric looked at his watch and pulled the lid over the keyboard.

"Military charters. The usual," said Gordon. "You?"

"Maintenance. Snow gear. Should have been done in the summer and now there's a big panic, of course. One of the ploughs seized up altogether."

"That's Healey's job," said Gordon. "You got ground operations always in a snarl because he won't do his job. His wife leading him around by the nose."

"Some fellas can't hack it," said Eric. "And Healey's one of them."

5

Carter and Isabelle had talked about his first marriage. He wanted to be honest with her. But he wasn't.

He should have told her about the dog off its leash, running circles in the rain. The circles expanding and the dog soaked, yellow-white fur plastered to its sunken ribcage. Starving and not caring. Leah in his boxer shorts, oatmeal sticking to the pot and the stale refrigerator smell, the Irish boyfriend and the girl who didn't exist, the dead mailman's guitar and all the old furniture shrouded in bed sheets.

Isabelle wouldn't like that tale. But there was nothing else worth telling. So he hadn't been honest.

It would soon be twenty-five years since he found the Telecaster.

The old mailman had died in his bed on the second floor of a red brick house. The room was narrow and sweltering. There was a patch of carpet still flattened from the oxygen tank, and a bedside table patterned with rings made by glasses or mugs. A tree branch tapped the window, and leaves poked through where it was wedged open.

The listing had said "electric guitar, good condition." Not much to go on for a trip across town and the thirty-minute walk from

Runnymede. But Carter badly needed a guitar because Leah had said, "You need a real fucking guitar."

When he arrived at the house, the door was blocked by two men carrying a couch.

One of them said, "We made our deal, lady."

"I'm watching you." A woman's voice from inside. "This paint job. Out of my pocket."

They were big men with scalps shaved to stubble. They moved as if the couch was no weight at all in their thick hands, down the steps and across the front lawn to a pickup truck. Carter guessed they were professional movers, hardly breaking a sweat on a July morning.

An enormous black woman emerged and stood next to Carter on the porch. She shouted something about the men leaving footsteps in the grass. They ignored her and drove away.

She turned to Carter. Tugged at a knee-length orange cardigan and touched a patterned headscarf. Lifted her chest and sighed, looked to the sky.

"Yes?"

"There was a guitar?" He had the newspaper in one hand, the ad circled. She took it and studied the ad, as if to remind herself what she was selling. Her long blue fingernails were like beetle shells and made scratching noises on the paper.

"Upstairs," she said, pointing overhead. "In the room where my brother died. He delivered the mail all his life."

The bed was precise, with a stiff white sheet and grey blanket tucked into the metal frame. The instrument was laid out in an open case on the floor, right where the mailman would have placed his feet every morning.

Carter was in love with Leah, and they were making music. Nonsense, most of it, meandering ideas pursued in the living room of a rented bungalow in Yorkdale. Scratchy guitars and stuttering synthesizers. Cheap percussion programs they didn't know how to use. Leah sang in the bathroom and the bedroom. She sang in every room. She wrote lyrics and discarded them, making up words as she went or reading from books opened at random. The neighbour's dog yapping outside all day. They threw food scraps over the fence, and Leah said they should steal the dog because the neighbour was starving it. Once they hung a mic out the back door, recorded the barking and tried to build a rhythm track from it.

They recorded everything, and often didn't bother listening back to what they had done. It was all forward motion, a snowplough bashing through each idea, clearing a path to the next one. The smell of the fridge was all over the house. There was something wrong with the fridge.

He had first seen her at the music shop on Queen, where she was often the only one working. Not a popular shop. Dim and musty, with condensation obscuring the front window. A few battered guitars and horns hung on display. But the walls were mostly bare, patches of it scored with hooks, showing faded outlines where instruments used to be.

Leah was in a band with her Irish boyfriend, Kevin. But that band was finished because they were moving away to take teaching jobs. He was already in North Bay. Leah was moving up in August. They would get married and teach at the same high school. It was all in place. But she was wavering. Carter could tell from the way her eyes wandered when she talked about North Bay.

Her band had made a few demos, and Carter asked to hear them. She handed him the headphones, and when the tape was finished he told her she was so lucky to have all that music.

She went to North Bay, and when she came back for Christmas break Carter called her. Don't come here, she said. But he went anyway and stood at the door of the bungalow until she relented and opened the door a crack and said, please go away. If you keep all this music inside it'll kill you, he said. She told him to mind his own business and tried to close the door. But he got his foot in, pushed against her and said he just wanted to talk, and she let him in.

Leah returned to Toronto for March break because he told her to. In June, he told her to start driving as soon as the last day of school ended, and keep driving all night until she got to the bungalow, and she did. The Irish boyfriend showed up a week later. Leah sat him down at the kitchen table while Carter hid in her bedroom. It didn't take long, maybe ten minutes. He heard the door and the car leaving the driveway, and waited a little longer before emerging. Found her cooking oatmeal, still wearing his denim shirt and boxers. They each took a spoon and ate from the pot. Leah said the sensible thing to do, the right thing and decent thing, was to get married and keep her job. Instead, she was being crazy, making crazy decisions.

"I blame you for that," she said, pointing the spoon at him. "I blame you."

For nearly a week after that they hardly left the house. It was all they could do to keep pace with the music. Black cables snaked and coiled around the bungalow. The finicky Tascam tape machine blocked the basement door. Leah's three keyboards took up half the living room. Tambourines, shakers, blocks of wood. Little black boxes with pedals, buttons, dials and glowing lights. The refrigerator smell. Tea cups and toast plates, an old sweater they shared, scratchy blankets, CDs and tapes spilling over each other, scribbled notes taped to walls. Cellophane stretched across the picture window. On the wall was a poster of Sam Cooke, wailing into the microphone. There was another poster, a woman in a pink bikini, spraying herself with a garden hose. The phone rang a couple of times every day. They never answered. The dog got off its leash and didn't even make a run for it. Didn't leave the yard. Just kept running mad, joyous circles in the pissing rain.

When Carter lifted the dead mailman's Telecaster, the neck was greasy from previous hands. Tilted to the bedroom window, the sunburst finish showed fingerprints and smudges. He found a stained dishcloth in the case. Ran it up and down the neck and body. He would keep the cloth. The strings were slack and lifeless against his thumb. There was no guitar stand, no amplifier in sight. He opened a sliding door to an empty closet with a lived-in smell. The door jammed on its runner and wouldn't close.

The enormous woman repeated her story to everyone who came through the house. It took several weeks for the mailman to die. She came to look after him, arranged for the oxygen and had a nurse visit. He recovered a bit of energy and started eating, but grew agitated. Said to leave him alone. So she went out every day, and one afternoon he died while she was out buying a chicken and vegetables. When she got home she called the nurse. Then she stuffed the chicken with garlic and lemon and put it in the oven. She looked Carter in the eye when she talked about cooking the chicken.

Carter wanted to tell her that his father had died in the palliative care unit, just a few weeks before. Watched around the clock, all vital signs tracked to the end. Would he rather have been left alone? He had died with his mouth wide open, and Joyce had tried to close the jaw. The flesh was warm and the unshaven face prickly, but the joint wouldn't give an inch.

Carter had flown back for the funeral and spent a few days with his mother. When he got back he told Leah that there was a girl back home, and he had gone to the girl's apartment and slept with her. The next day he had gone back and broken up with her. The day after that she called him and when he got there she went down on him. Of course, Leah hated the story and they had a fight.

The mailman's sister brayed in a honey-rich accent Carter recognized from Bob Marley songs. He didn't like her, but he didn't want to be racist. He had seen loud, assertive Caribbean women in movies and on TV. They were hefty and big-bosomed and wore headscarves.

She made him wait while she argued with a white-haired woman about the dining-room table.

"Of course you have to refinish," she said. "Price is set for the quality." She rapped her knuckles on the table. The white-haired woman drifted away, and the mailman's sister raised her voice to chase after her. "This is not for junk. There is quality here." She rapped the table again and turned to Carter.

"This guitar, then. I will trust you to give me a fair price." Her look suggested anything but trust.

Carter wasn't sure what he had. But he apparently knew more than she did. He knew it was a Telecaster. It had three pickups, and knobs and toggle switches that mystified him. No one else had come about it. He offered more than he could afford, though much less than it was likely worth. All the cash in his pocket, which was everything he had. Most of it borrowed from Leah, because they had to put everything into music now.

"Sit while I count your money."

The living room was filled with furniture, much of it covered in yellowing sheets. People walked through the open door, sniffing the air and lifting the sheets. When they let go the sheets billowed and sank, dust swirling in the sunlight that streamed through bare windows. Smaller items were laid out in the kitchen. A set of small wooden elephants. Old radios with broken dials or cracked casings. Assorted hats and a tweed overcoat.

She counted out loud, sounding angry. Carter feared she would take the guitar away.

Then he understood that the deal was done.

This was astonishing good fortune. But Carter was young enough to expect it.

They spent the next morning with another half-realized song. Carter toying with his new Telecaster and Leah cross-legged on a big red cushion that used to belong to her grandmother. The cushion gave her sinus trouble, and she wanted that congested, nasally quality because the song was about claustrophobia. They stopped to pee and eat corn flakes. Carter called in sick for his shift at the light-fixture shop. He would soon be fired.

74

"I used to think music was a dream state," she said. "But with you it's the opposite. A bigger reality, not an escape from it. It's all the triggers firing at once."

Why would he have expected anything less than good fortune?

/////

"Mr. Carter, it's Melissa Ryan calling from Howley Enterprises. Director of Resident Relations here at Howley. I've just been down for a visit with your mother today, and she's doing wonderfully."

"Okay. She was trying to call me. The other day."

"But Mr. Carter, we've already met. I was on your flight when you came to Gander a couple of weeks ago. We talked about your band."

The bay girl.

"If I had only known that your mother was moving in," she says. "I was tied up with the conference that week. But this is wonderful. I had a note to call a Mr. Carter, and I said to myself, I wonder is that him? And sure enough."

"It's funny how things work," offers Carter.

"Now, I want to apologize for this week's regrettable incident. The telephone call from your mother. I understand you weren't expecting to hear from her?"

"It's fine. No need to apologize."

"I've asked the duty nurse for a full report. We do everything we can to prevent such episodes. We'll be reviewing our staffing on that shift. And your mother's medication, of course."

"You just put her on some new pill. I just agreed to it a few days ago."

Pages flipping. Melissa Ryan hums a soft nuh-nuh-nuh-nuh sound to fill the brief silence. "We'll certainly be reviewing that. And of course the telephone left unattended. Clearly a lapse. If you wish to pursue this further I can give you the administrator's direct line. You can speak to her directly. As I said, we keep the lines of communication open."

Carter feels like a man joining a conversation in progress.

"I'd like to talk to her. My mother."

"We can arrange something, of course. Right now…" Flip-flip-flip. "We're already into the dinner hour and then the evening shift, which is of course a smaller complement."

"So I can't get her on the phone now?"

"You might want to consider the sundowning, Mr. Carter."

"Sundowning?"

"Pattern of fatigue and disorientation at the end of the day. We see general confusion and decreased awareness as daylight fades. Aggravation and mood swings. A widely recorded phenomena among seniors."

"Oh."

"I'd venture that your mother is at her best in the morning."

"Right. But in her message, she sounded upset, and the nurse said there was a complaint about her from someone?"

"A complaint?"

"It sounded like she was reading from a notebook, something like that."

"She's not supposed…I don't suppose you caught her name? The nurse?"

"No. But this complaint—"

"Don't you worry, Mr. Carter. I'm sure it's nothing. People live together, they're going to have their little squabbles. I'll look into all this and get back to you straightaway on Monday. Do you know I was driving home the other day and I thought, if only I still had that CD to put on right now. Haven't heard it in years."

"It's pretty hard to find these days. If I see one I'll send it along."

"Really? That would be wonderful. To hear it again, just me alone in the car. Sometimes you want to feel like you're nineteen or twenty years old again, only for a few minutes, don't you find?"

//////

Isabelle descends the stairs in her long black skirt. It's a sensible skirt, but then it fans out with a playful swish, adding a dash of whimsy and flattering her rangy build. Carter knows this because Isabelle has told him.

"So it starts at noon?" Carter asks, though he knows the answer.

"Yes," says Isabelle. "And we'll want to be there in good time. Saturday at the mall. You know." She stops in front of the hallway mirror and agitates the skirt, wiggling a little. "Shelley's coming next month."

"Shelley from fashion school?"

"Yes. Next month, around Valentine's. On her way to Windsor for something the producer needs."

The producer is Shelley's occasional boyfriend, who makes television shows. Carter has seen one of them, a reality show about three hotshot business types sent to revive a meat packing plant in a moribund small town.

"I just heard from her this morning," says Isabelle, smoothing her charcoal sweater. "It's just for one night."

The friendship ran its course long ago. But Shelley refuses to take her cue and fade away, so Isabelle grants her the irritable tolerance of family. Their safe topic of conversation is fashion school, with its shared memories of adolescent fervour. Shelley and Isabelle holed up in a dim little townhouse basement, with a mountain of by-the-pound clothes dragged home from Goodwill. The ancient sewing machine that jammed up if you didn't have just the right touch on the pedal. The Portuguese family next door always screaming, and the old guy upstairs taping Playboy centrefolds in his little kitchen window. A new girl every month.

What they never talk about is the turn that spoiled everything: Shelley's unwavering pursuit of Isabelle's brother. As Carter understands it, the two were never a couple, at least not in any conventional way. This didn't stop Shelley from claiming a stake in Ronnie's death. She wore the tragedy like a tattoo. Carter found it implausible, this high-pitched drama of doomed love. He suspects Shelley of being more enamoured with the drama than she ever was with the man.

Sam explodes in a huge, liquid sneeze, and his cereal spoon clatters to the floor. "Can I get a tissue?" he calls. Snot bubbles from one nostril. Carter snatches tissues for him, and picks up the tablespoon. Sees his distended face in the back of the spoon, frog eyes bulging. The reflection darkens as Isabelle enters the kitchen behind him. Carter hears the soft brush of the skirt as it slides over her frame. She insists that clothes must be "honest," but Carter sees trickery in the skirt, and loves it. The fine wool mesh is clingy, yet it hides the true expanse of her thighs and gives her slinky hips.

/////

Sam has been to the movies before, but not for a birthday party. Carter expects preschool chaos: tantrums, flying popcorn, vomit. But the children lie back in their seats, pinned down by the pulse and throb of coming attractions.

The feature begins, a cartoon set in a snowy kingdom where humans are dwarfed by gloomy palace rooms. Carter and Isabelle slip out of the theatre and walk the mall.

"How long since you saw Shelley?"

"She's never met Sam. She never saw me pregnant. So four or five years, at least. Look at this shit." She stops outside a shop and lifts the sleeve of a frayed, spangled jacket. "The girls who buy this garbage will end up with the worst boyfriends, and when they get treated like crap they'll come back and buy more. Abuse and recovery. It's a huge market."

Completing the mall circuit, they slip in to check on the movie. The Nordic princesses are pale and pink, their saucer eyes ready to reflect everything a child might invest in them. The princes are handsome in the sinewy way of purebred hounds.

Valentine's Day will be the anniversary of Ronnie's death. But the day always goes unmarked by Carter and Isabelle. Forgetting the anniversary is a transparent fiction in their marriage. Can the customary silence be maintained with Shelley around?

Ronnie Mullins was a diabetic with alcoholic cirrhosis, Hepatitis D, and an appetite for "whatever you've got," according to Isabelle. A disciplined addict, he was remarkably adept at hiding it from his parents, and even had the guys at the fire hall fooled for a few years. Until the diabetes caught up with him. The fire department put him on leave and he rarely left the apartment after that. Isabelle had a key, and one night she found him dizzy and cramping and shitting blood. The doctor said his colon looked like a war zone, his esophagus on the verge of rupture. He told Ronnie to stop drinking. Ronnie said he'd rather give up the crystal meth and stay on the booze. The doctor said the booze was killing him, but avoiding crystal meth was a good idea in any case.

Isabelle started overnighting at Ronnie's when she could, because he would try to stay straight for her. When Carter met her, she mentioned that she occasionally stayed with her brother, doing the fifty-minute commute between her apartment in Kitchener and his Etobicoke duplex. Ronnie was back in the hospital a few weeks later, his digestion jammed up with what little food he ate. They purged him and kept him overnight.

On the night he went in for the purge, Isabelle slept at Ronnie's side, in a chair. She called Carter before the sun came up and said it was like waiting for a strange old man to die. He's like a stranger lying there.

A few weeks later she called Carter and said, "Can you come get me? It's getting weird here."

"Where's your car?"

"One of his drug buddies took it."

He found her at the street corner at the end of the block, hugging herself against the cold.

It was twilight when they arrived at Isabelle's place. She wanted to go for a walk. Then she decided they would see the French movie.

The paramedics found the body that night, after the building super let them in. Too late, by about an hour. Carter looked up the movie online: 109 minutes.

Shelley came through Isabelle's door the next day, flinging her overnight bag aside and bursting into tears before Carter had any idea who she was. She said Ronnie was "too beautiful" and "too pure," and otherwise carried on like she was mourning in public, always mindful of the camera. She clutched Isabelle's hand and demanded every detail of the story. Isabelle explained how bad it got, how scared she was, how she sat shaking in the car all the way back to Kitchener, how she couldn't think straight and called 911 too late. There was no mention of the French film. The 109 minutes.

After the movie, the kids are penned in a room for pizza and cake. Most of the parents sat through the movie, and it wore them down. The small talk is desultory. Isabelle is on her phone.

"I Googled you guys," she says.

"Who?"

"Your band. I've never done that before. Isn't that funny? The pictures are sweet. You're all so, so young. She's very sexy."

"She had a look."

"So the top result for 'infinite yes' is an art exhibit in Texas. Did you know that? Then some spiritual thing, and a blurb for a self-help book. You guys aren't even on the first page."

"I know," says Carter. Sam turns to them and makes a face, pointing to his plate. Carter leans over him to eat the unwanted melon and strawberries. "Did you like the movie?"

"Yes!" says Sam. "Can I have a sister?"

Isabelle flicks at the screen with her finger. "More spirituality, religious stuff, infinite yes to all life offers, poem, another poem. Ah, here we go. Ooh, you were an independent Canadian band widely celebrated for its hazy melodicism and nocturnal urban aura."

"That's the standard band bio. It's replicated on a million sites."

"Wait, here's a message thread: 'semi-obscure mid-90s Canadian rock bands.'"

"I've seen that thread."

"You're here! Infinite Yes. One guy says, 'Ubiquitous background music of the time.' I guess that's a compliment." She scrolls. "'I had a friend who was obsessed with them.' Oh, here's a good one. 'You could tell the I-Y types just by looking at them.'"

A girl with black curly hair cries out, snatches something from the hands of the kid next to her, and they both collapse in tears. It brings the room to life, as the children break into laughter and squabbling.

"Look at this." Isabelle hands Carter her phone. "Have you read this?"

Album's impossible to find. Not in new or used racks, no iTunes, no Amazon. I've looked at yard sales and junk sales. – White Boy Wonder

They always said another album was coming. But I guess they broke up and that was it. A lot of us felt kind of jerked around when that happened. Like, what the fuck? It was like we owned the band or something. Ha! – spitfire

Isabelle is on her knees, holding Sam by both shoulders. "Teagan doesn't want a hug right now, okay? It's sweet. But I think the party has her a little upset."

Teagan's mother rushes in with a cake, and strikes up a hasty "Happy Birthday" chorus. Teagan's dad circles the table, dropping loot bags in front of each child. "Sorry," he says, and begins piling gifts into a garbage bag. "Supposed to be out of here by three."

"I emailed Will," says Carter. "Will who used to be in the band. I'm going over this week to talk to him and hear some of the stuff."

"I expected as much," Isabelle replies. "But we shouldn't talk about it around…" She points down, where Sam is giving her legs the hug that Teagan wouldn't accept. "All that cancer and divorce."

A boy pulls a T-shirt over his head and walks blindly into a wall, falling down and getting the biggest laugh of the day. He's about to do it again when his mother snags him by the wrist and pulls him away. "Natural performer," she says, shaking her head.

/////

Driving home from the mall, Carter asks whether it might be emotionally difficult for Shelley, to be visiting around Valentine's Day. Isabelle's response—"No, I don't think so," and a quick lane change—reminds him to leave well enough alone.

After Ronnie died, the police came around. Apologies, miss, but you were the last one to see him alive. It was dark when I got out of the house, Isabelle told them. Herb picked me up and we drove back here and called 911. I should have called sooner. I was scared. I wasn't really thinking. She didn't mention the French movie, nor did Carter.

When the police left, Carter said, "Well done."

Isabelle shrugged. "All I did was tell the truth."

He started waking in the middle of the night, counting the minutes and hours. The drive from Ronnie's, in rush-hour traffic. Then 109 minutes for the movie, plus previews and ads. What about in between? How long did they walk before the French film? What did they talk about on that walk? What did he think about?

Carter waited until spring that year, then asked Isabelle if they could talk about Ronnie, and what happened. Just the two of them, just to clear the air.

"This is the toughest year of my life," she replied. "If this is the relationship we both want, and I really believe it is, I have to have your full support right now." Then she asked him to move in. Offered to call the super and ask for an extra storage locker in the basement. There's a fee for an extra one, she said. But let's see if he'll waive it.

He might have let the whole thing go, if not for that strange old movie. The grubby little French town, everyone singing. The girl and boy are in love until he leaves, then it ends on both sides, not for any reason except separation. The film was absolutely convincing in depicting this.

///

The bay girl calls Monday afternoon, as promised. "That complaint you heard about. It was nothing."

"That's good. Can I call down there now?"

"Maybe after lunch? This morning we took them out to Deadman's Pond," she says. "You never saw a happier bunch. And Joyce had a grand time."

"Wouldn't it be getting a bit cool this time of year, down around the pond?"

"Oh, they're never off the bus. It's just a drive. They love to be on the move, our ladies. The men are a bit more stay-put, I must say. They do enjoy their pub night, though. No alcohol, of course. A few games and what have you. Of course on paper we maintain a strict policy of all activities open to all residents, regardless of gender or mobility issues or what have you. But between you and me we're still giving the men their pub night to themselves. We'll hope the feminists don't get wind of it. Don't want them down here on a protest march, eh?"

She's elusive, like his father. You get them on topic for a bit. Then a story or a joke, and they're off again. You're left grasping at nothing.

"They love to get together and tell the old stories, you know," says Melissa Ryan. "Old Billy George told a wonderful story the other night about his father going down to the whale factory in South Dildo every year. They'd drive the whales ashore, hundreds of them. Blood and guts, up to their necks in it. And at the end of it his father would bring home a big box of whale meat and fry it up with onions. Best feed he ever had, Billy says. So wonderful to hear the old stories."

"My mother was never really one for reminiscing." It was Carter's father who venerated the past with repeated anecdotes. Hauling the well water up the hill on washday. Aunt Blanche shearing the sheep and spinning the wool. Old Skipper Max, who never took a drop except on Christmas Eve, and on Christmas Eve he'd be legless. The night before Carter left for Toronto, his father had called him into the bedroom, pulled the oxygen tube from under his nose, and started talking about how all the boys in the cove used to split herring at two dollars a barrel. They'd go to school with the scales clinging to their boots and the smell coming on thick as the wood stove got going.

He pushed himself up in the bed, forearms quivering with the effort, and said, "Did I ever tell you about my first night in the tower, and we had the bomb scare? A DC-4 it was, Maritime Central en route to Vienna. Watching the boys talk her down, and my son I tell you that was nervous times. And here was me, a raw rookie. Didn't know but the whole town might be blown to smithereens."

The airport tale was more animated, with hands sweeping across the bed covers to suggest the expanse of the tarmac, and an arm raised to indicate a brilliant blue sky crossed with vapour trails. The striped pyjamas flopping around his shrunken frame.

Art Carter measured his life by the blurred acceleration of the twentieth century, from the fish-smelling schoolhouse to the control tower. He had been born into a world where it seemed nothing would ever change. Then the future was invented, and once he caught its slipstream he was pulled along to the end.

"Can I ask you something?" says Carter. "While we're talking about reminiscing."

"Of course," says Melissa Ryan.

"Back in the days when you used to come see my band."

"Yes?"

"Was everyone expecting us to release another CD?"

"Oh my goodness, yes! Or cassette or whatever. We were beside ourselves over it."

"So we left a lot of people disappointed."

"I remember everyone talking about it. But after that I was done grad school and I started my first job and of course everything's changing in your life by then. But I still have wonderful memories from those days."

6

The English girl bent her head to light a cigarette. Hunched to shelter the flame as if from a draught. Couldn't be more than nineteen or twenty. Maybe even younger, with those knee-high socks and turned-in toes. The boxy jacket handed down from a broad-shouldered aunt or sister.

Joyce waved. But there were too many people milling about, and the girl kept her head down. Joyce came around the counter and picked her way past the crowd huddled with their coffee and yesterday's ham sandwiches, and the nuns picking postcards at the novelty booth. Wove through a crowd of soldiers sprawled across the floor, looking more like schoolboys on an outing in their oversized fatigues, playing cards or sleeping against their duffel bags. Stepped around a handsome, olive-skinned man snoring on a bench, his stocking feet propped in the lap of his wife, who did the crossword.

The English girl had taken the farthest end of the farthest bench.

"Excuse me, Miss Peckford?"

The girl looked up, startled. Her lips pulled back around grey, crooked teeth.

Joyce sat next to her. "We've got your connection sorted out as far as Toronto."

"Toronto?" The word meant nothing to the girl. Joyce should have brought a map. She slowed her voice, as if addressing an especially thick child.

"Toronto is between here and Edmonton. You'll fly there, and they'll get you on your flight to Edmonton."

"Oh," said the girl. She buried the cigarette in the sand of the ashtray and tucked her hair behind each ear. Reached for her purse and clutched it with both hands.

"I will phone ahead to Toronto. I'll let them know you're coming. They'll arrange to get you on to Edmonton."

"Only, they won't ask for money?"

For God's sake. They had been through this. "Your passage to Edmonton is booked and paid for," said Joyce, in what she hoped was a firm but patient voice. "You will get a hot breakfast on board and dinner as well, after you leave Toronto."

Talk of in-flight meals didn't help. The girl went tight, and a crack in her bottom lip showed blood. Joyce guessed that she had made ample use of the sickness bag on the flight from Heathrow. It had been a bad night for turbulence, with every overseas arrival adding to the mountain of used bags in the trash bins behind the control tower. Late flights and missed connections had everyone scrambling to rebook. On cigarette breaks, the agents huddled in the restaurant or retreated to the baggage hold, cursing the arrogant Yanks and pushy Wops and the Frogs who carried on "like their shit don't stink," as Mose Whitehead put it.

Joyce escorted the English girl to the other end of the lounge, in view of the departure door. "You'll go through here when the flight is called, in about forty minutes." She held out the boarding pass. The girl looked at it but didn't make a move. Both hands on her purse.

"You'll need this," said Joyce. "Don't look for your bags in Toronto. They're checked through to Edmonton."

"I see," said the girl, who didn't see at all. Though she finally took the boarding pass. Held it tight until Joyce took the hand and guided it into her purse.

"Tuck it away until you need it. I'll come back and we'll get you on. Do you still have the toiletry kit?"

"Oh," gasped the girl, bringing her fingers to her lips. "But I brushed my teeth. Sorry."

"No, it's fine. Just keep it handy." Complimentary toiletries were for First Class only. But Joyce was indiscriminate with them. "You'll want to freshen up. You're in for a long day."

"Do they know if he's there?"

"Well, he's the one bought your ticket, so he knows your arrival…" Joyce stopped. Who was she to say whether the poor thing's fiancé would be waiting in Edmonton as promised? The girl had shown his photo earlier this morning. A puffy-faced soldier with sparse brown hair and a wide smile. Older than her by a decade or more. Overdue to settle down and fatten up on roast beef dinners and lemon meringue pie.

"We'll call Toronto," said Joyce. "And Edmonton. Don't worry."

"I believe she's expecting," said Mary, when Joyce resumed her place behind the ticket counter. They could see the girl, both hands on her purse. Grimacing. Probably holding her pee.

"No," said Joyce.

Mary narrowed her eyes. Her glasses were new, with a caramel-coloured frame and a diamond shape on each earpiece. "I don't know," she said. "Something in how she carries herself."

A pregnancy didn't jibe with the girl's story as told to Joyce. It had been a wartime romance. But her father said she was too young to marry, and she had given up hope when her soldier went home to Canada. Then after several years of silence he initiated an exchange of letters, the most recent of which had proposed marriage. Her family opposed the union until he sent the fare. Heathrow to Edmonton was four hundred dollars or more. A serious commitment.

"I'd say you could rob every house on her shabby little street and not come away with four hundred dollars," said Mary.

"Her man doesn't look like much," said Joyce. "Not from his picture."

"She doesn't look like much herself. But she won the jackpot. Putting an ocean between herself and Mummy. Every English girl's dream."

"Is it so bad over there?" Mary's husband was English, and had taken her and the kids home to Coventry for a visit in the spring.

"The rationing is awful," she said. "And Joe's sister, she never had the sense to get out. She's stuck now. Mother got her worn down to the bone. There's another one."

A hollow-eyed young woman limped past, one shoulder tilted with the weight of an overstuffed bag. Taller and thinner than the Peckford girl, but with the same glazed look.

"On the run from dear old Mum," said Mary. "Couldn't even afford a decent pair of stockings for the trip. You can bet there's some young buck waiting wherever she's going, ready to fill her up with babies."

///

Joyce had always known she would leave Cape St. Rose. She didn't make a fantasy of it. She didn't imagine herself at Parisian cafés or New York ballrooms, the way the other girls did when they flipped through their magazines. She just wanted to get out.

It was the death of her mother that set her in motion. Joyce had helped Mrs. Stoodley and her daughter wash the body and lay it out. Then she inherited the kitchen. Spent three solid days in there, while her father and Marty brushed off their Sunday clothes and faced the tide of mourners. Marty threw himself into it, gripping every hand and holding every hug, returning every blessing. He never stopped, not even for a drink. A drop of rum was good for Marty. Slowed him down and settled his nerves. Made him think a bit. But since his disappointment with the girl from Branch, he had given it up altogether.

Nothing changed after the funeral. Joyce replaced her mother everywhere except her father's bed. She was eighteen years old, and not so foolish as to imagine a radically different life. But even an ugly husband would be a more welcome sight than Marty, stomping through the door at the end of his shift and calling for his dinner. Always complaining about the gravy. Can't you do a gravy, girl? It's right bitter. From her mother she had learned how to clean and cook in anger, slamming dinner plates down on the table. But she wanted to slam them on her own table. For that, she had to leave.

Gloria had sent a mass card and letter, apologizing for not making the funeral. She sent a postcard as well, a map of the world with Gander, Newfoundland, in the middle. There were lines curving from the middle like red ribbons, connecting Gander to Europe and America.

Joyce showed the postcard to Father Coles, who said a little town had some gall to place itself at the centre of all humanity, and to Mrs. Pine at the school, who said the map ought to tell the glory of the British Empire. After that she kept it to herself, under her mattress. It was illicit, like the dirty picture she had found when she was sweeping Marty's room. A girl in nothing but her small clothes, bent over to point her bottom at the viewer, her head turned to show a shameless smile on her painted face.

Joyce's father was still a young man, younger than Marty in many ways. He would be fine without her. Wasn't Bridge Fallon already at his heels? Stopping him outside the church, just to mention she had been up to the hill that very morning. "...Oh, no trouble at all. Was up there anyway to see to Mom.... You got to watch the new graves especially. Gone right to dandelion if they get half the chance."

When the arrangements were made in Gander, Gloria sent the train fare. Joyce said nothing until two days before. I never would have thought, her father said. Of course he wouldn't. Marty was away, hunting bull birds down in the mouth of the Chute. But when he got wind of it he was back. He hauled her into his room and threw her on the bed, slapping at her with big meaty palms and scratchy calluses. Don't you go near that train, he shouted. From her back, Joyce raised her legs. He grabbed them, but she kicked until she saw an opening and got him good in the stomach. Felt her heel sink into his belly, which was harder then it looked. He sprayed her with spit, and doubled over gasping. Joyce was shaking. Smelled what she thought was blood, though there was no blood. Ready to lay in another boot, if he made a move to come back at her. Instead he gathered himself and walked out.

//////

Joyce had to wait for a seat at the lunch bar, and her tomato soup took forever. The woman on the next stool introduced herself as Alice Henley from central laundry.

"Awful mess coming off the overnight flights," she said. "The linens and uniforms."

"You do the laundry for the airlines?"

"Everything. Airlines, hotels. That serviette in your lap, that'll be through the wash by dinner."

Alice had a creamy complexion and healthy figure, hefty arms straining the short sleeves of her starched white uniform. She joined and twisted her hands, quick eyes taking in the crowd around them.

"Funny smell off the Europeans, eh?" she whispered.

"Sometimes," said Joyce. A rush of deplaning passengers arrived on a gust of fresh air, with undercurrents of bad breath, fuel exhaust and boiled vegetables. A passing whiff of vomit and toilets as the service crew got to work. The boys on the crew claimed to have a nose for every airline. The English and Irish smelled of old water. The French of their pungent, sweet cigarettes. Italians were spicy, Germans greasy, and so on. Joyce suspected it was all just talk, just men on their noisy smoke breaks. But one night a crowd of Greek soldiers came through, carrying a wonderful, toasty smell of sugared pastry on their billowing white costumes. Mary said she'd run away with any one of them, sight unseen.

"Awful smell off the stuff from the Russians," said Alice. "You don't want to even open the bag. Right cabbagey. And God only knows what they're up to here, with everything the Rosenbergs told them."

"Who told them?" asked Joyce.

"The Atom Bomb spies. Don't you read the paper? Sent to the chair, and it took two extra shocks to kill Ethel. Smoke coming off her. That's how nasty she was."

Joyce didn't read the paper. But there had been much talk of spies.

"And that's just the tip of the iceberg," said Alice. "Do you have children?"

"No."

"But look at you. You're bursting for babies. Once they start coming you'll want to clear out of here. No place for youngsters, old air force base."

But Gloria had already had her baby, and he seemed perfectly at home. Joyce had been to Chestnut Street just last night, and held him, all warm and powdery and washed clean. There was a deep scent from him that must have been the smell of fresh skin. New skin, bursting to life. Expanding like soap suds in a running bath.

"We'll be off the airport long before I have any babies," she said. The distant grind of heavy equipment was unrelenting lately. The sound of land being cleared for the new town site, a couple of miles east. "They'll put up nice homes in the new town."

"But the place will still be full of Russians and whoever. Negroes. Italians. My husband went through Italy with the Fusiliers. Took shrapnel at Monte Camino. He says the Italians know which side their bread's buttered on, and no mistake."

Joyce guessed Alice to be six or seven years older than her. But having a husband in the war widened the gap between them.

"He says around here it's just as bad as the war. You know when those poor people got cut to ribbons? Just standing there at the end of the runway? Back in '46."

"Oh, yes," said Joyce. She had heard the story on her first night shift, from Mike Devine. Half a dozen folks had been at the edge of Runway 14, watching the takeoffs and landings on a warm Sunday evening after church. The roar of the engines so loud they had no idea of the Lancaster bomber coming in behind them. Cut to ribbons, Mike had said, nearly drooling with excitement.

"Cut to ribbons," said Alice. "It was Henley drove the ambulance."

"Who?"

"Henley. Bernard. My husband. Picked them up and piled them aboard the ambulance. Piece by piece."

"Oh!"

"My God, don't be talking."

Gander took pride in its extraordinary tales of death and destruction. Everyone made a show of respectful silence, as if the tragedies were too awful to speak of. Then the silence would break, and you would hear about the tangled wrecks dotting the town's perimeter. Massive American bombers crushed like eggs. Lightweight single-engines impaled on spruce trees. The DC-4 slicing through half a mile of brush, bodies flung from the wreck with enough force to contort their features and tear off their boots. A Fortress bomber that disappeared into the lake, sunk so deep that no one would ever find it. The men who went up Dead Wolf River and hacked through two miles of deep woods to rescue the survivors of the Sabena crash, and which of them stayed behind to burn the bodies and how they couldn't even talk about it after. The disasters were usually unexplained, and this element of mystery was recounted with special relish. It's the strangest thing, they'd say. Clean mechanical record. Experienced crew. Fuel and weight conformed to specifications. The last radio transmission was normal. The next thing you know.... They would sit back, scratch the backs of their necks and shake their heads.

Alice laid her sandwich on its plate and rubbed her forehead. "No place for a child," she said. "For a decent family."

/////

Joyce got Flight 535 away and took a moment at her locker to unwrap a stick of gum and examine her fingernails. Resolved to stop biting them and stop picking at her cuticles.

Gert came through the swinging door and headed to the bathroom stalls. "Gord Delaney's asking for you out front."

"We're doing the tribute night for Mr. Wells," he said, when she appeared at the counter.

"Good morning to you, too."

"It's the seventeenth. Can you manage it?"

"Who's Mr. Wells?"

"School principal. Drowned last fall, remember?" He tapped the calendar taped to the counter between them. "The seventeenth. Whole town'll be out because the family's moving back to Plate Cove and we're putting up a few dollars to send them on their way."

"I didn't think my singing was up to snuff."

He waved this away. So her singing was fine? Or it didn't matter, so long as she was available? Joyce wanted to ask, but instead she agreed to do the show.

British Overseas offered the Caribou Club, and the ladies from the school put on a spread. The widow Mrs. Wells stood and smiled for every envelope of cash from the school, from the churches, from Captain Geist on behalf of the airlines, from Newhook's Jewellery where she worked, and from Oceanic Area Control where Mr. Wells had worked several summers. Joyce, still uncertain about the songs, sat in a corner, reading the words over and over from the sheet music.

Finally the line of well-wishers ran out. The widow thanked everyone and said she was very sorry to be leaving town. She spoke as though she had failed some kind of test. They gave her a big round of applause as she handed the microphone to Gordon, who said it was time to get everyone on the dance floor. The band played a couple of instrumentals, and by the time Joyce stepped up for her first song—sheet music in hand, just in case—a nervous energy had taken over the room. Everyone relieved to be done with the widow and her tragedy. The band didn't know how to respond, and the uncertainty held them back a little. That made it easier for Joyce, who remembered all the words and enjoyed herself, closing her eyes to sing. She didn't mind anything, not even the awkward moment when Dr. Duchene asked the widow to dance, leading her onto the floor and clutching her waist to his for "That Ol' Black Magic."

///////

Jules travelled, and when Joyce saw him around the airport he was only in town for a night, or not even that, before setting out again. The morning after the show for the widow Wells, Joyce spotted him in his truck and flagged him down. "I'll need a drink after work," she said. "We were out till all hours with the band." He offered her a ride.

"I'd like to play with them," said Jules, his unruly hair whipped by the breeze through the open window. "But I'm never around, and I'm not sure they're respectable, to be honest."

Joyce laughed. "You sound like my father."

He brightened, appearing to take it as a compliment. "Your father must have been in the war."

"No," said Joyce. "He had a general store. Do you really think the boys from the war are any more respectable than anyone else?"

"They did their duty."

War veterans were easy to spot, and nothing like her father. They were comfortable in transit, slouching through the terminal, not bothering to stifle their yawns. Swore at small things, but shrugged off genuine irritants like mechanical problems and weather delays. They asked where they were, and laughed when she told them. Another far-flung outpost. "Keep your jacket buttoned," Gert had warned. "They'll look you up and down, bold as brass, and don't give a hoot if you catch them at it."

"How long since your father passed?" Jules asked as they pulled up at the terminal.

"Oh, he's still very much with us."

"I'm sorry," said Jules. "I thought, the way you were talking…sorry."

"I could tell you anything at all, and you'd never know if it were true."

"Yes, you could."

Joyce had a mercifully quiet shift and Jules met her at the Big Dipper shortly after four. Ordered a whiskey for her but nothing for himself.

"Your crowd over at AOA," she said. "They've had a Stratocaster on the ground for two days now."

"Propeller number four," said Jules. "Feathering and stalling. They worked on it all day yesterday. It took off around lunchtime, I think."

"It didn't get out."

"No?"

"It started and gave out again."

Joyce had been delivering a mailbag to Flight 400 when the Stratocaster called across the tarmac, its engines firing one by one, like notes climbing a scale. She had heard the fourth note die.

"So you know all the business of this airport, do you?" He grinned at her.

"You get to know a few things."

They lingered long enough that she thought he might offer her another round. He didn't. But it was payday, so she and Rachel split half a bottle of whiskey from the Moakler fellow who kept a supply in his car.

/////

The band hardly stopped through the fall, into Christmas, and even after. They did the Rotary cookout at Deadman's, where Joyce lost her shoes. The Port Blandford Lion's Club, where only three couples danced. The RAF reunion, the Signals dance, the hospital dance. A curiously prim Catholic wedding at the Airport Club, and an Anglican wedding at the Skyways Club where everyone seemed sad. A mad circuit of Christmas dances. A farewell do for the Scandinavian Airlines station manager. Port Blandford again, with a few more dancers.

They juggled three drummers and occasionally did without guitar, because Martin Molloy didn't want to be at it every weekend. Joyce couldn't get out of work for a dance in Lewisporte or the Air Force party, so they went back to Gordon singing a few. The Lewisporte dance ended early due to a brawl, the barman with his head cracked open, and half a flat of Haig Ale gone missing, all blamed on a tanker crew that had docked for the night.

She knew the songs now, and knew the band. She still stepped on the piano a good deal. Gordon said it wasn't her fault. "Eric ought to be in a proper jazz combo," he said. "He learned his stuff down in the States, you know. Even made his way down to Kansas City for a bit. Saw Count Basie, in the flesh. You just ask him." Joyce thought a man of such ability and experience ought to adapt to the situation. Perhaps he didn't want to adapt.

But Joyce didn't mind any of it, not the difficult piano or Gordon with his nagging. Not the drunken fools, or having to push away their hands. Not the ridiculous hours or the train. She liked to sing, and liked how the microphone stand felt like a shield, protecting her from whatever shenanigans went on in the crowd. None of it bothered her anymore.

Jules must have seen the change in her, because when they went for their usual drink on a miserable evening in February, he was much bolder.

"They did well with you."

"Who did well?"

"The airline. Putting you behind the counter. A man's been flying all day, and the plane touches down in the middle of nowhere.

He's tired and he needs a wash. Then he looks up and sees a girl like you. A sight for sore eyes. I bet you could take your pick of those boys. Any one of them would love to rescue a girl like you and bring her home."

Joyce preferred seeing them in transit. Whenever she imagined a travelling man returning home, he was always diminished, falling into her father's habits. Rising from an old mattress that held the shape of his frame. Calling for his porridge as he lingered over his morning bowel movement, and don't forget to give it a drop of tinned milk. Leaving his shaving bowl on the counter, tiny bristles floating in grey scum. Scrubbing himself red with carbolic soap. Drenching his head before working in the pomade to set his hair smooth as a beach rock.

"Oh, but they wouldn't have me. I'm not respectable, you know," she said to Jules. "I'm out till all hours with a crowd of men in a band."

7

Will lifts his arms in the manner of a freshly scrubbed surgeon awaiting rubber gloves.

"Look," he says, using his chin to guide Carter's gaze from the left hand to the right. The fingers on the right bend sideways like trees in a gale. Two knuckles are bulbous and white.

Carter is in the doorway. The screen door crashes against the newel post behind him.

"That's what you get when you live the life. You see?" Will tilts to present the crown of his head. The shaved scalp shines blue in the streetlight, marked by lumps that must be scars. Fingers reach up, touching lightly on the scars as if counting them.

"That didn't tickle." Carter has an arm braced against the screen door so it won't crash again.

"You better believe it. Down my back as well." They're both shivering from the stiff October breeze.

"Can I come in, Will?"

The living room looks barely lived in. The coffee table and the sofa set look new. Carter had been expecting a shabby house, over-stuffed and eccentric.

"I'm a lucky man," says Will. "If Miriam wasn't here for me I don't know where I'd be."

Muffled voices rise in the darkened hallway, booming from behind a door. The television must be up on bust.

"Look," says Will, and raises his T-shirt to display a lean working man's torso. It's hairless, puckered and whorled down one side, the colour running to pink, white, crimson, and a rich, leathery brown. Carter is unclear on what happened in northern Alberta. A fire? About two years ago? More?

"Is it painful?"

"It's okay now," says Will. He reaches around and slaps the discoloured skin hard. "The feeling never came back." He slaps again, and drops his shirt back in place.

They are silent for a moment. Will looks at Carter like he's trying to place the acquaintance and how well they're supposed to know each other. They were never great friends. But there had always been a quickness in Will—the way his bass found the heart of a song; his ready grasp of numbers, details, money—that Carter can't see anymore.

"I really appreciate you doing this for me, a chance to hear the music."

"Yes, come on then," Will says, as if Carter has been lagging behind. "Jordan's in there, waiting on us."

The garage, like the living room, is fiercely lit, with three lamps and a naked overhead bulb. A young man with a brush cut and a black button in his earlobe sits in a wheelchair, facing an audio console, two computer monitors, keyboards, a pair of speakers, several slim black boxes, and a snaking mass of cables and power cords. It's all stacked on an old Formica table, which bows under the weight.

"Come on now, Jordan," says Will. "Look alive."

Jordan turns to look at them through the small ovals of his glasses. Beyond a smooth goatee, his face glows with razor rash, and his pimples are little eruptions of inner vitality.

"Bring up the master drive, the one with all the outtakes."

"Ready to roll," says Jordan. He grabs the wheels of his chair and shifts closer to the table. Taps at a keyboard to bring the monitors to life.

"Everything locked up this morning, you know. Had to reboot."

"You just got to be patient, Uncle Will."

"Now bring up the original mixer, like I showed you."

"I created a new mixer, Uncle Will. Do you want to see how it's done?"

"I know how it's done." Will stands over the boy. It feels like a standoff. Carter breaks the silence by introducing himself.

"Jordan," says the boy, working a mouse, opening files on the smallest screen. He's suspiciously well groomed for a soundman, in a shirt and tie under a light blue cardigan. But the wheelchair is a good sign. An engineer needs to sit still. In his last email, Will had praised his nephew's "flawless ear."

"You better not crash the system," says Will, still at his shoulder.

The system looks ready to crash. It's coated with dust and fingerprints. Old strips of tape are twisted around the cables, and the white keyboard is nearly black with grime. The small monitor, which has a long crack in its shell, displays the music as coloured strips across the screen.

"Relax, Uncle Will." Jordan taps the space bar, and the coloured strips start moving.

An electric tremor fills the garage, and expands to become scattershot guitar chords that Carter recognizes as his own.

Leah sings.

Callie wakes and says,
Something's moving inside

A touch nasally—allergies were her constant battle—but otherwise in good form.

Carter shifts on his feet. There's nowhere to sit except an old couch at the other end of the garage, wedged between a deep freeze and a dusty foosball table with several broken handles.

"Very rough," says Jordan. "Snare drum sounds like a side of raw beef."

Leah starts another line, but the guitar interrupts her with sustained notes that sound like random squeals, like spinning a radio dial between stations. The band grinds to a halt. The drummer, Colin, laughs and smashes his cymbals, does a rimshot like he's working a comedian's punch line. Leah coughs. Carter hears himself saying, *Okay, okay, okay.* He counts in and they start again.

It must be from the sessions they did that last summer, when they were breaking up and Carter was repeatedly constipated. The pharmacist gave him suppositories and warned him not to stray far from a bathroom. Leah inserted the suppositories, and the following afternoon they started working all at once. Every ten minutes he was setting down the guitar and dashing down the hall.

"Let's move on," says Will, reaching for the mouse.

Jordan nudges his arm away. "No, Uncle Will. There's a good take coming up."

Will takes the mouse, whacking it with his index finger and staring at the monitor. Carter remembers him as being always at odds with things, frustration tensing his body and contorting his face. This impatience had its uses in the group dynamic. But it didn't make him easy to be with. Carter and Leah had talked about replacing him.

"Goddamn it!" snarls Will. He jiggles the mouse furiously. The screen is frozen.

"I told you," says Jordan, rubbing the thin line of hair along his jaw. "You went too fast. The software is medieval."

"Jesus Christ."

"Seriously, Uncle Will. You've got to treat this stuff with kid gloves."

Will runs a hand over his waxy head, and points to the black boxes on an overhead shelf. "I had everything digitized. *Everything* burnt to these hard drives. Took me a week. This format, this was the industry standard."

"It was never the industry standard, Uncle Will."

"The guy told me they used it in Hollywood, and the CBC." Will grips his head and lets out a low moan. "We're going to lose it all."

"Hey, Uncle Will," says Jordan. He turns and lays an arm on his shoulder. "It's okay. It's going to be alright, man."

Will nods, his head still gripped by his hands.

"You want to go see Miriam for a while? Let's go see Miriam."

"No, I'm okay," says Will. He raises his head and squeezes the bridge of his nose. "You know, maybe I will take a minute to sit with Miriam."

Jordan takes Will's elbow. "I'm sorry, Uncle Will. I gotta look out for your triggers. My bad. Sorry."

"It's cool." Will lifts his head in a show of regal dignity. He stands and shuffles out of the room. Jordan bends down to restart a computer tower under the table.

"So, this software is a real mess," says Carter.

Jordan shakes his head. "Any computer less than ten years old won't even run it. The plug-ins, the drives, none of it is compatible. Uncle Will tried his best, but it's impossible for him to keep up. He needs to focus on his own health."

A twinge of guilt digs at Carter. He neglected the music and let it slip away. "It's a bad situation," he says.

Jordan shrugs. "It's been worse. The anxiety is the real issue these days. The medication helped, but then he had trouble with the side effects." He turns the wheelchair to face Carter and holds his hands far apart. "Big memory gaps. Like, he'd miss whole days, most of a week. So he had to get off the medication."

"And Miriam, his mother, she can handle it? She must be getting up there now."

"His mother? She died long ago."

"Oh…"

"Miriam's *my* mom," says Jordan. "Uncle Will's her brother. I don't think they were that close growing up? But Gran left the house to her, and Uncle Will came with it."

The computer is coming back to life with a rush of insect sounds, buzzing and whirring.

"We could lose everything," says Carter.

"Well, if we start soon I should be able to convert it to MP3, back it up on Pro Tools." He threads a hand between two of the units stacked on the table. "Or it could blow up. This unit throws a ton of heat."

Carter can smell the transistors cooking, the scorched dust and warm plastic.

"Nothing's future-safe anymore." Jordan clicks through several options as the computer returns to life. The ticking machines groan and flicker. "MP3, Pro Tools. Everything's going to be obsolete in no time. You guys got good buzz in the community. So let's get on it, get it out there. Get it released, get it in ads, industrials, sync rights."

"Sync rights?"

"Placing tunes in movies and TV shows, video games." Jordan produces a business card from his chest pocket.

Siege Fifteen Productions
Full Service Creative Solutions and Music Rights Management
Jordan Toytman, Founding Partner

"How did you get that flange effect?"

"Hmm?"

"You're the guitar player, yeah?" Jordan gestures to the screen. "On that tune just now, before it all crashed? What's that nice thing you had going? Not quite a flange. Never heard anything like it before."

"Just a chorus pedal on the board," Carter says, surprising himself with the automatic recall.

"How?"

"Speed on zero and depth on nine or ten." He can feel the ridged dials in his fingers.

A few minutes later the music begins again. Leah's alto catches and quivers, like she's pulling it from deep inside. *Didn't mean for her to suffer*, she sings. *Didn't mean her no harm*. The band provides a high, chiming bed of sound.

"This song is very together," says Jordan, and checks the cue sheet. "*Stendhal Syndrome*. Ring a bell?"

It doesn't. "We probably didn't finish it. Just a fragment." To Carter's ears the music feels pushy, demanding all the energy in the room.

Jordan laughs and slaps his tiny leg. "I gotta hear that last piece again," he says, working the mouse to scroll back and replay the instrumental break. "You bring it to A-major, a moment of suspense." His chin is lifted, a hand in the air. "Then you just whip it out from under us. You bastards. Now a G-minor section in the middle! Fuck, yeah! That's a total Mozart move! Someone in the band listens to Mozart."

Carter smiles. Someone in the band might well have been listening to Mozart, for all he knows.

They take in the next verse, and Jordan says, "Ah, too bad. Now you've lost it. You're fighting it, sweating it."

"But for thirty-two bars we were great."

"That's more than a lot of bands get, believe me."

The fighting and sweating feels more apt to Carter's recollection.

Will returns, carrying a tray. He hands Carter a mug of tea and says the bungalow suits him fine, as his knees and hip flexors are in a bad way. But no, he says, raising an index finger to correct himself. The bungalow isn't fine. It's perfect. He can scarcely believe the good fortune, the serendipity that delivered him back to the house he grew up in, exactly when he needed it most.

"Check this out, Uncle Will," says Jordan, and reverses the file to play the Mozart bit again.

"You and her together," Will leans into Carter. "You made sure nobody's ideas got through."

"What?"

"You and her controlled the music," says Will. "Nobody else's ideas got through."

"We all contributed."

"It took me a long time to forgive you for that. I see now that I had to. But it was a long time." Will's voice is casual, as though making small talk.

"This is so good," says Jordan, as the music snippet plays again.

"Five thousand dollars, right?" says Will, speaking up. "Five thousand at least?"

"That's right." Jordan hits the space bar to pause the music and takes out his phone. "I just gotta find something here, guys."

"Five Gs, if anybody gives a damn. Maybe you don't give a damn."

"But let's just back this up a bit." Carter shifts from Will's unblinking gaze and turns to Jordan. "What do you mean about a buzz in the community?"

"We do a lot of work with indie bands," says Jordan, pecking at his phone. "Work the clubs, produce demos and sessions, the gamut. People in that scene are shit hot on Infinite Yes. It's like whatever happened to that band? Wasn't there supposed to be another album? Great fucking band."

"No way. We were never that big."

"It's not about big. It's about reach." Jordan looks up. "You know that expression about the Velvet Underground?"

"No."

"Only 10,000 people bought the first Velvet Underground album. But every one of them formed a band." Lilting symphonic music rises from Jordan's hand. "Yes! This is what I was looking for. This is Mozart. Third Violin Concerto." The strings race, ease for eight bars, and race again. "Hear the soloist there? How he plays to the oboes? Don't even need a conductor, they're so locked in. Hang on." He tap-taps the phone, and the music jumps ahead. "Here we go. This is shit hot."

The music swirls. Will takes a big gulp of tea and says, "Remember that video you made in Colin's room? With the girl in Kingston? I got that video."

"I think I remember her," says Carter. A strapping, moon-faced brunette with a hoarse laugh. Dressed in a kilt and military jacket. "There was something wrong with that girl."

"Definitely something wrong with her. Where do those kids end up, eh?"

"But I didn't shoot any video of her." Will's memory must be ravaged.

"He's nineteen when he writes this," says Jordan. "The little punk. Just a little fucker. Hear those flutes?"

"Yes," says Will, moving to the edge of his chair. His tea sloshes over the side.

"A little pizzicato, just in here. Now this section," says Jordan. "It makes you think there's great drama coming, right? Wait for it. Here it is! But no! It doesn't happen! The joke's on you." He leans back and slaps his knee. "I used to hate that. Fuck you, Mozart! Asshole! It was my dad who helped me figure it out. 'You're so serious, Jordan. Let yourself go. Have a laugh at it all.' And then it was like the music opened up for me."

Jordan raises the phone overhead. His other hand dances in the air, conducting the orchestra as it creeps, swells and surges. "Now the third movement, so amazing. It's not in the notes. It's the band. They're rolling with it. Swinging it."

"Yeah!" shouts Will.

"This next part. So fucking wild." Jordan leans forward and for a moment looks like he might rise and walk. "Like he's sneaking up behind the orchestra and giving them a wedgie."

"Yeah!" screams Will, a line of drool rolling over his bottom lip. He turns to catch Carter's eye, a fierce smile on his face. "Yeah! Mozart, the little fucker! Go, you little fucker, go!"

///////

The following morning, waiting for the appointed call from his mother, Carter digs deeper into the Google results. There's not much beyond what Isabelle turned up. No evidence to back up Jordan's belief that Infinite Yes inspired thousands of bands. There are a handful of images, including several from Carter's brief Mohawk period. Leah remains astonishing, with her lean face and all that unruly red hair.

Will's garage was euphoric by the time Carter left last night. Jordan whooping and clapping at the half-finished songs and barely-articulated ideas. Will pacing the floor and muttering excitedly, shaking his fists when he heard a nice bass flourish. Carter didn't share the excitement. Listening only reminded him that the spirit in which the music was made is gone. He is middle-aged and calcified. He can't hear it. But Jordan is young, and still subject to the fervour of an unexpected key change, the mounting excitement of a chorus, the meditative cycle and goosebumped release of an unbroken riff.

The band got plenty of enthusiastic media in its day, usually in college papers. But Carter finds just one review online, a grainy scan from the *Fergus Elora News Express*. The writer cleverly dismisses Infinite Yes as "the musical equivalent of fascist architecture: Very striking from a distance, but look a little closer and you'll see there's no grass or trees, nowhere to sit, no shelter from the elements, and you have to climb a thousand steps just to get to the front door."

He's debating whether to keep reading when the phone rings.

"Mr. Carter?"

"Yes?"

"My name's Shanna. I'm calling from Howley Park. I have Mrs. Carter with me, if you'll just wait a moment?"

But there's no wait. "Herbert?" The voice is hoarse but firm, an exaggerated version of the rasp he grew up with.

"Hi, Mom. How are you?"

"Mrs. Daly says she'll marry that awful man. Can you imagine?"

"It's okay, Mom. Just use your normal voice. I can hear you fine."

"—two bigger fools in all my days."

"Is that why you called the other day? Because your friend is getting married?"

"She's no friend of mine. She's dumb as a post."

"But is that why you called?"

There is a muffling of the phone, as she leans in and whispers. "Someone's been coming and talking about the old days."

"Who is it? Who's been coming to see you?"

"Some girl. It's, I don't know what it is." A thickness creeps into her voice, like she might burst into tears.

"It's alright, Mom. We'll look after it. I'll find out who it is and she won't bother you anymore."

She's calling out to someone. The phone drops with a crack and Carter fears she might cause a scene. After a moment the phone is lifted again.

"Sorry, Mr. Carter. She seemed ready to talk, but now she doesn't want to."

"What's she doing? Is she alright?"

"She's fine, sir. One of the girls is giving her a hand there now. She'll settle down, get a cup of tea."

"Is she eating okay?"

"We get the odd one likes a good feed. But to be honest with you, sir, most of them lost interest long ago. They eats when we tells them. That's about it."

"You're Shanna, is it?"

"I didn't mean for her to get upset, sir."

"No, I'm glad you called. But there's been some girl coming around and talking to her. Do you know anything about that?"

"I'll...I'll make sure it doesn't happen again."

"I would appreciate that, Shanna."

Carter stays on the phone to call Leah. Sam has a check-up in Toronto in two weeks. It's routine, so Carter will use the trip to visit Leah. He has to get her on board with Jordan's plan.

"Is there anyone there to lend you a hand?"

"Oh, yes."

"Who?"

"I'm fine."

He judges this the right time to tell her about Melissa Ryan on his flight to Gander.

"The album saved her life how?"

"I think she meant that she was young and confused and alone. The music kept her company. Consolation, I guess."

"I see," says Leah, and the silence that follows makes a fool of Carter. Play a song, save a life. If only it were that easy.

He's downloaded Mozart's Third Violin Concerto, trying to hear what Jordan hears. Jordan was bursting with ideas as they listened to the old tracks. Remix and reissue the CD. A tentative online release of the second album—the "lost" Infinite Yes album—plus limited edition vinyl. Call in a couple of session players to flesh out the unfinished songs. Maybe even a girl singer, subject to Leah's approval of course. And financing. Jordan says the market is small, but ripe. The college kids who used to come to the shows are closing in on fifty and hitting peak income. Youth has a powerful pull as the last of it slips away. He's in for fifteen per cent. Carter warns him to lowball projected sales. He's a kid. His first real kick in the teeth is coming soon, and Carter doesn't want this to be it.

But they need Leah. Jordan's partner confirmed it. The band agreement specifies that three out of four have to approve before anything can be released. Colin disappeared and fell out of touch years ago, without a word. So it's up to Carter to talk Leah into it. The Mozart will build his resolve.

"Do you remember Suzy Q?" she asks. "From Grossman's?"

"Of course. I sat in her stool when we met."

"She died not long ago, and the bar had a little vigil for her."

"Oh."

"Suzy came to me after one of our gigs one night," says Leah. "I mean, this is twenty years ago, and she looked ancient then. We were feeling good that night. It was still those early days when we were loving it. And she comes up and grabs my arm and says, 'You fucking people, you're killing me.'"

"Ha," says Carter.

"So that makes it one saved and one killed. I guess we broke even."

/////

As a boy, Carter imagined the working world as a manicured campsite where cheerful men arrived every morning, keen for adventure. So he likes how the university campus slips away from the street, orderly and spacious, with wide walking paths, clusters of groomed trees, a curved footbridge over the narrow creek, and evenly spaced dumpsters in regimental formation behind a maintenance shed. Like the airport at home.

The foreign students, who presumably have nowhere else to go between semesters, have the campus to themselves in the first days of January. The slender Asians all wear glasses, and the bushy-faced Slavs look sullen. For a few seconds he falls into step behind a short black girl with swaggering hips. He takes a wide turn around three silent men in turbans.

Dr. Tang tugs at the strap of a lavender-coloured bicycle helmet as he knocks on her open door. "Hello, hello!" she says, clopping out from behind her desk in tiny black and yellow shoes. Her glasses are flecked with dirt, and she wears a metal clip around each cuff. "I hope you didn't bike here too."

"No."

"It's like they designed the place to slaughter us. Now," she says, shuffling back behind the desk and shaking the computer mouse. Still standing, she leans into the screen. "You're... Mr. Carter. Herbert?"

"Yes."

"Well, Herbert, welcome to the graduate program." She said the same thing the first time they met, in the spring. "Oh, but you're Mr. Carter from Newfoundland. Of course." She claps her hands. "Did I mention that my first job was in Newfoundland? At Memorial."

"Yes, that's right."

"I wanted you to meet Terry, yes?"

"Yes."

She dashes out the door and down the hall, bike shoes echoing. "Terry? Terry!" she cries.

A few seconds later she's back, breathless, pulling a man in a tweed jacket.

"I wanted you to meet Mr. Carter from Newfoundland," she says.

Terry perches on the edge of the desk and folds his arms. He is traditionally professorial, with his paunch and open collar and frizzy grey-white hair waving gently over a ruddy face. "Townie or bayman?" he asks, pleased with his command of the idiom.

"I grew up in Gander."

"Terry's field work is there," says Dr. Tang. She's shedding layers. A spattered safety vest, blue nylon shell and black turtleneck. "He's visiting from Memorial this semester."

Terry hitches thumbs in the belt loops of his corduroy trousers. "Any interest in aviation history?"

"My dad was into it."

"He'd get a great kick out of some of the stuff we're doing."

"He died years ago. In his bed." The added detail feels like a faux pas, so Carter smiles. Which is a worse mistake, because it makes him appear amused by his father's death.

"Let me show you," says Terry, pulling out a phone.

"You see!" cries Dr. Tang, coming around to grip Terry's arm. "We're all Newfoundland lovers here!"

"Though not all of us in the Biblical sense, Alice."

"Oh, Terry!" Dr. Tang's laughter bares long straight teeth and crushes her face into multiple folds.

"Alice met her lady friend there, you know. Young woman was already spoken for, but that didn't stop Alice."

"You're embarrassing me," shrieks Alice, gripping his arm harder. The act is well-rehearsed.

"Here we are." Terry hands the phone to Carter. The screen shows dark terrain dotted with tiny red crosses. "Every one of those is where a plane went down. The more accessible ones are long since picked over by scavengers. But lots of good work done by my teams over the years."

Carter recognizes the layout of the airport. Its intersecting runways look like a letter from a foreign alphabet. The lake is a ragged stretch of blue cutting through the image. The red crosses number a dozen or more. "I had no idea there were so many," he says.

"There's more. Those are just the ones we've surveyed."

There are two crosses in the middle of the lake. One of them must correspond to a favourite story of his father's, about an American bomber that lost an engine after takeoff and barrel-rolled straight into the water. Gone without a trace, undisturbed to this day. And given the oxygen-deprived depths of the lake, it surely remains as stainless and shiny as the hour it went down.

"Drop by some time and I'll tell you more. Crash sites all around that town. From the war mostly, but some after. Fascinating stuff. We're putting together a team to go back this summer. Just a bug in your ear." Terry stands and rocks on his heels. "Right, then. Cheers." He sweeps from Dr. Tang's office, as if urgently needed somewhere. A man well versed in the slivers of social intercourse. Knows when to make his exit.

Will chimes in with a text. *What's situation with Leah? Need her to sign off so we can push ahead.* He adds a postscript in a second text: *Is she playing straight? Could be messing with us re cancer story etc.*

Carter emails Jordan, with the text from Will copied. *I have to insist on total respect for Leah's situation or this will blow up in our faces. I'll be seeing her soon.*

It's time to shut Will out of the process, before his demons take over. The Alberta accident obviously made a mess of the man.

Leah's issue is different. She's embarrassed by the music, as was Carter for a long time. You only get one crack at being young, one chance to believe that voices and instruments can be used to dream your ideas into being. After that, you only hear a memory of that time, a second-hand experience.

For Infinite Yes, the golden stretch came about two years into it, when they had enough bookings to keep all four of them afloat without day jobs or side gigs. It was a nonstop churn, powered by Carter and Leah's burgeoning well of ideas and the belief that real money might yet come their way. Then Colin fell down the stairs of a townhouse in St. Catharine's. (This chick was blowing me, he explained, and everything started spinning.) He had to be replaced for three months, which cost them a bunch of gigs while they were breaking in a replacement who didn't really get it, and the record fell behind because they had to get back on the road, and then the van died and they scrambled to find another one. Leah went back on the substitute teaching list to get them through the cash squeeze. Colin checked out for a few weeks and went back on the booze. They finished recording the album, but some part of it was missing, something they couldn't name. It was over at that point. The rest was just wasted time.

That's their story, and Carter's job is to convince Leah that it's irrelevant. He should know as well as anyone how suffocating old stories can be. The Newfoundland he recalls is paralyzed by its stories, an interminable repertoire of legends, jokes, potted histories and well-worn lies, populated by the usual fools and heroes.

Jordan emails a reply, copying Will. *Understood. Sorry, man. Respect.*

8

Joyce and Rachel slept all morning. Woke to the sound of rain on the window and shared a cigarette. They could do this without either of them disturbing the covers. If they each extended an arm, their fingers met in the middle. Joyce lay on her back, sending long streams of smoke to the ceiling. The westbound arrivals ought to be underway, crossing overhead as they found their bearings on the radio range. But perhaps it was too early. A uniform grey sky had closed over the airport in recent weeks, making it difficult to guess the time of day.

A stinging spring rain came hard against the window, driven by the whistling wind.

"They'll perish in this," said Rachel. The cigarette butt hissed in her water glass.

"Maybe they've turned up," said Joyce. The hotel was dead quiet.

The town was consumed by the lost men. Two of them missing since yesterday. They had set out after breakfast to do some trouting, and were due back for dinner. By the time Joyce began her midnight shift the call had gone out: a couple of fools from out of town gone astray out around Boot Pond. All available men convening at the Airport Club. But the search couldn't begin in earnest until daylight.

"Ever been lost?" Joyce asked,

"No," said Rachel, her voice thick. "Hates the woods. You?"

"Once."

"For very long?"

"Better part of a day." Thirteen years old, prickling with distraction, Joyce had wandered off the path to the Chute on a fine morning in May. She knew her place until a shift in the sky threw her. It was a ripple of shadow that cast the world in a strange, yellow glow. The light started playing tricks on her, dropping the ground under her feet and pulling an alder away when she reached for it. She stared at the sky and listened for the Chute or the wider ocean, which she could follow home. An osprey tracked her, the shadow of its wingspan flitting in and out of view. At dusk, a red fox ran alongside her for a few paces, though her father later said she must have been seeing things.

"Weren't you afraid of the little people?" asked Rachel.

"No." She probably was, but couldn't recall. She lost all track of time and bloodied both shins without knowing it. Imagining her future as she stumbled blind. The whole shore brought to a standstill. Her father overcome, her mother keening, and Marty shocked into silence. Girls from school weeping hysterically, and a boy overwhelmed with grief, his secret crush exposed. Though she couldn't decide which boy.

"We should get over there and lend a hand," she said to Rachel. But her legs felt heavy, throbbing after five shifts in four days.

The second time she woke, Joyce inhaled the damp, oily smell that indicated plenty of traffic on the tarmac. She sat up and pulled on her socks. Extended a leg and rested her toe on Rachel's shoulder. A gentle shove.

"No."

"I'm starving."

They had the dining room to themselves. There was white pudding, split down the middle and charred on the grill. Fried potatoes and onions. Bread with real butter. Too much tea.

"We've got to go over and lend a hand," Joyce said.

Rachel tipped the sugar dispenser to make a little mound on the table. Ran a finger through it, drawing circles and swirls. "I'd rather go back to bed," she said.

Joyce envied the way Rachel could give herself over to a big, lazy lunch and a wasteful day off. Gaps in the schedule unnerved Joyce. To be idle was to be out of step with the place. The adjustment to days off staggered her.

She went for more bread and butter, spreading it so thick it showed teeth marks where she took a bite. In a couple of days the butter would be gone and they'd be back to watery margarine.

Voices approached in the corridor, and four, six, eight women entered the dining room, groaning and sighing and falling into chairs. Cup of tea, they cried. Cup of tea, for God's sake.

Alice Henley broke from the group and approached their table.

"I'm going to pee," said Rachel.

"Don't you dare." Joyce looked up at Alice. "No word?"

Alice shook her head. The first search parties had been out at the crack of dawn, she said. All day, teams of three and six trudging through deep woods. A truck dropping men down the logging road. Two punts out on Deadman's Pond and a Cessna in the air. Even spotters on the train from Alexander Bay. No signs.

"They should bring in the military." Alice pulled a tissue from her sleeve and squeezed it with her red hands. She was pregnant but not yet showing. "Jews," she said. "You don't know about them, see?"

"What Jews?" Rachel worked a polished fingernail between her front teeth. It was a substantial gap and she always picked at it after she ate.

"They're Jews, for God's sake."

"The lost fellows?"

"They could be out there to destroy the radar. Or up on Transmitter Hill cutting wires. Henley says you never saw a craftier fellow than the Jew." Alice always called her husband by his last name.

"They were trouting," said Joyce.

"Jews?" asked Rachel. "You mean like Scheffman?" Mr. Scheffman had a small shop at the Eastbound Inn. "The Jews were on our side in the war," said Rachel. "Weren't they?"

"The Russians wave a dollar at them and they'll do anything." Alice was standing straight now, her voice steady. "Henley says they don't know truth from lies. They don't even have the words for it, in their Jew language that they speak among themselves."

People said Alice's husband wasn't right in the head. Alice ought to have given up her job at the central laundry because she shouldn't be hauling those big loads with a baby on the way. But she was still at it because Henley couldn't hold a job at all. Everywhere he worked ended in some kind of blow-up. Lately he was pushing a mop around the hospital, and if he couldn't stick with that there'd be nothing left for him.

"Those soldiers you said came through the other night," said Rachel. "Were they Jews?"

"They were from Poland, I think," said Joyce. They hadn't looked like much. Weedy and hollow-chested.

"Poland and Russia, it's all the same," said Alice. "And Germans coming through here all the time as well."

"But the Germans," Rachel paused. "They switched to our side, yes?"

"A leopard don't change his spots. The Germans were sneaking around here during the war, you know. Sabotaging the bombers, Henley said. They had a girl here, too. A little steno girl with the ferry command. Spoke perfect English, like in the movies. And she was in silk stockings every day, and she disappeared after."

"Well, there's spies in the news all the time, isn't there," said Rachel. "Spies in the movies. Just last week at the Globe."

"Ruth Pinsent was the last one seen them," said Alice. "They bought a few supplies from her yesterday. Tea and sugar. Says they were right greasy looking. Dirty fellows with pointy noses. I'm telling you, they should call in the army."

Joyce had been to Scheffman's on her last payday, buying four pairs of nylons at thirty-nine cents each and putting a deposit on a shirtwaist dress from London. It felt deliciously careless to waltz into a store and cast off her money this way.

///////

The door to the Airport Club jammed, as it always did since Fox Connolly kicked through the plate glass on one of his sprees. The glass was replaced, but Connolly's boot had put the frame off kilter, and Old Dunphy said a new one was more trouble than it was worth. Every time Joyce saw him behind his bar he was telling someone that it was time to get out of these bloody old air force shacks. Get on with the new town site. Get it built so people can live properly and have a night out at a proper club.

Den Shea was in the foyer as if he had been waiting for them, chewing a sandwich. The sight of him—tie cinched to his neck under waxy, clean-shaven cheeks—made her alert to the seriousness of the situation. In times of trouble Den always looked his best. Hair combed and slicked into place, shirt starched, and somewhere in the panic of a chaotic day he always found a moment to take a razor to his craggy face.

"Wonderful, girls," he said, and clapped them both on the shoulder. "You'll want to lend a hand in the kitchen. Many mouths to feed. Joyce, love, take a moment to drop this off with Dawson and Tucker?"

"Frank Tucker?"

"That's right." He handed her a file folder. "They'll be updating the map."

Joyce said hello to Fred Yetman before she realized he was asleep on his barstool, arms folded and head tilted to the wall.

Men stood leaning on the bar, drinking from chipped white mugs. Others sank deep in leather-upholstered chairs, dark-eyed and damp. Even a crisis couldn't dispel the louche, lazy rhythms of a tavern on a rainy afternoon.

Frank sat at a table against the far wall, between the two washroom doors, playing cards with a man she took to be Dawson. They leaned back in their chairs, white shirt cuffs rolled over hairy forearms. The cards flew quickly between them, each one briefly aloft and skidding to a halt on the table. Dawson pushed the trick aside and started the next without delay. The map hung from the wall above them, sagging between its thumbtacks.

"You're to update your map," she said, handing the file folder to Frank. He laid it on the floor next to him and pushed his chair back, opening room at the little round table. "Hand of forty-fives, Joyce?"

She was in no hurry to get to the kitchen. She knew Maeve Vardy would be in charge. Maeve volunteered for everything, and insisted on running everything. Mary said she had a special way of spoiling a good cause. Joyce took the chair indicated and released the top button of her coat. Laid her gloves in her lap.

"How's Gloria?" she asked. "And baby Anthony?"

"The house is in an uproar, day and night."

Dawson snorted a laugh. Joyce recognized him now. Used to be the TWA station manager, always strolling the airport with a wet-lipped smile and ambling, open-toed gait. He had recently left the airline under murky circumstances and was driving a car for Star Taxi. The town seemed to attract men like him. Lean and hawkish, with tiny waists and jutting elbows. She would see them at Goodyear's or the Co-op with their equally severe wives. The women bustling and scolding dirty children. The men trailing behind and looking away, as if not wanting to be seen with their families.

"Now, Joyce." Dawson gathered the cards and tapped them on the table to make a deck. "Would you not say that this parchment before us is a fair and accurate picture of our beloved community?"

"Parchment?"

"He wants to know if you trust the map," said Frank.

"It's a surface chart," said Joyce. Why in the world wouldn't she "trust" it? She saw it every day. The weather office sent surface charts around the clock, along with upper-air, isotropic and adiabatic charts. Their arrival was always treated with great ceremony. The crackle of virgin paper unfurling across a desk. The damp, pulpy smell rising as men gathered round to frown at the curling lines and scribbled numbers, their neckties dangling over air currents and disturbances. Smoke rising from their cigarettes as if from the chart itself.

"See that bit of territory off the side of Runway 32?" said Dawson, dealing the cards. "Our friend Bern Henley doesn't believe this piece of territory exists. What does he imagine might be there in its place, I wonder?"

"Check."

"Twenty-five."

"Go on."

"Diamonds," said Frank, and gathered the kitty. "He never said anything didn't exist. It's a matter of proportion. From runway to pond, it can't be that big."

Dawson said something about proper scale. Joyce had the ace of diamonds and drew the five. So what was Frank going twenty-five on?

"Now Joyce," said Frank. "If you wanted to hide out, wouldn't you make for uncharted territory?"

"It makes no sense, the whole business," said Dawson.

Joyce took a trick with a ten and another with the nine, and Frank shagged up the next one by failing to follow suit.

"Henley don't know which way his arse shits," said Dawson. "Beg pardon, Joyce. Got his brains half blown out in Italy."

"Those are the fellows who win you the war. The ones who are so deep into it they'll never get out."

Joyce reneged on the five until Frank played the jack, and put him in the hole. Perhaps they were letting her win, as if she were a child and they were charged with keeping her amused.

"Aren't they just fellows who went fishing?" Joyce was trying not to take any of it seriously. It was hard to know when men were serious, the way they were always braying at each other.

Frank put down his cards and looked at her. "Tell you what," he said. "Head over to the old navy site. If you can get one of those boys to take off his headset, ask him what Joe Stalin had for dinner last night. I guarantee you he'll know, right down to the brandy and the pudding."

"Surely you've seen the B-47s landing here," added Dawson. "And the B-17s with their photo reconnaissance."

"You may have seen a distinguished-looking gentleman at the terminal a couple of Sundays ago," said Frank. "A Slavic sort."

Slavic? Joyce shook her head. Her knees jiggled under the table.

"None other than the Russian foreign minister, taking a little stroll on his stopover."

"And not his first visit, either."

"You wouldn't know the Russian foreign minister to see him, would you, Joyce?"

"No. Are we done with cards?"

"Dmitri, I believe his name is. I wonder did our friend Billy Scheffman drop by to say hello?"

"You might like to know, Joyce, that before coming among us as a merchant, our Billy did a stint in the Russian army."

"So he and Dmitri are old comrades, you might say."

"You might."

"It's a point of interest, if nothing more."

"Especially when you consider that Billy is of the Hebrew people."

"Which explains his success."

"Explains his flair for separating the Christian housewife from her dollar."

They talked across her, in a way that Joyce felt pinned to her chair. "Anyway, you'll need to update the map," she said. "That file I gave you. It's from Den."

"Now see here," said Frank. "Some of the great military campaigns in history were conducted without a map. The Romans, or Alexander the Great."

Dawson said something about Napoleon in Russia and they were off again.

/////

Joyce made the rounds with a big tomato juice can, dumping ashtrays into it. Old Dunphy dimmed the lights, throwing shafts of deep shadow over the room. Gord Delaney's wife, Fran, appeared with a steaming pot of beans and wieners, and scurried back to get the buns. You'd never know Fran and Gord were married, to see them on an evening at the Airport Club. Him running the band and her running the kitchen, not so much as a glance between them. People said they weren't happy, rarely seen together except at church. There was no sign of Gord today.

Men began drifting to the table, where Rachel towered over the used teabags, dirty dishes, overflowing ashtrays, and bread crusts marked by half-moon bites. She dug a ladle into the beans. The men lined up before her, dutiful and quiet, as if taking Holy Communion. Joyce laid out spoons and napkins.

"Are they Russians out there?" she asked one, laying a full bowl in his hands. "Or Germans?"

"Well, miss, I'd say they're awful fools, whoever they are. Out on a night the like of this." The man grinned at her, pleased to be singled out for conversation. "Did you know, miss, they had mind to blow this place to bits during the war?"

"Who? The Germans?"

"No, my love. The Brits. They had a plan to blow the works rather than see it fall to the Krauts, if it ever came to that."

124

"That's enough," said the next in line, a balding, stubby man in bib overalls. "Mind your dinner."

"Bern Henley got the Jack-a-tars out looking," said the next one behind him, and the group broke into giggles.

"The Jack-a-tars will find 'em for sure."

"Got the smell of the bog right in them."

"They say there's a bottle in it for them."

"That got their attention."

"The Jack-a-tars with a bottle? Look out!"

They were interrupted by a commotion near the front. Frank was shouting, though he didn't seem to direct it at anyone. His shirt was soaking wet, with pink flesh and a ribbed undershirt showing through at the shoulders. He must have been outdoors, or fallen in something.

"Cripes. Can't the wife come and get him?" someone asked.

"Gloria won't go near him in that state."

"He might find a friend among the Jack-a-tars."

Frank fumbled with a package of Viceroys, dropping several cigarettes as he made an unsteady path to the door. A crash of coat hangers as he slipped in the muddy foyer and tumbled into the closet. Open laughter rippled through the room, and a smattering of applause.

Joyce wondered if she ought to call Gloria and warn her not to let him in. He shouldn't be allowed in the house with her and the baby.

It seemed unlikely that men would carry on like this, if there were Russian agents about. Or would they? She didn't understand the Gander crowd at all. It was all a bit of a lark around here. You had to scratch the surface to get at the serious business of life, and people didn't like having their surface scratched.

/////

Nobody wanted to say, with dusk coming on, that the search might soon be for bodies rather than men. Joyce and Rachel were waiting on a tray of sandwiches—Fran Delaney had just loaded a boulder of ham into the meat slicer—when Maeve Vardy came through the kitchen door at great speed.

"Dirty dishes sitting out there gone rotten," she said. "You'd never run a kitchen where I'm from."

Fran, stout and slightly walleyed behind thick glasses, ignored Maeve and flicked the switch on her slicer.

A whirring motor set the blade spinning. Wriggling sheets of ham, veined white with fat, piled up on the butcher's paper.

"Anyway, there's news," said Maeve.

"News?" Rachel spoke through her full mouth.

"They've found someone."

"Why didn't you say so, woman?" cried Fran.

From the lounge came a burst of applause. They all ran from the kitchen to find a crowd gathered around Den. He stood on a chair, talking, black hair gleaming under the lights. "Word from the doctor is, if he'd been out another night all would have been lost. So thank you. Thank you, all."

More clapping, but Den raised a hand for silence. "If I may, if I may… Want to acknowledge our rescue team today. A full effort by the whole town." Vigorous applause. "You've all earned a drink," shouted Den. A roar of approval.

Music started up from unseen, crackling speakers overhead. Old Dunphy laid out bottles on the bar, one at either end and one in the middle, with stacks of tumblers. The liquor glowed gold and amber.

"Joyce?" It was Den, appearing at her side with a drink.

"They're safe?"

"There was only one fellow, as it turns out. I believe he's alright."

"But is he a Jew? Some kind of criminal?"

"Ah, some people just like to talk a lot of guff," said Den. He held his drink with two hands, turning it slowly. "Look, Joyce, I thought you'd like to know. It's that fellow Walser who was lost. I just thought…"

"Julian Walser?"

"Yes."

"Cripes," said Joyce, using her mother's favourite curse.

"He'll be alright," said Den. "He's at the hospital. Some bumps and bruises. Hard night out there."

Rachel had been dragged onto the dance floor by a pair of men who were now dancing a ridiculous jig around her, spilling their drinks. She laughed as if nothing could be funnier. With everyone on their feet the lounge was suddenly crowded.

Joyce returned to the empty kitchen to get her coat and bonnet. Fran was there, smoking furiously. The meat slicer still hummed, waiting for her to lean into the big ham again. Joyce had never seen such a machine before. Her father's slicer had a hand crank.

"Maeve bloody Vardy," said Fran. "Wouldn't run a kitchen where she's from? I wouldn't let my dog lift his leg where she's from. Bloody townie."

/////

She had been in the hospital once, to visit Gloria and the new baby. The medicine smells and church-like quiet had unnerved her. Tonight she appreciated the sharp, unsoiled air. It was a relief from the club, which was all mud and wet socks and whiskey.

Through the small window in the door, Jules looked much as he always did, hunched over a magazine. But the posture was exaggerated, his back curled as if under a burden. The arm holding the magazine was bandaged.

The head turned slowly at her knock, and Joyce saw the damage. One side of his face yellow and blue. Its cheek bulbous, as if he were a boy working on a jawbreaker. The eye above reduced to a red slit, though she felt its gaze.

He lifted a hand to beckon her inside.

"They gave you a room to yourself."

"Nobody wants to look at me." His voice was hoarse and slurred.

"You'll be in here for a while, I think." She held the door with one hand, as if just popping in for a moment.

"I'd like to get out soon. See a proper dentist. Come in, sit." He indicated a chair at the foot of the bed.

The bruised side had little knots of black thread in three different places, the biggest running along his jaw line.

"I trust you, Joyce," he said.

"You shouldn't talk."

"I wasn't lost."

"What?"

He pushed two fingers into his mouth. Wincing with pain, he pulled a blood-soaked wad of cotton from the swollen side and dropped it in a metal tray on his bedside table.

"I was never lost," he said. The voice was still laboured, but sounding more like him.

"You meant to stay out all night in the rain?"

"I was detained, Joyce. Delayed."

Joyce felt a tingle at the nape of her neck, and shivering goose bumps raced down her arms. She pulled her coat tight, though the room was stifling, heat coming off the radiator in waves. "Did you hear what people are saying about you? That you're a Jew?"

"So I am."

"But you were at church."

"My parents converted, turned Catholic. Before they had me. Before they left Austria."

"Can you do that?"

"All kinds have done it."

She wondered if he might be a bit touched after all those hours out in the cold and wet. His good eye looked glassy and marbled, as if looking inward rather than out at the world. It reminded Joyce of her mother in her final days, when her mind went bad.

"They came for me," he said. "Your friend was one of them." He wiggled his fingers. "The piano player."

"Eric Furlong."

"Right. They did this"—he touched the bandaged arm—"and this"—drew a finger across his brutalized features.

"Why in God's name would they come after you?" A drop of sweat rolled down her spine. This goddamn town and its nonsense. She was always trying to make sense of it.

"I didn't do anything, Joyce. If people are saying I'm Jewish, I suppose that was the cause."

Setting her things on the chair, she approached the bed. Lifted his shoulder to adjust the pillows and pulled the covers up around him. Touched his hair. "Is that good?"

He nodded. "Thank you."

Bracing her hands against the head rail, she leaned into him, close enough to smell the ointment on his wounds and decay on his breath. Laid a hand on the swollen cheek. His eyes widened.

"Now you'll tell me what's going on." Flecks of saliva hit his cheekbones.

"Joyce."

"Tell me." She pressed against the bruise until he emitted a groan that frightened her.

"You know I make runs to the base," he said finally.

"Yes."

"Two or three times a week. Parts and supplies from Argentia, mostly." The bad eye slowly closed, and she heard the lid release as it peeled open again. He touched her hand where she pressed the bruise. "Cripes, Joyce. Please."

She stood straight, and folded her arms. "Keep going."

"There's a woman, works evenings at the base. We got to talking."

"Who?"

"Never mind. The base."

"Talking how?"

"Talking, just... She was working nights. And..." Both eyes closed. "I always arrived at night, it seems."

Joyce curled her toes. The sweat coming off her was thin and gritty. "She works at the laundry?"

"No."

"She does." Joyce leaned into him again. Touched his stitches.

He gave a little gasp. "Okay, yes. There's a night supervisor, Mitchell. He'd be off playing cards, so she was the only one there. At the laundry. Do you see?" he said, as if the whole story hinged on the arrangement between the woman and Mitchell. "Anyway, she has a husband. So that's where the trouble starts."

Joyce backed up and gripped the rail at the foot of the bed. "You don't seem the least bit ashamed."

"And why should I be ashamed? A woman makes a fool of herself, she gets what's coming to her. I told her my next posting might be Bermuda or Rangoon. Let her believe whatever she liked."

"You brought this trouble on yourself, then."

"Yesterday I went trouting at Boot Pond." His voice gathered strength, sounding more like him. "These boys show up and throw me in a truck. Start driving, out past Union East and down some old dirt road. Barely a road at all. I had to lay in the truck so the branches wouldn't tear me to pieces. Stopped at an old cabin. Tore my clothes off. Took my boots. Said I could walk back to town if I liked. I sat in the back of the truck, freezing. Them in the cabin, drinking and playing cards. Rain started up. This morning they came out and knocked me around a bit and let me in the cabin for a bit. They said never lay a finger on another girl in this town, or it'll be worse next time."

"And Eric Furlong was among them?"

"He's a nasty customer. He said to me, 'You were lost last night, and we found you. Tell anyone otherwise and we'll be back.'"

"And here you are telling me otherwise."

"I trust you."

Joyce saw Eric's hands at the piano. The black grease worked deep into the creases and knuckles. The fingers striking sharp, staccato notes. Pictured those fingers curled into a fist. A nurse entered, and Joyce stared at the floor a moment. But on who's account was she being discreet? "You're disgusting."

The nurse stared straight ahead, silently lifting his wrist to take the pulse. "How are you feeling?"

"Not so well."

"I thought you were the sort to make his way in this world," said Joyce.

"What world is that?"

"The way everything's changing now, a man needs a good head on his shoulders. But you..."

"What do you mean, everything's changing?" Jules laughed in spite of himself, wincing as his mouth stretched. "A woman looks for trouble she bloody well gets it. That's all there is to it."

"You had best let him get some rest, miss," the nurse said without looking at Joyce. She picked up the tray with its blood-soaked cotton, the red so deep it was nearly black. "We'll get you a new dressing." She glided from the room.

"Don't play innocent with me, Joyce. That night I found you wandering around the Officers' Mess, well in your cups. A fellow could have done anything with you. Taken you anywhere. You're lucky it was me. I can still get you out of here, if you'll clean up your act and do your duty."

The nurse returned, scissors and dressing in hand, the quiet pad of her shoes surprising them. "Open wide, let's have a look," she said, perching on the edge of the bed.

"Come on, Joyce."

"That's enough," said the nurse.

"Don't you ever think about living somewhere else?"

"I already live somewhere else," Joyce said, and left.

/////

Mary brought her a coffee in the locker room. Joyce took the paper cup and ran a finger along the blue crosshatched pattern that swirled top to bottom like the stripe on a barber's pole. She had never been a coffee drinker until she joined TCA. The women drank it black and the men added long streams of milk and sugar.

Mary dropped into a discarded office chair, which rolled back and bumped the row of lockers. They had long been promised new furniture, but were still stuck with broken chairs and lockers salvaged from the RAF.

"Would you like a pair of shoes?" She produced a shiny black box. Not without a sense of performance, she lifted the cover, which held for a moment and released with a tiny puff of air. Parted the tissue with her fingers.

The camel-coloured pump felt like velvet in Joyce's hands.

"I can't imagine."

"Suede leather," said Mary. "I don't know how they make it. The silky end of the cow, I suppose."

"You can't give these away."

"Well, I could leave them in the closet, for all the good that would do."

Joyce gripped the shoe by its wedge heel. Light as air. Three slender straps across the front. Three gold buckles. She shook off her flats.

"Joe got them in Montreal. He knows I can't wear them, but he can't walk by a shoe store."

"But even if you wore them once. The Christmas dance."

The buzzer went, indicating a customer at the front counter. Joyce started to rise.

"Somebody will get them," said Mary. "A fifteen-minute break is fifteen minutes."

Joyce took the second shoe from the box in Mary's lap and stood to slip into them.

Mary's chair let out a metallic shriek as she leaned back. "Oh, my love. It's like your legs grew them."

"Thank you." The left one nipped at her pinkie toe. She sat and lifted the foot, rotating it, examining all sides.

"They're from Spain. It's all that spicy food they eat. Makes them randy, and they put it in their shoes."

"Mary!"

The buzzer again. "Girls!" shouted Mike Devine with a rap at the door. In a frenzy, as always. Racing around with a telex in one hand and a stack of reservations in the other. Crew schedules half done. Shouting for a weather report, as if it was someone else's fault that he hadn't paid attention. Mike was always flustered or on the verge of it, gasping for breath with his big mouth hung open.

Joyce slipped the shoes back in the box and folded the tissue paper back over them. "My mother," she said. "She never..." Her fingers left moist prints in the slippery black cardboard. "I mean, she wouldn't have *allowed* herself. Even the thought of it."

"I know," said Mary, and they both laughed.

///////

Gert kept her girls in line by force of shame and exposure. Lateness, shabby dress, scuffed shoes, smoking at the ticket counter, tawdry lipstick or eyeliner, too much perfume, stale breath, undesirable odours of any sort, curt manners, less-than-cheerful comportment, illegible cursive, "wild" hair, making a show of yourself, and other lapses were usually corrected with a glance and perhaps a quiet word. ("Run in the stockings, love.") Repeat offenders were chided before the whole crew. ("Now girls, we don't care what Catherine does on her own time, but she can't be coming to work with those big black bags under her eyes.") Only the worst offences earned a private audience with Gert, with the whole crowd catching every word of it through the paper-thin walls of her office.

Joyce knew she had it coming after a trio of air force men waltzed through the gate without proper boarding passes. She shouldn't have been working departures in the first place. Rushed over at a moment's notice to cover for Mary, who rushed home to cover for her husband, who was at the hospital with a finger bitten nearly clean off by one of the youngsters. The flight was called and the three airmen got through while Joyce was still rifling through the clipboard, looking for the passenger manifest.

She thought she might get away with it until Moncton telexed that they had been delivered three RCAF fellows now demanding passage to Montreal for the weekend, without so much as a ticket between them. Gert waited until shift change before calling Joyce in.

"Documentation," said Gert, snatching a piece of paper from her desk and shaking it before her. "You know bloody well, Joyce. Paper, boarding pass, ticket, waybill. *Something*. You know it's not our job to ferry those boys to their girly clubs in Montreal. Next time you tell them the war is over and they don't have the run of it anymore."

Joyce went straight from Gert's office to her locker and slipped out the side door, eyes averted. She was in no mood for the banquet at Gleneagles, even with lobster on the menu. Anyway, there was no time to mope, as the boys were gone ahead to set up and she was due by seven.

It was a big cabin, newer and nicer than Deadman's or Spruce Brook, with a higher ceiling and shiny tableware. Good, solid tumblers and hefty ashtrays that didn't upend when you crushed your butt in them. A banquet for management from Anglo-Newfoundland Development, and a dance for the whole staff. The workers and their wives gathered at the doors during pineapple upside-down cake, waiting for the doors to open. Joyce's mouth was dry and her tone thin. But she was mostly on the mark. When all hands were good and soused, Roland on the saxophone did his little routine of coming next to her and wrapping a hand around her waist. The fingers wandered up her ribs while he climbed a scale on the horn, until his instrument blared a high, urgent note and he brushed her breast a quick paw before scuttling back to his music stand. Men roaring and women tut-tutting on the dance floor.

Gleneagles had no piano, but Eric came along anyway and sat in on drums for a few songs. He bought Joyce a whiskey at the end of the second set, and sat with her at a corner table. When a small, grey-stubbled man came by to bus the table, Eric introduced him.

"This is my brother Aubrey. What are you doing here tonight, Aub? A few extra dollars, is it?"

"A few extra dollars," said the brother, who looked much older.

"Are you still down at the sawmill?"

"Oh yes, it's all lumber this season. A good deal of it headed out your way."

"Houses going up all summer in Gander."

"Not so much the pine as the birch." Aubrey propped a full tray against his skinny hip, and hardly noticed when the glasses and beer bottles wobbled precariously. "No end to the birch coming through. Like shit through a goose."

"Mind language, Aub," said Eric.

"Sorry, miss."

"It's alright," said Joyce.

"Some days they wants it rough, some days dressed," said Aubrey. "So you got to be on your toes, see?"

"And is it still the two women running it?"

"Missus Murphy and Chippy Steele," said Aubrey. "They got me up to nine dollars a day, so I calls it fair. Hard old maids, mind you."

"You'd do better with Bowater, I imagine."

"Bowater got Joey John superintendent, and I don't like his manner. I might go over to Point Leamington or Badger, catch on with a logging camp."

"Miserable work, that. Miserable pay."

"The union will put it to rights, I figures. Smallwood's a union man, see? So it's good for unions. Anyway, I calls it fair, what I gets from Chippy."

They were three songs into the third set when the crowd started calling for a man named Myrick. "Come on now, Myrick!" they shouted. "Tell us a story, Myrick!"

Gordon indicated that the band should stand down. Joyce went to pee. When she came back a man was at her microphone, telling a laboured tale about a lady with a wooden leg. His rubbery face was remarkable, twisting into grimaces of agony and surprise. The crowd roared. He continued with rhyming stories about dead goats and buckets of squid and Lacey Simms losing her bloomers in a gale and how Edgar Mouland nearly went mad trying to work the pocket grinder down at the mill. This went on until well after the bar closed and the lights were up, until a flushed man with scars around his mouth started in on a recitation called "Pisspot Pete." He was interrupted by several others, who said the tale wasn't fit for mixed company. This seemed to break the spell of the room, and people began drifting to the door.

Eric offered Joyce a ride back, with a short detour to drop Aubrey at the road down to Appleton. The prospect of hanging about for the train was exhausting, so Joyce got in the truck and sat between the brothers. For a few minutes they drove silent, Aubrey breathing loudly through his mouth and dabbing his nose with a rag.

"Thought about starting my own operation though," he said, as they bumped and rattled in the dark.

"What kind of operation?" asked Eric.

"Sawmill. In Glenwood."

"How would you do that, Aubrey?"

"Cobble it together. There's ways."

"Don't be at that, Aubrey. Take a steady pay packet at Bowater or ANDCO."

Aubrey took a mouthful from the bottle he had been holding between his thighs. "I don't much care for this, though. Whatever it is." He held the bottle to the light of the dashboard and squinted. "Spur Cola."

"It's what they drink in St. John's."

"No doubt," said Aubrey. He rolled down the window and tossed the bottle. "I don't know that anyone expected that music you were playing."

"They danced," said Joyce.

"They danced, yes."

Aubrey had them stop at a trail only he could see. The night swallowed him.

"Did you ever see the like?" said Eric, reversing the truck to go back the way they came. "'Start my own operation.' Bloody fool."

They backtracked to the main road, drizzle picking up, and Eric talked of his family. "Seven brothers. Five of them still in Placentia Bay at the salt fish or the herring or whatever they can manage." He shook his head. "They can have it."

It became hard to talk as Eric picked up speed, the truck rumbling and kicking up gravel, rocks ringing sharp off the underside. They hit the airport road, freshly resurfaced, with a jolt and a satisfying purr of asphalt. Runway lights blinked through the trees out Joyce's window.

"Come for a drink," said Eric.

"At this hour?"

"What hour is that?"

"It's late."

"No harm in it."

"There's nothing open." She gripped the door handle and leaned toward it, as if she could direct the truck. But they were already past the hotel and turning towards the airport.

"Well, I'm going for a drink," said Eric, as he pulled to a stop at the terminal.

Joyce sat listening to the ticking of the engine, watching the rain blur the windshield. Finally she climbed from the truck and caught up to him inside. "I suppose you find this funny."

"Not at all. A nightcap is no laughing matter."

Their voices echoed down the terminal concourse, which was silent except for the buzz of overhead lights and the distant skitter of a telex machine. Bodies were scattered about, slumped in chairs or sprawled on benches. The only one awake was a skinny girl behind the coffee counter with a paperback.

The leather-padded door to the Big Dipper was shut, its small oval window dark. Eric thumped a hand on the door. A sleeper sighed. The coffee girl shifted on her stool, coughed and turned a page.

"We should go," said Joyce.

A bolt released and Parsons the bartender let them into the empty bar. Eric nodded and asked for two Scotches. Parsons didn't look especially happy, but he set his mop in a corner, bolted the door behind them. Eric directed Joyce to the nearest table.

He said that he and Aubrey had gone to California during the war, working the sawmills and box factories. "Should have stayed down there. They were desperate for men. Aubrey's problem is he's too proud to work for another man for very long. This foolish notion to start his own operation. He'll starve."

"My father would never work for another man."

"I don't mean to disrespect your father. But Smallwood got the right idea. You get the experts in here, Europeans, Canadians, to show us how it's done. You get your steady pay and baby bonus and the old age. Never mind scraping by with your own fishing boat or your own sawmill."

Joyce held the first sip in her throat and felt it down to her toes. She had been shivering all the way home from the damp. Parsons mopped around them. Apart from Eric's drink order, the two men had not exchanged a word.

"Newfoundlanders, see? They hardly know there's a world out there." Eric stared into his glass. "Most places it's the same five families staring up their own behinds for the past two hundred years or more."

There was a spill of change on the bar. Parsons counted up the evening's take, mumbling numbers as he flicked coins into an open palm.

"Those two women must be turning a dollar, though," said Joyce.

"What women?"

"Your brother said he works for a couple of women. They have the sawmill in Appleton?"

"Yes, well, we'll see. The Bowaters could run them out of business just like that if they chose to." He snapped his fingers on *that.*

It seemed to Joyce that if the sawmill women were paying Aubrey nine dollars a day and the lumber was coming out as fast as they could make it, they must be doing alright.

The coffee girl stared at her paperback, sucking at her teeth as if to dislodge something. There would be gossip, but Joyce suspected she was already being talked about. She didn't doubt that Gloria talked about her all the time. Gloria loved gossip, and always laced the barest facts with the most salacious speculation. Then she would say, "Shame on me for even saying that, for even thinking it," and shiver with pleasure. Joyce saw now that she'd never be rid of Gloria, and so never completely rid of Cape St. Rose.

Outside, Joyce insisted on walking home.

"Walk? Nonsense."

"It's just around the corner." The drizzle had stopped, and the air felt mild compared to the cold of the truck.

"Alright then," said Eric, tossing his keys in his hand. "Now look here, maybe we could do this again, only at a more decent hour? On Thursday? Payday and all. What do you say?"

"No," said Joyce. But her feet wouldn't move beneath her until she gave the honest answer. "Yes."

"I could see I was winning you over," said Eric. "Just a matter of time. Ha."

It seemed like a long time since she had spoken the word with any kind of conviction. "Yes," she said again, because it sounded so good, with its affirmative hiss at the end. Then she started away at a good pace, the porch light of the hotel already in sight.

9

The basket of assorted jams is a mistake. Six small jars nestled in straw, with a package of biscuits and a veil of pink cellophane. Carter holds the basket in his lap, eyes smarting from the glare of the morning sun as a cloud of snow lifts and sweeps over the car, hard grains pelting the windshield. The drive to Toronto was going fine until Isabelle decided to pass a bus. Now they're trapped in the middle lane, hemmed in by transport trucks on either side.

He tries to recall the label on each jar. Pomegranate, apple, blueberry, lavender. There's a dark one, blackberry or black currant, and a green minty one. Carter pictures Leah scooping jam in the morning, her hair wrapped in a towel. He was supposed to visit her at her apartment. She called last night and said she was in hospital due to a bowel blockage, and insisted he come regardless. She sounded good, though her voice was tight and gave some of her words a childlike squeak.

He has prepared his case on behalf of the music. Last night he listened to the Mozart again.

The transport trucks work in tandem, racing ahead and dropping behind, as if they find great sport in keeping a Suzuki hatchback stuck in the middle. Sam is mostly silent in the back seat, watching videos on Isabelle's phone. He occasionally cackles, and the phone makes the whooshing sounds of something moving at great speed. Isabelle will drop Carter at the hospital and take Sam for his check-up with Dr. Hurley. They used to dread these trips. The fifty-minute drive. How the doctor twisted his brow and pressed the stethoscope to Sam's chest. The yawning silence as he listened. But now the visit is routine, and the doctor has suggested they can soon stop coming altogether. The electrical pathways are secure. The tubes and valves robust. Though the gallop remains, Sam's heart beats without the ragged slips or swishes that signal trouble. The dread has receded to join the other fears wrapped into the core of their days.

It's a poor choice, bringing fruit jam to a bowel blockage.

"Can I leave this with you? Maybe I'll just chuck it?"

"Bring it," says Isabelle, doing a shoulder check. "It's something. Anything to brighten up a hospital room."

"I know what they're up to," says Isabelle, as the lead truck kicks up another wave of snow. "He'll give a little extra gas any second now." As if on cue, the truck roars with acceleration. Isabelle does a shoulder check and brakes hard for a moment. There's the blare of a horn behind them. But there's daylight on Carter's side, an open slot in the left lane. They fill the slot with a quick jerk of the wheel and another pump of the brakes. They're free. It doesn't even feel dangerous.

///////

The man in the next bed is worse off. He's young. Averts his eyes as Carter enters, ashamed to be sick and in pyjamas while his peers are out in the world, staring at phones and driving too fast and talking loudly in bars. The tendons on his neck ought not to stick out like that. One of the tendons seems bent, as if it recently collapsed. Carter flinches at the thought and a nurse pulls a curtain around the young man and there's Leah just beyond the curtain.

She tells him about the three stages of chemo and radiation coming up. Then a break and another three stages.

"It's metastasized to a couple of places, so they're picking targets. Like back here." Leah taps behind a shoulder. "Shrink the tumour so I can breathe better."

She extends a hand to catch the shaft of sunlight from the corner window. Her complexion has a yellow hue, like the inside of an apple. The lines on her face are deep but familiar. They always showed when she sang, when she climbed the register or held long notes. Now they're permanent.

"So this latest problem," says Carter. "It came out of the blue, sort of?"

"Monday afternoon. Kevin gave me a hand." Her voice runs aground, the words trapped in her throat. Carter stands—he's been in the chair at the end of her bed—and lifts the plastic cup from the bedside table. Holds the straw for her. She swallows and he feels the effort of it, the Adam's apple crawling up her neck and descending. "I have to drink more water. They said if I was better about drinking water I might not be here." She points to the dangling bag on its rack, with the tube running down and into her forearm. Its liquid is clear, but doesn't look like water. Carter imagines a sugary gel.

She's still fighting it, jaw clenched and eyes fixed at the foot of the bed. He returns to the chair and looks away so she can finish the fight in private. Kevin must be the old Irish boyfriend from North Bay, back in the picture. Or maybe there's a new Kevin. Carter knows little about Leah's life and relationships, though he's revealed much of himself in the years since their divorce. During her first bout with cancer he would drive into Toronto to sit with her. Emboldened by his new relationship with Isabelle, he talked too much, and apologized to Leah for interrupting her life and derailing it with music.

He certainly hadn't planned to talk about how Ronnie died while he and Isabelle watched a ridiculous French movie. But it came out. He'd been sitting with Leah, listening to her talk about treatment and pain. Laying a hand over the nipple, she'd pulled one side of her robe open to show the red crescent of her radiation scar. This prompted him in some way, and he started talking.

When he'd finished, she said, "You remember the movie so well."

"What?"

"The way you describe it. The colours and the actors singing. The heartbreaking scene at the end."

"It's just this weird movie we saw."

"You spent as much time on it as the whole rest of the story."

He didn't go see her for a long while after that, not trusting himself around her.

Leah touches the basket of jams on the bedside table, pressing her fingers against the cellophane to get a better look at the labels beneath. "That was a nice story," she says. "The one about the woman you met travelling. That album saved my life, or whatever she said."

"Yes." Carter was searching for a way to introduce the topic. "It's for people like that. We should get it out there."

"Get what out there?"

"The album again, and the unreleased tracks. Just for the audience that's there. There's a buzz in the community."

"What community?"

He launches into his argument, setting it up with the story of Colin's fall, the money troubles, the van crapping out. How circumstances cheated the band and incited the decline.

"That's not what happened," says Leah, interrupting him. "We were playing great back then. We could always play."

"The point is that none of these details or how you remember it or I remember it, none of it matters. Because it's not our music anyway."

"A song about my dead sister and her mental breakdowns? I'm pretty sure that's mine."

"We changed the name."

"From Clara to Callie. You think nobody knew? You think she didn't know? The way you kept leaning on me to finish that song. I said it was a bad idea, and you just leaned on me until we did it."

Carter won't rise to this. "It's not ours. It belongs to that woman I told you about, who saw me on the plane." Melissa Ryan's grip on his bare arm. Her hair and red throat. It prompts a stirring in his crotch, and he marvels at this boyish moment, his dick defiant, rushing ahead against his wishes. "Everyone like her. We have to honour those memories. I mean..."

"Honour the memories? Like the time you locked me in the house for a week?"

"We locked both of us up, to finish writing the album."

"Right. Except you took my key, and warned me not to go anywhere. Not even for a walk."

"We both agreed to it. For the music."

"You took my key. You hid it from me."

Maybe she's not so different from Will. Looking to settle scores. The cellophane crackles as Leah pulls a jar from the basket. "Would you mind?" she says. It's the green one. Carter twists the lid until it pops. When he hands it back, she has produced a spoon from somewhere. He watches her lift a dab of green and lay it on her tongue.

"You're not being reasonable, Lee. I mean, this is a lot of strain for you right now—"

"Oh, fuck off," she says quietly. "Just..." She holds up a palm and tilts her head back to rest on the pillow. Closes her eyes.

"There might be a little money in it. You could use the cash. We all could."

"Those kids at our shows." She lifts and shakes her head as if waking, and goes in for another green spoonful. "They had to grow up too, I guess. Or maybe they stay like that their whole life? Weirdos and loners."

"Maybe we helped them grow up."

"Sad little kids. Lonely and confused and horny. Like us."

"We helped them, I think. Gave them a place to be. Maybe we even helped them get laid."

"Not likely. But a few of them might have had a really nice wank after the show. I suppose that's something."

///////

"It's bad," says Carter, buckling his seatbelt. "It's moving along quicker than anyone expected."

Isabelle pulls into traffic and turns to look at him, which she almost never does when she's driving. "That's a shame."

"It's all about radiation and chemo and tumours. They're targeting one in her shoulder. Then the bowel thing. A big rush of problems now."

He emailed Jordan while waiting for the car. *Everything's changing quick. She's down to months, possibly weeks.* When she's gone, won't Carter and Will make a majority, two out of three remaining band members? They'll be in the clear. He's pretty sure that's the case. Jordan's partner is looking into it.

Within a few minutes they are cruising west on Eglington with relative ease, escaping Toronto in daylight, before rush hour. Sam falls asleep immediately, his head lolling against the door and wobbling with each bump.

"We're going to release the music again," he says, confidence buoyed and dick still tingling in the wake of its unexpected half-boner.

"Really?" Isabelle taps one fingernail repeatedly on the steering wheel.

"Yeah. There's potential, for sure. Licensing for movies and TV, that sort of thing."

"They want to see Sam again in the summer."

"What?"

"Dr. Kim asked us to come back in June."

"I thought…" Carter tries to piece it together. "I thought today was routine."

"It was."

"But June is only…" He twists the rear-view mirror to get a look at Sam. Eyes closed and head dipping. He jerks his chin, fighting the sleep.

"Dr. Kim is new. So."

"Is he young?"

"She. Yes, she's young and she's new and she never saw Sam till today. We should be grateful. Do you know how hard it is to see a specialist?"

"What did she hear?"

"A little rush, she said."

"That's not routine."

"A little rush in one valve. It's there on his chart."

"Dr. Hurley never mentioned it."

"He did, way back. You just forgot."

"But he didn't say 'rush.' That wasn't the word."

"Carter! Christ, I don't know. Rush, swish, whatever it is. I'm trying to listen to her, trying to follow it."

"I'm sorry. I'm just trying to figure out what changed."

"Maybe nothing. It's a new doctor. She can't just read what the last guy gave her. She has to get in there and hear it for herself. So I don't know."

"Well, we have to get a clear picture from her."

"There's never a totally clear picture. There's always… Next time you can be there and ask all the questions you want."

They drive silently, Isabelle merging left and left again as lanes consolidate and options narrow, pushing them west.

"I'm just surprised," says Carter. "Because Hurley used to say, maybe another year and we could stop coming. Maybe a final appointment."

"It's a condition. It's built into him. There is no final appointment."

146

The screen opens on the archaeology lab, and there's music blaring, harsh and jangly over the little speaker. Carter knows the guitar riff, a little pleasure pill of F/D/F sharp/D sharp. Frantic tambourine and boxy drums. A man with a thick, swirling ridge of hair reaches offscreen to stop the music.

"How's everything in St. John's," shouts Terry.

"February," says the man on the screen. "Surviving."

"Snow day on Monday, eh?"

"You can just talk normal," says the man, his hand looming large as he adjusts his monitor. "I can hear you fine."

Terry turns the screen so that it faces Carter. "Say hello to Morris, one of our grad students back on the Rock," he says. "Morris, this is Herbert."

"Hey," says Carter.

"Pleasure," says Morris.

"Herbert here might be on the dig with us this summer," says Terry. "He's from Gander." He leans in so he and Carter both appear on camera. They're Skyping from Terry's office, which is overheated and crammed with books and papers.

"So I have to tell you this one," says Terry. "We're right in the thick of it last summer. Hot as blazes. You never thought Newfoundland would get so hot. And it's nothing but marsh and bog, and you know we're all going to end up in it at some point. But it's poor Morris every time! Four times he went down, and the rest of us dry as bone. A couple of weeks later his wife wakes him in the middle of the night and says, 'Cripes, Morris, you've still got the smell of the bog on you.' The heat must have baked it right into him."

Morris smiles, thin fingers adjusting his glasses. "I went down right up to here," he says, laying a hand at his chest above a prominent belly.

"Cataloguing today, Morris?"

"That's right."

Terry turns to Carter. "Every item from a dig has to be cleaned, photographed, measured, and assigned a catalogue number."

Morris lifts a clipboard and reads, "United States Air Force B-24 Liberator. Crashed on approach, 26 kilometres from Gander, February 14, 1945. All ten on board killed."

"So this was where we did well last summer," says Terry.

Morris pulls the switch to illuminate a floor lamp. He opens a locker and begins expertly identifying the scraps on the shelves. A throttle and gyroscope mount from the cockpit. A segment of fuselage lining patterned like honeycomb. It's hard to see in the glare of the lamp.

Terry flips open a second screen on his desk to show the Google Earth image of Gander and its surroundings. "Fourteen wrecks from World War Two. Here's where we're at." He taps a red cross which is labelled B-24. Terry slides his finger around it. "Bog everywhere, as Morris can confirm."

Each cross has a label. *Canso, Hurricane, A-20, Hudson, Lodestar.*

Morris belches loudly and excuses himself. Carter glimpses a trashcan spilling over with greasy takeout bags. Morris doesn't look like a field-work guy, whereas Terry is born to it. Every inch the hunter and digger, built for cargo shorts and heavy boots, for hearty meals cooked on a Coleman stove and eaten from a rocky perch. Confined to civilization, Terry's most vital energies are held in abeyance.

"Where's Arrow Air?" asks Carter.

"Ah," Terry pushes up his glasses. "That's around the lake here. We stopped by to see the memorial. But there's nothing for us to do there. You're old enough to remember that one, I'd say."

"I was in high school," says Carter. "It was ..."He doesn't want to say. It was thrilling, to be fifteen years old and have epic tragedy so close at hand. "It was crazy. The whole town was in shock, I guess. But we went to school, same as usual." The boys in grade nine were giddy with news and rumour. Not just a big crash. A super-fuck-ing-humongous DC-8 stuffed to the gills with American GIs. A fire? More like a fucking fireball, man, ripping right down to the lakeshore. Two hundred and fifty burning bodies. Not just burning. Incinerated. Like, even their dog tags melted. At lunchtime the boys streamed into the school parking lot to watch the black smoke rise and spread. It was just off the highway and not even as far as the old cemetery. Close enough to ride their bikes, and several boys declared they would do so after school, and never mind the slick December roads. Forget it, said Todd Philpot. The CIA will have it locked down. That night Carter's father said the motels were booked up for miles with all the reporters come to town.

"People there still talk about it, eh?" says Terry. "About conspiracies and cover-ups."

"The day it happened people were already saying it's a bomb, it's terrorists." Todd Philpot had spoken of it with grim assurance, narrowing his eyes like Clint Eastwood. "This is heavy shit, boys. The heaviest. Welcome to the real fucking world, boys."

"In fairness to them, I think everyone knows the official report doesn't hold up," says Terry. "So it invites all kinds of wild speculation. But you have to be wary of that sort of thing in our line of work."

"What sort of thing?"

"Letting your imagination run away with it. Getting sucked into the idea that you're chasing a big secret. That only happens in the movies. You'll find bits and pieces of people's lives. But you have to resist the urge to fill in the gaps. We know only what we know."

People said the ground was still smouldering two days after the Arrow Air crash, hot enough to warm the feet of the men from Search and Rescue. They turned Hangar 21 into a morgue. Nicky Gill's father did security detail there, and he said the remains they brought back were just the tiniest bags. People said some of the Search and Rescue boys never went back to work after. Some of them lost their marriages.

Morris opens a small set of drawers and sets the laptop on a table behind him, half sideways. "Smaller items here. More personal." He brings individual pieces to the screen. A house key, several buttons from U. S. Air Force jackets, and a tarnished lapel pin of silver wings. "Navigator's wings. We've got a set of radio operator's wings here somewhere too."

A large freezer bag holds pieces of parachute, its white nylon stained like a smoker's fingers.

"This is the kind of stuff we retrieve," says Terry.

Carter examines the Google Earth image again. The town is a grey-white blur, like a patch of overcast sky. He finds the main shopping square, with Alcock Crescent at one end and the patch of wood behind the old post office, where a girl was killed when Carter was a baby. He recalls the frowning, hairy-browed woman who came to see his mother once. There was a great fuss over the visit, with his mother changing in and out of her cardigan. He was shooed from the house as soon as the visitor arrived. It was his father who later revealed that the hairy-browed lady was mother to the boy who did the killing, and she hardly ever left her home anymore.

"You should come along this summer," says Terry. "Always a great crowd. Always good fun."

Carter has never been easy in the company of men. As a teenager he couldn't master the knowing grin or internalize the banter, with its scatology and sodomy and sporty belligerence. Couldn't lie convincingly about girls and lemon gin and the stains on the back seat of Dad's car. In the end, he settled for being an outsider, slightly disdainful of the manly world. Leah was a good buffer against it during the band years. Carrying himself as a brooding artist helped maintain a distance as well.

Morris tilts his laptop to show several lumps of iron laid out in plastic tubs, bathing in a bluish liquid.

"Morris?" calls Terry. "Where are these from?"

"Langdon crash," calls Morris from behind his camera.

"So this is from the same dig, last summer. The sodium hydroxide baths will clean these pieces for us. Takes six months, sometimes a year or more."

"Why is it called the Langdon crash?" asks Carter.

"That was the pilot's name. He has a grandson who is very interested. Contacted us from Minnesota. Several of the bodies were never found, and his grandfather is one of them. No remains whatsoever."

//////

Joyce wants to Skype, according to Shanna, the nurse at Howley Park. *I did a demonstration this morning during Coffee Time,* she writes. *It was a bit confusing for many of them. But Mrs. Carter was quite interested. She asked if we could use it to talk to you.*

Carter is also a bit confused by Skype. But he's seen Terry do it, and Isabelle. He and Shanna settle on a morning, and after a couple of false starts, a naked pink face fills the screen.

"Hi, Mr. Carter!" Shanna licks her upper lip with a slithery tongue, and the motion breaks her mouth into fragments. "Are you getting me okay?"

"Yes. But you're very close." He's never been so close to a face without kissing it. Her hazel eyes are huge, and one front tooth is set at an angle, creating a small black gap.

"Sorry!" Shanna laughs and backs away. "Is that better?"

"Yes. That's good."

Even with distance, her gaze is discomfiting. Shanna's face radiates childlike vigour. Her russet hair is chopped short around the ears, sprouting frosted tips at the crown.

"I'm in your mother's room now. Do you want to say hello, Joyce?"

Carter expects some sort of introductory…something. But Shanna shifts aside, leaving him to look at a rosy blur of a bare wall. There is rustling and mumbling, and the screen darkens with his mother's green fleecy. A glimpse of her small, leathery hand. Then her head appears, her small, sleepy eyes peering from a bloodless face.

"Hello, Mom."

"Herbert. Well, isn't this something." Her eyelids flutter and she squints.

"Does the screen bother your eyes, Mom?"

"No," she says. Her voice is strong but out of sync, trailing behind her lips. Her hair is pulled back the way it should be. The picture brightens—perhaps Shanna has opened a blind—bringing out the red of her nose and the liver spots at her temples. She appears to have cold sores at both corners of her mouth.

"I'm well," she adds, before he can ask. "The jewelry box is gone. Someone's after taking it. But you know, I don't mind."

"I think we'll find it, Joyce," says Shanna, off camera. "We're going to have a good look."

A hand rises and waves, making a blurry streak. "Nothing in it worth much anyway. Old cheap stuff." Joyce smiles. "Is everyone well? Your wife and the little boy?"

"They're good. It's too bad they're not home to say hello. That's where I am right now, you know. At home in Ontario. "

"I know, my dear. That's why I asked." She's chiding him gently. Before he can respond, she resumes talking. Her thoughts ramble in the way one expects of old people, mostly concerning the food, which she doesn't mind, and the weather, which she does. She peers slightly to one side, as if there's something over his shoulder. Her questions are ordinary and direct—health, happiness, career, the boy. How old? What's he like? Where will he go to school? But Carter is unsettled by her clarity. This is not the ill-defined Joyce he saw two months ago. Her face bobs about and crumbles into pixels, but reassembles when she stays still for a few seconds.

She asks him to fetch a picture of Sam and hold it up so she can get a good look.

"Can't you send it somehow? On the computer?"

"You can email it to me," says Shanna. "I'll give you the address."

"What do you make of that nonsense some people are getting on with?" said Joyce. "About Canada. Got their head in the clouds."

Shanna leans in, showing half of her face. "Her and Mr. Johnson had a bit of a discussion the other day, about Confederation and how the vote went."

"That's great, Mom. I thought you were never interested in all those old arguments."

"I'm not interested at all. Only you can't let people talk nonsense. Someone's got to set them straight. Do you recall how I poached eggs for you as a boy?"

"Eggs?"

"Yes. We used that saucepan with the little cups for the eggs?"

"Yeah, I do remember," says Carter. It was a variation on a double boiler. The cups were cradled in a frame that sat on top of the saucepan, with water simmering below. You could lift a cup out and turn a domed egg bottom-up on your plate.

"I said at breakfast the other day, they should get a couple of saucepans like that. Because it's the best poached egg you ever had. And this old one at the next table, she wouldn't hear of it. That's the lazy way, she says. You don't poach a proper egg like that. What was her name?"

"Mrs. Vincent," says Shanna.

"And she from Lumsden. Sure what would they know about it down there?"

"Mrs. Vincent's from Cape Island."

"Which one is Lumsden?"

"Mrs. Gibbons."

"Anyway, it's all the same crowd. All married to each other." Her mouth falls open and her eyes squeeze shut with an almost silent laugh, delighted with the confrontation. "Sure what would—" She

153

makes two attempts at finishing the sentence before giving way to another phlegmy wheeze of mirth.

The moment of hilarity seems to disorient her. After recovering and wiping her eyes she turns her face from the computer. Carter talks to her. But she shakes her head, uncomprehending. "Turn it off, turn it off," she says to Shanna. Though she still seems in good spirits. She pushes from her chair and shuffles offscreen.

"Okay, Joyce," says Shanna. She leans in to work the mouse and asks Carter if they can Skype again soon. "Just the two of us, if that's okay. Couple of things I want to update you on."

"Okay," says Carter.

"It's nothing urgent, only—"

"Turn it off now please. Turn it off." Joyce's hand reaches in, slapping at the keyboard. They disappear.

/////

Joyce had looked curiously two-dimensional on the screen. The light in the room gave her no depth, or maybe it was the pixilation. Her voice had been unmistakable, nipping at the words and jumping smartly into any lull in conversation. Not once did he have to remind her that Isabelle had replaced Leah, or repeat Sam's name. When she started in on music—how it brings meagre rewards, "and I don't just mean the money"—he told her he had given up music for good, and she never mentioned it again.

Computers never scared Joyce. She'd worked for a phone company in the eighties, when they overhauled the long-distance system and computerized it. She even modelled the new rigging for the local paper, in a photo captioned CNT *operator demonstrates new computerized 4000-line digital switiching exchange.* Carter's father had clipped it, circled the spelling error in red pen, and posted it on the fridge. Joyce looked good in the picture. Every inch the modern working woman, poised at a keyboard in her crisp blouse and smart shag cut, smiling at what might have been a very large microwave oven across her desk. She had little patience for those who flinched at the new technology. "Some of the girls are terrified," she had said. "Sure it's not going to bite you."

A few years after she was widowed, Joyce purchased a computer of her own, and her first emails to Carter included links to websites poring over the details of the Arrow Air crash. The pages were text-heavy conspiracy arguments, including one that accused the American government of bombing its own soldiers. Carter was at the height of his powers then, the band working steadily and college kids swooning over his wife. His grand plan to leave Newfoundland had worked out even better than he could have hoped. The air he breathed seemed charged with music. He had little appreciation for his mother's predicament: barely sixty years old, widowed and alone. He had scoffed at her computer noodlings and written a lengthy email advising her to find a more productive use for her time. It was not one of his better performances.

10

Eric heard that Pan-Am was looking for new station agents, and applied for the training program in New York. An operation that size would surely prosper for years to come, he reasoned, and getting in now opened the possibility of working anywhere in the world. He was turned down, much to Joyce's relief. Eric didn't possess the patience for the half-witted passengers and countless bumbling oversights she dealt with daily.

The rejection troubled him, but no more than a day or so. More and better opportunities were sure to come his way. Eric didn't so much search for jobs as search the world for wonder and possibility, spending long evenings in his easy chair, the floor around him strewn with his magazines and newspapers. He was dogged in his concentration, reading softly to himself, often repeating a line or paragraph several times over until it made itself clear. He might call Joyce over to show her the latest developments in skyscraper design, or read to her about how potatoes were being bred for greater yield. One night he asked her opinion on a series of magazine illustrations proposing "a revolution in the household kitchen." But she didn't get to say much. "You see what happens with better design," he explained, tracing his finger over the strips of chrome trim on the stove and refrigerator. "Just by making it more pleasing to the eye, it becomes an easier place to work. And nuclear ovens, for quick cooking."

"Nuclear ovens!" Joyce couldn't imagine it, not after seeing the newsreels of bomb tests in the American desert.

Eric's kitchen wasn't much. A filing cabinet for a pantry, a hot plate and coffee pot on an old office desk. But the tiny electric refrigerator was the first Joyce had ever seen in action. The rest of the apartment she liked. On Page Street, well away from the tarmac, with a second easy chair for her and a nice big picture window looking to the woods. The worst of it was the Murphy bed, which partly blocked the bathroom door.

His next job idea was to work the network of superhighways that would soon crisscross America. Hard labour, but with his years of experience he'd rise to foreman or beyond before too long. After that he had a notion to return to California, where the next generation of airliners would be conceived and built. Opening a magazine page that folded out to double size, he showed Joyce the sketches for an airship that would hold hundreds of passengers and crew, with dining rooms, libraries, tennis courts, private quarters, and a ballroom with full orchestra.

"But can they actually make it?" asked Joyce, perched on the arm of his chair.

"Sooner than you think," he said. "Maybe we'll be the house band. What do you say?"

He stored his records in a case that looked like a toolbox, each disc nestled in a velvet-lined slot. The case had a lid and a handle on one side, so it could be latched and carried like luggage. The record player was similarly built, resembling a briefcase made of blond wood. It might stay latched a week or more, and then he'd play every record, working through the case from front to back, late into a single evening. Or he might fixate on a song and hound

Joyce with it. One night he insisted on playing "Mood Indigo" for her, to show her how it was done.

"Please don't," said Joyce. "Mood Indigo" was among the songs she had been trying to master. It was beyond her, the words felt false in her mouth.

"You're being foolish," said Eric, holding the disc by its edges so Joyce could read *Duke Ellington & His Famous Orchestra* stamped on the black RCA Victor label.

Whoever sang it for Ellington would surely fill the words with all the hope and sorrow and solitude that Joyce couldn't muster. If she heard it done that way she would never sing it again, and she had to sing it because Gordon had worked out a solo for it—the muted trumpet groaning like a sheep being sheared—and was determined to play it.

"No," she said. "I'll walk out."

"You're the singer," said Eric, but seemed to sulk a bit. Joyce thought him a bit foolish for making such a fuss over a song, but it wouldn't matter much longer. Singing would be over for her once she was settled with children.

/////

Fran Delaney was in an awful state. It had started in the winter, when she stopped going out. Not for groceries, said Mary. Not even for mass, said Gert. Sleeps all day. Won't answer the door. Gordon's looking after the youngsters, said Mike Devine. They say she hardly talks to them. Won't let them near her. Her own children! said Mary, pity turning to disgust.

People asked Gordon, how are things? Good, he always said. Not bad. The band had a wedding in June, for the general manager at TWA. Joyce watched him closely that night, but it was the same Gordon. Counting in every number, and flexing his knees with the tempo. Tilting an ear and pursing his lips at the trumpet. On the slow songs especially, his instrument purred with a warm, drowsy tone. His face belied the effort, bursting red and wide-eyed. On long notes his chin inflated like a bullfrog's.

Fran disappeared on a fine night in September, in slippers and housecoat. Constable Reid caught up to her easy enough. Found her in the middle of Radio Range Road, he said. The red velvet of the housecoat lit up like a Christmas tree in his headlights. She must have been through the woods, going by the tree needles she carried and the mud caking her slippers. At the hospital they kept her door locked, said Malcolm Follett, whose wife worked at the hospital reception. Afraid she'll bolt in the middle of the night. Not even able to clean herself, said Gert. And she used to be the life of the party, said Malcolm. Loved a hand of cards. And those beautiful cakes, said Mary. First gone at any bake sale.

A week later the band did the MET office anniversary party. They opened with "Got a Feelin' You're Foolin'" as usual, and the tempo lagged right out of the gate. Gordon lifted his shoulders, urging them to pick it up. Ivany panicked on the drums and soon the band was chasing itself. The anxiety was contagious, sweeping across the hall like bad news. Everyone was thinking about Radio Range Road and the velvet nightgown and muddy slippers. They sat clutching coffee cups and dessert forks, Baked Alaska dying on their plates. Dance floor empty and every eye trained on Gordon.

Ivany settled down, and the moment passed. Dancers came out, and the rest of the evening was uneventful.

"If you can't play your best show on your worst day, you might as well pack it in," Gordon said.

Fran came home from hospital. But Mrs. Tucker next door started taking the kids every day. Then Mrs. Kendall for a while. Father Kiloran offered an intercession "for all those troubled by illness we cannot see, and for their loved ones." People saw Gordon eating at the airport on his days off. So they started dropping by with tuna casserole and three-layer meatloaf and fresh buns. Gert did up her cheesy green beans and onions.

Joyce knew Gordon's sweet tooth. So she and Gloria tried a recipe for no-bake chocolate butter balls. They ate two each and Joyce found them a bit mushy—a mistake to whip the butter, perhaps—but they loaded the cake tin and drove over. They found Gordon strolling his front lawn, trying to pick a spot for a maple tree. The maple sat behind him, leafless, with a brin bag tied around its roots.

"It's not a good time to be planting," said Gloria.

"I suppose not," said Gordon. He wiped his hands on the thighs of his creased slacks, lifted the lid of the cake tin, popped a glossy brown ball in his mouth, and said, "Hoo, hoo, hoooo!" Tilting his head back as if doing a bird call. The house behind him looked dark and lifeless. But the front door was open. Gordon's trumpet case sat just inside the door, as if he might dash off to a dance at a moment's notice.

"My stepmother went mad in a similar way," said Eric. "It seems almost a regular thing with girls. Ever see it in your family?"

"As a schoolgirl, I had a terrible crush on a boy I saw in films," Joyce said. "I was lost in it altogether. Like I wasn't even in the world anymore."

"That's not at all the same thing."

He was right, of course. Still, she recalled it as a time that might have easily spilled over into a kind of madness. The boy and his sister appeared in a series of films brought round to the school by Father Coles. The films were meant to teach modern standards of health and hygiene. The importance of containing odours and fluids and appetites. The priest introduced the films by reminding the class that true Christians were clean and sturdy in body, mind, and soul.

The boy didn't have a name, and Joyce didn't give him one. She watched him complete his studies and paper route. In snug white T-shirt and dark trousers, he touched his toes and flattened his frame for perfect push-ups. He scoured his hands and arms with soapy water, laid out fresh clothes on his bed, conducted polite and cheerful conversations with schoolmates of either sex, and refused the company of boys in blue jeans or messy-haired girls with dark, budding lips.

By the end of grade eight, Joyce was the tallest girl in class, and woke at night with throbbing in her legs and hips. Father Coles always carried the smell of church, of candle wax and incense. Combined with the darkness of the room, the dust motes dancing in the projector's beam, the scorched smell from the film, and the thick air of boots and wool socks drying near the woodstove, it made the film days sacred and profane. Cast back into Cape St. Rose when it was over, she would leave school and walk home in tears, or sometimes not go home at all until well after dark, when she would turn up cold and dirty, hardly aware of where her feet had taken her.

///////

"We might finally be getting somewhere," Eric announced, the next time she stepped through his door.

"Who?"

"A company's been formed to explore the potential up in Labrador." He rapped a finger on the folded newspaper. "This is the real thing. The Americans are in on it. The Brits. Brazil."

Joyce liked that nothing seemed to discourage him. She had begun to notice how the men around town made a show of thwarted ambition, wanting a witness to their torment. One night Joyce stood in the doorway of her room for a good ten minutes, listening to a strange man explain how he had been cheated out of a position with the RCMP. The man had come calling for Rachel, and didn't seem to believe that Joyce had no idea where to find the girl. But I always treated her with respect, he said. I wouldn't dream of disrespecting her. All the fellows who fell for Rachel were mad for respect. They would repeat and hang on the word as if they had just invented it. The RCMP reject lingered longer than most, as Joyce stood with one hand on the door and the other closing the collar of her housecoat at her throat. Finally, he asked if she would like to go for a drink, and when Joyce refused he went on his way.

Eric was certainly a cut above such men.

Joyce stood over the hot plate to make a melted-cheese sandwich, while Eric circled the apartment, slapping the newspaper in his palm. "Not just hydro, it says here. Minerals, smelting, uranium enrichment. It's like nothing you can imagine." He flipped down the Murphy bed and pulled Joyce to it. She had to delay him long enough to unplug the hotplate, and delay him again in the midst of his excitement to make sure he put on the safe. "Very good to take charge there, Joyce," he said after. "Well done."

It was too late for the cheese sandwich when he pushed the bed back up. Joyce had to get home and clean up in time for work. She dressed quickly while Eric lathered up to shave. She was straightening her skirt, reaching behind to free a bit of fabric snagged in the zipper, when she heard him suck a quick breath. Then she saw his fist, the white shirt cuff flapping back, and the bulging blue veins in his forearm.

Joyce saw it and heard it and buckled at the waist, as if all she had to do was make room for it. The fist swept in and stopped just short of her belly, brushing the front of her blouse. The rest of him carried forward so that his cheek touched hers. It left a dab of shaving soap on her, its sharp mint filling her nose.

Joyce rocked on her heels for a moment. Watched a drop of sweat roll down behind his ear. Her hands were still behind her, a thumb and finger tight on the zipper tab.

"I had you then, Joyce!" His voice thick and wet. "I had you going that time!" He backed away and did it again, this time a roundhouse under the chin, so close that she felt the breeze.

"Christ, Eric." The words died in her throat. She backed into a chair and sat, her chest was shuddering and her stomach still clenched. "Goddamn it, Eric. What was that?"

"Come on, love. Got to be on your toes." He was grinning at her. "I don't …" She wiped a tear that clung to her eyelash. "Why did you scare me like that?"

"Ah, just a game, love. Bit of fun." He had already turned back to the mirror, and she caught his glance in it, still grinning, then pursing his lips to scrape around them. "How about you and I go up to Labrador?" he said, tapping the razor in the bowl. "Live in a company house and build that big bloody dam. By God, we'll have the run of it up there."

11

"In the fucking clear," says Jordan. "It's all over the band agreement. Once she's gone, you and Will are calling the fucking shots."

The relevant wording arrives via email a few minutes later:

From Clause 12: In the event that a Band member dies, his or her estate and heirs will assume the rights of a terminated band member. From Clause 6: Terminated members shall have no rights related to the use of the Band's music and artwork, including decisions related to performances and master recordings.

Carter allows himself a fist pump, and takes a moment to settle himself before calling Jordan back.

"Let's not act like it's a celebration. Someone's dying here."

"Sure," says Jordan. "Hang on." There is a thunderous crash like a room coming down on him.

"Where are you?"

"Banquet hall on Keele. Almost got taken out by a stack of chairs. Anyway, when she's, you know, gone, it'll drive media. Media's definitely on board. Already getting feelers from *Now*, maybe the *Star*, maybe the *Globe*, definitely the CBC."

"Really?"

"We're looking at cameos for the unfinished tracks. I've asked around and groups like Snowblink, Lowell, they're like, yeah, let's do it. I've got feelers out for Doug Paisley, which would be huge. Just feelers right now."

"These are big bands?"

"These are first-line, second-line names at indie festivals. You could drive a tribute show with these names. Maybe festival slots." Jordan pauses while something scrapes across the floor. "You play at all now?"

"Guitar? It's been ten years or more."

"I think Uncle Will would be game."

"I don't...I have no feel for it anymore."

"We can cover for you. Surround you guys with a nice little band, like a trio. It'll be a tribute to Leah. With some of the girl singers, especially, it's a feminist thing. Like, she didn't do the diva thing. Didn't do tits and ass."

"Everybody wanted her," says Carter.

"Wanted her?"

"Everyone at our shows." He shouldn't be talking about sex. Jordan, with those pipe-cleaner legs, probably can't fuck. "They all wanted...to be with her, I mean. The guys and girls both."

"Okay," says Jordan, and laughs. "We can work that angle too. That's feminist too, right? But I'm being serious, man. This is a chance for you guys. This is validation."

///////

It's his turn to put Sam to bed. After his bath and an episode of *Bubble Guppies*, Sam asks for the Zamboni game.

"Ten minutes, that's it," says Carter.

Zamboni was a stocking stuffer last Christmas. A sturdy block of die-cast metal with smooth rubber tires. Its driver grips the steering wheel with both hands, though his head cracked off a long time ago.

A fine head it was, too. Dark eyes and a curling brown moustache. An officious blue cap to match his overalls.

Initially, the Zamboni game served as a framework for the usual mayhem. Sam raced the vehicle around the floor of his room, resulting in delightful disaster at every turn. But the game evolved, with the Zamboni taking on a deeper purpose. It is a seeker. Sometimes it wants to find someone—usually a stuffed toy—who will be the driver's companion, to ride shotgun and be the eyes and ears he once had. More often, Zamboni sets out on a melancholy search for the missing head.

This is new, this inner life. Zamboni never used to be troubled by the missing head. It just disappeared, attracting little notice. But now the head is a phantom limb. Zamboni gets frustrated, discouraged, despairs of ever finding it.

At least he isn't fighting stuffed toys anymore. He got past that.

Sam sits his father on the bed. He kneels and brings his face to the carpet and whispers to Zamboni, encouraging, nurturing hope. Almost kissing it with his perfect red lips. Carter knows how this will play out. So he stops Sam and asks whether there is any point in continuing, when every search for the head ends the same.

"He'll find it someday," says Sam. "I know he will." He starts Zamboni on its journey. They're headed for the ruins of a Lego castle behind the bedroom door.

"I don't think so, Sammy. It's been gone a long time. I think it's gone."

"Don't worry, Dad. It's just a pretend game."

Sam is old enough to know that not every kid has to see a special doctor in Toronto twice a year. When he confronted his parents last year, they tried telling him that it's a privilege, that he's very lucky to see such an important doctor. Then they said, we're just taking extra-special care of you because you're an extra-special boy. This made Sam angry. He picked up the false cheer in their voices, knew he was getting the brush-off, and responded by shutting down, refusing to talk or eat.

Finally they explained that his heart is different, so different that it needs regular check-ups to make sure it's working the way a heart should. This rang true, because it is true, and he accepted it with minimal fuss and worry.

"Okay," calls Isabelle over the stairs. "Time for story and lights out."

Sam pushes the door shut. "Come on, Zamboni. Dad. Come on." With his feathery new haircut and roguish pyjamas—crimson with white piping—he's too cute to be trusted. A playboy, a smooth operator.

"Where are we going?"

"The ocean." He sweeps his arm. "Let's pretend all this is a big ocean. I think his head got in the ocean."

/////

That night, Carter and Shanna are back on Skype. Shanna appears in a T-shirt with a frayed collar. It could well be a bedtime shirt, given that it's nearly eleven in Newfoundland. A strange woman giving Carter a glimpse of her pyjamas while Isabelle pads around upstairs, the path of her footsteps marking her end-of-day routine.

"I owe you an apology for any trouble I caused your mother," says Shanna, her face ringed by a fuzzy blue border. "I apologized to her as well."

"But you were great with her when we talked."

"But before, when she was on the phone with you. That's me she was complaining about. The one asking too many questions."

"Oh. Well, she's prone to getting aggravated. Seems like the two of you are good now."

Shanna's minimal hair and watchful eyes suggest an unadorned life, intensely focused. "But I wanted you to see that we've made progress. I'm not putting any pressure on her or anything."

"I know," says Carter. But Shanna is still talking.

"—sharp, because of the argument."

167

"What argument?"

"When she and Mrs. Vincent went at it about poached eggs. The way it engaged her. It was wonderful to see. And arguing with Mr. Johnson about Confederation. Mr. Johnson is from Ferryland, and I guess they were all for independence down there years ago. You'd know better than I."

"Of course." Carter doesn't even know where Ferryland is, though the name rings a bell. He studiously ignores Newfoundland, not wanting to be associated with its idiosyncrasies and foibles, or the tiresome expectations that come with being ID'd as a Newfoundlander in Ontario.

"Mr. Johnson started in on his case, about a nation throwing itself away in 1949, and Joyce wasn't having any of it. 'Your crowd would still be living on hard tack and tea. Misery and poverty,' she said. That got Mr. Johnson going. He says, 'There was never a harder-working man than my father.' And Joyce says, 'Any fool can work hard to no purpose and no gain.'" Shanna laughs. "The whole room came to life. It was wonderful."

Carter recognizes Mr. Johnson's argument and its sour vanity. He recalls the preening Newfoundland nationalists encountered during his one year at university in St. John's. Their cultivated savagery and exaggerated accents, faces pinched and lips pursed, as if union with Canada made everything smell bad.

Isabelle has descended the stairs, the floss popping as she runs it in and out of her molars. She glances Carter's way, in the direction of Shanna's delighted cackle, and carries on into the kitchen.

"Well, thanks for the update," says Carter. He didn't tell Isabelle that he had arranged another Skype with Shanna.

"The specific method I work with is called narrative care," says Shanna. "It's storytelling therapy, basically."

"Storytelling?"

"Too often the system treats the nursing home as a holding pen. We just watch over them until the body shuts down. Is it any wonder that the elderly become depressed, when we treat them like they're dead already?"

"Yes, I see." Her argument demands agreement.

"By inviting them to share life stories, we're engaging them and valuing their experiences."

"Mom was never much for talking about the old days. That was more my dad's thing."

"That's completely understandable. So I let it be. But I take her outside for a cigarette sometimes. I've got the habit myself, I'm sorry to say."

"That will make you comrades in arms for sure," says Carter.

"Then she started coming to our storytelling group on Mondays. I didn't ask her. She just came along. I want you to know that."

"Is that where the Confederation argument happened?"

"Yes, and the eggs." Shanna pokes at her glasses. "I have to say, Howley Corp is a bit suspicious of my methods."

"What's Howley Corp?"

"They run the home. They have nursing homes all over the continent."

"I could put a call in, or an email. I actually know one of the management people from years back."

"That would be great. Thanks. You know, we're not supposed to let the residents get upset or agitated. But if they're engaged, a little disagreement can't do any harm. Just to see them light up."

His mother lighting up. He'd like to see that.

///////

Isabelle goes to bed with an Advil for her throbbing ankles, and half an Imovane. "You had your guitar out."

"Just for a look," says Carter. He had pulled it from behind a chair in the spare room and held it in his lap. There wasn't much point bloodying his soft fingers on the dead strings. "Have I played since we met?"

"Not that I've seen. But I thought you might at some point. Are you going to have a band again?"

"No. But I might end up playing a bit. With a band. For a short while."

"I honestly think Sam is going to be fine," says Isabelle. She pushes up on her elbows and turns on the lamp.

"Me too," says Carter, looking up from his pillow.

"No, it's not just being hopeful. It's a feeling I got from watching Dr. Kim. So with this thing you've got going, okay, you get the leeway you need. One of the cardinal rules with teenagers is you let them sleep as much as they want and eat whenever they want, insofar as that's possible. So that's the model I'll use here, with you and this music thing. Insofar as it's possible. That's more than fair, right?"

/////

The lamp is still on when Sam wakes them from the foot of the bed.

"Will I know if my heart don't go right?"

"Jesus, Sammy." Isabelle shields her eyes against the lamplight, and strains as if trying to recognize him. "Come up."

He wedges between them, and reaches to pull Carter's arm around his waist. "Is it working now?"

"Show me your belly." His mother shifts down the bed and puts an ear to his chest. "It's perfect, Sammy, and we're going to make sure it stays that way."

"Not perfect." He frowns.

"But almost perfect, Sam. Give me your hand." She presses his palm where her ear was. "Feel that? Thump-thump, thump-thump. So strong."

"Keep going, heart!" calls Sam.

Moments later he's asleep, leaving his parents wide-awake, their worst fears indecently exposed.

12

Joyce thought it might be more than just a headache. More than just the humidity. She waited, wiping down the baseboards and putting a wash through. A mild cramp sent her to the bathroom and she thought, "That's it." Stood up from the toilet to see the red cloud in the water, circling the paper.

"Alright then," she said out loud, dabbing herself. "Alright then."

She sat in the kitchen to think about it. Instead of thinking she looked out the window to the tops of the birch trees, watching the light change as clouds raced past the sun. Watching the birds flit in and out. The pace outside seemed too quick.

///////

It's true that she missed mass from time to time. Working, or stuck somewhere with the band, waiting out a snowstorm or a late train. She didn't sing in the choir. Had told Maeve Vardy she'd drop by for Wednesday rehearsal but never did. Father Kiloran didn't seem the kind of man to keep account of such things. But what else would bring him up her front step? And what was Gordon doing at his side? She wasn't about to take any lectures from him. Not on matters of worship.

Joyce started to remove her apron, then left it. How else should they expect her at eleven o'clock in the morning? She glanced in the mirror and tucked a lock of hair back under her scarf. It fell out again.

Through the front door window, both men seemed to examine their shoes. Joyce put a hand to her stomach to settle a gentle stirring inside, like a spoon turning in a teacup. Her lunch was ready, just laid out on the table when she had caught sight of them walking up to the house. One knee began to shake.

At the creak of the hinges both faces looked up and filled the doorway. The whole town smelled like tar from the paving crews and she nearly shut the door again to lock it all out. Nobody said anything and she was sure she would slam the door if one of them didn't talk soon. Gordon put two damp hands on her, one holding each bicep. She hated that.

"Joyce," he said. "There's word from the airport." He faltered, throat growling.

"An accident," said the priest. "That is ... Can we talk inside?"

Just last weekend, Eric and Gordon had talked of the trapper who found the B-25 that went down north of Deadman's Pond; how he stuck a frozen arm in his backpack and took it to the airport as proof. It was the sleeve on the arm that confirmed it. Only American pilots had leather jackets. He found the tobacco too, and kept it. Tobacco was scarce during the war, after all. It was a well-worn anecdote, recounted this time for the benefit of the new drummer, a fellow who had arrived from Winnipeg to help plan the new town site. He had been duly impressed and horrified.

Joyce tried to concentrate as Father Kiloran parsed the useless details. A homily, delivered in his gravelled monotone. "Eric left this morning, you see. Flying Maritime Central Airways to Labrador." Why would this priest come around assuming he knew something she didn't? Then he said, No survivors. She heard that part, and stopped listening. Pictured the trapper and the frozen arm.

When he said something about God's mercy she knew he was finally done.

She said, "I was poaching an egg for lunch."

She let them lead her into the kitchen, as if she had to show proof of the egg, sitting on its square of toast, perfectly cupped. She had found the poacher in the back of a cupboard a few weeks before, when Eric took possession of the house, and had called Gloria to ask how it worked. It was awfully clever, the way the water bubbled in the bottom of the pan, cooking the eggs from below. She had been eating poached eggs just so she could watch the process.

Joyce sat at the kitchen table. If she felt anything, it was more like foreboding. Like the story was incomplete. Like there had been a crash and Eric might or might not be alive, pending further news. Joyce had been denied the moment when hope still nags. The disaster was confirmed before she understood it, before Gordon and Father were in through the door.

Gordon brought her a folded strip of toilet paper.

"Can't find a tissue," he said. "Sorry."

Joyce held the paper tight, turning and twisting it. It was so much more substantial than the crumpling, flaking stuff her father kept in the outhouse. On a summer morning like this, her father's voice would carry from behind the door, humming a tune. If he wasn't anxious about work he might be in there half an hour or more.

A fat teardrop landed on the back of her hand, another hit her thumbnail. She was crying, after all. Still she held the paper. Turning and twisting. Someone shut off the stove, where water still bubbled in the poacher.

Gordon hovered like an obstruction. He was by her side, one knee on the floor. She got a whiff of the whiskey smell before he placed a drink in her hand. It smelled like that song about wanting rain but getting only sun, and being blue like the sky.

Her throat felt thick. It didn't want to let the whiskey pass.

"She's not breathing so well," said Gordon. "Do you want a doctor, Joyce?"

"No," she whispered. Perhaps she did. She turned to Gordon and said, "What are you doing here?"

Father Kiloran must have still been there as well. But later she would have no recollection of him in the house. Just a grim, cassocked figure ascending the steps, his shiny red cincture whipping in the breeze.

Gloria arrived at the back door and Joyce was there to meet her. Apparently expecting her. She'd brought Anthony, asleep in his stroller, and left him on the back step.

"Dear God, Joyce," she said. "We never know. We can't possibly know."

Know what?

Gloria stood away from Joyce, and circled her waist with her arms to untie the apron. Then she gently lifted it over Joyce's head, barely touching the hair, and tossed it on a chair. It would stay with her, the burnt cotton smell of the apron.

Joyce opened her dry mouth and lifted her chest, seeking a good breath of air. Gloria's breath came in big, convulsive gulps. She was red and hot and swollen, teary-eyed even at the best of times now that she was pregnant again.

"Remember how beautiful he looked?" Gloria's words garbled through her tears. "That night at the Allied party?"

Joyce didn't share the memory, but felt the power of it. Eric at some party. Playing the fool. All the girls wide-eyed. ("Any one of them would snap him up in a second," Rachel had warned her.) An essential part of the man had been unavailable to her. The part of him that turned up at these parties.

The sky was blue outside the kitchen window, and she didn't think she could stand that anymore. Or the egg and toast, cold on the plate with knife and fork on either side. Joyce walked down the hall to the bedroom, shut the blind and sat on the bed.

"I'm sweating," she said, and pushed a hand into her blouse to lift it from her skin.

"The baby. Your poor baby." Gloria sat next to her. "Father Kiloran will pray for your baby."

"There's no baby," said Joyce. "I was late, that's all." She kicked her slippers off and kneaded her toes into the rug.

A descending roar shook the window blind and the lamp at her bedside. Flight 850. One o'clock already? The clock on the table confirmed it.

"Give me a moment, will you?"

Gloria left and started to pull the door behind her, but the thought of being fully enclosed in one room gave Joyce a twinge of panic. "Leave it," she said. "Push it open." Through the door she saw Gordon in the kitchen, his eyes averted from her. She appreciated him for it.

She let herself imagine Eric in a wide clearing of the woods, pacing irritably and pausing to sit on a downed tree trunk, not far from where the plane lay twisted and smouldering. Checking his watch and shielding his eyes to scan the horizon. Where was that bloody rescue crew? The light changing as clouds passed over the sun. Black smoke billowing from the wreck, carried away on the breeze.

///////

The loss of the PBY Canso —an amphibious twin-engine 22-seater, thousands produced during the war and later refurbished for civilian use—left the airport faintly embarrassed. The crash did not demand heroic effort. There was no grimly determined rescue team trekking into the wilderness and battling the elements. A daring airlift of survivors was not required. Saintly doctors and nurses did not work round the clock to save lives.

The plane had simply failed to gain altitude, and clipped the treetops about two miles off Runway 32.

The man from DOT would eventually conclude that the pilot had done his best. Maintained control and brought her down flat enough for the belly to carve a long furrow in the bog. A violent landing, yes. Hard enough to break a man's neck. But maybe not if he was strapped in. The bog was wide and soft, with plenty of room. After the initial shock of impact there might have been a moment when they believed they had a chance. A moment before they saw the boulder. They must have seen it. The aircraft met the boulder with enough force to cave in the nose and send an unmounted compass a good 200 yards through the windscreen.

The wreck cast a broad circle of nylon, leather, plastic and canvas scraps, long shredded strips of rubber tire, life jackets, rescue flares, buttons, buckles, twisted scraps of clothing ripped from suitcases, shoes, cigarette lighters, and keys. One engine disappeared in the nearby pond. A cabin door lodged between dead trees. A thick husk of fuselage, emptied by the impact of the boulder, was angled to catch the sunrise on a clear morning and reflect it for miles.

/////

She told Gordon not to introduce her as Eric's fiancée.

"What should I call you, then?"

"Don't call me anything. Call me Joyce."

Eric's father and brother had arrived by mid-morning, the day after the crash.

"They went down to the Drill Hall for the identification," said Gordon. "And they've been there ever since. At a bit of a loss, I think."

The old Drill Hall on Foss Avenue had been commandeered as a makeshift morgue. "They're using the shooting range downstairs," Gordon explained. "Cooler down there." Of the eleven dead, only Eric had lived in Gander. The rest came from around the island, with the exception of an American from Maryland. Men trickled into town throughout the day—fathers, brothers, uncles, in-laws—identifying bodies and waiting until Magistrate Clowe saw fit to release the remains for burial.

Joyce and Gordon pulled up in Eric's truck, and Gordon said, "There's the brother." A man sat on a folding chair with a hand cupped over his eyes, watching as they approached. He shook Gordon's hand and turned to Joyce. "I'm Teddy." His forearms were burnt red, with white patches where skin peeled away.

"Joyce Pelley."

"You knew my brother?"

A rush in her stomach like a long drink of cold water. "We hadn't known each other quite so long, but..." She took in Teddy's face. Red like the arms. "I only knew him since last year. I got here last year."

"Is the skipper about?" asked Gordon.

"Dad!" Teddy turned to call over his shoulder. His neck was dimpled, with a loose pouch of flesh under the ear. An old wound, maybe. Or a surgical scar. "Dad, come over a minute!"

"Oh, there's no need," said Joyce. "We don't have to interrupt."

"Is that the wreck?" Teddy lifted his face. "The smell, I mean? The burning?"

Burning bodies. Joyce pushed the thought away. "Oh! No, no. That's just trash. They're burning trash over at the base."

"Over behind the curling club," said Gordon.

"But it's close by? The place where they went down?"

"Just beyond Runway 32." Gordon lofted a hand overhead, in the direction of the airport. "They barely got airborne."

"We all met because of the band," said Joyce.

"Well now, me and Eric go back a ways before that," said Gordon.

"Of course," said Teddy. He looked from one to the other without a spark of recognition. She could see that Eric had never mentioned her.

A white-haired man appeared from the shady side of the building. Small, but with a perfect bowling ball middle. The belly looked firm, protruding like a pregnant woman's. He wore a dusty dark suit and a plaid shirt buttoned to the neck. He walked with a roll, one side rising and the opposite shoulder pitching, like an unseen hand was yanking at the left side of his trousers with every step.

"Dad, this is Joyce Pelley. She and Eric were close."

"Well now," said the old man. He reached for her hand and lifted it. "Well now, my dear." His eyes were small bluish pools, nearly swallowed in doughy flesh.

"I only…" said Joyce. Her throat closed and tears gathered, sinuses aching with the pressure. "I knew him with the band." Teddy sank back into his folding chair.

"That's alright now," said the old man. "Going up on the Labrador, was he?"

Joyce nodded, biting hard on her bottom lip. "Just for a few weeks. He had a few weeks work up there." They had argued about it. Joyce thought it unwise for Eric to quit a good job at the airport for six weeks work somewhere else. Eric argued that it was nearly twice the pay, with travel and board included. And couldn't he always find something when he got back? Wouldn't there be all kinds of jobs in Gander, or anywhere, once he had eight weeks experience as a rigging foreman?

They hadn't said much that morning, though he had thanked Joyce several times after she gave him a tin of sweet biscuits for the trip. Nice ones from Browning and Harvey.

The old man released her hand. "His mother had great hopes for him, you know. If only he'd stayed put."

"Dad, please," said Teddy, without looking up.

They paused as an EPA mail plane made its groaning ascent over the hangar, banking lazily to begin its northern trek.

"He was never one to stay put," said Joyce.

"You fellows must be starved with all this waiting around," said Gordon. "We could get a bite to eat."

"I was just talking to a fellow." The old man pulled a white hanky from his pocket and wiped his nose. "A fellow, and he was saying…"

Another swipe across the nose. "He was saying about the service they got planned. Did you know, Ted, they'll have the priest and the Anglican fellow and whoever all up there on the altar together? Each man taking his turn? Who's your parish priest here, love?"

"Father Kiloran." Joyce raised a hand to wipe the tears tickling her eyes, but they had already dried in the sun.

"And he doesn't mind having the Protestant fellows on the altar? What a sight! Won't that be a sight, Teddy?"

"We won't be here," said Teddy, raising his voice.

"What's that?"

"They say we'll get hold of him tonight. We can take him home on the overnight train, if there's room."

"What about his passage?"

"The fellow at the station says there's no charge. He says they load up all the baggage and mail and what have you, and if there's room we can put him on, and there's no charge. If there's no room we got to wait for morning."

They spoke as if arguing, as if each had lost patience with the other. But they didn't appear agitated. Teddy tilted back in his chair and squinted into the distance. The old man stood over him, hands on his belly, lips parted and moving slightly as he whispered to himself, repeating what he had just heard.

"I've got to make me water," said the old man.

Gordon took him by the elbow. "We'll go around to the Elk's Club. You been in Buchans many a year, I suppose."

"Since twenty-six, when they collared the Lucky Strike."

"Twenty-six!" said Gordon. "You must have been there for the first bucket of ore." They disappeared around the building. Teddy looked up from his chair and said, "You can stay at the house with my missus. I'll stay at Dad's."

"The house?"

"In Buchans, for the funeral."

"Oh," said Joyce. "But I have to work."

179

"The house will be quiet, you know." She said nothing, and he added, "We've no youngsters, me and her, and the wake'll be down at Dad's."

Joyce found a tissue in her purse and lifted her feet one at a time to wipe her shoes. The hot wind had left a fine layer of dust. "I just don't know. Of course, you're his family, so…"

"It's alright, love," he said finally. "Never mind."

"I just don't know what I would be…"

"It's fine. Never mind."

They both lit cigarettes, Joyce flicking her lighter rather than bending to share the flame from his match. She was relieved not to be pregnant, but that didn't fully account for the liberation she felt.

"I wonder will they take the sacrament?" said Eric's father when he returned.

"Who's that, Dad?"

"The crowd when they come to the service. What's to stop any of them taking the Holy Communion, putting their tongue out for the host, as bold as you please?"

/////

Joyce's bed was littered with cards. Chaulk's, Eaton's, the Co-op, DOT, the weather office, Oceanic Control, the Skyways Club, the Naval Station, Shell Co., TWA, Royal Dutch, Trans Ocean, Pan-Am, Gert and the girls at the ticket counter. A bottle of whiskey from the boys at the Bristol Building. A note from the wire chief at CN, who had briefly courted Joyce a few months ago.

"I don't know who I am, or what I am in all this," she said. "I just insulted his brother, anyway."

Footsteps sounded in the hallway, and she sighed with relief as they continued past their door and on to the stairwell.

"Go somewhere," said Rachel, lying on her bed with a paperback.

"Go? Where would I go?"

"Anywhere."

"Cripes, Rach. I can't just disappear."

"Why not? Every day you put people on those airplanes."

Joyce waved this away and they fell silent. Rachel read. Joyce rubbed her eyes and temples and neck. The next set of footsteps stopped to knock. "Joyce?" It sounded like her lips were right at the crack of the door.

"It's open."

Katie let herself in, leaning against the door as she closed it. "I'm sorry. Is it alright I came?"

"Everything still grounded?" asked Rachel, taking the measure of Katie in full stewardess guise, hat, eyebrows, and all.

"Everything, till after supper at least. I'm sorry, we haven't… Katie Hogan."

Rachel offered her name without rising from her pillow.

"Is it alright I came, Joyce?"

"Of course." Joyce had no idea what was appropriate.

"Joyce should get out of here," said Rachel. "I told her to go away somewhere."

"Oh!" Katie looked to Joyce. "I can get you out, you know. As soon as we're flying again. Do you want to go to Montreal for a bit? You can have my apartment."

Joyce recalled rising from the toilet and turning to see the clockwise swirl of reddened water, a darkened fold of toilet tissue at its centre. She saw it as though looking down from a great height. By then everything had been sealed. They were already down, no survivors.

"I can't go," she said. "Not now."

"Of course you can," said Rachel.

"We went off the same runway three years ago," said Katie. "It was nothing. Only we skidded off into a snow bank, and everyone was fine, only I had headaches for a bit, and sometimes still. But, I'll stop now." She was still pressed up to the door, hands behind her back. Like they kept her in the room against her will. "Everyone's afraid, only they won't admit it. I can't be around them tonight."

Joyce shared a tin of wieners with Rachel for dinner, got cleaned up and went to the drill hall, where Maeve Vardy was to lead the rosary. The shooting range in the basement was long and cool and dim, with plain coffins laid side-by-side along the far wall.

They began with the Agony in the Garden, and carried on with a mix of the sorrowful and glorious mysteries. Joyce picked through her beads and swayed gently on her knees, stumbling over the Hail Holy Queen, as always. She muttered what phrases she could recall—"… send up our sighs…this our exile…"—and emerged slowly back into the room. There was quite a crowd, three dozen or more.

"I understand, Joyce," said Maeve, pulling her aside. "I went through it all in the war, when Toby's ship was lost. It's a sisterhood, really. So many of us." She produced a sheaf of paper from a folder. It was thick, cream-coloured paper scripted with fancy black letters. *To everything there is a season…* began the first page. "Will you do a reading for the general service, Joyce?"

"I don't know," said Joyce. "Isn't it every church? You want readings from the different bibles? Whatever they use?"

"I got the sister-in-law of the pilot. They're Baptist. Is it Baptist? Anyway, Father Kiloran agreed to it, whatever bible they use."

"I might be in Buchans," said Joyce.

"Oh, well then."

Gloria came to Joyce's side and clutched her hand. "The children are doing the offertory," she said. "Father Kiloran can't be letting old Reverend Wiseman have his way all the time."

"Each crowd gets their prayers and blessings," said Maeve.

"You don't have to do a reading, Joyce."

"That's up to Joyce," said Maeve, turning a shoulder to block Gloria out.

/////

Joyce waited until the hallway was silent, then crept from her room to the telephone. She called Den. As good a confessor as any.

"Should I go to Buchans?"

"It'd look awful queer if you don't," he said. "Why wouldn't you?"

"I'd have to go as his fiancée."

"Yes."

"It's wrong."

"Ah."

"Not wrong. But it doesn't feel honest."

"Ah. How bad would it be, to be there?"

"Easier than here, I'd say."

"People go to funerals with all kinds of feelings. Nobody's completely honest about it. Don't mind that."

"I already said too much, to one of them at least."

"You won't be held to it. You're in shock, like everyone. Will you be alright, Joyce? Want me to come with you, as your brother, or uncle?"

She considered this, declined, and thanked him. Called the Eastbound Inn, had Finley on the night desk track down Teddy.

"I'll come with you," she said.

He sighed. "We're leaving first thing."

Morning dawned pink. The skipper dozed as soon as the train pulled out.

"We'll introduce you as the fiancée," said Teddy. "Will you agree to that?"

Joyce nodded, tugging at her hem.

"Then we'll talk no more about it," said Teddy.

///////

For two days the crowd pressed into the old man's house, bringing in the smell of the town. A grinding, smouldering odour. The smell of friction. The brother Joyce had met before, the one working for the sawmill women in Appleton, spent most of the first day outside, pulling rotten planks off one corner of the house. The others implored him to come in, not to ruin his good clothes. "Look at this," he replied, holding up a plank and pulling it apart. "Rotten.

Look." There was a brother who worked the Lucky Strike Mine, a brother with one eye who had helped cut the drift to the Oriental Mine, and a brother who said the Maclean would be the deepest pit of them all, just you wait. There was a brother who had won two Herders playing defence for the Miners, and a brother who had burned the theatre down by letting the film overheat in the projection room. The women mostly spoke on the run, in and out of the kitchen. They were all older than Joyce, except a cousin near her age whose husband never showed, and a novice with the Presentation Sisters who couldn't have been more than sixteen. There were little boys who stuck pencils in each other's ears and were sent outside whenever someone noticed that they had come back in. There was an ancient man who had towed the very first ore sample across Red Indian Lake so it could be shipped overseas for testing.

"Do you meet the movie stars in Gander?" asked the brother who had burned down the theatre. He had a florid face, as if he had been permanently scorched by the blaze. "Did you meet the ones who came to do a picture with Jimmy Stewart. Did you know about that?"

"No," said Joyce.

"Jimmy Stewart wasn't in Gander," said Teddy.

"And that's what he was," said the brother who burned down the theatre. "They made a picture. And when they were done they had a big dinner laid out for the whole crowd of them. Sixty pound of lobster, that's what they ordered. I have it on good authority."

The girls always talked about stars spotted at the airport. Monty Clift last week. Ida Lupino, coming in soaking wet on a Sunday morning. Bob Hope on the radio while his flight refuelled. In his cups, said Den. Joyce didn't pay it much mind. But she knew the heightened buzz that ran through the airport when someone special was sighted. She had been shocked to look up one day and see Bobby Darin striding by right in front of her. Hands in his pockets and a nice blue checked jacket. Disappearing into the men's room.

The casket sat under the front window, closed. Joyce wondered whether it might be empty. Alice Henley had told her that there were empty caskets for some of the poor folks who had been cut to ribbons on the runway back in forty-six, because what was left of them couldn't be put in a box.

The young novice, Sister Rosalia, led the rosary on Thursday night. Her slender throat puffed and quaked as she rang out the mysteries in a high, clear voice.

Teddy kept his distance, but he and his wife sat next to Joyce for the funeral. There was a big turnout, though the service felt drab and perfunctory after the drama of the wake. Back at the house, the parlour felt empty without the body and attempts at conversation died in the rattle of unsteady cups on saucers.

When Joyce brought down her small, sturdy case in the morning, she found Teddy and Sister Rosalia standing inside the front door. They looked as if they had been standing there for some time.

"She'll accompany you to the station and carry your bag," said Teddy. The sister looked fearful, standing next to Teddy with her hands hidden and her wide, dark eyes on Joyce.

"Oh, but I can carry this. It's nothing."

"Well, you'd best get underway then," said Teddy. "Goodbye, Joyce. We'll remember you in our prayers."

"Thank you for everything," said Joyce, and would have said more. But Teddy was out the door.

Sister Rosalia walked quickly, though they had plenty of time. "This way," she said. "This way." Joyce knew the way. The railway station was almost in sight of the house, at the end of a path that ran down a small slope and alongside the tracks.

They walked in silence until the girl turned her wide eyes to Joyce and said, "I was nearly spoiled, you know. We had a lodger who...I could have been spoiled."

"I don't understand, Sister."

"When Father took in lodgers, there was one who tried." She looked away again, hugging one arm to the other. "I kept away from him. Once he caught me at the washing, and meant to force a hand. He pulled at my clothes. But then he stopped before anything else happened. He seemed to be in pain, and then there was a dark spot on his trousers. He said it was because I was filthy."

"What's your name, Sister?"

"Rosalia, since I took my vows."

"Before the vows."

"You mean my baptismal name. I was Elizabeth Margaret."

"Elizabeth, why are you telling me this story?"

"I never told anyone before, outside the Order."

"Don't you think you should keep it that way?"

"But what if it might help someone else?"

"How can it help anyone?"

Elizabeth stared at the ground. "Well, I, I didn't want, I mean, just because a girl is spoiled..." Her voice trailed off in what might have been a sob. With her cameo face and fulsome, straight teeth, the strands of black hair escaping her wimple, Joyce thought it awful foolish for her father to have invited strange men into the house.

Elizabeth stopped walking. The path had taken them parallel to the railway tracks, and they were close enough to the station that Joyce recognized several men and women waiting on the platform. She had met them during the wake. A little boy stared at her as he reached into a wrinkled bag and crammed candy in his mouth.

"Do you have your permissions for the train?" asked Elizabeth. "From Uncle Ted?"

"Yes. I have everything." Teddy had presented the required papers to her that morning, and had done so with some ceremony, explaining that travel on the branch line was restricted to persons with written permission from the company.

"Uncle Ted says he doesn't blame you, and he wanted to be Christian about it so he let you come here." She spoke quickly, and pressed both hands to her legs, flattening her habit as the wind picked up. "He says Uncle Eric was awful, how he…he carried on. He says Jesus is merciful. You'll find some literature for your journey. You have my prayers. My prayers are with you, I mean. Goodbye." She hurried away, the habit lifting behind her.

Joyce dropped her suitcase beside her and opened her purse to retrieve the brown envelope stamped *Anglo-Newfoundland Development Company*. In the folds of its officious documents she found a pamphlet: *The Next War: A Call for Christian Vigilance Against the General Slackening of Moral and Social Standards*. She opened it to a page marked by a white strip of paper.

The Good-Time Girl

A decline of parental responsibility was an unfortunate by-product of the war effort, as well as a diminishing influence of religious and social values. Having grown up in a time when the stable life of home, church, and school was disrupted and threatened by the Japanese and German Peril, young people prone to social and mental defects emerged with no sense of responsibility. Left unchecked, these defects led to a licentious deviation that has been particularly damaging for young women.

It is this subset of the community's wasted and wanton that produces the 'Good-Time Girl.'

She is self-centred, valuing little beyond personal enjoyment and committed to little beyond her own gratification. She is morally and emotionally unstable, with a tendency to reject discipline and control.

Joyce turned to the front of the pamphlet. Pages flipped in the breeze, and she caught it at the table of contents: *The Jewish question. What happened to daddy? Idle hours and delinquency. Healing the wounds.* The corners of this page were decorated with small line drawings. A smoking man in a fedora, a shapely woman drinking from a glass, a crying baby, and Jesus on the cross.

Boarded and seated, she returned to the bookmarked article and browsed it, registering phrases at random. *...personal adornment... the venereal stain...she often does not trouble to wash and is sluttish about her undergarments.*

She took a TCA linen napkin from her purse and wiped her shoes. Tugged at her hemline a couple of times—she was travelling in the troublesome skirt again, the one that hung on to the seat while her legs slipped forward and out. She held the pamphlet tight in one fist until a man came around selling the raspberry drops she and Gloria used to gorge on every Christmas. Then she dropped the pamphlet to the seat beside her and bought the candy.

/////

Christmas was approaching. She asked Gordon what bookings the band had, and said she wanted to sing. They hadn't replaced Eric. A lot of halls and clubs didn't have a proper piano anyway.

The change was immediate, and so obvious as to be embarrassing. They heard it in the sure-handed flow of a tune, in new spaces that let a little air into a horn solo or a crescendo. The band sounded cleaner, like the grit had been washed from it.

The only difference was Eric's absence.

Joyce flew to St. John's and found a rippling plum-blue cocktail dress with a high neckline and a pearl-beaded bodice miraculously cut to her size. The first night she wore it, she had the extraordinary sensation of opening her mouth and the music coming with hardly any effort, the words forming and settling back on her like mist. It stayed like that for many nights after, and she had the cocktail dress nearly worn through by summer. Occasionally, a song might put a lump in her throat for no reason. A simple line she had sung dozens of times overwhelmed her one night with its perfectly matched string of words—*glitter... gleam... dream*. She had to skip the final chorus, feeling stupid and embarrassed until Gordon struck up the next number.

Gordon needed the band more than Joyce did. Fran was getting out again, picking up a few groceries at the Co-op or driving Matilda to Girl Guides. People said it was good for her, a fresh start. The way she shuffled about with little steps and big, wide eyes, hardly exchanging a word with anyone, was an embarrassment trailing Gordon's every move. But people still danced to songs about romance and eternal love. Gordon had been right all along. It was a kind of playacting, a dress-up game.

Every show the band did now closed with Gordon taking the microphone to sing "Days of Wine and Roses," while Joyce stepped down from the stage and danced with any man who offered. Sometimes other men would cut in and the band would give the song an extra couple of turns, until everyone waiting could have his twirl. Some of them treated the dance with great solemnity and ceremony, and Joyce suspected these were the men who pitied her. Others were flirty and breathy, with crawling hands pulling her to their hard hipbones. These must have been the ones who understood that she had never truly been Eric's fiancée, though she had never mentioned this to anyone except Den, who was airtight.

"Is that what people are saying?" she asked Gloria one afternoon. "That I'm good for a bit of fun?"

"Oh, goodness no!" cried Gloria, though neither of them pretended the answer was truthful. "It's not like if we were back home," she added. "It's not like you're spoiled goods."

13

The video arrives with no identifying details. But the dark, unadorned space can only be a motel room.

Carter opens it while brushing his teeth. Isabelle and Sam are safely below, bickering over breakfast.

Shadowy limbs move. A flick of hair. It's a woman dancing. The window behind her is a square of sunlight, and she's silhouetted against the glare. She pivots, showing a round cheek and an arm topped by a T-shirt sleeve. There's no music. The woman laughs and hugs herself, the arms rise, bringing a dark shirt overhead. It falls behind her and the light catches the white of a bra and armpit. The dancing resumes. Her arms twist behind and the bra drops while she turns away. A small, shadowy breast, side-on. A hand reaches and pulls her back to face the camera.

The picture freezes in a blur of flesh as Carter drools a gob of toothpaste, slurps it back, and gags on it.

"Everything okay up there?"

"Yeah." His eyes water. He hacks painfully into the sink and gargles. The email from Will included no message, just the attachment and *video* in the subject line. Carter watches again with his headset plugged in. It starts with male laughter and indecipherable voices, except when Colin calls, "For the boys, for the boys!" in a sing-song voice. The sunlight in the window is reflected off the grill of a parked vehicle—the blue one that took them through the last couple of years.

He's expecting the hand this time. It emerges from the screen's edge, touches her shoulder. There's laughter as it slides briefly for a stroke of the breast, and takes her arm.

On third viewing he focuses on the moment of laughter as the girl exposes herself. It's almost lost behind Colin's loud, approving "Yeahhhhhh!" The laughter belongs to Carter. As does the hand.

She dances again, and he watches the quick movement of the hand, the fingers turning to quickly cup the breast as the girl turns. The grip on her arm is firm, with the thumb wrapped around her bicep.

/////

"Aunt Kat had an eye. A brilliant eye," says Shelley. "The family let her down, leaving her all alone in that big old house, way out on the Durham County Line. Poor Kat."

Isabelle and Shelley tumbled through the door a few minutes ago, carried on the winter wind, toting heavy bags from the market and liquor store. Isabelle announced that Sam was staying with his grandmother in Hamilton, then the two women set to work on a window-fogging, stove-spattering Spaghetti Bolognese, "like we used to make." Bacon spits in the skillet and onion skins blow across the floor. "Spag Bol!" the women cry. "Spag Bol!"

Aunt Kat lived in her kitchen and her sewing room, Shelley explains as she smashes garlic cloves with the side of a knife and stirs them around the bottom of the pot. In an old house she inherited from her parents. She spoke in a hushed voice, produced enormous meals for the extended family, and was rarely seen to take up a plate. Eating at Kat's house left Shelley stricken, as if the loneliness had been poured into her cooking and shared around the table.

"But what an eye. She could *see* clothes on a person. She did a bit of knitting and sewing over the years, but nothing much. A brilliant, wasted eye."

"I can't believe you never told me about her before," says Isabelle, her cuffs red with tomato juice.

"I had no appreciation. I thought she was just a silly old woman."

Shelley opens a bottle of white and fills champagne flutes. Carter takes his glass and sits on a stool against the wall, keeping his distance.

"You could have learned so much from her," says Isabelle, nearly shouting. She's been possessed by a nervous gaiety since Shelley clomped into the house, kicking off purple sneakers and greeting them both with mock kisses. (*Mwa! Mwa!* Pressing her face to one cheek, then the other.)

"She never had the chance," says Shelley. "The chance to just hide away and make clothes and use her imagination and make mistakes."

"To make dueling bandage skirts with her best friend."

"Exactly."

Carter has heard about the dueling skirts. In Shelley's occasional visits, he has heard all the favourite tales from the idyllic fashion school days. How Isabelle and Shelley spent hundreds of hours with their pencils and scissors, labouring over sheets of tissue paper and rolls of cheap fabric. Every day they dug into their mountain dragged home from Goodwill, raiding it for buttons and ruffles and strips of leather or tulle or denim. The whole apartment stank of sweat and polyester and mothballs, of old closets and basements. The mountain produced treasures, like the gold buttons for Isabelle's high-waist capris, the green serge for Shelley's asymmetrical skirt, and the endless supply of Lycra for their naughty line of dominatrix yoga wear. They found occasional coins and crumpled bills—including a memorable cache of eighty dollars—an old baby picture, which they framed, a pair of unwashed black underwear from the Gap (ladies petite), also framed, and a knob of driftwood kept as a talisman. There were church bulletins, keys, tickets and tokens, fossilized wads of chewing gum and used tissue, court summons, mouldering food scraps, and mouse shit.

"Will your mother be alright with Sam?" Carter asks. The woman has lately complained of nerves, and how children make her anxious.

"Oh yes, they'll be fine." Isabelle holds the bottle of olive oil overhead, tipping and twirling it to send a spiraling stream into the stockpot.

But Shelley isn't finished with Aunt Kat. It all came to a sad end. They left her alone out on Durham County Line all those long dark winters, until finally she went mad and they put her in the home and sold the house.

"Shameful for the whole family, all of us, to let it happen like that. I was so wrapped up in my own life. If I could have it back, I'd go live with her."

"Aww," says Isabelle, and reaches for a brief, one-armed hug, cheek to cheek. Glasses are refilled.

There was a very bad scene a few weeks before Ronnie died. As Isabelle tells it, Shelley went to see him without telling her. Isabelle found out and drove into Toronto, where there was an ugly confrontation. Carter isn't clear on why she found the possible relationship so abhorrent. Couldn't Ronnie use a woman? A reconciliation at the funeral, with a heartfelt hug, could have been the perfect, final grace note between them. But Shelley insists on the tether. They still have fashion school, after all. They were closer than lovers back in those innocent days, sharing a double bed in their basement apartment. Occasionally they would even "make out like teenagers," according to Isabelle. "Just a comfort thing," she called it. "Just kissing. We were both so lonely." But surely, with the two of them in the same bed every night… "Your mind goes there because you're a guy," Isabelle insisted. "It was just kissing."

Carter has never been good at drinking. It puts him to sleep. But today the buzz from the wine is fortifying. It burns a little, as if glowing inside him.

Shelley turns to him and says, "What about you?"

"What?"

"Your younger days, what were they like? You were in a band. There must have been some wild times."

"It was great, but its time was brief." This is his stock answer.

"But what was it like?" Shelley lowers her voice to a purr of comic seduction. "Didn't the girls throw themselves at you?"

"Not at Herb," says Isabelle. "He was married."

"That's a shame," says Shelley. "Did people come to see you?"

"It was a big soap opera, and a big break-up at the end." He's being unfair. It doesn't account for the way music, or the idea of music, pulled like an undertow. But he can't give a name or purpose to this force. It's why he's had trouble arguing his case with Leah.

"But what was it like when it was wonderful? What did you love best about it?"

"My Telecaster."

"What's a Telecaster?"

"A guitar that can make you believe anything."

"Really? I bet that came in handy. This was the nineties, right? Would I know any of your songs?"

"I doubt it."

"Can I hear some now?"

"Not now. But we've got plans to get them back out there."

"Are your songs embarrassing, like someone reading your high-school poetry? Horrible feelings and heartbreak?"

"No." The comparison is not entirely off the mark. But he chafes against the touch of glee in Shelley's voice. "Maybe a bit young and foolish. But it shouldn't be dismissed because of that." He shrugs. "It's old."

"Carter left all that behind long ago," says Isabelle, dumping ground sausage into the pot. "We both let a lot of things go when we got married."

They switch to red for dinner. Carter breaks the cork and has to push the rest of it in to pour. They drink and spit flecks of cork. Soon he is finding out things he never knew. His wife hates her hair, and has never found a style that can minimize the expanse of her forehead and the impossibly thick bridge of her nose. Also, even her most carefully selected shoes look absurd, big planks at the end of each leg.

The women push away empty plates and continue gnawing on chunks of baguette.

Shelley says the lemon-drop A-line jacket was the best thing Isabelle ever made, and she never, never ever should have shown it to Callahan.

"I remember how she held it," says Isabelle. "Like I just handed her a lump of dog shit."

"Like it was a personal insult or something."

"I can't believe my tuition helped pay the salary of that … that *cunt*."

"That *cunt*," says Shelley, and they let the label fill the air between them. Carter sits back, giving them room to relish it. He's never liked this dining room. It's more of a dining nook, too small for he and Isabelle. They loom over each other's food and get entangled trying to help Sam. With Shelley taking Sam's chair, it feels like the three of them are huddled in a secret bunker, knees touching.

They talk about boys.

"It was all out of anger," says Isabelle. "Like, not hate, exactly."

"No."

"If you thought about it, you'd never, you know?"

Carter knows he has gained access to a raw, rich female moment. But what he wants is to see the video on a bigger screen. The laptop sits on the cabinet behind him.

Shelley spies a bottle of grappa at the back of the bar shelf. It's been there forever. She opens it and pours shots for the three of them.

"Mmmmm!" says Isabelle, and Shelley pours another round. They talk about TV. Shelley's guy is making a documentary about women who visit men in prison, men they've never met, and fall in love with them. Isabelle says she saw a documentary about Kurt Cobain, and it was so full of shit. The poor, tortured artist, too sensitive for the world. She takes her wine to the couch. Why can't an artist be like anyone else? Why can't he go home after a good day's work, put dinner on the table and put the kids to bed? She settles into the couch, tucking her legs. Makes a pistol with her fingers, puts it in her mouth, and throws her head back. "If that's your idea of a hero," she says. She leaves her head back, resting on the cushions, and closes her eyes.

Carter excuses himself and heads upstairs, sitting on the bed, squirming with anticipation. Watches three times, turning his phone sideways and back, concentrating on the moment before the picture freezes. His hand touches her shoulder and slides down to the breast. The girl flinches and starts to turn her back. Carter takes her bicep and says, "Over here." Or that's probably what he's saying, just as he's cut off.

Will is dangerous. He has to warn Jordan that Will is dangerous. He hasn't heard from Jordan for a few weeks. *Smart just to lay low,* he wrote in January. *Keep it quiet until, you know.*

Will is dangerous, he writes, and sends it.

/////

Morning is unseasonably warm, stirring odours of sticky alcohol and acidic tomato, with an underlying gym-locker rot. Carter sweats, his head in a vice. The young laughing man in the motel room is stronger than him. Stronger and younger, with a head full of ideas and a guitar. The lead singer is waiting back in his room and the girl in front of the camera is topless.

Shelley has receded since last night. Her face is small, and sharpened by its frame of greying hair. The hair tapers to fine points that curl around each ear. Her skin, which radiated liquid orange in the candlelight, looks dry.

"Are you going to give me your music?" she asks, breaking the silence over coffee. "Maybe we'll use it? We're always looking for music for our films."

"Talk to Jordan Toytman," says Carter. "I'll get you his email."

"They're in a bit of a holding pattern," says Isabelle. He can see her wavering over whether to mention Leah and her resistance, her decline. "Legal things to work out."

He's been waiting for the right time to mention that he's mentally set aside late summer and fall to devote himself to the reissue. Possibly to rehearsal and shows, assuming Leah is gone by then. Jordan sent him several names of potential singers. Carter Googles them. Young women on the indie scene, daring and feminist and "sex positive." One of them is a thin, painted blonde who used to be a stripper.

"Anyway, Carter's an archaeologist now? He's going to travel this summer, go digging in the dirt."

"Anywhere sexy?" asks Shelley.

"I'm going to Gander in June."

"Where?"

"In Newfoundland," Isabelle explains. "Carter grew up there. It has a big airport and it's full of plane wrecks."

"Not full of them," says Carter.

"This is Herb's new life. He and his new professor friend, they're going to go dig up old plane wrecks."

"But that's awful," says Shelley. "A plane crash is horrible. It ought to be left in peace."

"They go back to the war, most of them. It's long ago now."

"But I don't know about digging things up," says Shelley. She peels chunks of wax from the base of a collapsed candle. "Supposing you find bodies, or bones of people?"

"There's no bones," says Carter. He has no idea if this is true.

"It's history now," says Isabelle.

"My mom lost her father in the war. She never got over it. She wouldn't want anyone digging him up."

"We're not digging up graves."

"It's the local people who are in charge, right?" says Isabelle.

"Yes. Memorial University. Terry and his students. I'm just lending a hand."

Shelley asks about Gander, and Carter tells her about the mural they made in high school. A big blue sky filled with airplanes of every vintage. An outsized Gander Airport below, its runways spanning the breadth of the wall, and *Crossroads of the World* scripted in gold across the top. The only one in the class who could really paint, he tells them, was Barb Felthem, a sulky, green-eyed girl who had famously touched Wally Forbes's crotch in exchange for two cigarettes, leaving her hand there while a hooting crowd counted three steamboats.

They erupt in hysterical, hungover laughter, with Isabelle wiping her eyes.

The woozy surge of energy burns out as Carter drives Shelley to the bus station.

"Are you and Bella okay?" she says, as he pulls into the curb.

There are little bursts in Carter's head, like small balloons going pop. "Absolutely," he says.

"It was just something you said. Kind of strange."

"Last night?"

"We were talking about music and film, and you said there was a French movie you saw once with everyone in it singing. Around when Ronnie died. You said you and Bella can't get away from that movie. Do you remember?"

"No," says Carter. He gets out of the car and retrieves her bag from the back. "It must have been drunk babbling. We're fine."

"I mentioned it to Bella this morning. I mean, not what you said. Just the movie, and she had no memory of it at all. She said she never heard of it."

14

The teddy bears tumbled from the box in sickly shades of yellow and pink, with muddy red eyes that looked like scabs. Over three hundred teddy bears donated by the St. John's Boys Club—the hard-won result of who knows how many bottles collected and cold-plate dinners sold—and all so tragically ugly.

"A merchant clearing out poor stock," said Ingrid, the Red Cross interpreter from Toronto. "Something doesn't sell. So when a charity comes he offers a discount, or a two-for-one." Using one edge of the scissors, she cut the seal on a second box. More of the same. "For the children, it doesn't matter."

"No." Joyce squeezed a pink bear, its fur greasy on her fingers. "It's a sin all the same." She dropped the bear and wiped her hand on her slacks. Reached into the fusty, tangled innards of the latest clothing donations to separate the most essential items—winter coats, boots, hats, scarves, long johns, and sweaters.

She had given up trying to distance herself from the refugees. Over three thousand Hungarians had passed through the airport since last week, en route to New York or Montreal or Toronto. Plenty more to come, what with the Russians killing everyone and setting fire to everything. Joyce had watched several newspapermen talk to a barber from Budapest, with Ingrid at his side to translate. I got out with the clothes on my back and a razor to defend myself, the barber said. I saw their bayonets cut down women and children. Bodies trampled under their boots. If they found out you fought against them, they killed your family and friends and neighbours. Ingrid struggled with the translation, and said later that it was impossible to get people's stories straight. The barber had been small and handsome, with a luxurious white moustache like the man in the Monopoly game. He had borrowed a clean jacket before meeting the newspapermen. Combed the moustache before they took his picture.

Joyce had stopped reading the papers after the barber's story, had stopped eavesdropping as well. Instead she took to watching the Hungarians as they entered the makeshift relief centre, a curtained-off section of the terminal. They fumbled with glasses, formed orderly and near silent lines for soup and fresh clothes and washrooms, and repeatedly checked their pockets for important papers or money or small items to be held and worried like rosary beads. They rarely embraced or even touched each other. Joyce liked the children best of all. How they shook off the shyness and disorientation, blinking back to life, desperate for release after countless hours trapped on a slow air force freighter. Before long they would be laughing and carrying on, riling their parents.

The latest group had just been packed off to Montreal, bellies full, teeth cleaned, bowels voided, faces and armpits scrubbed, pads changed, cheeks shaved, and hair combed. Less than ninety minutes earlier they had stumbled into the airport, lifeless and slack-jawed.

"No shortage of help today," said Ingrid, arranging the ugly bears on one of the plywood tables that lined the back of the room. With another flight due in a couple of hours, the volunteers had mostly stayed on, clearing dishes and wiping down tables. Card games were starting up. Beth Ann McCurdy was winning. Her husband

Dave had been with the band for ages, his big bass so reliable that no one gave it a thought.

"Sure that's not even cards!" Beth Ann cried, slapping Dawson on the shoulder of his Star Taxi windbreaker. "You'll go on anything! That's not even cards!" Dawson hunched in his jacket and grinned.

"Here comes your friend," said Ingrid, touching Joyce's hand.

Andor strolled into the relief centre at a leisurely pace, toes out and legs wide, greeting the volunteers like a plant owner touring the shop floor. He leaned into the soup tureen, sniffed, frowned, nodded. Took his time selecting a new toothbrush from the toiletry table. Shorter than Joyce and impossibly thin, with long ears down the sides of his long head, he looked like a dissolute magician in the clothes he had chosen: grey flannel schoolboy pants cinched under a billowing bright red shirt. The shirt was surely a woman's blouse.

Andor was one of the sixty-five men who had been stranded in Gander for the past three days, waiting for their freighter to be repaired or for a replacement plane to show up and complete the journey to Toronto. People said they were resistance fighters who had spent weeks hiding in the woods before finding their way to Vienna. They were sleeping on cots at the old Eastbound Inn, irritable with the delay. They slouched about during the day, smoking, dozing, eating little, complaining of headaches.

Andor was different. He never stopped moving and made faces like a comic actor. The first time Joyce saw him he was digging through the donated clothes, trying on colourful outfits and striking ridiculous poses for anyone who wanted to watch. She had laughed and offered him a cigarette. He lit it, puffed thoughtfully, wrinkled his lumpy red nose, and muttered something that Ingrid had refused to translate until Joyce badgered her. "He says, I hope you American girls are sweeter than your tobacco."

She didn't need his foolishness today. Joyce was desperately tired, and due back at work at four. She turned her back and went to work with a box of used toys. They smelled of metallic paint and mould and cardboard, and a salty tang that could only be children's saliva. In her exhaustion she couldn't suppress a wave of emotion at the touch of each object, an awareness of the human presence in every toy. The nicks and scratches on a battered wooden boat. A baby's teeth marks in the lid of a jigsaw puzzle.

"Question, Miss Joyce."

"Yes?" Joyce turned and pushed back her hair, a strange plastic object in one hand.

Andor perched on the table and searched for the English words.

"Why does your Eisenhower, does not, send armies to save Hungary?"

"Ha-ha," said Joyce, with a roll of her eyes. Andor laughed, showed his yellow teeth. He raised this question every day. The first time he asked, Joyce had told him this wasn't America. The second time, she had snapped, "He's not my bloody Eisenhower," which was apparently the funniest thing Andor had ever heard. Now it was their running joke.

Joyce reached for her cigarettes and laid two on the table. Andor tucked one behind an ear, and took matches from his pocket to light the other. Like all of them, he had grey circles around his Chinese eyes, and always seemed slightly out of breath.

He beckoned Ingrid, speaking Hungarian to her in a low, gravelly whisper.

"He wants to know, is your heart pure and strong and worthy of the love of a Hungarian man?" said Ingrid.

"My heart is tough as an old boot," said Joyce, examining a fine black velveteen skirt with a rope-tie belt. "You wouldn't get a steak knife through it."

Andor turned an ear to Ingrid, then whooped with laughter and raised his puffy sleeves to clap twice. Joyce reached under the table, where she had stored a thick canvas shirt, nearly new. She tossed it to him. "Tell him that blouse smells."

Andor caught the shirt and made a great show of surprise and delight, long ears lifting and flexing as his face split with a smile. Clutching the shirt to his chest, he bowed deeply and blew Joyce a kiss, skipping away to the dining area, where Gordon was wiping down tables. Snatching the towel that hung over Gordon's shoulder, Andor propped a shoe on a chair and began buffing it.

"Get out of it with your foolishness," said Gordon, and snatched the towel back. Like a mime, Andor twisted his face in mock bewilderment and shrugged his shoulders.

"He'll be back here before long," said Ingrid. "Where his hijinks are more appreciated."

/////

The goal was to have each planeload back in the air in two hours. But everyone talked as if the Hungarians might settle in Gander and never leave. Gloria said they should be put to work straight away building houses and roads. They'd be happy for the work and do it for any wage. Den Shea said there was sure to be Communists among them, and soft-hearted kindness was exactly what they were counting on. Mike Devine said the first thing that happens when a crowd like that settle somewhere is the foreign men go after the women and the local men are shut out altogether. Alice Henley had heard that Hungarians ate soup made from cherries, and they wouldn't be very happy with the pitiful cherries around these parts. "They want to go to Nova Scotia," she said. "Up to Digby, where my father's from. Gorgeous cherries." Rachel said there ought to be more military around to keep them quarantined, as they might carry diseases.

Rachel feared everything since her marriage to the fellow who ran the fire department. They had a house on the new town site and Rachel worked hard to leave behind her old airport days, with all the parties and boyfriends. She called Joyce occasionally. But they never crossed paths anymore.

Joyce didn't say much, but she understood that the Hungarians had come from violence. Some of them must have killed and lied and stolen to save themselves. What if they still carried this violence with them? The fear never surfaced when she took a shift at the relief centre. But later, when she recalled their faces and their restless, twitchy bodies, the way they huddled and shivered as if unable to get warm, she thought that some of them would surely kill and lie and steal again if they had to. She knew that a jolly, outgoing man often held awful things inside.

The Hungarian crisis had brought all manner of stranger to the airport—Red Cross staff, military men, nurses from St. John's, customs officers, out-of-town volunteers. The place felt lighter with so many strange faces. None of them knew Joyce's history. They didn't feel bad for her or treat her like her best days were behind her. In the two years since Eric died, Joyce had been circled by a few men and been set upon by a couple of widowers encouraged by Gloria or Mary. She had allowed none of them more than an after-work cup of coffee. She was social, playing bridge and stepping out weekly with the TCA bowling team. Last year they had recorded the highest team score of the season, duly reported in the *Beacon* sports section the following Wednesday. But the streets around the airport were quieter now, with so many moved into town. Hardly any children around, unless their parents drove them up for the hospital or the rink.

Chaulker's Store was the last one Joyce could walk to, with the rest moved to the new town square. Joyce had her name in for one of the apartments going up on Elizabeth Drive, though everyone said it was more expensive to live in town. Gloria said the town taxes were robbery.

She returned to the relief centre the following afternoon, and walked in as Maeve Vardy grew very curt with a teenaged girl who refused to exchange her filthy dress for decent clothes. "Look at this," said Maeve. "Nice sweater set, and slacks to match. Just your size." The young woman backed away. Her black hair was short and bristly, with patches of exposed scalp showing red welts. Ingrid stepped between them, speaking gentle Hungarian to the woman, who replied in a shaky voice, near tears. "She thinks you want her to undress here, out in the open," Ingrid explained to Maeve.

It was a small group off the latest flight, and there wasn't much to do. They picked through the food and clothes with little apparent interest. Alice Henley distributed towels and cakes of Sunlight to those lined up to wash. Joyce helped bring dirty dishes to the commissary, passing through the room being used as a clinic. The girl Maeve had scared sat with her skirt hiked up and stockings rolled down, showing bruised and bandaged legs. A nurse changed the dressings while the girl stared unblinking at her wounds, as if committing the sight to memory. The battered legs looked strong and her exposed neck was straight and sturdy. Joyce was sure she would live many years.

"Your friend got out this morning," said Ingrid, when Joyce returned to the clothes station.

"Andor? Got out?"

"Flew out to New York."

"But…But they're going to Toronto."

"New York or Toronto, it's all the same to him. He didn't want to wait any longer, so he talked his way onto a planeload bound for New York." Ingrid shrugged and apologized—"*Boch-uh-nut*"—to a grey-bearded man who held up two odd shoes, the last ones in a wooden crate. A boy in a ragged shirt approached. "Hello. *Fogota-tash!*" Joyce said in the phonetically crude Hungarian she had picked up. She pulled a blue dress shirt from the box at her feet. "*Ked-vuh-led?* You like?" He snatched the shirt and scurried away.

"What a shame," said Ingrid, lifting the shoe crate and tossing it back with the other empties.

"He's only a boy. Scared out of his wits."

"I mean about Andor. That you didn't see him to say goodbye."

"No, no. Don't be ridiculous."

"He left something for you." Ingrid pulled a small box from a wrinkled paper bag, the light rippling off its shiny black surface. "A jewelry chest, I think."

"Goodness," said Joyce. She took the box, which was much heavier than it looked. "It's got a racy picture." The lid was painted with a brown-skinned woman on a couch, her robe opened in a v down to her navel. "Where do you suppose he got this?"

"When the invasion began, some of them managed to get away with a few valuables, like jewels or money. I talked to one man who took his liquor with him."

"Took his liquor? Dragging bottles of liquor around with the Russians after him?"

"The liquor is what saved him. They came up against a Russian tank, and the tank commander let them through, as a trade for the liquor."

Joyce examined the brown-skinned woman on the lid, her breasts fully outlined and barely covered by the robe. Threaded gold lines looped and curled around and down the sides of the box. She opened the lid, wondering if it might be a music box. The blue carpet inside darkened when she ran her fingers against it, and the extra shelf that hinged from the lid held a small bracelet. But no music played.

"Is there anything in there?"

"Just this." Joyce held up the bracelet, made of smooth, polished stones linked together.

"I'd say he started out with a box of jewelry, and bartered pieces for food or passage," said Ingrid. "He had a message as well."

"Andor? What message?"

"He said." Ingrid shook her head and sighed in exasperation. "He said, 'Tell Miss Joyce my great adventure is over. From now on my life will be like any other.' He was nothing but jokes and nonsense, the entire time he was here."

"Oh, but I would have been disappointed if he didn't leave us with nonsense."

"It's gotten him this far, I suppose."

//////

The Christmas Eve refugees stayed a few extra hours so they could have turkey dinner with all the trimmings. The school choir sang and the gifts from the toy drive were ready because Mrs. Bowe and the other teachers had stayed up all night sorting and wrapping them, marking each with a B or G and a number to suggest appropriate age.

Joyce spent all afternoon in the kitchen, using an ice-cream scoop to add a ball of mashed turnip to every meal. Maeve Vardy was at her side, dousing each plate with gravy.

"Father Kiloran says they're mostly Catholics, of a sort," said Maeve. "They looked very devout when we did the blessing beforehand."

When everyone had their pudding, Joyce took up a plate of turkey and dressing and found a stool in the rear of the commissary kitchen. Racks filled with dirty dishes wheeled through the door, and steam plumed from sinks being refilled for another round. "Look alive now, girls," called a voice, just as several plates crashed to the floor, raising laughter and a round of applause.

"Joyce!" hissed a voice behind her.

She turned to see Gloria's husband looking through a barely opened door.

"What are you doing in the pantry, Frank?"

"We're ready to do the gifts for the youngsters. Come here."

She stepped in and he closed the door behind her. Joyce blinked, adjusting to the glare of the overhead light bulb. He was a few drinks in, she could tell by the minty candies he sucked to mask his breath. He always had a few in when he played Santa for the Airport Club kids' party.

"Give me a hand with the jacket, will you? Can you get the first three buttons for me?"

Frank held an old pillow across his waist while Joyce pulled the two sides of the threadbare Santa jacket together. She had to kneel to do the buttons. "They'll pop," she said. "The buttonholes are nearly gone."

"Christ, Joyce. You're a saviour." He groaned, and the pillow belly swayed toward her.

"You can manage the rest." Joyce stood and backed into a shelf, knocking over two cans of peaches. The pantry was large, but crowded with crates and flour sacks and beef buckets, the walls lined with tinned fruit, tomatoes, peas and carrots, coffee, lunch meat. A crate of potatoes smelled earthy.

"Give me a hand with the belt, though?"

She crouched again, and took the strip of black vinyl hanging from either side of the jacket. He kept the pillow in place as she ran the belt through the plastic buckle and cinched it.

"Do they know who Santa is, I wonder?" asked Frank, as she stepped away.

"I don't know. They'll be grateful either way."

"Do you get lonely up here now? With most people moved to the new town site?" He asked this as if it were the next obvious question.

"That beard needs replacing," Joyce replied. The white mass of curls had shriveled on one side. Someone must have left it on a radiator.

"Remember that?" asked Frank, using his chin to indicate over Joyce's shoulder.

She turned and recognized the costume hung from a hook on the door. A head-to-toe bodysuit with a zipper up the front, patterned in faded diamonds of green and yellow. It was more of a jester's outfit. But Joyce had worn it during her first Christmas in Gander, acting as Frank's elf at the children's party.

"Nobody wore it this year," said Frank.

"What happened to that girl you had last year?"

"Her husband won't allow it," said Frank. "But no one ever wore it like you, Joyce. You've still got the figure for it. You know that, don't you?"

She touched the sleeve, wondering at her brazen confidence of three years ago. It had stretched around her like a second skin. "Where's Gloria? I thought she was bringing Anthony and the twins."

"Anthony's terrified of Santa. When I pulled off the beard and said, 'Look, it's me, Daddy,' he cried even louder. But Joyce, you'd fit nicely into that costume still. How about it, eh?"

"No."

"Come on now. For a lark."

Joyce opened the pantry door. "I imagine they're ready for you."

"A house full of screaming youngsters, it makes you remember the old days. How good you had it."

"Merry Christmas, Frank. I'll see all of you for dinner tomorrow."

/////

She helped with the dishes and slipped in for a look at the party. Frank was on his feet, empty sack over his back. The children were gathered around and calling to him in their strange language. Some clutched dolls or teddies or colourful objects. "Bulldog," shouted Frank, and paused. Ingrid leaned into him and whispered in his ear. Frank nodded, and roared what sounded like, "Bulldog-Kara-Choneee!" The kids laughed and clutched at his legs as he started wading through the crowd. He touched their heads and bent for kisses. He threw his head back and arched to the ceiling until Joyce thought he might fall. The pillow bulged out from under his jacket. The suit was filthy. "Ho! Ho! Ho!" he boomed. "Bulllllllldog-Kara-Choneeeeeee!" The grown-ups were clapping in time as "Jolly Old St. Nicholas" played on the phonograph.

209

The noise echoed around the room, bringing others from the kitchen. "Good lord," said Beth Ann. The parents hadn't moved quick enough, and one young man was bowled over by the child mob. Frank trudged through the crowd, the kids swarming him, grappling at his legs and sleeves. Mike Devine thrust himself into the middle of it, raising his big arms. "Now, now, boys and girls," he shouted. "I think we all need—"

Frank called out something, and the children must have understood because now they were jumping and screaming, drowning out the music. From the sack he drew a handful of candy.

"I didn't know there were so many," said Joyce.

"It was all families, this flight," replied Beth Ann.

"Isn't it beautiful?" said Maeve, wiping a tear away. "They're all God's children. Even the poor Jews."

Candy spilled to the floor. The kids dove for it.

"I meant to tell you," said Beth Ann. "Gord Delaney—"

The shrieks from the children hit a higher register as more candy rained down from Frank's hand. Then another handful, landing at Mike Devine's feet. The children attacked, nearly toppling him before he could back away.

Frank finally escaped through a fire exit, with Mike doing his best to hold off the horde. A little boy in a green cardigan slipped through the door. Mike, teeth gritted and hair askew, grabbed the tail of the cardigan and dragged him back, handing him to an old woman who landed a good cuff at the back of his head. The boy started crying, cuing an outbreak of tears around the room. Several older boys appeared to be fighting in the corner, running hard at each other and tumbling to the tiled floor. A little girl sat alone not far from Joyce, sobbing and pulling at her fine yellow hair.

"Gord Delaney and Fran. They're moving to Halifax in the new year."

"Moving?"

"For work. They haven't told anyone. But Dave got wind of it. Gord's been hired to run the show up there. It's closer to Fran's family as well. They'll have a bit of help."

Joyce counted a pulse in the arch of her foot. She had never known Gander without Gord. Never sung without him. "Could Dave lead the band, do you think?"

"Dave's going to give it up. He says there's nobody to lead the band, really. And he's tired of it."

The children began to slow, voices turned hoarse. The criers sniffed and snotted. The fighting boys slumped in exhaustion. The room trembled in aftershock. Joyce sneezed twice from the dust they had kicked up. The boy in the green cardigan sprawled on the floor, wiping a sleeve across his hot face. The yellow-haired girl hung over the shoulder of a birdlike man, her mouth open and eyes glazed.

"It couldn't go on forever. God knows I could do to have Dave around the house more. We were in such a rush to get in. The yard's a shambles, and the basement half-done."

Joyce wiped her nose. The Hungarians were on their hands and knees, men, women, and children, gathering the remaining candy. Who knew when they might see such bounty again, or where?

"Never mind all that," said Beth Ann. "Are you working tomorrow?"

"I'm off until four on Boxing Day."

"There'll be a crowd making the rounds tomorrow night."

"I don't know." Making the rounds was tiresome. Trudging through the snow. Fumbling with boots in a darkened foyer while your stockings soaked in melted snow. Warm drinks and mixed nuts in an overheated living room. And just as you started to get comfortable someone would be shouting Come along now, come along, forcing all hands back out into the black night, feet freezing and sweat chilling, on to the next house. Last Christmas a fellow from Atlas Construction had vomited in Nel Anstey's lap. It was like he was taking aim, the way he lurched at Nel and let fly. A few feet to the left and he would have hit Joyce. "Everyone's so spread out now. You can't just dodge to the next house."

"The boys will drive. But listen now." Beth Ann glanced behind her, as if checking for eavesdroppers. "Those new boys started last month at Air Traffic Control? They're coming with us. Not one of them married, Joyce."

"I don't know."

"Top dollar at ATC is a fortune, Joyce. Best salary in town. Wouldn't you rather have a fellow like that, instead of dirty old Frank Tucker pulling you into the pantry?"

"I didn't let him do anything," hissed Joyce.

"Of course not. But that's how a fellow treats a girl when she's footloose."

As long as she remained single, she had to endure it all. The pity and hushed whispers. The dancing boys who brushed their lips to her ear and worked their fingers into her waist. The besotted men who pulled her into the pantry, sighing as she dropped to her knees to help with their buttons and big pillow bellies.

The room was nearly silent now. Parents lined up for the washrooms with the bodies of their spent children draped across them. Exhaustion seemed to sweep the room all at once.

"Don't be sad about the band, Joyce. It's someone else's turn."

"I'm not sad."

"A lot of people just want records now anyway."

"They can't leave right after Christmas," says Joyce. "We've got a booking for New Year's."

"And that'll be it, then. By next New Year's, you can have your own night on the town, maybe with a fellow to take you out."

15

Before flying to Gander, Carter writes: *Be ready. I have a feeling something's going to happen very soon. We have to be ready to roll and get on it quick.*

Tumours advance, creeping over the back and blooming in the lung. Rogue cells seek out glands and organs, working inside and multiplying, scorching everything in their path. A phallic nub of cancer pushes at a bone, breaks through and sinks deep, feeding on the marrow. These visions are disgusting in detail and texture. But if he could share them with Leah she would nod in recognition. He has a strong urge to see her again. He fantasizes about another bathroom-stall moment, and a long look at the ruined body. She stopped returning emails and calls after the bowel blockage visit.

Carter lingers over the email as his flight is called, and shortens it.

Be ready. Something's going to happen very soon.

He sends it to Jordan.

/////

The motel off the Gander Bay Road is new to him, as are the streets that curl away from it and wind around Cobb's Pond.

"All this was woods when I grew up," he says to the apple-cheeked girl on the front desk.

"Look out if the wind changes," she says. "The sewage plant up off Rowsell Avenue is maxed out. If we get a breeze coming this way..." She shakes her head. "Oh my God."

Carter sits on the slippery, floral-patterned bedspread and calls Terry, who says, "Welcome home, Newfie," and explains how they'll start with a visit to the Globe Theatre dig, which is the dissertation project of a student named Red. Then they'll stop to review last year's work at the B-24 Liberator, and see how many sites they can hit in the days following.

Carter calls home. Sam has an electrocardiogram later this week. He's had one every year, but doesn't seem to recall the other years.

"He didn't eat," says Isabelle. "He wouldn't let me say goodnight. I told him he's fine. It's routine. But he won't talk about it."

"He'll bounce back."

"How's your room?"

"Fine. A bit cramped." There is a notch cut into the door so it doesn't jam against the dresser. The bar fridge in the corner won't open unless the bed is nudged sideways. The bed rolls easily on its wheels, but nudging it blocks the door to the small closet.

"He'll be fine," says Isabelle. "It really is just routine."

"According to the doctor."

"According to you."

"How so?"

"If it was anything other than routine, you would have stayed home for it."

Terry pulls up at six-thirty in the morning, giving the horn a couple of rude blasts.

"They say this neighbourhood stinks to high heaven," he says, as Carter straps in.

"We're waiting for the wind to change."

214

"We're lucky." The dusty hatchback rumbles past Carter's high school. "No flies yet, with the cool air."

The old Globe Theatre is a grassed-over foundation at the corner of a dirt road. The students from Memorial are there, four men and two women, drinking from mugs. A pot steams on a nearby Coleman stove. Birds flit noisily in branches. The airport is a sea of asphalt hidden beyond the trees, close enough that they hear its machinery drone and creak in anticipation. But the sky is quiet.

"This used to be the old Legion, here on the other corner," says Terry, nodding at another overgrown patch. Carter helps him unload backpacks and a bag of tools. "And houses, up and down all these roads. The chapel and schoolhouse. Drill hall."

The Memorial crowd finish their tea, toss the dregs into bushes and rinse mugs with water from the kettle. One of them is Morris, who did the Skype tour of the archaeology lab in February. Carter places them all around thirty years old, except the one they call Red. The faded copper of her hair places her closer to Carter's age. The hair is woven into beaded dreadlocks that click and clack with her every move.

There is much preliminary grooming. Velcro peeled back and pulled snug at cuffs and waists. Zippers zipped to the chin. Pants tucked into boots. It's June, and still cool enough for extra layers. They've already cut away much of the brush around the foundation, roping off the footprint and opening several excavations. Carter is assigned to a patch of clay where the front entrance used to be. Next to him is a small grad student wrapped in clingy athletic fabric. Her name is Andi, and her Italian father came to Newfoundland as an offshore engineer and married a girl from La Scie. The dark hair and slender oval face look glamorously European. But she's muscular, with thick calves and a belly roll that looks far sturdier than Carter's ring of flab. She twists her hair into a bun and tucks it under a ball cap.

He shudders at the slugs and centipedes, sweeping them away with his trowel. It's reminiscent of childhood, when he used to poke around in newly-cleared building lots behind the house. He has no idea what he's doing, but his trowel comes up against a lump of thick glass. Andi hears it and joins him, crouching and probing the dirt, their heads nearly touching, her breath strong and steady. Together they expose a clear glass bottle, fully intact, with *Gordon's Gin* in raised letters across the front.

"Looks new," says Morris, leaning into his trowel. He's wider and hairier than Carter remembers from Skype, with a ponytail halfway down his back.

"Maybe," says Andi. "Gordon's haven't changed their bottles much over the years."

"You know old liquor bottles?" asks Carter. His exhalations stir the strands of hair at her ears.

"Some of them," she says, brushing dirt from the thick glass and narrowing her eyes. "Pop bottles, too."

"How?"

"Been to a lot of websites. A few stores downtown. Water Street Convenience has a nice collection."

They take turns examining their find, sniffing the neck and running fingers over the embossed letters. In Carter's hand the bottle vibrates with the approach of an incoming flight. It passes to their right, thundering and sputtering, a FedEx logo on its tail.

He stands because his knees are killing him. There's a sting up his left arm, and the breeze gives him a shiver, chilling the sweat on the back of his neck.

"Come on," says Andi, bouncing on her haunches in their black-and-purple microfibres. "I bet there's more."

Bottle pieces emerge all over. Red and Andi make their guesses: Coke, Pepsi, Canada Dry, Hi-Spot Lemon Soda, and Keep Kool. "Probably from the seventies, eighties," says Morris.

"Not the Canada Dry," says Andi, stroking the green glass. "See the cross-hatch pattern? That's gotta be from the war."

Coins are found, and chunks of ceramic. Red turns up two

unopened packs of chewing gum, their labels washed white. Terry circulates, occasionally crouching to dig a probing hand in the dirt. After a standing lunch of gas-station sandwiches, the team splits. Red will stay on the Globe with two others. "The rest of us are going deep woods," says Terry, his index finger picking out Carter, Andi, and Morris. "That egg sandwich was a mistake," says Andi, as Terry's car bumps up an old logging road.

Using a trail originally cut for a memorial service, they easily access the b-24 Liberator. Terry leads them through survey exercises, and Carter is quickly exposed as the new guy, fumbling with the line-and-compass, incurring a nasty scratch on the waist as he stretches to pull the tape through a maze of trees. He steps into a puddle that is much deeper than it looks, and falls sideways, soaking one side. Morris offers a slow clap.

A mossy furrow leads to an engine, rusting and stripped of its skin, aluminum scraps scattered about like confetti. Circling it, they disturb moths that flutter at their shins. The propellers disappeared years ago. "Scavengers love props," says Terry.

A rounded tail piece is wedged in the ground, still painted military green. Terry runs a finger over a scattering of small holes. "See this? Buckshot. Young local taking target practice."

"Idiots," says Morris.

"So this one went down in a snowstorm," Terry continues. "1945. We found good stuff a couple of years ago, including the radar array, in good shape. This is our greatest hit, you might say." Using the metal detector, Morris and Andi turn up several buckles, likely from disintegrated kit bags, and a lapel pin bearing an eagle insignia.

They're packing up when Carter spots what seems an ordinary piece of metal trash in the tall brush. "Looks like an old video game," says Morris. "Like the Atari my brother had." Terry helps Carter hack away a couple of branches, and Carter peels off a layer of moss. The piece is too chunky to be anything recent. It has a black facade and a switch with the instructions, "return slut before cocking" printed below. Morris snickers. Terry takes the object, turns it in his hands. "This is the bomb release console." He touches the switch. "The bombardier flicks this and lets fly." He flicks the switch. "Still works! Well done. Good find."

///////

Though he tucks his cargo pants into his socks, Carter takes fly bites at the back of each knee, and a big one dangerously close to the groin. The itch is maddening, he sleeps poorly, and endures the next day in fretful exhaustion.

The morning starts with a look at a Hudson bomber from '42, down an old woods road, surveyed and catalogued a few years ago. "This is not the crash site," says Terry, as they size up crushed landing gear and a flattened aluminum frame. "It was pushed aside back when the Trans Canada went through. Where we parked on the highway is actually much closer to where she went down. The lesson is, always consult historical records. You'll only get part of the story on the ground."

Turning the hatchback down a nearby logging road, they set out for the Maritime Central Airways Canso from 1954.

"Fresh survey," says Terry. "Never been down here before. Post-war crashes are a different kettle of fish. Commercial airlines, casualties generally in double figures. Eleven killed with this Canso. Flew too low and clipped the trees."

The logging road narrows, branches closing in and slapping the windshield. When they can go no further, they leave their cars and walk the rutted road until it opens to a meadow of knee-length grass. Horse flies and stouts hover on the thick, warm breeze. Birds arrive and depart with sudden violence, crashing through the tops of trees. The ground begins to suck at their boots.

After a lot of pointing and squinting, Morris leads an approach from the west, only to sink ("I'm up to my tits!") within minutes. Rounding the bog on a more arduous southwest approach, they come up against a muddy creek, where Andi belly-flops in the muck. Fat stouts circle happily in the sun as she pulls herself up and bends to retrieve her sunglasses.

"Maybe next year," says Terry.

They retreat for lunch, Morris and Andi use Terry's hatchback as a shield while they change into spare clothes, and they head up the highway to try their luck with the RCAF Hurricane and USAAF A-20, which collided during manoeuvres in '43. They spread out and cut a wide circle. But an afternoon of fighting the brush reveals no sign of either wreck. Carter gets another soaking on the way out. Waving at mosquitoes and half-blinded by the sinking sun, he goes to his knees in a quiet stream.

/////

"What's the matter with you guys?" says Isabelle. "You can't even find the stuff? Didn't anyone bring a map? A compass?"

Carter rakes at his fly bites, nudges the bed with his knee so he can open the closet. "We did see one. A Hudson bomber they dug out years ago."

"Did people die in it?"

"People died in all of them." Carter tries to recall Terry's potted history of the Hudson. "Four of them in this one."

"Who were they?"

"I don't know. Two from Australia, I think." He's pretty sure Terry mentioned Australia.

"But you want to know, don't you? Otherwise you're just looking at junk."

"Two Aussies for sure. They're buried in the old cemetery next to the airport.."

"You'll have to get me on the cell tomorrow," says Isabelle. "We'll be at the hospital."

"His appointment's not till Thursday, though."

"Dr. Kim wants us to check in tomorrow and stay overnight."

"Why?" Do they already know something? Are they anticipating trouble? Some horrible flaw requiring emergency surgery?

"They're doing a test where the results take twelve hours," says Isabelle. "So it's easier."

"Maybe I better come home."

"No. It's just part of the test. If we had somewhere in Toronto we could probably stay there. It's just overnight at the hospital because it's easier. Seriously."

"Tomorrow night."

"Yes, just for tests."

"This new doctor, he's young, right?"

"She. Fairly young, yes."

"A bit keen."

"Why is that…What do you mean?"

"I don't want some young hotshot who sees every kid as a science experiment."

"She's thinking for herself instead of just reading his file. How is that a bad thing?"

"How many kids like Sam has she had?"

"You can ask, if you ever meet her." Her shoes clop-clopping into the hallway. "Come on, Sammy, please. Shoes. Have you called your mom?"

"Yes," Carter lies. "Going to see her tomorrow, probably. I'd just feel more confident with an experienced specialist, is all."

"You're arguing against the best possible care for your son. I have to admit, you always find new ways to surprise."

///////

Red joins them on the third morning, and demonstrates how to walk when a stretch of bog can't be avoided. Quick and light. Lift the back foot before the front is fully landed. Feels almost like gliding. Carter prances like a dancer.

"Anyway, it doesn't always work," she says. "But try to avoid water, even if it looks like nothing. If there's bog, stick to the tree line. And if you need to grab a branch, try for the var because the needles are softer."

"Var?"

"Var, yes. I thought you were from here."

"Never spent much time in the woods."

Red smiles and her dreads go click-clack as she shakes her round head. She has a creamy brown complexion, but no foreign accent. "It's a brighter green than the spruce, and not so prickly," she says.

A man inherits the outdoors from his father. But Art Carter never held a rifle or set a rabbit slip, knew nothing of outboard motors or snowmobiles, owned no hip waders or heavy plaid shirts, and burned grocery-store fire logs in the fireplace. An occasional gift of wild game from a neighbour was eaten with great respect, in the manner of travellers at a foreign table who know they must scarf down the strange national dish. To have no interest in the woods was an embarrassing secret for a man who grew up in Bonavista Bay in the 1930s. Carter recalls his father amongst men, feigning comprehension and laughing too loud at anecdotes of fishing, snaring, and shooting moose and turrs.

They make the 30-minute drive to Benton, set out on a snowmobile trail, and are thrilled to find the RAF Ventura on a stretch of open, dry land, as if laid out by a curator.

"Another one from '42," says Terry, looking over his notes. "Went down a few weeks before the Hudson."

The chunk of fuselage is a crumpling grey husk, as if the aircraft had molted and returned to the sky in fresh skin. Carter bends at the waist to enter it, a protective hand to his head as he steps through puddles of brown water on the floor. The inside of the hull is scrawled with messages.

"This one says, 'Kyra I love you. You bitch,'" shouts Morris, following behind him. Everyone laughs.

"People often date their graffiti," says Terry. "Let's record it. It's part of the site."

Carter and Morris crouch in the fuselage to record the dates. The earliest is from Tony in February of 1974.

The rest of the wreck is easily accessed around the clearing. Carter asks whether the pilot might have aimed for this spot, in hopes of a survivable landing.

"Could well be," says Terry. "No casualties, so full credit to him."

Wind pulls the measuring tape off line, so the site has to be mapped with a theodolite and surveyor's level. Red stumbles over the tripod and nearly smashes her head on a boulder, escaping with a nasty scratch at one temple. Terry calls everyone together for a brief refresher on site safety.

Andi and Morris make their way to a smaller section of fuselage, which stands on end.

"The crash didn't do this," says Morris, as Carter approaches. "He points up to the ragged edge, just beyond his reach. "See that cut? That's an axe. That's scavengers. Looks like they chopped away a piece and dragged it this far and gave up. Couldn't get it through the bushes."

Andi leans against the fuselage, wedging one heel in an oval window, and raises her camera. Part of the serial number appears over her head: AJ47. "Oh no!" she cries. "Look!"

Next to her, in black paint, is an expertly rendered pair of legs rising in a v. The feet are turned out, and a black triangle fills the space where the legs meet. Below the triangle is a large black dot in the centre of rounded buttocks. The artist's caption reads, *Pink or stink, take your pick.*

"That's disgusting," says Carter, in deference to Andi.

"Oh, it's just...boys," she says, and giggles.

There were boys in Carter's class who circulated such pictures, but he had always been too fastidious to laugh. It was another of his youthful failings, this excessive seriousness that scorned the absurd and the vulgar, and scorned the boys who reveled in it.

"What's interesting," says Morris, "is their urge to write them-selves into this scene." He slips away to perch on a rock. Produces a notebook, and chews on the end of a pen.

"What's his story?" asks Carter.

"Morris?" Andi raises her camera and stalks the piece from several angles. "Morris is all in."

"All in on what?"

"We all know where the job market's at. Of course we'd all love to be Terry in twenty years. But you may as well buy lottery tickets. So you've got to think about alternatives. Not Morris. He's going for it."

On his rock, Morris looks skyward, and bends over his note-book, scribbling quickly.

"Seems to have a lot on his mind," says Carter.

Andi waves at a persistent fly and ducks into the bushes to cap-ture the hidden side of the fuselage. "Morris really wants to be the professor type. He's working on a paper for a big conference this summer, and likes to make a show of it."

"About all this?"

"Plane wrecks and modernism, something along those lines."

She emerges with needles in her hair. "Can't go without captur-ing this," she says, and shoots several close-ups of the vulgar picture.

"I guess it is well done," says Carter. "Look at the calves, and the backs of the knees."

"Well done, except for this part," says Andi, tapping the back triangle. "He got to the most important bit, and couldn't finish it. So much agony over one little opening. He lost his nerve."

The site is rich—iron spikes, aluminum framework, an engine and wing piece they still haven't looked at—so they stay through lunch, sharing Vienna sausages, cereal bars, and cans of Coke. Andi asks Carter to follow her up a shallow hill and keep a discreet watch while she relieves herself. Terry has a habit of rambling, and last year nearly walked into her with her pants at her ankles.

He's standing guard when his phone chimes in the zippered, waterproof chest pocket of his jacket.

"There's a signal up here," he says.

"Order a pizza," calls Andi.

Leah has checked into hospital and the doctors have left no doubt that she will soon be released from her pain. She mostly sleeps now because of the morphine. But she has clear and lucid moments, and has left directions for when she is gone. These directions have been witnessed by the family and family lawyer and captured on video. Please accept my assurance that there is no doubt or ambiguity as to her specific wishes.

///////

His eyes race over the email twice more before he registers it's from Kevin. Kevin from North Bay, back in the picture after all these years.

Andi comes to his side, tugging at her jacket. "Anything urgent?"

"My ex is dying."

"I'm sorry."

"I sort of knew it. I had this feeling it was going to be now."

"I felt like that first time I was pregnant. Before I knew, I kind of knew." She looks at him. "But are you sorry? I'm not sure I'd be, to be honest. I'll tell everyone you need a minute."

She leaves him at the crest of the hill. She has kids?

Can he see Leah? What would he say?

I may be in Toronto soon, he writes to Kevin. *Would like to have a final moment with her.*

Below him, the group has already set out towards the wing-and-engine array, which is half-submerged in a small pond. Terry says the pond was likely created by an exploding depth charge.

As he expected, the travel site quotes obscene prices for Gander-Toronto on short notice. But if his first priority was Sam, Isabelle might agree to it.

He writes Jordan. *Any progress with the festivals? Singer auditions? Session players?* But sending the message brings on a rush of doubt. How foolish, to be in a band. The posing and posturing and heaving dramatics. The childlike need to be heard and applauded and taken seriously. Picking a silly band name, as if they were a gang of boys in a tree house. And isn't there something pathetic about fans? A little gang of followers sniffing at your heels like lost dogs.

From the crest of this ridge, Carter sees that they aren't so far into the wilderness. A couple of strips of highway show through the woods, and hydro wires strung along a line of towers. Further on, streaks of blue-grey sky on a flat horizon indicate one end of the airport tarmac, with the circular antenna of the military radar station rising beyond. It might be an hour's hike away, if the ground were passable.

His eye is drawn back to the crash site and four bodies trudging single file through knee-high grass, making for a half-submerged, gnarled hunk of machinery. Andi is in the back, young legs rising and falling, black ponytail wagging from the back of her ball cap.

Carter steps behind a long boulder. Seeing Andi's wet spot, he straddles it and unzips.

It's a rich confluence of events. Leah approaching death while he searches ancient sites of death and destruction. Carter surrounded by the trappings of flight, past and present, as he contemplates all the things he has taken flight from. The circular route that brings him back to Gander, to the past where he once obsessively plotted the future. His mother unacknowledged since he arrived. The thrill of watching Andi stumble in the thicket as he adds his hot stream to hers.

The mystery at the heart of it all is his inexplicable need to see Leah again before she dies. Why? What possible difference could it make to sit before her one more time? It's more in his body than his head. He twitches with it. He finishes pissing, and pauses. Runs his thumb up his cock and down again, and circles it with two fingers.

He could. Right here. But the energy quickening in him isn't lust. Or it could be, but that would waste it. His blood races, strange and familiar.

For the first time in years, Carter has an idea that demands music.

16

Joyce was at the living room window waiting for the phone to ring when the garbage truck rounded the corner. An old dump truck purchased cheap from the air force. The driver's face hung in the window. His partner jogged along the sidewalk, trying to keep pace. They shouted at each other. The truck slowed to let the walking man catch up, and sped away just as he grabbed the side mirror to hoist himself aboard. The walking man tried to hang on, but fell and tumbled. There was more shouting, the two of them sunburnt and grinning. The walking man slapped dust from his green overalls.

"Boys," said Joyce. "Boys and their games."

A few days ago, Arthur had suggested she might adopt a more generous view of the people around her.

"Like who?"

"People in general," he said. "It's a shame to be so negative. Think of the boy. Think of the lessons you'll want to impart."

"If people are fools the child ought to know it."

Joyce could see him weighing whether to take up the debate. Then he opened his newspaper and said, "I'm sure it's very hard, your first child and all."

"It's nothing to do with Herbert," she replied, and they let it drop.

Nearly ten years they had tried for a baby before Herbert was born. Arthur had been terribly agitated during the pregnancy, suspecting, as Joyce did, that it might be their only chance. But Herbert was well into his second year now. There was no need for Arthur to still be after her about every little thing.

Still, his words had worked into her, as they always did. She respected him more than anyone she had ever known. His dignity, the way he carried himself in the world, she found intensely romantic. She loved his seriousness and intense focus on the few things that truly engaged him, his complete immersion in a task or book or argument.

She resolved to do better, resolved not to fly at him so hard next time.

It had not occurred to Arthur to ask whether her mood had anything to do with her father. Nearly a week since she told him her father was dying, and he hadn't said a word about it. The two men had never met, as Joyce was long cut off from the family by the time Arthur appeared. A letter announcing their marriage had received no reply.

Gloria had called last Thursday, when Joyce's leg cramps were so bad she could barely make it to the phone. It's your father, said Gloria. Mom says he's taken to his bed and won't be getting up again. They've put a mustard poultice on his neck but it won't do any good. Mom's down there every day, as long as your brother allows it.

The estrangement was all Marty's doing. Arthur understood that, though Joyce had never mentioned the other reports that had trickled in from Gloria's mother over the last few years. How Marty tortured the old man beyond all endurance, hectoring and belittling him, keeping him locked up in the house, hardly feeding him. Turning away all visitors, refusing their pies or puddings or even a meal of fish.

The garbage truck lurched to a halt in front of the house, shooting a black cloud from the smokestack over the driver's head. The smoke was heavy, threads of it sinking and hovering over the new pavement and new lawns that wilted in the choking dry summer. Arthur had stood for council last fall, on a proposal for new garbage trucks and more efficient collection. For two weeks he had turned his collar against the September rain and dodged the muck of streets not yet paved, knocking on the doors of new bungalows and townhouses. Coming home with his raglan soaked through and mud nearly up to his knees. Changing into clean slacks and filling his pockets with breath mints. Back out again until well after dark. Joyce washed the slacks every morning. The mud was impossible. Thick clay churned up by construction and black earth from lawns newly laid.

Arthur had rehearsed and tailored his argument so as to be irrefutable. Battered old air force dump trucks were poorly suited to garbage duty. They broke down constantly, scuttling the weekly collection schedule and eating up countless hours of maintenance and manpower. The investment in a fleet of proper trucks would be recouped within a decade. But people didn't want to hear of anything that might raise taxes. Some were still upset about paying any taxes at all. We should have just stayed up at the airport, they said. Government land and government services. Arthur had not polled well.

The walking man grabbed the trashcan at the end of the driveway and used his other hand to swing aboard the truck. With deft sleight of hand he removed the lid, tipped the can bottom up, returned it to the curb, and dropped the lid back in place. The truck lurched to the next stop, billowing smoke. Joyce and Arthur had been among the first residents of Alcock Street, surrounded by the shells of half-completed houses. The neighbourhood had filled up in the two years since, but a fresh timber smell hung in the air. There were sewer smells too, and a chemical scent that made Joyce nauseous when she was first pregnant.

The gentle snoring from Herbert's room meant Nan Carter was asleep in the rocking chair, with Herbert dozing in his little bed next to her. His midday naps were deep and impenetrable, and his grandmother slept just as deeply. Joyce didn't have to think about dinner, as there was chicken and potato left from last night. Arthur wanted chicken every Sunday lately, now that the stuffing was to his liking. It was his mother who set her straight on it. "Your savoury isn't fresh," she told Joyce one Sunday. "If your savoury's no good you'll taste nothing but onions. And real bread crumbs, mind you. None of those big chunks."

The creak and clap of a screen door brought Donna Primm into view, hugging herself as she crossed the street. The garbage men paused to watch, and Joyce stepped out to meet her on the step.

"Did you hear about that poor girl?" asked Donna, her fine cheekbones glowing. She was very pale, but flushed easily with all the young blood pressing beneath her skin. "Beat up and left for dead behind the post office?"

"Dead?"

"Well, no. But she was beat awful bad. Her family is new in town." Everyone was new to Donna. It was only last year she had arrived from North Bay and moved in across the street with her remote and gorgeous pilot husband. The wind tugged red hair from her scarf and whipped it around her neck. "Anyway, they've arrested a boy, and I believe you know the family?"

"Which family?" Donna often counted on Joyce to flesh out her gossip with telling details of history and reputation.

"Tucker?" Donna peered at her quizzically.

"Anthony Tucker?"

"That's it."

"He didn't. A little girl?"

"She's eleven, twelve years old? Something like that."

Joyce got a chill like her blood drained dry. "I grew up with Gloria Tucker. She and Frank got me my first job here."

"How awful for them."

"I held him, Anthony, when he was just a couple of days old. In the old Banting Hospital."

"He hit her with a junk of wood."

"I remember thinking it was a funny place to have a baby, a place full of sick people. We were all born at home when I grew up." Joyce said this to push away her first thought: that Anthony was capable of it. The obvious suspect. He had turned strange during high school, always clowning around. Gloria used to say she couldn't get a sensible word from him. He had failed a grade, and had no apparent interest in anything. Joyce didn't see Gloria much lately. But she saw Anthony when she drove past Sears, where the young crowd gathered in the shelter of the wide front steps. He was always shouting and carrying on, a curly spray of hair swinging around his spotty face.

"Do they have other children, besides this boy?" asked Donna.

"Three." Frank would be at the police station by now, called away from work. Gloria wouldn't go there with him. She'd stay at home with her private shame. It was up to Frank to appear at the station on Reid Street, whispering, "Yes sir....Yes sir" as the officer explained the situation. Then a short visit with Anthony, the two of them lost for words.

"There'll be nothing for them but to leave town now." Donna pulled a pack of Viscounts from her jacket. Joyce thought about pouring drinks. But lately the whiskey gave her a funny feeling, as if this house and this street were foreign to her. It had started after Herbert was born. A kind of vertigo after one of two drinks. A third one usually got her back on her bearings.

Herbert's feet pounded in the hallway. He arrived at the screen door, clutching at the mesh like a prisoner and pressing his face to it. "Mama!" he shouted, and sputtered a laugh.

"How's your bum?" said Nan Carter, coming up behind him.

"I better go," said Joyce. "I should call Gloria, see if she needs anything."

231

"No word on your dad?" asked Nan, rubbing her sleepy eyes as Joyce let herself in.

"No." Perhaps her father was already dead, and Gloria's mother was lending a hand. She would phone after the body was washed and dressed, the hair combed and the stubble shaved. Or she was consumed by her own grief. Her oldest grandson in jail.

According to reports, Joyce's father hadn't been the same since he dug the water line into the house last summer. With electricity finally come to the Cape, he didn't want to be hauling water from the well anymore. So he dug a two-foot-deep trench and ran a length of pipe from the well to the house, where he put in an electric pump to draw the water. The project had set off another confrontation with Marty. Nobody could quite grasp what the fight was about—their battles had always been unfathomable—but the result was that Marty refused to help and Dad had worn himself out digging the trench alone.

He'd be waked in the front room. All hands would turn out, as her father wasn't one to make enemies. A few might come across from Arnold's Cove, and maybe a few of Mother's crowd from Rosaru. They had met when he went there to work the whale factory. Three days they'd wake him, and Marty would make a meal of it. The only son in his mourning clothes, circling the room with his sad little smile. Claiming his hugs and caresses from the women. Lingering just a moment too long with all of them. All except Nell Hinchey. Poor Nell would stand inside the door, suffering his indifference, clutching the blueberry buckle she had baked from berries picked just that morning. Nell had long ago betrayed her favour for Marty, the worst mistake you could make with him.

If Joyce dared to show, Marty would keep her in the kitchen to clean fish or pick the turrs he shot that morning. Joyce hated picking turrs. You had to ruffle their feathers to let the water in, then dunk them in hot water just long enough to get them loose. She always scalded her arms, and if the temperature wasn't right—just below boiling—it could turn into a mess.

But Gloria's mother said Marty never went hunting and fishing anymore. Made his dinner at the shop, opening tins of ham and salmon and bone-in chicken. He couldn't get to church on Sunday without stopping to catch his breath, mopping his brow as he steadied himself on somebody's gatepost. Joyce was picturing the wake as it might have been when she left Cape St. Rose, eighteen years ago. Nell Hinchey was surely married by now, with grey hairs sprouting from her chin and children climbing her sausage limbs.

There had been a time when it seemed Marty and Nell might settle together. Back when Marty was trim and fit and could swim to Birch Island and back three times running on a summer's day. But he was rough with her. Nell's father had come over one day to complain about it, Marty sending her home with her dress torn up.

Joyce pulled a bowl from the fridge and a spoon from the drying rack. Chunks of apple and celery suspended in green Jell-O. She had to eat. If Arthur came home tonight and found the Jell-O salad untouched, she'd be in for another lecture about her appetite. Arthur was a gentle soul, but he had a poor way of talking to people. It had surely cost him votes.

Herbert was off again, a Frankenstein monster staggering on stiff legs, arms extended. He had been walking for a month, and still delighted in the mechanical wonder of it. Laughed at his great tumbles, even the hard ones that left him bruised. The dining room chandelier chimed when Herbert crashed to the floor. The toilet water rippled.

"Come to Nan!" Arthur's mother scooped him up and stilled the churning legs against her broad body. She was remarkably strong for a woman past seventy, and quick too. Her territorial claims were modest. She ate anything. Kept herself tidy. Joyce hadn't wanted her moving in just as Herbie was born. But she was a saviour in that first year, taking shifts with the baby while Joyce tried to sleep.

Joyce walked to the pharmacy in the afternoon.

"Quiet little girl," said the druggist. "Grade seven."

"How bad is it?"

"She's in hospital, is all we've heard." He dropped the ointment tube in a bag. "Young people today. They're gone mad. You know the boy, and his family, I think?"

"Gloria and I grew up together. Haven't seen her much in the last few years."

"And he's with the weather office."

"Frank? Yes. He was always very cheerful. But he always seemed sad underneath..." Joyce trailed off, uncertain of whether to mention his drinking or whether he even drank at all anymore. She had long avoided him.

She followed the sidewalk across the town square to the post office, where an empty police car blocked the trail that curled behind the building. There wasn't much to it. Just a few trees caught between streets, with a small, weedy pool where the older children gathered in summer to catch and torture frogs.

/////

Arthur's mother said there was something about seeing men on the moon that drove young people mad. "Like people can do anything, because there's no sense to the world anymore. When I was a girl, you always knew there was an order to things."

Donna Primm crossed the street again. The three of them met on the sidewalk, with Herbert in his playpen on the front lawn. Donna's hair was gathered in a bun now, with damp strands sticking to her neck. She had been stretched out in a lawn chair sunning herself for a good part of the afternoon.

"They say the girl might die," said Donna.

"It's like a sickness, teenagers today," said Nan. "The drugs and whatnot. You should move somewhere else," she said to Donna. "This is no place for children."

"We aren't ready for children yet."

"And why would you? If you have your pills, or whatever, why would you bring a child into this world?"

This was strange coming from Nan Carter, who could quote Pope Paul's encyclical against birth control. "A man who grows accustomed to contraceptive methods may forget the reverence due to a woman, and reduce her to being a mere instrument for the satisfaction of his own desires." Nan had long suspected that Donna, bursting ripe but still childless, must be on the pill. Donna walked around the neighbourhood in blue jeans and flip-flops, had spent the whole summer lying in the yard in a tiny bikini. The house came with a lovely little garden and she hadn't done a thing with it. Just yesterday, Nan had grumbled about Donna's freckled nose and large hazel eyes, as if they were the telltale features of a sinner.

"We might go to the airport for an ice cream," said Joyce. "Do you want to join us?" She loved the new terminal, though she had left work before it opened in 1959. The reach of its ceiling. The smooth ascent of the escalator. The leather seats. The mural with its strange faces and shades of colour she had never seen before.

"Is your husband off at four?" asked Donna.

"Yes."

"He'll have plenty to say about this," said Nan.

It was Arthur's favourite dinner-table topic of late. Something must be done about the young people, so they aren't just hanging about idle. He liked to quote a statistic from a few years back, which identified Gander as having more children per capita than anywhere else in Canada. "So it's not like we didn't see this coming." Fearful stories had been circulating. Katie Hogan's boy was rushed to the hospital in a marijuana stupor. That pretty Tessier girl ran away with a fellow in a van, and her parents hadn't heard from her in a year. A family on Earhart Street gave their twin boys the run of the basement, with a separate entrance, and now it was nothing but parties day and night.

235

Arthur had met the deputy mayor to propose a committee of concerned citizens. "A rational approach," he called it. The committee would sit down with young people to hear their concerns and get them organized in some fashion, so they wouldn't be traipsing around town with their long hair and blue jeans. Don't lecture them on the dangers, he said, because young people relish danger. The issue is idleness. Fill their idle hours in a productive manner, so they have to keep their wits about them, and all but the dreamers and ne'er-do-wells will soon lose interest in cannabis and ear-splitting music.

Joyce found the music crude. But she could understand the appeal. The wildness in it, how it spoke to the great dramas of youth.

She had given up singing when she got married. A few of the old band still scratched together a show for the occasional New Year's Eve. But everyone liked to play records now, and with the young people mad for their electric music, the old songs she used to sing would soon be forgotten.

Last year, Arthur had nearly bought a Chevrolet Biscayne. But Reg Pritchett was the sales manager at Chev, and when he started reminiscing with Joyce about their times with the band, Arthur stiffened and withdrew. They ended up going to Ford.

Her memories of the band felt like they came from another century, or another world altogether.

"I suspect we'll all be murdered in our beds," said Nan. "This town. It's terrible."

"It's not just this town," said Joyce. "People get beaten and killed all over. Didn't Arthur's Uncle Selby kill his wife? Just up the road from your house? Arthur says he threw her over the stairs."

"That's just talk. She fell over the stairs. She could hardly stay on her feet, what with the bad hip and the bunions. It's different now, with all the young people and the drugs."

Herbert smacked his lips and coughed wetly. Joyce crossed the lawn and reached into his mouth to free a chunk of cream cracker.

The opposite cheek bulged with a huge lump of meal. She went after it with a crooked forefinger.

"Ayyyggh," said Herbert.

"Don't bite," hissed Joyce, catching his eye. She pulled the soggy lump out and flicked it to the grass. "You've got to watch him with food, Nan."

The jet crossing above had to be an air force fighter, with its high-pitched roar coming over them in waves.

"Ice cream would be nice," said Donna. "Did you speak with your friend after? The boy's family?"

"There was no answer." A white lie that Joyce would correct later. She had to call Gloria eventually, drop over with a meal or something. And she was still counting on her for any word from the Cape.

A crowd lined up for ice cream at the airport, burnt-red children chaperoned by sweating fathers or surly older siblings. You would never know from their faces that a girl had been beaten nearly to death by Anthony Tucker. Joyce, Nan, and Donna strolled the perimeter of the lounge with their twirlies, pushing Herbert in his stroller.

"Hello, Joyce," said Mary, as they walked past the Air Canada counter. "That can't be your boy? He's some size!"

"I thought you retired," said Joyce.

"I keep trying."

"There's no one around at all today," said Joyce.

"Nah. It's nothing like it used to be. I'd love to come out and sit for a cigarette, but I'm trying to quit."

"Me too." They laughed and Mary disappeared through a door, into the inner workings of the airport that Joyce was no longer privy to.

"You know, they're casting about for a freight clerk at EPA," said Donna. "Just part time."

"Oh, no. I'm through with all that."

Herbert wanted to walk when they stepped out into the court-yard. But he wailed when a 737 came in, sending an oily gust of heat their way. So they made for the car. Across the tarmac and the old airport road, the horizon showed a ragged, sun-scorched thicket where the streets and buildings of the old town site used to be. People called it the "Army Side" now. Donna said that when teenaged boys talked about "going to the Army Side," it meant taking a girl there in a car. Joyce believed her, as Donna was not much older than a teenager herself.

Driving home, Joyce cut through Kolsou's parking lot and into the town square to avoid the post office. The events of the day resurfaced, and she chided herself for stepping away from the phone with her father on his deathbed and Gloria in desperate straits.

17

The mural is freakishly extravagant. A riot of earthy colours, crowded with mutant birds, exotic flora, and ungainly human figures cut at hard angles, their faces blank and arms held aloft.

"Almost a holiness to it," says Morris. He draws his index finger left to right. "You can see where it references pilgrimage, martyrdom, revelation. You can even read it as a post-apocalyptic vision, as befits the era."

"It scared me when I was a kid," says Carter. It unsettles him even now.

"Who did it?" asks Red.

"*Flight and Its Allegories*, by Kenneth Lochhead," says Terry. "Have a good look around. Everything we've been looking for out there, the power of those plane wrecks, the spirit of that history is in this room. This terminal opened in 1959, when flight was still considered one of the wonders of the modern age."

"One of the great Modernist rooms in the country," adds Morris.

Andi bends to examine the floor, touching its enormous burnished tiles. "It's so earthy, but at the same time..."

"Mondrianesque terrazzo floor," reads Terry. "Makes you wonder why can't we still have airports like this. Winnipeg used to have a beauty, and that's gone. Everything's a box now. Or a glorified shopping mall, like Toronto."

What strikes Carter is the scope of the room, spectacular and worldly. His childhood perspective is uncompromised. But it's faded badly, inevitably. The mural seems to have a film over it, and cracks split several of the tiles. The air is stale, infected by the mundane domestic lounge next door.

"I suppose you know this place well?" asks Terry.

"We weren't allowed in here after they restricted it to international flights," says Carter. "But I saw it a couple of times, on school field trips."

"Typical Newfoundland," says Morris. "Cut people off from their heritage."

"Everything is so hard and straight." Andi makes angles with her hands.

"Herman Miller couches," says Terry. "Eames chairs."

"I can't believe we could lose this place," says Morris, spreading his arms.

"Apparently, the utilities alone run about a million per year," says Terry.

"Not to mention maintenance, and just keeping the place up to code," says Red. "Plus, there's nobody here but us."

"Christ," says Morris. "Heritage hasn't got a chance around here. Can't even get the archaeologists on board."

"It needs a creative solution," Terry intones. "Preservation isn't for purists. Taking a hard line is how you lose the battle."

"There must be some part of Newfoundland that hates itself. Like, this urge to burn the whole fucking thing down." Morris walks away.

"Wants to be alone with his boner," whispers Red. She heads further into the room, to the curved sculpture of birds.

Terry lifts his hands, thumbs touching, to frame the mural. "It doesn't work," he says. "It's the one major flaw in the room. It bullies the imagination." He heads for the stairs to the upper level, taking them at trot. Andi and Carter turn to the other end of the room and walk up the stalled escalator. "First escalator in Newfoundland!" calls Terry.

"Look at him go," says Carter. Morris is below them as they reach the upper level, busy with his notebook. "He writes in that thing like he's trying to kill it."

"At least he's passionate," says Andi. "What about you? Is this stuff really what you want, or are you just doing it to do something?"

"For a long time I was in a band. It used up all my passion, I think."

"What did you play?"

"Guitar."

"Guitar god? You don't seem like the type."

They lean into the rail and look down on the main floor.

"What about you?"

"Came at this kind of sideways," says Andi. "I started in film studies."

"Movies?"

"I believe that's what they're called. You know, Terry's wrong about the mural. Without it, the room is too orderly. Inhuman, almost."

It was the order of the airport that most appealed to Carter as a boy. The flat land and open view, the precise tree line and groomed green spaces.

"Do you know French films?" he asks.

"Oh, yes." Andi gathers her hair and drops it over her shoulders. "Better than I care to."

"Do you know one called *Umbrellas of Cherbourg*?"

"Who made it?"

"I don't know."

"Sounds familiar. Hang on." Andi works her phone, and catches her breath. "Catherine Deneuve's in it!"

241

"She's big?"

"Big?" Andi laughs. "Oh my god."

"Anyway, there's a lot of singing in it."

"I probably sat through a sleepy Monday morning screening at some point. Yeah, the still looks familiar. I'll ask my friend Bridgett. She stuck with film studies. I kind of drifted on. What do you want me to ask her?"

"I don't know. It just, stayed with me, I guess."

"I totally get it."

///////

Carter's phone erupts, waking him from a nap. Sam and Isabelle are on their way to Sick Kids by now. But the message is from North Bay Kevin.

At this point we must restrict visits to immediate family. Thank you for your thoughts. I will call you in person when there is any news. This is a courtesy due to you because of your previous relationship with her. Please respect our privacy during this difficult time.

Prick.

He calls Jordan. No answer. "Very urgent that you get back to me with anything you know," he tells voicemail, and emails the same.

///////

It's dart night at Mitch's Lounge. "Mixed league every Tuesday," says the bartender. Beyond the pool table, dark figures flick forearms to pierce brightly lit dartboards. Thunk, thunk, thunk. Murmurs of approval or consolation. Then the next group, chins lifted and right arms raised, like ballet dancers poised to begin. Thunk, thunk, thunk. A voice cries out: "Yes, b'y!"

Terry pulls together three tables next to the bar. Carter sits in a corner, wedged between the door and a line of lotto machines.

The machines are unused, but still ping and whirr like a parking lot carnival. Andi sits between Morris and Red, well out of Carter's range. There are two young guys he doesn't know, bearded and man-bunned. Probably from the Globe Theatre dig.

By waiting until Saturday, leaving at five-thirty in the morning with no checked bags, and sitting in Halifax for nearly three hours, he can get to Toronto and back for under $900. He could get it close to $800 by staying an extra day. But he can't. He can't skip out on the dig like that. Three days max. Kevin won't stop him. Prick's not even immediate family himself.

Carter will see Leah Saturday afternoon, and tell her the band earned its legacy. He'll vow to protect it. If he can look her in the eye and tell her that, if she can hear him, she'll believe it.

Then he'll take a day to see Sam.

Thunk, thunk, thunk. A round of applause and voices. A scream rises above it all, a short-haired woman jeering at the other team.

A grey-bearded man in green rubber boots approaches the bar, glances their way, and stops. "Terry Purchase! You're not back again?" he shouts.

"Hawco, you miserable son of a bitch!"

"Jesus Kerrr-rist!" Bodies part so the men can lean across the table and lock hands.

"Hawco here saved our tails last year, pulled us out of the muck with his big old pickup."

"Back for more, Doctor T. Still digging for gold, are you?"

There is laughter and shouting from the dart game, and the short-haired woman pumps her fist.

"Oh yes," says Terry. "And how'd you make out with the moose last year?"

His friend inflates his large face and heaves a sigh, removes his ball cap to scratch a thinning scalp. "Two days over on Dead Wolf Pond," he says. "Cows? My Jesus, by the dozen. Only saw the one bull, and he must've been three hundred yards off."

Terry chucks his chin and snorts, as if disappointment at Dead Wolf Pond is all too common.

"You got a bull-only ticket, you're never gonna fill it over there," says Hawco.

"Hawco is a hero in this town, my friends," says Terry raising his pint. "How many pots of soup did you make for those Americans on 9/11?"

"Oh, a good deal of soup," says Hawco.

"Don't be blowing smoke up his arse," calls a woman with a cigarette, standing outside the fire escape door. Carter catches Andi's eye. She smiles and shrugs as if to say, how did we end up here?

Carter excuses himself to the bathroom, where an old 3-D photo of Joey Smallwood hangs over the sink. Joey sits with a contemplative hand to his chin. His blue shirt matches the blue map of Newfoundland behind him. Carter leans to one side, narrowing the angle to get the blurry 3-D effect. The island recedes, and Joey jumps out, especially his thick black glasses and the don't-fuck-with-me glint in his eye.

Laying his phone on the back of the toilet, he selects the flight, declines travel insurance, lounge access, the air miles discount, advance seat selection, and the prepaid onboard café voucher. Clicks through to review his itinerary. Hesitates again.

Nine hundred bucks is reasonable, for a flight leaving the day after tomorrow. But it's still nine hundred he doesn't have. Carter saves the booking and gives himself until midnight to decide.

"Everything okay?" Andi meets him outside the washroom, as if she's been waiting.

"Me? Yeah, fine. Actually," he waves the phone as if news just arrived. "My boy has to go to the hospital."

"Oh no!" says Andi, her eyes flying open wide. She swallows quickly and clears her throat. "I mean, Jesus, what happened?"

"It's a heart condition. Or we're not sure. It might be."

"The poor kid. Poor you." A hand on his arm. "How old is he?"

"Four. It's nothing. Chances are it's nothing. They keep saying it's nothing. But he has to keep going back."

"Is he sick now?" She waves away smoke drifting in from the nearby fire escape.

"He's never been sick. But he has an appointment tomorrow."

"So sorry," she says, and touches a moist palm on his cheek.

Terry is in full flow with his 9/11 tale. "Jimmy Meisner is with air traffic control," he says. "He comes to work that morning and he can't believe it. The radar. The radar blocked, *blocked* with aircraft." He raises a finger and twirls it. "Thousands of people with nowhere to go."

"That's right," says Hawco, who has pulled up a chair.

"Now, Jimmy knows what it's like to seek safe haven, because his own mother came here to escape the Communists," says Terry. "So he calls his wife and says, I hope everyone in this town got the spare room ready. I hope they got the basement ready."

Bob Dylan sings from the ceiling. Hawco leans back and roars in unison. He's standing on the road. It's raining on his shoes. Lord knows he's paid his dues. And on to the next verse.

/////

Andi sits with her feet dangling, struggling to stay upright on the slippery floral bedspread. She pulls her arms from her windbreaker, letting it fall behind her. Presses her knees together, as if trying to take up the smallest possible space, and silently accepts a drink. It's warm in the room—there's a film of sweat on her upper lip—but Carter can't open a window because the wind has shifted.

Hawco plants himself next to Andi, pouring shots in plastic cups and handing them around. The students sniff the drinks—rye whiskey, which Hawco acquired from the bar—and take careful sips.

Red sprawls on the bed behind Andi and Hawco, her dirt-caked boots dangling. Terry perches on the bar fridge. Morris sits on the dresser.

Carter accepts his drink of rye, and picks his way through knees and feet to find space just inside the door. He checks his phone, half expecting something from Isabelle.

"Ready?" says Terry.

Morris will read them a draft of his conference paper. Just the introduction, where he lays out his theme. "Hang on," he says, shuffling papers and smoothing his beard. "Okay? Are we okay?"

"This is a two-minute elevator pitch," Terry announces. "He gets two minutes to tell us why we should care." Red snorts a giggle. "Okay, go."

"Okay. So I'm going to start with this. This is the opening, so it's super-important." A tug of his hair. "Okay. In 1912, Pablo Picasso produced a still life called *The Scallop Shell*, one of the foundations, sorry, foundational works of Cubism. Cubist art, I mean. The piece included the reproduction of a cover from a pamphlet about aviation. The title of the pamphlet, featured prominently in the piece, is *Notre Avenir est dans l'Air*, excuse my French, which means Our Future is in the Air."

Morris removes his wire-rimmed glasses and rubs the lens with the hem of his shirt. Hawco shifts in his seat. "Refills for anyone who wants it," he says, raising the bottle by its neck.

"So, I'll have, you know, a slide projected for the Picasso thing," says Morris. "Okay. So. Picasso and his colleagues saw in aviation an analogy for their own work, which was conquering new dimensions, expressing new energy, and rejecting nostalgia. Their age was one of optimism, excitement, and the breakdown of the old order. In its early days, aviation was seen as an embodiment of energy, youth, transgression, danger, immediate experience, and the breaking of new boundaries." He looks up. "Yeah?"

Terry nods for him to continue.

"Today we view technology with suspicion—embracing it, while at the same time worrying that it drains away the energy of true experience. This was not the case a century ago. The new technology of flight was seen as a source of renewed energy and vitality."

"You say 'energy' a lot," says Red.

"Okay. Cool." Morris makes a note. "I mean, I'm just roughing it out right now. Okay. Almost done. So, beauty is nothing but the beginning of terror. Quoting the poet Rainer Maria Rilke. For proof, he might have pointed to our early fascination with flight, or to the current growing field of aviation archaeology. Okay, that's it."

"Hear-hear!" shouts Red from flat on her back.

"Good start," says Terry. "You'll want to shore up the leaps between modernism and romanticism. Just smooth that path forward."

"Yeah. I mean, it's just the two-minute thing."

"Are you going to link it to the airport?" asks Andi. "I mean with that mural, it's perfect, even more than Picasso."

"Picasso gets their attention, right off the hop," says Morris.

"True."

Red holds out her cup for a refill from Hawco. "So you're probably going to get into the whole thing with authenticity and pastiche?"

"Yeah, totally," says Morris. "Like, you've got the original wreck, which is totally real. Then comes the other stuff, like the graffiti, and trash left by hikers and scavengers. It's total pastiche."

"No," says Red. "Pastiche is deliberate. It has to be self-conscious about what it borrows. The sources."

"This is more how we experience it."

"That's just randomness, Morris. Don't read so much into it."

"There's human agency in those sites." Morris twists, trying to address Red, who is still on her back on the bed. "We made them."

"Oh, so the plane intended to crash and kill a bunch of people and leave a pile of mechanical garbage." Her hand rises and swoops it down.

"Why are you hung up on intent?"

"I see what Morris is driving at," says Terry, adopting a conciliatory tone. "Newfoundland feels so ancient. There's still a wildness to it. And to see these machines that used to be so state-of-the-art, to see them broken against this ancient beauty."

Morris grunts. Red smirks.

"How about a tune!" calls Hawco. "How about it, hey?"

"Not that song," says Terry. "I know the one you're thinking of. Not with ladies present."

"But we sing it every year," says Red, who sits up and takes the bottle from Hawco to pour another round. "The ladies don't mind at all, right?" She looks to Andi, who shrugs.

"Oh, we'll keep it clean, keep it clean," says Hawco, and starts in, keeping time with his foot.

Away, away, with fife and drum
Here we come, full of rum
Looking for women to pat on the bum
In the North Atlantic Squa-ha-dron

Carter checks his phone again. Still nothing from Isabelle. But Jordan has surfaced.

Sad, even if everyone saw it coming. Just wanted to let you know that plans had to change to adapt to Leah's wishes. Sorry to shut you out of the process like that, but she's been driving the bus on this. Respect.

"Come on!" shouts Hawco. "Who wants the next verse?"

Terry sings:

The RAF are on the bit
Giving Hitler lots of shit

Applause for Terry as Carter returns to the Air Canada booking page. The red-eye is still there. Same price. But his booking has expired.

"Come on, Herb Carter," shouts Terry. "Don't be hiding back there. You got to learn a verse or two."

"Refills," cries Red.

"Just one more," says Hawco. "Couple of fingers."

Carter refreshes the website and picks his flights again. His "confirmed booking" appears again. And somehow, the cost of his return fare just went up by over $400. He backtracks to "book my flight," and the cheap flight he picked, the Tango Plus or whatever the fuck they call it, is gone. He logs off the system and logs back on again.

Terry continues with a verse of the song about pilots taking pills and shitting from Yarmouth to Gander.

The cheap fare is definitely gone. Terry finishes his bit—*in the North Atlantic Squa-ha-dron*—and they're all clapping and shouting. Carter will straighten out the flight and announce that he has to go home for three days. When he tells them why they'll slap his back and raise a toast. Andi will send him off with a sustaining hug.

But he'll be goddamned if he's going to pay $1,270 for a round trip that was close to half that price an hour ago. Carter dials the number provided on the booking page. Outrage won't get him anywhere. The airlines are numb to it. Far better to be disappointed. Don't they have family emergency fares or compassionate fares, something like that? Carter recalls getting some sort of deal when his father died. He'll hold Leah in reserve, play that card if he's stonewalled. Do ex-husbands qualify as family? Surely, in a case of life and death. He could leave out the ex.

All our agents are currently assisting other customers. Tinkly piano plays in Carter's ear. He knows the tune but can't place it.

Red stands. "The one-six-one—"

"Not that verse," says Terry. "There's no need."

"But who cares?" says Red. "Who gives a shit? I don't."

She looks to Andi, who smiles and looks away, as if interested in something on the wall.

"Heave it outta ya, missus," cries Hawco, who has an arm strung around Morris, who shies from the embrace.

Red tips back her head.

The one-six-one crew number four
Went out one night to find a whore
With her legs spread wide
You could fit inside
The North Atlantic Squa-ha-dron.

Carter's phone announces an incoming call from Isabelle, but he can't risk it. If the airline answers and he's not there, he'll lose his place in the queue.

Hawco whoops and claps. The others follow suit, and drinks spill over. Terry smiles. "Ha-ha!" shouts Hawco, clapping Red on the shoulder. "You don't mind, missus! You don't mind at all!"

The room telephone rings on the bedside table.

"I imagine that's management," says Terry, and reaches for the phone. "We're keeping somebody awake."

"Let me handle it," says Hawco. "I know the b'ys." Terry hands him the receiver.

"Who's next?" shouts Red.

"Hello, sorry to keep you waiting. This is Evan speaking. How may I help you?"

A person! "Oh, hi," says Carter. "Yes. I was online, and, well, I was booking my flight…"

Hawco holds the room phone to his chest and silently mouths, "It's your wife."

Carter points to his cell. "Just ask her to give me two minutes."
Hawco offers a thumbs-up.

"I'm sorry, sir. Can you speak up, please? How may I help you?"

"One moment," says Carter, and heads for the quiet of the bathroom. It's locked. He knocks. They're roaring behind him now, several voices singing about the pilot buggering the wireless boy.

"This is Evan, sir. Can I help you?"

"Just one moment." Carter opens the door to his room and steps outside. He turns to shut the door behind him and Andi is standing there, trying the bathroom doorknob. Then Hawco appears, and the three of them are at the threshold, breathing the fetid night air. Hawco looks almost comically solemn, his eyes downcast. Carter's chest floods with panic. *Sam. Please, not Sam. It's supposed to be just routine.*

"Is it Sam?" he asks, pulling the awful words from his throat. He grips the doorjamb to steady himself.

"Who?"

"My wife, when you talked to her."

The bathroom door opens and Morris emerges. "Whoa," he says. "This town reeks." He, Hawco, and Andi are bathed in a flood of brilliant bathroom light, the shit-sticky night air curling around them. The others have moved on to another verse.

In Newfoundland when it got hot
We used to fornicate a lot

"You have a friend named Lee?" asks Hawco.
"What?"

Only the fools would be pulling their tools

"Do you wish to continue this call?"

In the North Atlantic Squa-ha-dron

"Lee? Or Leah, is it?"
"Yes."
"She passed away tonight. Your wife wanted you to know."
"Oh, I'm sorry," says Andi.
"Holy shit," says Morris.

"Sir, can I help you?"

Andi takes Carter's fingers for a moment. The stink rolls over them, yet she still smells like outdoors. Like black soil and dust. He loves youth, with its clear eyes and fresh dirt and elastic limbs.

"Then it's not Sam. Of course it isn't."

"No sir. This is Evan speaking. Do you wish to remain on the line?"

18

She never got to see Marty after. She waited too long. He was admitted to the Health Sciences on Monday, and she put it off for a day or two. Finally on Thursday she packed her bag for the drive into St. John's. Then the phone rang. It was Marty's wife to say he was gone.

"I'm so sorry, Esther," said Joyce.

"And all that time we wasted dragging him into St. John's," she said. "We should have left him to die in bed."

"Arthur died in his bed," said Joyce.

"Anyway, we're leaving today. Take him back home."

Joyce kept packing. But now she'd be driving to Cape St. Rose. After so many years.

/////

She set the bag in the front hall and called Donna across the street to water the plants.

"Father O'Rourke is back," said Donna.

"What do you mean?"

"Back in town."

"Not back with the church?"

"No, no. That's all over."

Joyce couldn't imagine Father O'Rourke showing his face again. Nobody could have such gall.

"Where did you hear this, Donna?"

"It was all the talk when I dropped Cathy at school. They said he's back to look after a few things, and it was all a misunderstanding. He didn't run away with the Philpot woman from the choir. He left his vocation according to, you know, all the correct procedures."

"But of course he ran off with her. They had the room together in Clarenville."

"People are saying that's all lies."

"But where's the Philpot woman?"

"No sign of her. I suppose her family knows."

"But Donna, surely…"

"I suspect what happened was, she thought better of it. An ex-priest, and not a very good-looking one either. I'd say she had her fun and moved on."

Joyce needed food before the long drive. Bacon and eggs. She still couldn't believe Father O'Rourke would show his face again. When he and the Philpot woman disappeared in August, people had been grateful it was a grown woman he'd taken up with. Not like the sick priests who prey on little boys, or those disgusting Christian Brothers who ought to be shot.

/////

Joyce didn't mind the four-hour drive, even with the wind leaning into the car and the little gusts of dry snow. But the overpass down to the Cape nearly killed her. It took a big turn and climbed up to loop back over the highway, with the wind coming hard and nothing to break it. There was a thin layer of snow with little curved peaks, and she slowed as she hit ice patches, until one of those patches sent the car fishtailing. She whipped the steering wheel this way and that, and her mind stupidly called up a scrap of an old song. It repeated in her head until finally she came to rest sideways, with the back bumper

254

kissing the guardrail. She was shaking and cold—suddenly the car was frigid—and she didn't know how long she sat there before a man tapped on her window. Joyce was singing to herself as she rolled down the window. There was a noise behind him, which turned out be an idling pickup. She said she was fine. He wanted to know where she was going, and insisted on driving her there, with his wife following in the truck. Joyce said there was no need, but she was grateful for the company. During the drive he asked a lot of questions about her family. "So's I can place you," he said. She answered the questions until he said, "Yes, my dear, sure I know your crowd."

At the old house, the fellow and his wife insisted on going in and paying their respects to Esther. Of course, they stayed for a cup of tea and mentioned how they found Joyce with her car askew in the middle of the road, singing to herself. So for the rest of the weekend, Joyce was treated like a frail old lady on the brink. They wouldn't let her help with anything. She was spirited away from the wake when the late-night drinkers took over—"You don't want any part of that dirty old crowd," said Esther—and treated regally at the reception following the service. Her privileged status allowed Esther to avoid her most of the time.

In nearly fifty years since she'd left, Joyce had never been back home. She had always imagined her desertion as a dramatic episode. The girl who boarded the train and never looked back. Resented and envied for escaping the place, which crippled those left behind as surely as poison in the well water.

But of course the Cape turned out to be no different than anywhere else. Everyone left. Emptying out was the ordinary business of outport Newfoundland. There was a teacher and two students, a school janitor with not much to do, and a crowd of old folks lining up to see the nurse who passed through every Friday. The church was closed, her father's old store long abandoned. Joyce couldn't imagine why anyone would stay at all. Or why anyone had put down stakes in the first place, for that matter.

She met a man who said he remembered Joyce as a girl, coming around with deliveries from the store.

"Everyone's looking for a resettlement offer," said the man. "Take the money and buy a house somewhere. Or pocket the money and move in with the kids. But we're not small enough to get the government money yet, and not expensive enough. Those little islands, serviced by the ferries? Cost a fortune. Government can't wait to close them up."

"Would everyone want to leave?"

"Here? I'd say everyone would come around to it. What about Gander? Wasn't there talk that the airport was finished?"

"It's doing nicely these days, I think."

"How do they make a go of it?"

"Private jets, you know, and air freight and the military. Emergency landings too." Joyce wasn't sure exactly how the airport managed to stay in business.

"Another one of Joey Smallwood's boondoggles," said the man. "Along with his chocolate bars and his hockey sticks and the rest of it."

"But Smallwood had nothing to do with Gander."

"He had his hand in everything."

At the funeral she had a good chat with the younger cousins on her father's side. Most of their kids were in Edmonton. Joyce talked about how she had almost moved to Edmonton once. TCA was looking for ticket agents to transfer out west, to Edmonton and Winnipeg. But then she met Arthur.

She told Esther how Father O'Rourke had run away with the Philpot woman from the choir, and then come back.

"They've got no shame," said Esther. "You won't see me back in church after today. Not until I'm in my own box."

The shaking from the near-accident persisted all weekend, right through the burial and the careful drive back. A steady vibration inside, as if her bones were ringing. It stopped when she got home.

Then it flared up again, coming at her for a few minutes at a time, and waking her at night.

Donna dropped by to return the house key. "Bill O'Rourke is gone back to school," she said. "Gone to do welding."

"Who?"

"Father O'Rourke. He's going to get his welding certificate and make a fortune offshore."

"What kind of fortune?"

"With Hibernia, I imagine. The rigs."

Father O'Rourke. Had she really taken Holy Communion from a man out for his welding certificate? Joyce wanted to say she would never set foot in church again. But she had made such vows before, and always drifted back. So she held her tongue.

///////

A week after Marty passed, she still hadn't told Herbert. She called, and caught him in the middle of his new job. At a bakery, of all places. Joyce had never known him to show an interest in the kitchen. He said he would call back in an hour. She put on her laundry from the trip and went through the pantry to clear out a few forgotten cans and bag them for the food bank.

The hour was up by then, so she sat at the kitchen table, next to the telephone on the wall.

When Herbert called, she said, "Your Uncle Martin passed away last week."

"I never knew him, did I?"

"No. We fell out of touch."

"You had that picture, though, of the two of you. Was he sick for long?"

"Oh, for ages. He finally got married a few years ago, and I started getting Christmas cards from his wife. There was always a report on his health, and it was never good."

"Did you see him before he died?"

"I meant to. It happened very quickly." But then, she had also missed her father's death, and hadn't young Herbert carried out his move to Toronto when they all knew Arthur was in his final weeks? "Esther was with him, that's his wife. And she has a girl from her first marriage, who was there as well."

"So no cousins on your side."

"No. It's a good thing they're not counting on the Pelleys of Cape St. Rose to keep Newfoundland populated. We've done poorly on that front."

After a while she asked about the divorce, and he said it was finally done. No children, and no assets to speak of. A simple division. But Herbert didn't sound relieved or renewed. He was still wounded, still enumerating his grievances.

"I hear she's moving to North Bay. Trying to get back with the guy she had before me."

"What she does is nothing to you anymore."

"Just interesting that she's showing her true colours. I heard there was another guy she's been out with too."

So nothing much had changed. A young woman was still held to account for her boyfriends, and it was treated like the only part of her story that mattered. But a man might be on a spree all over town, and people thought it hardly worth remarking on. Oh, by the way, he's having it off with so-and-so now...

He asked about the funeral. She didn't mention the incident on the overpass, or the shaking and how it had stayed with her. Joyce had no idea how long she might have been sitting there, the car sideways across both lanes, singing, before the tap on her window.

"Was it strange to be back there, after so many years away?" asked Herbert.

"It's not half the size it used to be. Your grandfather's old shop is long gone." She had known the Cape at a glance. The pebbled shoreline. The landwash with its fringe of kelp and shining blobs of beached jellyfish. The salt-stained streets and houses retreating from the sea, backing right up to the crooked trees screwed into the face of Bald Hill.

"The weather was raw," she said. "I almost forgot about that. How the wind comes in off the water. Everyone walks around with their faces scrunched up against it."

/////

Two days later Herbert called again. "Have you given it any thought, Mom? What I said about maybe selling the house and moving in somewhere so you're not alone all the time?"

They hadn't talked about any such thing, and Joyce was about to tell him so. But she hesitated. It sounded familiar, as if she had been rehearsing thoughts for this very conversation. The shaking inside started. She lifted a hand to see if she was shaking on the outside as well, and yes, it trembled a bit.

Perhaps he had said something about moving, and she just forgot.

"Give me a few weeks to think about it," she said.

"You're lucky, with Dad's pension. Dad did very well. I saw Gander on the news the other night."

"What for?"

"It was a nice story about 9/11, and all the flights that had nowhere to go because the Americans closed the airports. And you guys put up thousands of people, fed them and looked after them. Most of them never even heard of Newfoundland before."

"Oh. Well, I was away that week, I believe." She had been home all week. Hadn't gone out much, and hadn't answered the phone either, for fear that someone would ask her to take in strangers. She wanted no part of it. When it was over and the stranded planes were sent on their way, she could feel the town empty out and the silence descend. She could feel it from inside the house, without even cracking the door.

"How's Leah?" she asked.

"You and I were talking about my divorce already."

"Yes, that's right." Her mind was misplacing things, so exhausted was she from the trip.

"Are you alright, Mom?"

"The drive down to the Cape, it was hard. Middle of winter."

They finished the call, and Joyce ran a bath. She locked the bathroom door behind her, because you never know. The heat was almost too much, billowing steam around her. It would soon be time to get out of the house. The pipes were always banging behind the sink, like they used to in the old hotel at the airport. Shingles were blowing off the roof, and the fellow Anstey who ploughed the driveway every winter wasn't as prompt as he used to be, not since his wife left him. She wouldn't share any of this with Herbert. Not yet, or he'd be down here to rush her along.

It must have been Arthur who taught her what to do when the back end of a car starts waving about. Cut the wheels in the same direction. Or did the body have an instrument that automatically took control for such moments? A finely tuned bundle of nerves that could read and correct dangerous shifts in momentum.

The song came back to her as she rolled wrinkled toes over the faucet. Not the song, but just the one line. May this bliss never end. Over and over it had played in her head, for as long as it took her to stop the vehicle. May this bliss never end.

She couldn't recall the title of the song, or any of the other words. But she remembered the day she got it right. The band was setting up in one of the usual rooms—likely the Airport Club— and a few of the men were passing the bottle around. Christmas, maybe? Joyce was testing her microphone with a few lines from that song, whatever it was, when she was jarred by the realization that she had been singing it wrong all along. It wasn't just about heartbreak. It was about loving the heartbreak. She had to sing it as a woman abandoned and suicidal, but also more alive than she had ever been during the affair itself. In that moment, she knew exactly how to shape the words. It might have been a passing thing, long gone the next time she reached for it. But she had it in that moment. What a shame they were only rehearsing, with no crowd of dancers to share it with. But of course it would have been lost on them.

19

Sam's appointment has been postponed a week. "Receptionist said Dr. Kim had a family issue. I believe last time we were there she mentioned an elderly mother."

"Yes. I get it." Carter doesn't care shit for the doctor's life and troubles.

"They worked really hard to fit us in. They moved things around for us."

"So it's urgent. If they squeezed us in for next week. They want to get him in as soon as possible."

"Or they just want to be helpful, Carter."

She passes the phone to Sam, who answers yes to three questions and asks if he can have macaroni and cheese again tonight. A long silence then, as he stops talking and lays the phone down. Carter waits for Isabelle to notice and pick up again.

"I'm sorry about last night," she says. "Interrupting your party. But when the guy called, he really wanted you to know. I think it was one of the first calls he made after she passed."

"No, I'm glad you let me know."

"Did you call him back?"

"Yeah. I haven't been able to get him."

"Who is he?"

"Old boyfriend."

"Well, they'd be tied up with the arrangements now. You might not get him for a couple of days. It was just business about the music, he said. Things to wrap up."

"He doesn't get a say."

/////

They ride silently in the elevator until a man pushing an empty wheelchair gets off at the third floor, leaving them alone. When the door closes, Joyce begins to sing: *East of the sun, and west of the moon, we'll build a dream house of love, dear.*

Carter can make out every word, though the voice is barely above a whisper, and she falters on the high note. She inhales with a gentle wheeze. Her lips barely move. *Up among the stars, we'll find a harmony...*

She stops, clears her throat and works her mouth, showing the tip of her red tongue. The line begs completion. The elevator opens to the ground floor. Joyce says, "Is this it?"

Howley Park still feels like winter, warm and enclosed. But it's the first truly fine day since Carter arrived. As they pass through the main door, a woman behind the front desk cries, "Some day out there, Joyce! Going up to twenty-four. No, twenty-six! I believe it's twenty-six."

"I don't think it's right," she says, lowering to a bench in the shade. "Digging up old things like that. They ought to let it rest."

"Archaeology is a way of studying history, I think."

"People live as best they can. They want to be left in peace."

He tells her about the aircraft wrecks still there after all these years, and the gin bottle at the Globe Theatre.

"Crowd from Air France drank all the gin," she says.

They don't talk for a few minutes, and Carter half-expects she might sing again. She doesn't.

"I told them I'm not going to that place down by the lake."

"Okay."

"They can't even feed themselves down there. Can't even wipe."

"I think you're doing great where you are, Mom. Fantastic, really."

/////

Melissa Ryan backs away as Carter takes a seat, choosing a chair at the head of the table. She introduces a nurse with pink and blue streaks in her black hair, an older nurse with a scowl and a pageboy cut, and a thin balding man who takes notes.

"And we've already met," says Carter, reaching for and not quite touching Melissa's sleeve. He turns to the thin man. "It's the strangest coincidence, but years ago I used to play in a band, and Melissa here used to come to the clubs and see us!" It's the sort of small-world camaraderie that Newfoundlanders always indulge in. But Carter's attempt falls flat. They're already seated at the table flipping through binders.

Joyce is strong, according to the older, scowling nurse. Sturdy as an ox, and not prone to aggressive behaviour. Doesn't lash out like some do. She assures Carter that he wouldn't believe how some of them lash out. The most mild-mannered, they can turn on a dime.

The one with the pink and blue streaks in her hair reports that Joyce was talking the other day about a little girl who died. Very upsetting for the other residents. Melissa Ryan asks if this was during Shanna's narrative therapy. Maybe Joyce shouldn't do the storytelling sessions anymore, not if it upsets her.

"Mom's really done well with the narrative thing," says Carter. "She's really engaged."

"She's really come out of her shell, that's true," says Pink-and-Blue.

"What else do we have, Denise?" The roll of Melissa Ryan's turtleneck lifts her head in a regal manner, and the hair is pinned into a tight helmet.

Scowling Nurse turns pages. Two high-anxiety incidents last week. No, month. Last month. Some dependence for ambulation.

Partial dependence for bathing and dressing, also elimination. Increasing dependence in behaviour management, though not aggressive, as previously noted.

"Now those scores, we can see a trend," says Melissa Ryan, scribbling. "She is approaching Level Three care, though it might be a ways off yet. You're familiar with our New Horizons facility, just down off the highway?"

"She says she won't go," says Carter.

"Just something to think about. Transitioning is not a move, it's a process, Mr. Carter. What's the occupancy down there now, Judy?"

"One bed available, male," says Pink-and-Blue. "As of this morning."

"So nothing's happening soon. We want to plan ahead. I'll ask Natalie to flag Joyce for transition, possibly in the new year."

They review directives, noting the Do Not Resuscitate order with approval. They review her whiskey protocol. Two drinks per day, before meals. Melissa Ryan wonders if this might be cut back to one, given Joyce's confusion and anxiety of late.

"I don't think that would be wise," says Scowling Nurse.

"Now," says Melissa Ryan, gathering the papers in front of her. "Joyce has a hospital appointment this week?"

"Yes," says Pink-and-Blue, reading the file. "Friday morning at the eye clinic. Get her cataracts checked."

"Would you like to accompany your mother to this appointment?"

"That's when I fly back to Toronto. So I can't. Sorry."

"That's fine. We'll have a couple of staff take her. You'll see a small charge for that." Melissa stands. "Mr. Carter, could I ask you to stay behind a moment?"

"I understand that you had to stick with your protocol," says Carter, after the boardroom clears. "With someone taking minutes."

"Mr. Carter, if I can ask you." She's putting caps on pens and fixing them to her binder. "Please don't mention that old music anymore, or…" She flaps a hand as if dispelling a bad odour. "…all that business from the past."

"Of course," says Carter. Her love of Infinite Yes is flirtatious, though innocent, and she wants to keep a professional front on the job.

She looks up to meet his eye. "I contacted my old roommate and told her we had met. She's the only one who would appreciate the coincidence. She's out in Corner Brook, with Western Health, and we got to talking. First time in many years." She pauses while someone passes in the hall. Goes to the door and closes it. "Of course, we all had our wild oats to sow back in those days, and I knew that she went off with that fellow a few times. He was in your band."

"Colin?"

"Yes. And the things that happened, what she went through, if only I had known." Melissa hastily gathers up her binder and several folders, hugs them to her chest and returns to the door. "I don't hold you responsible in any way, but she had no idea what to do, being so young."

"I'm sorry, but what went on?"

"From now on, any communication must be solely about Mrs. Carter and her care." She puts a hand to the doorknob. "I told her to go to the police, you know. Even after all these years. But she never will, she made that very clear. So if you're still in touch with this man, you need not warn him."

"We haven't been in touch for years," says Carter. But she's out the door, closing it behind her.

/////

Carter walks the wrong way down the hall, finds a woman bent at a closet door where he expected the elevator to be. Shanna. She pulls out a canvas sack nearly as big as herself.

"Hello, Mr. Carter," she says. "I heard you were on the Gander, as the locals say."

"You're not local?"

"I'm from Mount Pearl. A resident says to me the other day, 'I know a joke from there, about a man with a wife named Pearl.' But I didn't let him finish."

She's diminutive, barely up to his chest, with a tattoo of thorny roses covering one arm. The sack is weightless, thrown over her shoulder with ease.

"I was just sitting with Mom a little earlier," says Carter.

"What does she have to say for herself today?"

"The crowd from Air France drank all the gin."

"I don't doubt it. We could chat for a bit, if you have time?"

She leads him to a room, bright and sparse, its tiled floor big enough for a dance. Wooden tables are pushed against walls and plastic chairs stacked high. A piano occupies one corner.

"You bring in people to play?" asks Carter, gesturing at the piano.

"Occasionally, and we have sing-alongs as well. Haven't gotten a note out of Joyce yet."

Joyce's elevator song is too private to mention.

Shanna tugs the lace on the canvas sack.

"We just reviewed her file," says Carter.

"Always a good idea to review the file. Her meds and directives." Shanna sounds tired, lacking the brash spirit of their long-distance conversations. Her white T-shirt is scuffed, as if she's been moving furniture.

"They said she's having trouble with old memories," says Carter.

"Is that how they put it?" She frowns at the tangled lace.

"They thought the storytelling sessions might have brought out bad memories."

Shanna pulls the bag open and flips it. Colourful plastic objects tumble out, the pins and balls of a child's bowling set, bouncing and clattering on the tiled floor.

"There was a girl who got killed or something?" says Carter. "She was talking about that?"

267

"Yes. Last week. More about the boy who did the killing, really. We didn't let her finish that one. It was too upsetting for some of the others."

"I gave you a vote of confidence in the meeting. I told them that the storytelling has been great for Mom."

"I'm having second thoughts about it, to be honest. I'm not sure whether to keep going with it."

"Oh." Carter searches for a response while orange and yellow pins slip from her arms and spiral across the floor. "Would you like a hand?"

"You could get down eight or ten chairs and line them up about here. Thanks."

Carter hoists a stack of chairs and begins separating them. Shanna stands the pins in a triangle. "The other week, Joyce starts talking about a man she knew once," she says. "So we all listened, and she said how this man was carrying on with other women while his own wife went mad and lost her mind. She said their names, and there was another resident, a gentleman who knew the names. Because it's a small town, you know." Shanna steadies the last pin in the triangle and backs away. They're so lightweight a mild breath of wind might topple them. "So the other gentleman got angry, and they had words. Come on in, Mrs. Hanlon."

A stout woman enters, with waxy skin and hair so sparse Carter can follow the trail of brown spots on her scalp. She presses forward under her own steam, followed by several others leaning on walkers and canes, eased along by the gentle patter of two nurses, and settled into the row of chairs. Joyce enters last, on the arm of a nurse Carter has never seen before.

Keeping a distance from the bowlers, Carter and Shanna take chairs next to the doorway. The stout waxy woman is given first turn. She stands gripping the ball with two hands while the nurses say, "Come on, Miz Hanlon. Right at those pins." Carter wills her to bowl a mighty strike, but the ball spins sideways from her hands and rolls under a table.

"She had another one about a brawl at the airport," says Shanna, voice low. "A fellow is knocking his wife around, and someone steps in, and soon they're all into it."

"She must be imagining things."

"With Joyce, people get nervous because she names names," says Shanna. "She doesn't say, the priest ran off with a woman in the choir. With Joyce it's, Father So-and-So ran off with Mrs. Such-and-Such. That's going to cause trouble. And she gets a bit racy. They ran off to Clarenville and broke the bed at the Holiday Inn, that sort of thing."

A man with a full head of rippling white hair stands and tosses the ball quickly, looking embarrassed. But when the pins fly he claps his hands and kicks a leg in delight.

"So Billy George, one of our oldest residents, well into his nineties, he starts talking the other day," says Shanna. "He's out hunting rabbits one summer. There was no rabbit season back then. You could go anytime. He sleeps in a lean-to out in the woods, and in the morning an airplane passes overhead. Maritime Airways, flying awfully low. Then he hears a terrible noise, and he starts walking toward it, and it's in pieces. Dead bodies everywhere."

The nurses applaud heartily as the pins scatter again. Joyce has been watching the game with a rigid smile like he's never seen before. Her eyes move quickly to follow the action. She doesn't seem to see Carter and Shanna.

"He tries to help, but there's nothing to be done. All dead. So he starts walking back to the airport to tell them what he saw. And at his feet there's a biscuit tin with barely a scratch on it. He's ravenous, so he eats the biscuits while he walks. Joyce got upset."

"Was she angry?"

"She just said, 'Stop it. Stop it.' Turned her head like she was trying to block it out." Shanna twists her head and shoulders and tucks her chin. "And Billy seemed pleased with himself. Like he wanted to upset people. Or maybe he's getting Joyce back for the stories she told." Shanna checks her watch and claps encouragement for the next bowler, a small woman reluctant to release a hand from her walker. "You can see how it might not be so healthy to have them share these things. And if the families get wind of it…"

They watch the woman with the walker, a nurse holding her from behind and cradling her arm. "When I swings your arm, you let go the ball," says the nurse. Surely this woman needs the next level of care more than Joyce.

"They talked about moving her to the place down by the lake," says Carter, as the ball bounces high, clearing the pins altogether.

"New Horizons."

"Maybe you could vouch for her? So she can stay here?"

"Nobody wants to see mom or dad sent there," says Shanna. "They all think it's for someone else."

Joyce takes the ball and bowls without hesitation. Her throw veers left. Too much English on it. Looks to be a clear miss, but it clips the edge of the last row. The red pin falls, and the green one next to it, and surely the others will follow. She has already turned away.

"There won't be any storytelling down there," says Shanna. "It would turn into an awful racket down there."

///

On their last full day, the team takes one more crack at the 1954 Canso, this time with Hawco as a guide.

"You got to take the long way in, from the airport," says Hawco. "Even then it gets mucky. No solid ground out that way."

"Everything okay at home?" asks Andi, as they set out on the spongy clearing at the end of the runway.

"Yeah," says Carter.

"Your boy, and then your poor ex-wife. What an awful week for you."

"Minty berries," says Hawco, plucking from a bush at his feet. The berries are white and dusty, as if rolled in icing sugar. "Really nice." He tosses them in his mouth.

"A friend of mine, his mother died while his parents were getting divorced," says Morris. "So it got really complicated. I hope you don't have to deal with anything like that."

"No," says Carter, trying for curt finality.

"Coyote scat," says Hawco, as they gather around what appears to be a deposit of ordinary dog shit. "They're thriving these last few years. You hear them at night. And moose droppings here too. Watch your step."

They begin to follow him more closely, seeing the woods through his eyes. Fresh sawdust at the foot of a spruce means termites, which will have it hollowed out by summer's end. A bird skipping along the ground is a whiskey jack, and will come eat from your hand if you're still long enough. Clusters of bright red berries are plum boys—"That's what we always called them"—with a rich raspberry flavour. Another bird departs a tree with the blurring flick of a branch. "Grouse, I believe," says Hawco.

Their boots are splashing with every step now, and they straddle an ankle-high stream. Hawco stops and reaches into the water, coming up with a frog no bigger than his thumb. "You'll never go hungry in the woods," he says, and drops the creature at his feet.

Terry squints at his GPS. "Now," he says. "I believe…I believe…"

A departing jet casts a quick shadow over them.

"According to my notes, there ought to be a pond here," says Terry. He pulls out a photograph and examines it.

High grass obscures the ground, which smells deeply of rot. Terry double-checks the coordinates. Red runs the metal detector, and they all hear the telltale click of the needle as it hits the high end of its scale. "There's a ton of crap under here. Maybe the whole thing sank?"

"Let me see," says Hawco. He takes the picture from Terry and holds it up against the horizon. Steps forward and drops a few inches. "Okay, nobody goes any further than this," he says, extending arms like a tightrope walker. "Missy with the camera," he says.

"Andi."

"Andi, love, come here with that camera."

She advances slowly, each step announced with a squelch. Hawco mutters instructions. She takes a few careful steps to the right, sinks slightly, stabilizes, and raises her camera. A flickering horsefly descends, lights at her waist, and makes its way to a protruding shoulder blade as the shutter fires repeatedly. "Can I get a hand here?" she says.

Carter finds a path. He and Andi lock forearms, she tugs with her back leg and swears as the foot comes free, leaving the boot behind. Soaks her white sock reaching to get it back.

Retreating to safe territory, they compare the pictures. The dog-eared photo is a black-and-white of shimmering water, with a shadowed mass emerging at an angle. A note scribbled in the border identifies the object as *Maritime Air Canso 1954 – 11 killed.* The window of Andi's camera shows the grassy marsh, spreading out in almost the exact same shape as the water in the old photo.

"And look at the horizon," says Terry. "It's a perfect match. This is the place. You'd never know anything happened here."

"Can that happen?" asks Carter. "A pond can disappear like that?"

"There's a gully out to our cabin, not half the size it was when I was a boy," says Hawco.

Red gives the metal detector another wave. The needle clicks frantically.

///////

"Let me tell you now," says Terry. "I'll tell you how they found the Dolan crash, just a few miles east of here. She went down in the middle of winter, see? And they didn't know where, exactly."

They're nearly back to the cars, but the blackflies are out. Hawco found a nearly dry trail for the return trip, so they can keep a quick pace. Terry shouting his story so they can all hear.

"They had—"

Red grunts, waving an arm around her. Carter tugs at his clothes, like the flies are underneath and all over him.

"Fuckin' cunts," growls Morris, swiping at an ear.

"Car," shouts Andi as they round a birch grove, and she breaks into a sprint.

They toss the gear aboard and seal themselves in the two cars, phones going off as they slam doors. They're back in cell range. Carter has two missed calls from North Bay Kevin.

"Oh my Jesus," says Hawco, swiping at the windshield to kill intruders.

"After the crash," says Terry. "And … a trapper … out—" He gasps for breath.

"Fuckers," says Morris, and slaps his window, leaving a bloody smear. He and Carter are in the back seat, with Terry and Hawco in the front.

Carter hits callback as the car starts moving. We've never met, have we, Kevin? But we were in the same house once. I waited in her bed while she sat you down in the kitchen and told you to fuck off back to North Bay.

"Mr. Carter. Right. Thanks so much for ringing us back. I was calling in my capacity as Leah's executor. She had asked me to clarify some things for you."

"Now's not a great time, actually." Carter's voice trembles as the car rolls over broken pavement. "Can we set a time to talk later?"

"I'm afraid I'm busy later. But I understand the producer will be sending along the songs."

"What?"

"Jordan Toytman. The producer. He oversaw the project. He'll send you the completed songs." The smooth Irish lilt is off-putting.

Carter turns toward the car door and covers the phone with a hand. "I think there's a misunderstanding. Jordan and I will be working on the songs. That deal is in place." He adopts Kevin's formal tone as the car passes the old town site and the Globe Theatre dig.

"Ah, no." There's the Irish thing again, crooning *nooo* like they're out for a pint. "No, the project has been completed. Your performance and songwriting credits will be—"

"The project hasn't started yet. We were waiting..." This guy hasn't got a clue. Never did. "We're going to honour her work, so..."

"Leah had no wish to return to the music." Kevin is firmer now, like they're arguing over a pint. "You left her no choice. I helped with the financials. Reluctantly, I have to admit."

Morris turns to the back window of the car, slapping wildly at blackflies with his hoody. Carter shakes his foot, the pulse racing in his arch. "That's... it's illegal, without my knowledge."

"We held to the letter of your band agreement," says Kevin. "Leah and the lads, Will Conway, Colin Stevenson. They all signed off on it."

"Colin?"

"We brought in a few session players. Played a bit of guitar meself after. Your songwriting and performance credits will be honoured, if there's income."

This dickhead is talking about something else altogether. Probably Leah had old tapes of a couple of tunes and decided to finish them. "Okay. You send me those songs and whatever else you have. I appreciate being kept in the loop. But where did she find Colin?"

"He gave his approval from the west coast. Lives there picking fruit. Fallen on hard times, I suppose. If you have further questions, I'll put you on to our lawyer."

What a dick. Morris hands him the jacket. "Get the ones on your side?"

The car picks up speed as it hits the highway. Terry will skirt the town rather than drive through it to meet the women at Mitch's Lounge. Carter lashes at the flies, but they scatter with the breeze from each swing, and the rear window is angled to prevent a direct hit. He'll call Jordan tonight. If Leah finished a couple of songs on her own, they can live with it.

"Whoa!" cries Gilly.

Carter grips the seatback as the car pulls at him. Morris pitches forward and back. There is a brief screeching of tires behind them. A shadow crosses the car. Carter turns to his window. "The other way," says Morris. "No, you missed it."

"Did you see the fucking antlers?" Terry pulls the car to the shoulder.

"That was a monster." Hawco cracks his window.

"If that was even a second later, we wouldn't have been able to stop."

20

Always too many of them everywhere. In and out of her room. Hello, Joyce! Morning, Mrs. Carter! Going through her things, telling her how to dress, scrubbing and vacuuming, delivering pills in little paper cups. And talk coming out of them the whole time. Through dinner and through her bath. They wouldn't even leave her be on the toilet.

She made sure they left her alone with her whiskey. Bring me a drink and go on about your business. She made that clear from the start.

"One of you is enough," she said to the second boy in the car. "You can go on and do something else."

"That's alright, missus," said the boy, reaching across to pull her seatbelt snug to her chest. "We'll have you home for tea in no time."

But she didn't want him sitting right there, next to her. There was a big fellow up front to drive, and that was enough. Why did they always have to be on top of you?

"Is she buckled in?" asked the big one in the front.

"Yes, we're ready to roll," said the boy, doing his own belt.

"I don't need the both of you."

The boy laughed. "We're all along for the ride, missus." He was fine-looking, though. Spotless face, and rings of hair like you just took the curlers out. The fellow up front, she couldn't tell. All she could see was a greasy mat of black hair at the back of his head.

They hit a bump and tossed in their seats. "Oh!" said Joyce, and put a hand to the seat in front of her. The boy touched her arm.

"It's just a visit to the doctor, missus. We'll be done in no time."

Joyce didn't want to see any doctor. But there was no point in complaining about it. Want or don't want—that was all over for her.

It was a hot day, with the empty sky turning a deeper blue at the horizon. She saw flashes of it between houses, the blue behind tall backyard trees.

"This is Memorial Drive," she said. She knew the long driveways, the generous spaces between houses.

"That's right." The boy touched her arm again.

"I'm not going to that place down by the lake," said Joyce.

"It's just to see the doctor, missus." But they were turning onto the highway, and the lake was out there, just down the hill.

"Can you stop the car?" She raised her voice to reach the big one up front.

He turned, and she got a good look at him now. Thick head and fleshy shoulders. Freckled.

"There a problem back there, Boyd?"

"No, no. We're just going to the hospital now, Missus Carter."

The big one caught Joyce's eye in the rearview mirror. Probably Scottish, with the freckles, and that fierce look they get. "You're alright now, aren't you, missus? We're just out for a little jaunt, that's all. Don't you mind Boyd. Boyd don't know the war's over."

She looked at the boy. But he stared straight ahead and didn't answer.

"Eric is like you," said Joyce. "Brazen, like. Knows he's a charmer. Can't help it."

The boy rubbed his ear. The big one was poking at his dashboard, and thin music came from the door. It was down around her knees, a reedy voice with an empty wash of rhythm behind it.

"Don't turn on that radio," said Joyce. She hated the way they always had the radio going. Always in the hallway and in the kitchen. Every door you passed was another big racket. A wonder she wasn't gone deaf.

"Shut it off, Reg," said the boy at her side. The big one turned and wrinkled his face.

She felt sorry then, and envied them.

"You don't even know what it's like to have a baby fight you," she said. "Twisting away because he doesn't know his own hunger." What was the point of telling them more? They'd never need to know how finally you get the baby to feed and he's like a dog on a bone. Little bolts of pain right through you. Then he spits up the blood he draws, pink milk shooting all over you, and all over his sleeper. And of course the nurse makes a spiteful sound and whisks the baby away as if you wouldn't know how to get him clean. Then she's back, saying "Get yourself covered up now, Mrs. Carter. Your husband's here." Snapping at you. "And that's what I won't," says Joyce. They don't like that very much, a woman deciding for herself what her husband can see.

"I couldn't wait to get free of those nurses," she said. But she wasn't home two days before Herbert shows the pimples behind his lips, creamy white ones. He's got the thrush, got it from her own milk.

"Like I fed him poison," she said. Her companions in the car pretended not to hear. Young boys, hardly off the tit themselves.

Joyce turned to the good-looking boy and saw three white scars stroked across his chin. So he was a clumsy one. Like Herbert. Though was any boy as inelegant as Herbert? All arms and legs and that big head smashing into everything like a wrecking ball. Falling out the car door and pitching over the handlebars of his bike.

She gripped the armrest as the car took a turn.

"You see, missus?" said the big one. "It's just the hospital. You been here many times, I'm sure."

The car curved around back, where a narrow road hugged the rear of the building. They stopped in a shaded spot tucked between a brick wall and a grassy square. A man was driving a tractor over the grass, a little green thing whining and sputtering. The square ran up to thick woods, and the woods sloped all the way down to the lake.

"You see?" said the boy. "We're not taking you to Horizons."

It's her fault, the thrush. That's what her mother would say. Your own fault for having all those bad thoughts. She's always thinking them. Even when the baby settles down and he's lovely, with big eyes and bubbles popping at his lips. Gurgling like he's laughing. Even in those moments she's thinking terrible things, and there's an awful dread when Arthur's on his way home from work. She doesn't know why. She can hear her mother. It's alright to think bad thoughts. But if you let them linger they spoil your milk, and the milk spoils the baby.

"Run in and check, will you, Boyd?" said the big one. "Make sure they're ready for her?"

The boy disappeared. The big one said, "You just sit tight now, missus." He got out of the car and wandered further down the snaking driveway, where he lit a cigarette.

They had her now, trapped in the car, and could do whatever they wanted.

She had been to the hospital many times, and it never looked like this. What kind of fool did they take her for?

Nothing to the seatbelt. They didn't give her much credit if they thought that would hold her.

The big one paced back and forth in front of a row of dumpsters. Not watching.

She had seen him moving his hand around on his armrest, working the locks. She snaked her arm between the driver's seat and window. Pushed and tugged at whatever buttons and levers her fingers could find, and landed on a smooth bump the size of a fingertip. Pushed it, and heard the whole car release.

Those fellows were charming, and so full of themselves. Boys had been like that ever since Joyce was a girl, always nudging and pushing at her, this way and that.

She gripped the doorframe to pull herself up. The heat surprised her. The fellow on the tractor circled around a weeping willow. The big one stood with his back turned and his head bent, as if saying a quick prayer. Smoke rising from his head.

Just a few steps behind the car, where the grassy square ended, was a shallow ditch that led directly into the woods. Joyce stepped down and back up the other side. Got hold of a spruce branch for support, and hoisted herself into the low bramble and scraggly trees. She moved quick, stumbled to one knee, stood and brushed her slacks. Low branches tugged at her cardigan and whipped her legs. Her hand was stinging from the spruce needles. A downed tree tripped her to her knees, and something pulled across her forehead.

She felt for her glasses. The glasses were gone. No matter.

Perspiration blurred her eyes, drops of it rolling down the side of her nose and to her lips. She felt for her glasses again. Walked into another downed tree. A high one this time, it punched the air from her. Every breath became a stab in the chest.

But here was something like a path, a trail finding her. Just like it always found them, Joyce and Marty, out causing trouble on summer nights. Even without Marty she could find her way back. She'd catch a glimpse of the water and map her way from there. Or she'd hear the Chute or find the slope. Or find Spence, who was always out in the woods.

Once, she was lost altogether and it was nearly dark and she thought about calling out. Then she heard Spence, clear as day. Spence who came out of his mother too soon, walking along with his rod and tackle and belting out some old song. She asked where he had been fishing because they were nowhere near the brook. But Spence just kept up his singing, and she followed him like he was the Pied Piper. Only took a couple of minutes before he found the main road. Didn't say a word. Singing, the whole time.

Marty nearly came out of his skin when he heard. "Bloody Spence. Did he touch you?" "No," she said. Though he touched himself a bit, because he always did. She didn't mention that to Marty, because Spence would have got a beating.

Joyce sank to the ground for a rest, the cardigan catching and hitching up the back. She reached to free it, and free her hair. The damp earth chilled her bottom. Her insides released and she wet herself. Couldn't help it.

The woods were a tangle. But the sky calmed her, just to look up at the rich, deep blue. There was a song about the infinite sky, with its wandering clouds, and the singer wondering where the clouds go. The sort of thing children wonder about, or people who are just falling in love.

That was a pretty song. It came on the radio when she was in labour, and she felt herself carried away by it. Surprised her that a song could still do that.

When Herbert was born the doctor said to her, "I heard you at a dance one night, and the way you sang, you could talk a fellow into anything. Did you always sing like that?"

"I always tried," said Joyce. She was near tears from failing to get the baby to latch.

"Well then," said the doctor. "I'd imagine you're responsible for a few babies born around here."

A thread pulled hard up her throat and out between her teeth. Only a bit of spit or something. She stood, and put her hands on her knees to stop them shaking. Made her stomach settle.

That's better.

There was sun coming through the trees, and a steady drone approaching somewhere beyond.

She had liked it when the doctor said her singing was responsible for the babies. The way he laughed when he said it. She liked to think how a song might make a fellow feel that life was stretched out in front of him and beyond. How he might feel it in his body. He and his girl dancing and carrying on and then back out into the night. Headed home to make the baby that's been waiting inside her.

The overhead drone shifted to a lower pitch. The first morning arrival, banking for its final approach, buffeted by the headwind. The shift schedule gone to pieces. Men rubbing tired eyes. And what would become of all those young girls? They didn't even know where they were.

Joyce started walking again, taking her time. The woods brighter now, with sunlight breaking through. All she had to do was find her bearings. A trail was sure to emerge, or a logging road or the railway line. She might get a glimpse of the radar station. Before long an arrival would pass overhead, and she could follow it to the tarmac, where the midday flights were running up their engines.

Her chest went tight, and she took a moment to steady herself. But nothing came up her throat. It was different this time. More like her body was excited, the anticipation wrapping around her. She stepped around a big tree trunk and caught a foot on the roots. But she wouldn't fall this time. She kept on, headed into the sunny woods and looking to the vast sky beyond. Home was out there somewhere.

21

Carter and Terry check their bags and a small crate of artifacts. They exchange hugs with Andi and Red, who are returning Terry's hatchback to St. John's. Morris left this morning, driving west to visit family in Port aux Choix.

Terry asks to see their seat assignments and takes it up with the agent.

"Look at the size of him," he says, pointing at Carter. "Can't you find something up front? A bit more leg room?"

The agent taps at his computer and looks up at Carter. "Are you from here?"

"Oh, he's very much a local boy. Very deserving of your best service."

"I think you went to school with Nick Skanes?"

"You're Nicky's brother?" Carter spent enough hours at Nicky's house to recognize the family look. The small eyes and downturned mouth with its little overbite. "How is he?"

"Divorced twice, five kids," says the ticket agent. "But he's fine. Lives in Florida, managing a condo unit."

"That's great."

"So you can do something for our friend here?" asks Terry.

"Wish I could. We're overbooked as it is." Nicky's brother stabs the keyboard again and sighs. "Oh my." This sounds exactly like his mother, who used to make Carter sit in the kitchen to talk about school and future prospects and it's criminal the government won't do anything to help young people.

"It's busy," says Red. The lineup for security snakes halfway across the terminal, which is no bigger than a modest grocery store.

"Do you think they made this one ugly on purpose?" says Andi, looking around at the windowless room in its varying shades of brown. The renowned international terminal is walled off, a glimpse revealed by an open door behind the ticket agent.

"Now, listen up," says Terry, gathering Andi and Red to him with a touch of their elbows. "Morris has to corral those ideas. Promise me you'll keep after him, Violet."

"He doesn't like it," says Red, acknowledging her given name.

"He needs it. He's only got a few weeks. All his wild ideas aren't enough. He's got to nail them down. And Andi, you'll keep working through those ideas you had about public engagement?"

"See how neatly he puts everyone in their place?" says Andi, as Terry strolls to the washroom. "The golden boy gets to have the brilliant, out-of-control ideas. His female colleague is supposed to hold his hand—"

"Or whatever else needs holding." Red makes a stroking motion with a fist.

"—and my job is to make everyone like us. Public freaking engagement."

Carter is flattered to be taken into their confidence, to be taken as an enlightened male.

"Do you think you'll be back next year?"

"In Gander, you mean? Not sure," says Red.

"I don't know," says Andi. "Plane crashes aren't really my thing. I might transfer to Manitoba. I would, if it wasn't for Harry."

Carter is jolted by a pang of jealousy. Why Manitoba? Who's Harry?

"I mentioned your French movie to my friend Bridgett," says Andi. "I'll show you what she sent me. I'll forward it. It's great."

The legroom isn't so bad on the plane. Carter is helpless when forced into small spaces. He'll end the day with aching knees and hip flexors and a crick in his upper back no matter where they seat him.

Terry closes his eyes. Carter calls Isabelle before the order comes to shut off phones.

Sam has a new confidence, she says. She told him how a machine will take a picture of his heart, and it will show what's going on. It makes complete sense to him. He trusts the machine. It's the doctors that make him nervous.

"We looked it up online, how it works," she says.

"Should he be seeing that?"

"It was his idea. We saw how the pictures come out. They look like ultrasounds. He loved it. Best machine ever, he said."

Sam doesn't fight the world, but he can be hard and mulish, denying what doesn't please him. So how does an ordinary medical apparatus, one that could deliver very bad news, become the "best machine ever?" Does he trust it because it's a machine, its workings fully explicable? Or does he have faith in the mystery of it, a device that can show him his own heart?

The plane rocks as the propellers catch and sustain a low note. Carter receives the email forwarded from Andi's film friend:

Les Parapluies de Cherbourg! Still breaks my heart. First movie for a very young Deneuve, so that's a thousand little deaths just watching her. Simple domestic drama. Gorgeous muted colours. They sing every line and for a second you think wtf, and then it just grabs you. The tragedy isn't that love dies - happens all the time after all. It's that we let it die so easily.

Carter's latest message to Jordan finally prompted a reply. Last night, as he packed his filthy outdoor gear.

In my job you find out pretty quick how bad people hate each other. It's like something about music really sticks the knife in, you know? I used to work with these two old guys. Best friends, nicest guys you ever saw. Sang these gorgeous folk ballads. You'd die to hear the harmonies. Moved a ton of units on the festival circuit. Then one of them calls me up and says we're going to remix the album, and when I get to the studio he means remix as in replace the other guy's tracks. Literally erase the other guy and overdub the harmonies himself. He says I got to let him do it because the contract says he calls the shots. But the other guy got wind of it and he shows up, pounding on the door. I won't let him in because I'm scared as fuck, and he's screaming. I said no fucking way I'm doing this. Go hire someone else. I heard after there was restraining orders and all kinds of shit. I mean, these guys used to go hunting together so they had shotguns.

Terry, who appeared to be dozing, turns and says, "Do you still play music?"

"How did you hear about music?"

"The guy who checked us in, in Gander. I was chatting with him after."

"I used to jam with his brother back in high school. Two or three times a week we'd be down in Nicky's basement, because his mother didn't mind. But I don't play now."

"My wife is from Bosnia," says Terry, leaning into Carter as the plane banks left. "Her uncle was a violinist, and the family always said music saved him during the war."

"Because he could play?"

"No, that's the amazing thing. Several months he was in a concentration camp. Torture, almost no food or toilets. You'd probably want to die. But he was a tremendous student of Mendelssohn, and every day he played Mendelssohn in his head. Symphonies, violin concertos, piano, whatever. Beginning to end, note for note. All the instruments and notes. All in his head."

"That's amazing."

"He swears he would have died without it. He used to talk about how all the great composers left him speechless, except Mendelssohn. He always felt as if he and Mendelssohn were having a conversation."

"Did you ever hear him play?"

"I never knew the man. He died within a few years, before I met Anna. The camp ravaged him, I guess. But they always say it was Mendelssohn got him through it. Hours he would spend in his head with his music. Completely removed from his body."

/////

The baggage area is dimly lit and Spartan, bigger but not so different from the little brown room in Gander. Arriving passengers negotiate the space with strained, end-of-day civility. Carter turns on his phone. He has no missed calls or messages. Nothing from Isabelle. But a string of emails stack up, all from Will:

Subject: *article in Now Magazine*
Late Singer's Final Wish: '90s Indie Band Completes Final Recordings From Vault

Subject: *TV sync deals*
For immediate release: Siege Fifteen Productions Reaches Extensive Licensing Deals for New Music from Infinite Yes

Subject: album preview

Siege Fifteen Productions invites you to enjoy <u>an exclusive</u> <u>preview of "Legacy,"</u> the new album by legendary indie cult band Infinite Yes, featuring previously unreleased tracks.

All the emails are copied to Isabelle.

Carter clicks on the link to his exclusive preview, which takes him to iTunes.

Legendary indie cult band. That's a new one.

There is a man next to Carter, their elbows touching and jostling in the traffic. He's unwrapping a sandwich. Terry lingers further ahead with his phone.

The first suitcase comes diving down the chute as the file opens:

LEGACY

Infinite Yes >

SONGS   RATING AND REVIEWS   RELATED

Name	Artist	Time
1. Umbrellas of Cherbourg	Infinite Yes	4:55
2. 109 Minutes	Infinite Yes	1:49
3. Ronnie and the Crystal Meth	Infinite Yes	4:09
4. North Bay	Infinite Yes	3:12

Carter stops reading titles. He shakes, deep in his bones. People are crowding around him, hustling through to get within reach of the carousel. He touches the first song, finger trembling on the screen, and hears himself. His Telecaster lays down a figure, Colin and Will kick in with a tempo that surprises the ear. He doesn't remember this tune, but it's a key and chord change he's used before. He's borrowing from himself.

The man with the sandwich hears it, too. He and Carter seem to be the only ones standing still as the luggage plummets from above, and hands reach to grasp. Worn and stale from flight, people stagger and strain to retrieve massive suitcases and body-sized duffels. The man turns his chewing face to Carter as a second guitar, a strange guitar, comes in at sixteen bars to set a melody. Then a voice, lower and brighter than Leah's voice, begins humming along.

One more email appears.

Subject: A Survivor's Final Triumph
For immediate release: In her last interview before her recent death from cancer, the voice of cult favourites Infinite Yes recalls the emotional and psychological abuse that tore apart her band and marriage, and how she fought through fatal illness to achieve the triumph of a final Infinite Yes album.

The man with the sandwich is chewing in time and gently nodding his head on the second and fourth beats. It sounds nothing like Infinite Yes. He wants to ask the man what he's hearing. The nice bit shifting A-minor-to-G, is that it? It could be the lazy slide of the tempo, before Colin leans in to pull it back. The slippery imperfection of it set against the churn of the baggage carousel.

Carter's phone rings, interrupting the music. A call from Howley Park. He mutes the ringer, mutes email. Carter jacks up the music as the voice begins to sing.

The first line says something about a final afternoon. A body pushes through, bumping his shoulder. There is an announcement about belongings left unattended.

He has to know these songs before he sees Isabelle. Has to know them fully. But the sound is foreign to him. Leah has reimagined the music in a way that won't let him in.

The man takes a huge bite of his ham and cheese, and pushes at his lips to fit it all in, head still working on two and four. Then it nearly falls apart. The momentum stalls, an A-minor hanging for a desperate moment. The man tries to swallow, twisting his face with the effort. Then Carter's Telecaster rises to resolve the line. The strange voice starts singing about blood and betrayal and love's final days. But it's Carter building the song with a rush of sound and colour, pitching the band into a chorus. Carter and his guitar cracking open all the potential in a music he has played but cannot hear.

ACKNOWLEDGEMENTS

Like many who grew up in Gander, I've always been fascinated by stories of the early days, when the town was a hub of international aviation and post-war prosperity.

Thanks to Kay Donahue, Cecilia Nolan, and Frank Tibbo for sharing their memories of that era. Other essential resources include *The Best of Aviation* and *Early History of Gander*, both by Frank Tibbo; *Life at the Crossroads of the World*—an anthology of stories and memories compiled by the Gander Seniors Club; the Gander Airport Historical Society website; and material from the Centre for Newfoundland Studies at Memorial University.

This story is a work of fiction. I have taken liberties with historical detail and embellished where I saw fit. The version of Gander presented here is an invention, as are the characters and events.

I am grateful for the close reading and feedback of Sharon Bala, Melissa Barbeau, Carrie Ivardi, Matthew Lewis, Lisa Moore, Morgan Murray, Gary Newhook, and Susan Sinnott. Lisa Daly helped with details of aviation archaeology and plane-crash sites in the Gander area.

Kate Kennedy and Leslie Vryenhoek are heroes in the field of editing. Thanks also to James Langer, Rebecca Rose, and the entire team at Breakwater Books.

This novel could not have been written without the generous financial assistance of the Canada Council for the Arts, ArtsNL, and the City of St. John's.

Finally, thanks to Danine Farquharson and Tess Fitzpatrick, who make everything possible.

JAMIE FITZPATRICK is a writer and broad-caster in St. John's, and a member of the Port Authority writing group. His debut novel, *You Could Believe in Nothing*, won the Fresh Fish Award for Emerging Writers in Newfoundland and Labrador. He most recently contributed "Like Jewels" to the short-story anthology, *Racket: New Writing Made in Newfoundland*.